*This book is for Kate Miciak,
with thanks
for all the brilliant years*

PLAN OF PARIS

Scale 1 : 31,500

English Mile

0   1/4   1/2   3/4   1

Metres

0   250   500   750   1000

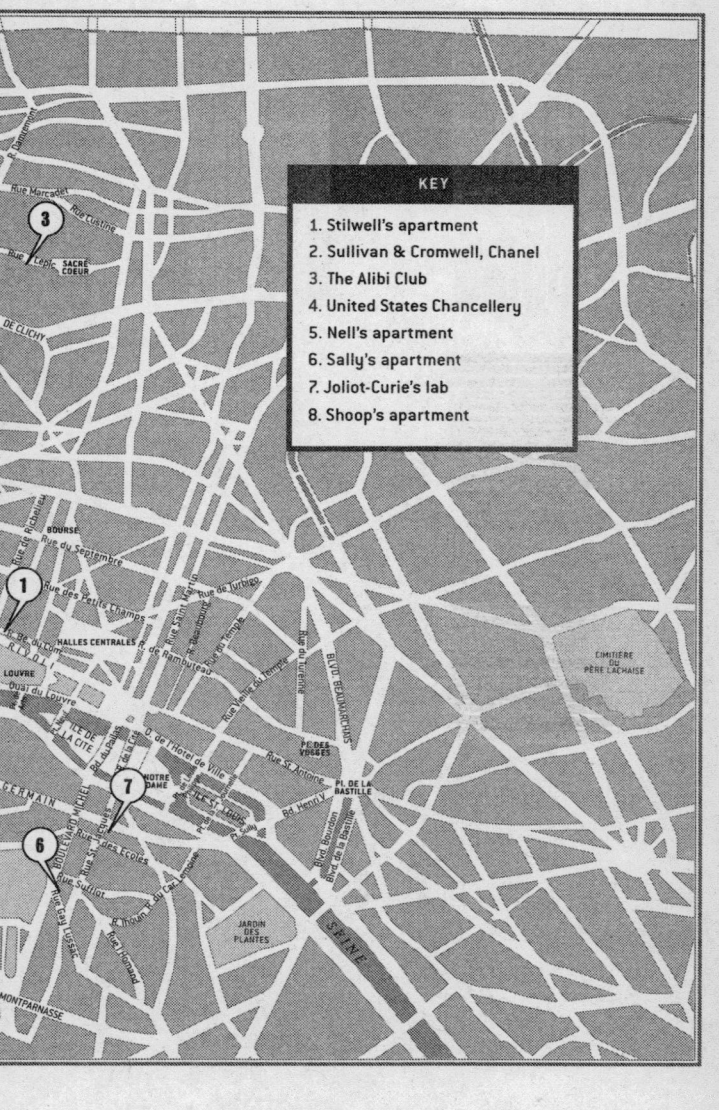

KEY

1. Stilwell's apartment
2. Sullivan & Cromwell, Chanel
3. The Alibi Club
4. United States Chancellery
5. Nell's apartment
6. Sally's apartment
7. Joliot-Curie's lab
8. Shoop's apartment

PROLOGUE

March 12, 1940

There were nine people waiting in the stuffy room that faced the aerodrome's tarmac, ten if you counted the sleeping child swaddled in a blanket in the Italian girl's arms. Three women, six men, several nationalities, and the brazen churn of propellers beyond the frosted window. Each of the waiting passengers was desperate enough to leave Oslo in the dead of night and dead of winter, so the air hummed with suppressed violence and restlessness and incipient hysteria. No one spoke.

Jacques Allier had his back to the wall nearest the door, an evening newspaper grasped in one gloved hand, the other thrust in his pocket. The unheated room was freezing, but his skin was beaded with sweat and his hidden fingers clutched a gun.

The clock read three minutes until midnight. The plane would leave at 12:07. Allier's passport had been taken ten minutes ago and not returned. The man named Demars—who had all his luggage—was inexplicably missing from the aerodrome, and this was only one of the factors contributing to Allier's sweat. He hated to fly. When he'd undertaken this operation he'd asked for a submarine out of Brest. A destroyer from Tønsberg. He'd gotten an eight-seater with ice on its wings and no guns to speak of.

He was praying he'd be allowed to board, although Allier was one of those who could not believe in God. Not now.

He was a spare, bland-faced man in the good cloth coat and spectacles of a banker, mid-forties perhaps, clearly European but shockingly unmilitary for the times. His eyes drifted away from the damning clock— the man Demars was still missing—and roved indifferently over the faces of his fellow passengers. Two men arguing politics in Dutch. A gawky boy in his teens, his looks feverish and his hands drumming nervously against the arm of his chair, fingers spilling cigarette ash onto the linoleum floor. A gray-haired woman stolidly eating pickled herring from a waxed paper box furnished by an Oslo shop. None of them spoke. None made eye contact. Only the tall, burly blond fellow in the impeccable camel-hair coat was staring openly, a slight smile curving his lips, at the Italian girl with the sleeping child.

And who could blame him? Allier thought irritably. She was exquisite, with her fur collar grazing her faintly flushed cheek, her dark knot of hair shining beneath the arc of her hat. Her fingers were gloved in ostrich skin; the frail hunch of her shoulders might reflect the penetrating cold, or the solicitude that kept her bent, Madonna-like, over the face of her infant. Was she even twenty? Her passport and ticket lay on the hard wooden bench beside her; like Allier, she was bound for Amsterdam in the dead of night.

Turn back, he urged. *Go north. Go west. Go anywhere but home.* He had caught one glimpse of her mouth, curved like a G clef, and her eyes, disconcertingly blue in an olive-skinned face. The blond hero opposite had glimpsed them, too.

"Madam," the man said gently in Italian, "you look chilled to the bone. Perhaps a cigarette?...If I were to light it for you...?"

The girl ignored him, failing to so much as lift her head. Allier exulted in this, in the snub offered the blond hero who might from his looks have been Norwegian or even English but who Allier knew now was German—a broad-shouldered, perfect German in civilian dress lounging in the very aerodrome where he, Allier, had elected to escape. This could not be coincidence; this was part of a plan. The fact of the German presence meant that Allier was already a dead man. Demars and the luggage would not be coming.

He tossed the folded newspaper into a waste bin and moved casually toward the door leading out to the planes. One of them bound for Perth, the other for Amsterdam. The propellers whined in the cold, the pilots worried about ice. It was possible that they would all be told to go home—to try again tomorrow—and for Allier there would be the certainty of an armed escort at some point along his route back to the French legation, a sudden flurried movement into an enemy car, a bullet in the temple after how many agonizing hours of interrogation? He continued to stare through the waiting-room window, his gloved hands clasped behind his back. Conscious of movement. Some kind of rank closing behind.

It was barely two weeks since he'd vaulted up the marble steps of the Armaments Ministry and accepted the fake passport in his mother's maiden name. *Freiss.* He was Michel Freiss of Salzburg, aged forty-one, a banker with no interest in this phony war between France and the Germans that had been going on for seven months now without a shot fired. That night he'd taken the last train across the border, bound for Amsterdam, and then by slow degrees traveled north to Stockholm and finally Oslo. There were five days of negotiation in a tiny snowbound town near the Telemark mountains, ponderous dinners and pledges of eternal friendship and risky flourishes of the French flag. Oblique counsels in the legation, none of the usual diplomats in on the secret, and the lights burning all night in the German intelligence pavilion across the garden wall.

"You're famous," the French ambassador assured him with a twisted smile. "Everybody wants to talk to you. Our people caught this the day you left Paris."

It was a decoded German radio transmission he carelessly handed Allier: *At any price intercept a suspect Frenchman traveling under the name of Freiss.* What the ambassador had not bothered to point out was that Allier had been betrayed before he'd boarded the night train to Amsterdam.

Who? he asked himself now. *A spy in Dautry's office? Somebody at the bank?*

The two-beat note of a police siren was audible, suddenly, in the distance; insistent, rising, certainly closer.

Perhaps it was the lab. One of Joliot's people. Or fucking Demars. He's probably sold the luggage.

"Mr. Freiss," said a voice at his elbow.

He turned, caught the untroubled face of Norwegian Border Control. A woman, neatly uniformed. Her clipped hair so fair it might almost be white. She was offering him a bunch of papers, but he ignored her extended hand. The police sirens had pulled up to the aerodrome door. The butt of his gun twisted in his fingers, slippery with sweat. In a matter of seconds the door would burst open, a clutch of men tripping over themselves in their haste to seize him. He might have time to take one of them down—the big German, perhaps—but there were these women, that child in the Madonna's arms...

"Your passport and ticket for Amsterdam," Border Control persisted. "Everything is in order. You may proceed to the tarmac."

He glanced over her head and met the German's eyes. The man was still smiling faintly, the same indulgent look he'd turned on the young Italian princess, who was rising now from her seat, magnificent and indifferent. *He's let me run all this way so he could follow my trail,* Allier thought. *I'll lead him no further.*

He took his passport and ticket from the woman's hand and without a word held the door wide. The Italian girl flicked him one glance from her arresting blue eyes as she passed; not even this, Allier thought, was comfort before dying. Then he and the blond hero followed her into the cold.

There was confusion about the planes: A huge black Daimler had driven straight onto the tarmac and thrust itself between them. A man was running distractedly beneath the wings, shouting inaudibly over the clatter of the engines and barely avoiding the propellers. His driver pulled an astonishing number of suitcases from the idling car. The police and their sirens were silent now, beyond the runway gates; it was the Daimler they had escorted through the streets of Oslo, wailing right up to the Amsterdam flight. Allier felt his face flush with heat and his hands clench: *This is what hope feels like. Terror and a clenched fist.* He recognized the dapper, black-haired figure pirouetting beneath the fuselage; he recognized the suitcases. Demars's driver was loading them even now into the belly of the Perth plane.

Allier counted them as best he could across the distance and darkness. *Thirteen,* he thought. *Please God let there be thirteen.*

Demars collided headlong with the German's camel-hair coat; whiskey fumes and cigar smoke wafted through the frigid night air.

"Pardon, most esteemed sir." He spoke Norwegian and he clutched the German's sleeve like a spoiled child. "Which of these is the Amsterdam plane? Have I missed it? I must at all costs make the Amsterdam plane!"

They argued the destination of both flights, the Daimler's right to park in the middle of the tarmac, the abuse of police escort, the advisability of arriving on time. Allier kept walking. He did not look back. The Italian girl boarded the Amsterdam plane with a grimace on her face, the saintly infant now screaming in her arms. Allier's ticket fluttered to the ground. He pulled a second one—stamped for Perth—from his breast pocket.

As the Amsterdam pilot taxied toward his takeoff, Allier caught a glimpse of the blond German under the tarmac lights: hatless, his coat flying back like wings, running hopelessly after the wrong plane.

·

Fog diverted them. As was expected.

They landed near dawn in a town Allier had never heard of, somewhere on the east coast of Scotland. A small field, quite deserted, the waiting-room windows blacked out with painted canvas. The pilot gave him tea. From politeness he tried to drink it.

"Did you hear?" the man asked him. "The Germans shot down that plane. The one bound for Amsterdam last night."

Allier thought of the young Italian girl, the two men arguing in Dutch, the child that would have been wailing, certainly, as the flames bloomed in the cockpit and the frantic pilot beat them back. The long tight fall into the North Sea, implacable as a destroyer's hull.

He set down the tea.

"What have you got in all those suitcases?" the pilot asked curiously. "The crown jewels of Norway?"

Allier glanced at the man. The truth was a breach of security but the pilot would never believe him, anyway.

"Water," he replied.

AMERICAN BUSINESS

MONDAY, MAY 13, 1940

CHAPTER ONE

Later, they would remember that spring as one of the most glorious they'd ever known in Paris. The flowering of pleached fruit trees and the scent of lime blossom crushed underfoot, the chestnuts unfurling their leaves in ordered ranks along the Champs-Élysées, the women's silks rustling like wings as they hurried to dinner—all had a perilous sweetness, like absinthe. Sally King, who had lived in the city for nearly three years now and might be acknowledged as something of an expert, maintained that even when it rained Paris was ravishing. The streets shone in the sudden torrents regardless of grime or automobile petrol or the piss in the open urinals; they glistened with a brilliance that was consumptive and suicidal.

She was surging against the tide of people on the Pont Neuf that night, across the narrowest point of the little island that sat like a raft in the middle of the Seine, having already fought her way past the shuttered bookstalls of the Quai de la Tournelle. She did not move swiftly, because the French heels of her evening sandals caught in the cracks between the paving stones. It was dark, blackout dark, and she would have liked a taxi but there were none to be found. She could sense the panic in the hunched shoulders and too-rapid steps of the Parisians, some of whom turned despite their fear and stared at her openly: Sally King, tall and angular, all her beauty in the impossible length of her legs, the clarity of her frame beneath the candy-wrapper gown.

She had been living among them long enough now to perfect her schoolgirl French and she understood the spattering of rumor and fear. *They've broken through the line. The Boches are through at Sedan. The army is in retreat—*

The news from the Front had blown through the city like a boiling wind. A whisper on the northern outskirts. The report of a friend of a friend. The streets were blazing with half-truths and exaggeration under the deep blue dusk of the shaded lights, and most people were milling south. Sally pushed north, toward the Right Bank and the exquisite little flat fronting on the Louvre. Philip Stilwell's place.

He had left her waiting at a table with a splendid view of Notre-Dame, conspicuously alone at La Tour d'Argent, not her favorite restaurant in Paris but certainly the most expensive. It was unusual for a woman to arrive without an escort but Gaston Masson, La Tour's manager, was accustomed to the peculiarities of Americans. If the rest of his diners chose to speculate on the cost of Sally's dress, her probable immorality, her purpose in waiting nearly an hour for a man who never showed up—she was at least decorative, and hence valuable against the backdrop of the Seine. Her face, with its high cheekbones and too-wide smile, was said to be famous. She was freakishly tall. She carried a gas-mask case instead of a purse and wore last year's Schiaparelli—an economical gesture in time of war. Shocking pink silk, embroidered with acid green bugs.

"Perhaps M. Stilwell is delayed," Masson observed apologetically. "If the Germans have broken our line . . . if they have crossed the Meuse and even now are on the march through Belgium . . . a lawyer might have much to do . . ."

But not tonight, Sally thought as she picked her way across the ancient bridge. *Tonight he was going to ask me to marry him.*

The note had come at five o'clock, hand-delivered by one of Sullivan & Cromwell's messengers because she had no telephone in her flat in the Latin Quarter. *Sally dearest I might be a little late for dinner this evening as I've an appointment with a member of the firm . . . Ask Gaston to seat you and order up a bottle of champagne . . .* A lawyer's wife, she'd thought, would have to adjust to such things. But Philip had never come; and rudeness was unlike him.

At the end of the bridge she hesitated. The darkened bulk of the Louvre loomed on her left. Without its usual blaze of light the city seemed forlorn and spectral, the people muttering through the streets like an army of the dead. Sally heard an air-raid siren shrill, and the high-pitched tinkle of breaking glass. A woman sobbed. Gooseflesh rose along her bare arms and she understood how solitary she was, how vulnerable. She ought to head for a bomb shelter, but nothing had fallen on Paris during the tedious eight months of phony war, so she squared her shoulders and walked toward Philip.

Another woman would have doubted herself. Assumed that he hadn't shown because he didn't love her. That simple thought never occurred to Sally. She had mapped Philip's soul quite thoroughly during the long months of the past winter, her job abruptly over, the whole question of her future hanging in the balance. She knew he'd been worried for weeks, and that it had something to do with S&C—with his work at the law firm of Sullivan & Cromwell.

They'd met the previous August, Philip new to Paris and losing his way on the Rue Cambon, searching for S&C's door and stumbling instead into the House of Chanel, which sat at number 31. Sally had been descending the famous staircase—Coco's preferred runway—to the admiration of the men and women seated expectantly below. It was Mademoiselle's fall collection, the last collection she would design for years, as it turned out. Sally had worn one of Coco's little black dresses, very chic and timeless in the usual manner; it was Chanel who'd made black fashionable when it had always been strictly for mourning. That August the color was disastrous, a presage of Poland's martyrdom, all diesel fumes and charred steel.

Philip watched the entire show from the doorway, and when approached by one of the *vendeuses,* stammered something about shopping for his mother. Sally'd agreed to have dinner with him, although she never really ate during the couture season. It was the beginning of an affair that had carried her headlong to this final night, the empty chair across the snowy linen, the curious gaze of the Paris streets. *A meeting with a member of the firm,* he'd said. And something had gone wrong.

Philip, she thought, fear knifing jaggedly through her. *Philip.*

She'd hung on all winter and spring in her apartment in the Latin Quarter, believing the news would change—hostilities would end—Hitler would go away. She rehearsed the truths Coco had taught her over the past three years, her inner voice less cultivated and more Western: *Raise the waist in front and a girl looks taller. Lower the back, and you hide a drooping ass. Dip the hemline in the rear because it'll hitch up along the hips. Everything's in the shoulders. A woman should cross her arms when her measurements are taken: that way she allows for enough give.*

He lived just off Rue de Rivoli where it met Rue St-Honoré. An old limestone pile arranged around a courtyard, a tall double doorway flung open all day. Some dead aristocrat's *hôtel particulier,* long since sliced into flats. Not a fashionable address, but Philip was too young and too foreign to know that. He wanted the heart of Paris: a view of the river from his salon, the cries of the knife-grinders beneath his window, church bells crashing into his bed at all hours of the night. Cracked boiserie and parquet that screamed underfoot. Mirrors so fogged they resembled pewter. Sally had lived in Paris longer but Philip loved the city better, loved the heartiness of her food and the guttural accents and the birdcages on the Ile St-Louis. Sunday mornings the two of them threw open the shutters and leaned on the windowsills, their shoulders suspended over the street, staring out at the world until their eyes ached.

She had four blocks still to walk when she saw the phalanx of cars from the *préfecture de police*. Philip's double-doored entry sprawled wide. Catching up her gas mask and silk dress, she began to run in the vicious sandals, straps cutting into her feet.

He was tied to the mahogany bedposts by his wrists and ankles, blood spattered the length of his nude body. She stood in the bedroom doorway swaying slightly, the police still unaware of her presence, and studied him: slack mouth, startled gray eyes, the lattice-work of ribs too embarrassingly white. The armpits monkeylike, the gourd of the hips and the knot of pubic hair at the groin, glistening with wetness. The erection still flagrant, even in death. Philip's penis, alert and red, something she'd touched once in a car. The whip forgotten on the rug beneath him. There was another man, also nude but a stranger to her, dangling from the chandelier. His toes were horribly callused, the joints blistered yellow.

Her mouth twisted and she must have gasped something in English—Philip's name, possibly—because one of the official French turned his head sharply and saw her, incongruous in her shocking pink gown. He scowled and crossed the room in three strides, blocking her view.

"Out, mademoiselle."

"But I know him!"

"I'm sorry, mademoiselle. You cannot be here. Antoine! *Vite!*"

She was grasped by the arm not ungently and led from the apartment, past the divan on which they'd had quick suppers, past the shutters they'd thrown open, a pair of highball glasses half-filled with drink. The wastebasket had overturned, and a few shards of glass were scattered on the threadbare Aubusson. She was dragged beyond the obscene figure dangling from the chandelier and into the hallway, where she began to shudder uncontrollably and the young man, Antoine—he wore a regular gendarme's uniform, not a detective's khaki raincoat—stood uncertainly clutching her elbow.

"Sally."

The quiet voice was one she knew. Max Shoop, who ran S&C's Paris office, in his elegant French clothes, his eyes remote and expressionless. They would have called Max, of course. She turned to him as a small child turns its face into its mother's apron, whimpering, her eyes scrunched closed.

"Sally," Max said again, and put an awkward hand on her bare shoulder. "I'm—sorry. I wish you hadn't seen that."

"Philip—"

"He's dead, Sally. He's dead."

"But how...?" She pushed Shoop away, eyes open now and staring directly at him. "What in the world..."

"The police think it was a heart attack." He was uncomfortable with the words and all that had not been said: the meaning of the whip, the determined tumescence. Two men dead with a simultaneity that suggested climax. But Max Shoop was not the kind to admit discomfort: He maintained a perfect gravity, his face as expressionless as though he commented upon the weather.

"Who," she said with difficulty, "is hanging from the ceiling?"

Shoop's eyes slid away under their heavy lids. "I'm told he's from one of the clubs in Montmartre. Did you ... *know* about Philip?"

"That he was ... that he ..." She stopped, uncertain of the words.

"My poor girl." Lips compressed, he led her away from the flat, toward the concierge's rooms one floor below. The good stiff shot of brandy that would be waiting there.

"It's not," she insisted clearly as he paused before the old woman's door, his hand raised to knock, "what you think, you know. It's not what you think."

CHAPTER TWO

The revue at the Folies Bergères didn't end until midnight, so Memphis never made it to the Alibi Club until one o'clock in the morning. Spatz knew exactly how the routine would go: The limousine and driver, the boy with the jaguar on its leash, Raoul hovering like a pimp in the background, his hands never far from his wife's ass. And Memphis herself: taller than a normal Parisienne, thinner and tauter, the muscles under the dark green velvet gown as coiled and sleek as the big cat beside her. She would pause in the curtained doorway as though searching the crowd—the Alibi Club was a true *boîte de nuit,* a box of a room holding maybe ten tables—and the effect would be instantaneous. Every head would turn. Every man and woman would rise, and applaud her again for the simple fact of her existence, for the whiff of exotic sex she brought into the place, of jealousy unappeased.

Spatz had seen it all before, month after month of his enslavement to Memphis—which had endured somewhat longer, he reflected, than most of his amusements. He was content to sit alone, nursing a cigar, a plate of hideously overpriced oysters untouched before him. Hundreds of people lined up outside the Alibi Club, but only forty would be ushered through the entrance ropes—and only Spatz was given a table in a corner by himself. Spatz's careless patronage paid the bills. The fact that he was German and officially an enemy of everyone in the room was immaterial. The man's French was perfect; he drew no attention at all.

He was a broad-shouldered, elegantly clad animal of the highest pedigree: Hans Gunter von Dincklage, coddled son of a mixed parentage, child of Lower Saxony, blond and inhumanly charming. Spatz meant *sparrow* in German. The name did not immediately suit him until one understood his habit of darting from perch to perch, whim to whim. His official title during the past few years was diplomat, attached to the German embassy, but the embassy was closed now because of the state of war and Spatz was at loose ends. He had spent the winter in Switzerland but had drifted back to Paris as the guest of a cousin who lived in the sixteenth arrondissement. His wife he had divorced years ago on the grounds of incompatibility. His enemies pointed out that she had Jewish blood.

He had done nothing of real note in all his forty-five years except play polo well at Deauville.

A girl in fishnet tights was passing gin, but Spatz preferred Scotch. He had just palmed the heavy glass, feeling its weight as a comfort in the hand, when a man slid into the empty seat beside him.

"This is a private table."

"I don't care," the man snapped. "I've been hunting

for you for *hours,* von Dincklage. You're *ridiculously* hard to find."

Spatz considered him. Fussy and small, with a toothbrush mustache and the sort of clothes that proclaimed the high-paid clerk; the sharp wet eyes of a blackmailer. He thought he could put a name to the man.

"You're Morris," he mused. "Emery Morris, am I right? You work for old Cromwell's outfit over near the Ritz."

"*Sullivan* and Cromwell," Morris corrected. "The New York law firm. I am a *partner* there."

"Call me tomorrow at home. I don't do business here."

Emery Morris glanced around him with a moue of distaste. "You'll have to make an exception. There is a matter of the *gravest* importance—"

But Spatz was ignoring him. He'd risen to his feet, his birdlike gaze fixed on the curtained doorway and the tall black goddess framed in the swinging curtains.

Memphis had arrived.

"What the *hell* you mean Jacquot's not here?" she breathed through her smile—her gap-toothed smile, practiced noon and night in the huge gilt mirror that hung in her salon off the Rue des Trois Frères, her dusky face melting into the shadows. She didn't care who saw her miming for the mirror, naked in the full-length glass, turning while maybe Raoul or somebody else looked on: *I'm just a little black gal from the hills of*

Tennessee, I don't know how I'm gonna survive in this big ole white town, you think I should go in whiteface and make the Frenchies do like Memphis, everybody wearing whiteface all the time like we gonna die of hunger and cold one day.

"I told you," Raoul muttered, fingers nervous in his pockets, face twisted in a grin. It was the carnival barker grin of a man who pulled the strings, except only Memphis decided who held the end of her rope and it hadn't been Raoul for a long, long time. "He never showed up. Baby, let's make the rounds and go. My skin's crawling just standing here. We got a train to catch."

"I ain't goin' nowhere," she murmured, her eyes on a bald man sitting in the front row, his look foolish as a bloodhound's, one of her regulars; she thought his name was M. Duplix. "I'm goin' to do my show." She swayed her long body in Duplix's general direction and smoothed his domed head with her gloved hands, crooning something her mama'd taught her years ago— sweet baby Jesus, how many years ago? Memphis was twenty-six this summer, and the years were just a string of beads around her neck. Married for the first time at thirteen. A runaway six months later and married again, this time in Chicago. A dancer in Paris by the time she was seventeen. A star by the time she was twenty, touring Scandinavia and Berlin where the riot police were brought out to protect her, degenerate that she was. Married most recently to the man who set up the Paris tour, the man who'd made her a household name: Raoul, the French Jew, thirty-nine and change, with his curling black mustache and his vague stories of titled Russian royalty, the connections he'd lost somewhere along the way. With her body and baby-cake voice and his smarts they'd made money hand over fist, most years, the Depression notwithstanding. Memphis never walked away from a show. Memphis never stopped dancing. She did ballroom teas off the Champs-Élysées at four and the Folies at ten and the Alibi Club at one A.M., and if she slept nobody but her lovers knew it, twisted in the fine linen sheets in the late hours of morning. Memphis sang for her supper and Raoul's, too. Raoul owned the Alibi Club; it was the one thing that kept them together, despite the endless bickering over money and the strangers she couldn't resist. He tolerated her string of men for the money they brought and the way they amused her; Memphis was too exhausting for one man to manage alone. In his own way, Raoul never stopped dancing, either.

They were both aliens, outsiders, the Jew and the Negress from Tennessee, leading the chicest city in the world with their daring and their jazz and their exquisite clothes. Fascists of every stripe and country hated Memphis and Raoul, hated the riffs they sold like cocaine on the streets of Montmartre. *Degenerate music,* they called it. *An alliance of half-apes and the Jews who train them, circus performers, shills.* The Fascists hated the German Kurt Weill, they hated Irving Berlin and Dizzy Gillespie and Josephine Baker, and they mounted an official exhibition of Degenerate Music to prove it. The show catalog had a black jazz trumpeter on the cover, a yellow Jewish star sewn on his lapel. Memphis framed the page with her name and hung it on the Alibi Club's wall.

She kept singing in that breathy croon, like a baby-doll girl in a candytuft dress, a little baby girl to bounce on your lap and make love to all night long. She breathed her way up and down the scale, smoky and sighing, through all the tunes Raoul decided would fit her range; he had the latest records flown in from New York like other men imported caviar. Memphis never sang the same song twice unless the man paid for it. Memphis always made him pay, whoever he was, and each and every one of them loved her for it—loved the bold crassness, the unabashed demands, the brazen greed. Memphis snatching a thousand-franc bill from an open hand, Memphis taking her revenge for all the years of closed hotels and barred dining rooms and exclusive toilets where only white people could pee, and singing while she did it. Offstage she was like something dead or thwarted; onstage, the footlights bathed her skin in a glow so rare she seemed luminous, incandescent, the whitest black woman on the face of the planet. On the rare days she couldn't perform—voice gone, throat scratchy from overuse—she fretted at the corners of her room like a penned dog.

Everybody knew now that the Nazis had broken through the line at Sedan, and Raoul was certain they were coming straight for the Alibi Club. *We've got a train to catch,* he'd said. *Before the knock comes on the door, baby. Before the truncheons fall and the pit opens and nothing and nobody can save us. You know what they do to Jews and blacks and people like Jacquot? Yellow stars. Pink triangles. Deportations and labor camps. No wonder fucking Jacquot never showed up for work.*

She was blowing kisses now to the regulars and making eyes at Spatz, sashaying her ass in his general direction just to tell him that she was his alone, his doll-baby with the electric fingers and the voice that purred in his dreams, even as she tried to stuff the panic back down into her shoes. Memphis would not be leaving, no sir, no way, no matter how many jackbooted Nazi shits marched into Paris in the morning, no matter how much Raoul begged and cried. Memphis was staying. A town full of soldiers meant a town full of money—a club full of pockets to burn—meant the world this girl was born to rule. Memphis was *staying* whether Raoul left or not. If she ran away again, she'd die.

On the small raised platform that served for a stage at the Alibi Club, everyone could hear her. That was what she loved about the place: when she opened her mouth here, the world fell silent. She settled herself on the stool in the center of the room, and sang.

"Strange," Spatz murmured as he studied her through a hanging veil of cigar smoke, composed as a statue in the circle of light, "Jacquot's missing. He normally twirls around while she sings. A number in black tie and tails. I wonder if he's ill?"

"He's *dead*," Emery Morris said flatly. "That's what I came to *tell* you. Dead in a flat off the Rue de Rivoli. I *saw* him myself."

"Alone?"

"*No.* With one of our people."

The admission cost Morris something and for a

second Spatz had no idea what it was. The lawyer had a reputation for discretion in Paris. Emery Morris was supremely respectable and unshakably trustworthy. There was a wife who kept to herself somewhere in the suburbs, a disinclination for drink even in the name of friendship. No sexual liaisons. No suggestion of a sense of humor. It was Spatz's business to probe for weakness in the men he encountered; he guessed Emery Morris's was a lack of imagination.

Jacquot the cabaret flame, the careless homosexual. Found dead with an American lawyer. Spatz's mouth knotted in a smile.

"I'm shocked."

"You *know* what he was," Morris spat out bitterly. "A *wretched* little *pervert*—an unnatural...he took *money* for what he..."

"Indeed. I'm simply astounded that his taste ran to Americans. For all his whips and cruelties, Jacquot was a snob. Your man killed him, I suppose?"

Behind the neat wire-rimmed spectacles, Morris's pupils flared slightly. "Probably the other way round. It is a *sordid* business and we've *got* to keep it out of the papers at *all cost*. With the war news, thank God, the suicide of a *queer* is hardly front-page stuff."

"But your dead lawyer?"

Morris leaned closer, his voice low. "That's why I've come to *talk* to you. We've got a *problem*."

He was gone by the time she finished singing, and Memphis never saw him go: The bright lights blinded her to the faces beyond, the tables that were filled. She sang for nearly an hour, then broke for a glass of champagne— so dry it burned in her throat, not at all the thing for singing, but the cut glass looked right in her elegant hand and it was important to work her image. She chatted with the regulars as she snaked among the tables, not wanting to look behind her for Raoul, who would be furious with impatience, his mind full of timetables. She cursed Jacquot for failing her; she would have to go home early, and then it would be the whole thing all over again: Raoul wanting to run. Raoul threatening her. Raoul.

There was a hand on her shoulder—not Spatz or her husband but An Li the driver, a Vietnamese Memphis kept for his exotic value, lithe and fastidious in his neat uniform. He bowed apologetically.

"M. Raoul took the car. He asked that I give you this, madame."

She snatched the slip of paper; scanned it hastily. Back home in Tennessee there were people who dared to say she couldn't even read, but Memphis had made sure her second husband taught her and she was always learning, always reading; she spoke French now and read the Paris papers. Her vision was slightly blurred tonight from the smoke or the lateness of the hour, or maybe it was the panic again, creeping up from her shoes, those precious shoes she bought in the Rue St-Honoré, the best lizard- and snakeskin, the pointiest toes.

Baby, Jacquot's dead and there's a cop at the door and if we get mixed up in police business we'll never get out of Paris. Baby, you close the club and you get our money

*when the bank opens tomorrow and you tell everybody
we're going on a long holiday because Memphis Jones
won't sing for the Germans. Meet me in Marseille as
soon as you can. I'll be waiting at the Hôtel
d'Angleterre. R.*

She crushed the slip of paper beneath her heel.
"Take the big cat," she told An Li, "and go on home.
Tonight Memphis is gonna party till dawn."

CHAPTER THREE

Sally King was shivering uncontrollably. The May night was cold, so she'd allowed Max Shoop to light a cigarette for her as he tucked her into the cab. It was lurching now along the Rue St-Honoré, and ash spilled down the silk gown. Sally didn't care. She would never wear this Schiaparelli again: she loathed its bright pink color, its swarming bugs, obscene as the last glimpse of Philip's body; the smudge of ash could serve as mourning.

Max had paid the driver to take her back to her apartment, but in the darkness of the muttering streets, the hordes of people still milling desperately toward the southern reaches of the city despite the lateness of the hour, Sally felt sick with claustrophobia. The dry, wracking spasms of hysteria and disbelief she'd stifled with a shot of the concierge's brandy were threatening to surface again. She closed her eyes and took a drag of smoke, willing the stuff to clear her brain.

We'd suspected for some time that Philip was disturbed, Max Shoop had said in that wretched room at the base of the courtyard, stinking of burnt sausage and mold. *Philip had been acting strangely. Secretive—distrustful.*

He saw plots everywhere. Probably because he felt guilty himself.

She'd tried to match this picture to the Philip she'd known—tried to think back to the last time she'd seen him, two days before as he walked briskly through the Place des Vosges. The pollarded trees were beginning to leaf; somewhere a soprano was practicing her scales, and the sound had spiraled in a lovely wash over the ancient square, echoing in the vaulted arches. He'd raced the last few feet to where she stood and caught her in his arms, heedless of whoever might be watching. *Springtime in Paris,* he'd exulted. *Who says there's a war on?*

Philip, guilty? Philip, disturbed?

She said nothing to Shoop about the note Philip had sent her, the alleged meeting with a member of the firm. It was obvious even to Sally that Philip's time had been spent differently. The image of his sprawling body—the penis bright and hard—the glazed eyes staring past her—sprang unbidden to her mind. The hand holding her cigarette trembled.

The chief thing, Max had said, *is to keep the truth from his parents. Wilson Stilwell is a judge, for Chrissake. No hint of scandal—we owe his family that. Will you accompany the body home?*

The body. Philip, at twenty-eight, a corpse.

She stared through a window fogged with cigarette smoke as though Paris itself had died. The crowd of midnight refugees was so thick in the Rue du Pont Neuf that the cabdriver cursed and abruptly threw his car into reverse. He turned west, up the Rue de Rivoli, in the opposite direction from the Latin Quarter. Sally was too numb to protest.

I want you out of Europe, Sally, Max had said. *Before all hell breaks loose, understand? I'll talk to somebody at the embassy tomorrow—*

The embassy.

They had reached the Place de la Concorde, and there it was: the United States' chancellery building, where the State department and the Army people and a few guys who worked for Commerce kept their offices. Though it was spanking new, it looked forlorn and unloved in the blue glow of blackout lighting. The chancellery gave out visas and dealt with such messy affairs as repatriating the dead, but Ambassador Bullitt actually lived elsewhere, in an elegant town house gifted to the American nation. Not even the Germans could faze Bill Bullitt; the U.S. ambassador would still be pouring champagne for anyone who held out a glass. Sally had met him at the embassy Christmas party: a barrel-chested, bald-headed dynamo who'd looked her up and down with the eyes of a connoisseur. She'd been wearing the same dress she was wearing now.

"Driver," she said clearly, "I've changed my mind. Take me to Avenue d'Iléna—Ambassador Bullitt's place."

It was Joe Hearst who won the right to talk to the most famous American girl in Paris, the one who'd been photographed by Horst, whose face had graced

Vogue during the autumn shows of '39, the impossibly tall young woman with the high cheekbones and the wide smile. She'd been recognized by one of the State department wives as she mounted the steps alone, uninvited to this party for Premier Paul Reynaud and the French Minister of War, Edouard Daladier, two men who perpetually swapped cabinet positions and cordially despised each other. Mims Tarnow remembered Christmas, remembered the shocking-pink gown, and although she was enough of a snob and a Radcliffe woman to feel herself superior to Sally King, she understood it was her grudging duty to report the gatecrasher to Bullitt's chargé, Robert Murphy.

Murphy fingered his lighter while Mims whispered in his ear, his head cocked toward the entrance foyer where more than a few of the French guests were already donning their wraps. Bullitt was known as "Champagne Bill" for his lavish parties, but with the news today out of Sedan nobody felt like celebrating; besides, Daladier's mistress refused to speak to Reynaud's. Sally King had paused uncertainly just inside the doorway, her expression blank and wooden. Her gas-mask case hung like the chicest of accessories from one sculpted shoulder; a smear of black trailed down her skirt as though she'd been grazed by a dirty fender somewhere.

Murphy felt a surge of impatience. *Innocents,* he thought. *Impossible innocents. They shouldn't be allowed out alone.*

"Find out what she wants, Joe," he muttered to the

political secretary standing silently at his right hand. "Thirty francs says it's passage home."

Joe Hearst had been in Paris for nearly eighteen months. Before that it had been Moscow. Before that, Geneva and Nairobi. Hearst was thirty-five years old, educated at Yale, a diplomat's son. He spoke five languages. His wife had left him suddenly the previous winter and nobody at the embassy could forget the fact. They betrayed their knowledge in awkward gestures of sympathy or poorly disguised glee. Only Bullitt, who'd had numerous women—who'd lived in a palace on a cliff overlooking the Bosporus with the notorious Louise Bryant—only Bullitt seemed to assume Joe Hearst still had a career. The rest of them were waiting to hear he'd been ordered home.

Hearst crossed the marble floor with an air of indifference, one hand in his pocket: a tall man in evening dress, body too gaunt for the breadth of his shoulders, eyes hawkish, deep gray, intimidating in their directness. The girl in last year's gown stepped backward as he approached. Apprehension flooded her face.

"Miss King, isn't it? Joe Hearst." He bowed—one of those European habits he'd acquired from childhood—and held out his hand. "We met at the Christmas party."

"Did we?" Her voice was frail as rice paper. "I don't remember. I'm looking for Ambassador Bullitt."

"I'm afraid the ambassador is engaged. May I be of help?"

He was playing his stock character: the mannered diplomat, too well-bred to be offended by a gate-crasher, intent upon blocking access to the Great Man. But his mind was wandering as he recited his lines, his eyes taking in the expression of bewilderment that lurked in the girl's face, the wisps of hair that had slipped from her chignon. *Like she's been knocked on the head*, he thought. *Or raped in a corner. What the hell happened to her?*

"It's the three glasses," she said irrelevantly. "I didn't really see them at the time but later, in the taxi, I remembered. Two on the windowsill. One smashed in the wastebasket. They don't make sense, any more than a word Shoop said."

Hearst frowned. "Are you unwell, Miss King?"

Her eyelids flickered and she swayed slightly, fingers convulsing on the strap of her gas-mask case. He guessed she'd carried it instead of an evening bag; everybody did.

He reached for her elbow and led her without a word into one of the wood-paneled rooms to either side of the entrance foyer: intimate rooms, with fireplaces in which nothing burned, a couch or two, shelves of leather-bound books, a single oil of the Hudson River School mounted over the mantel.

She sank down onto a fauteuil and stared blankly at her shoes.

"What is it?" Hearst asked gently. "What's happened?"

"Philip's been murdered," she said.

CHAPTER FOUR

The man known simply as Jacquot had lived in a number of places during the seventeen years he'd called Paris home. As a young man fresh from the provinces he'd sought a boardinghouse where the meals were provided by an indifferent cook; hopeful of securing a place in a reputable dance company—Diaghilev's, perhaps—he'd regarded the poor quality of the food as inducement to keeping his figure. In his thirties, the dream of classical ballet long since laid to rest, he'd held a coveted role at the club known as Shéhérazade—and had enjoyed a brief romance with the exquisite Serge Lifar, the most famous ballet dancer in Paris, then in his first youth and fame. In this period, too, Jacquot had acquired a taste for cocaine that proved ruinous to his looks and pocket. The worldwide economic depression of recent years, combined with his own advancing age, had further blasted the promise of his boyhood: In the past few months, Jacquot had descended from trysts on the Boulevard Haussmann and champagne at dawn, to a two-room flat in a rat-infested quarter of the twentieth arrondissement, not far from Père Lachaise cemetery.

Max Shoop had reached Jacquot's meagre place à few minutes past two A.M., having disposed of the police at Philip Stilwell's apartment and all their insinuating questions. It was they who'd told him the identity of the hanged man and the address of his flat. Shoop was almost finished rifling Jacquot's pathetically few belongings.

The main room held a stove and sink in one corner; these Jacquot had curtained off with a drapery of faded velvet. A divan of similar material, a scarred wooden table that served both cocktails and dinner; a shelf with a few books and photographs—one of them Lifar's dark profile, signed. A portrait of Cocteau. A feather boa, worn once in a production long ago. This was a public space and Shoop found nothing here of interest to himself.

The inner room was private, however, and here Jacquot had allowed his fancy full flight. The walls were lined in midnight blue silk, the bed draped à la polonaise. A writing desk with a modernist sculpture—possibly Braque, probably a copy—held down the view from the narrow window. It gave out onto a featureless alleyway and the collective washing of the tenement opposite.

Shoop had allowed himself a moment to gaze around; had considered briefly the vivid impression he received of carnal appetite and sexual abandon; and then gave himself up to the plunder of the desk.

He was a precise man, scrupulously self-controlled; a man of acute intelligence and subtlety who might have run an entire nation. He had settled instead for being a lawyer in Paris, where life was elegant and his freedom was complete. In New York he was pigeonholed: Max Shoop, Amherst 1910, Columbia Law. In Paris he could be anything: a criminal, a seducer, a builder and destroyer of worlds. In Paris, with his French wife, he might not even be American.

For this job he wore gloves. His eyes felt no strain in the blackout darkness; he carried a small flashlight with a blue lens, its beam narrow as wire. He stacked the miscellany of papers and bills the dead man had left behind in neat piles. He was searching for something he could not name but would recognize when he saw it. Shoop was calm—Shoop was always calm—but he was conscious of the passage of time. The police ought to be arriving at any moment.

He had just abandoned the desk and was opening the door to a clothes wardrobe when a key turned in the front door.

A key. In the hands of a friend, or the law?

Shoop froze. His silver head may have darted toward the window, but not even a man of his narrow frame could squeeze through the opening it offered, and the street was thirty feet below.

He slid noiselessly into the wardrobe instead.

And if it were the police? What then?

He would be discovered. Questioned. But Max Shoop, American citizen, managing partner of Sullivan & Cromwell's Paris office, could talk his way out of anything.

His feet were resting on a pair of ancient patent leather tap shoes. He quelled his breathing, ears strained to catch the sounds from beyond the wardrobe door.

A single pair of feet entered the flat. Light, staccato, hesitant footsteps uncertain of their ground. *Not* the police.

"Jacquot? Yoo-hoo, baby..."

A woman's voice—rich and breathless, an American voice. Shoop eased open the wardrobe door slightly and studied Memphis Jones, her back to the bedroom and her impatient body arrested in movement: no doubt wondering, Shoop guessed, where her dance partner had got to. He would simply wait for her to leave.

But she foiled him, turning swiftly to the bedroom and crossing it without hesitation. She wasn't looking for Jacquot any longer; there was unmistakable purpose in the beguiling face. Shoop caught the scent of roses mingled with cigar smoke as her current swept past him. Abruptly the sheets were torn from the bed and she was sliding deft hands under the mattress. With a whispered curse, she moved toward the desk. Another vulture turning over the bones.

The careful piles he'd made of Jacquot's papers held no interest for this woman; she scattered them like leaves. Then she turned without warning and yanked open the wardrobe door.

They stared directly into each other's eyes.

"Miss Jones," Shoop acknowledged. "A pleasure."

"What the *hell* you doin' in there, white man? And how come you know my name? *Shit*." She backed two steps toward the bed, her poise momentarily deserting her.

"Nobody in Paris is ignorant of your name." If he'd been wearing a hat he might have raised it to her. Irony was one of Shoop's more conscious arts.

"I asked who you are."

"Max Shoop. Attorney-at-law."

It was clear the name meant nothing to her. The jazz singer's eyes narrowed. "What you want with Jacquot?"

"I might ask the same of you."

"He didn't come to work tonight. I pay the man's salary, I want to see him in the club, you understand?"

"I do. But Jacquot's dead, Miss Jones—and I don't think it was his body you were looking for under the mattress."

Her eyelids flickered. "Jacquot took some cash off me a few days back. I need it now."

She never questioned the man's death, and she didn't mourn him, either, Shoop thought. "There's no money in the flat, and the police are coming. It could be awkward for you if you're found here."

She threw back her head and laughed. It was a sound so childlike and joyous he was startled.

"You think I was born yesterday, mistuh? You think Memphis is the kind of girl who does what she's told? I don't leave without my money—and if the police ask questions, I'll refer them to my lawyer. Mr. *Max Shoop* can tell 'em why he's hiding in Jacquot's closet."

He studied her face—intent and calculating, unmarked by weariness or her sleepless night. She was a force of nature, Memphis Jones, relentless in her self-absorption.

He decided she could be used.

"How much?" he asked, drawing his billfold from his pocket.

"Enough to get me to Marseille. Call it ... two thousand francs even."

"You could buy a train ticket for a couple hundred."

"Not on any train what's leaving today. Whole *world* wants to buy their way south *today*. And I ain't waitin' for tomorrow. Nosir."

"I'm surprised," Shoop said slowly. "A girl like you ought to jump at the chance to charm half a million soldiers."

"I maybe would have," she agreed, "except for the fact that my man left town last night with every last penny we'd saved. *Go to the bank tomorrow, Memphis. Tell 'em we're leaving town, Memphis.* Only the banks aren't paying a dime on Jewish accounts this week because of the Germans comin' and them banks thinkin' they'll get a windfall of hard-earned cash, you know what I mean? Ain't no accounts this little girl can touch today. You give me the money, mistuh, I walk away."

"It's not that simple."

She cocked her head, frowning at him. Shoop guessed he was the sort of man who turned up once in a while at her club: moneyed, aging, his appetites tightly buttoned beneath a starched white collar. She thought she knew what he wanted.

"You lookin' for a piece of sweet Memphis ass, mistuh? 'Cause if you are, I got to tell you I don't sell mine for a piddly-shit two thousand francs. And maybe there's no amount of money in the *world* would convince me to sell to *you*."

Shoop considered the offer, the episodes that might ensue. A faint singing in his brain at the thought of attitudes the woman could strike, at certain hours of the night.

"I want information," he said carefully, "about one of your men."

"There's a lot of those, mistuh." She sank down on Jacquot's bed and crossed her legs, looking profoundly bored.

He drew a fountain pen and checkbook from his breast pocket. Wrote a tight signature under the sum of a thousand dollars—redeemable for cash at the American Express office. At roughly thirty francs to the dollar, it was enough to get Memphis anywhere she needed to go.

He held the check under her nose.

Her eyes, rich and warm as fresh-cooked caramel, flicked up to his; he almost lost his resolve and begged her to take him.

"Which guy you mean?"

"The German," he answered softly, closing her fingers on the check. "The one who haunts your club. He calls himself *Spatz*."

CHAPTER FIVE

"So the guy was queer," Bullitt mused as the long black car nosed its way west toward the Bois du Boulogne, "and the girl can't accept it? *Bullshit*. Sally King's one of Coco's girls. She's no innocent."

The ambassador pulled a gold cigarette case from the pocket of his dinner jacket; Joe Hearst offered his lighter. It had been as the embassy was closing—Sally sent off at last in a taxi alone, the final stragglers sauntering down the steps—that Bullitt had thrown his hand casually on Hearst's shoulder and commanded, "Ride with me."

That might have meant an hour on horseback in the Bois before breakfast—one of Bullitt's inveterate habits—but tonight it referred to the car and driver and the trip west to the château he rented in Chantilly. Bullitt hated to be alone. Particularly in the wee small hours.

The yellow flame flared now under his chin, a jack-o'-lantern grimace, the face shrewd and hard in the flickering light. He was from one of the best Philadelphia families, a true blue blood of the old school—and yet at moments Bullitt looked like a gangster. The mix of breeding and brutality drew women like flies.

"She didn't pretend to be innocent," Hearst replied calmly. "She didn't deny the circumstances of the death. She's bothered by a third glass in a room with only two bodies."

"The glass was broken," Bullitt said dismissively. "What do you do, Hearst, when you've dropped a glass? Toss out the pieces and fetch another."

"But why use the cut crystal at all? From the sound of things, the night was better suited to swigs from a bottle or puffs on a hookah. I agree with Miss King: The detail doesn't fit."

"Sally's pretty enough," Bullitt observed. "You want to lift her skirt?"

"I'd like to send her back to the States on the first available ship," Hearst answered. "With the corpse, if possible."

"I'm acquainted with Stilwell *père*. The Judge, I should say. It's a damned shame. This fellow—the queer—worked for Sullivan and Cromwell, I understand."

"Yes. That's why it's particularly interesting," Hearst said neutrally. "The Dulles brothers."

The Dulles brothers.

John Foster and Allen, one the highest-paid lawyer in the world and the managing partner of Sullivan & Cromwell—and the other a new-minted partner at the same firm. Both men were socially connected on several continents and had been educated at Princeton.

Bullitt was a Yale man. He despised the Dulles brothers.

"God!" he snorted furiously. "Have you seen the unremitting *crap* Foster's pushing in the *New York Times*?"

"Yes, sir. I have." The newspapers were sent by diplomatic pouch and generally arrived within a week of publication.

"Dulles calls Roosevelt a traitor to his class! Insists we've misunderstood the Nazis—and should elect his friend Lindbergh instead. Trumpets free markets and debt relief as the foundation of peace. The world's going to hell in a handbasket and all Foster Dulles can think of is how to turn a buck. He was always a mercenary little shit, Foster."

"I didn't know you were acquainted, sir," Hearst said woodenly.

"*Years*. The bastard showed up at Versailles in 1918—not as a *delegate*, mind you; not as a *State department* body. As a *lawyer*."

Bullitt had attended the Versailles Conference, of course, as an official negotiator in President Woodrow Wilson's entourage.

"Foster shipped out from New York on pure speculation and crashed the most important diplomatic conference since Waterloo." The ambassador expelled a gust of smoke as though the taste were bitter in his mouth. "Eventually we all went home and left Foster to it. He made himself indispensable to the Allied Powers as an instrument of *compromise*. You know why he could compromise, Joe? Because Foster Dulles hasn't a principled bone in his body. Now the Germans pay him by the hour to say we screwed them at Versailles. Dulles is the biggest Nazi apologist in New York—and the wealthiest. We should shoot him for *treason*."

"But his brother—"

"Oh, Allen's all right." The cigarette tip waved in a glowing arc. "Fucks around on his wife, of course. I like a guy who knows how to live. Too bad he left State for S and C—but they say he needed the money. Buys his wife jewelry whenever he's feeling remorse. I doubt a State department salary runs to Tiffany's these days."

Or to Balenciaga, or Cartier, Hearst thought with a nod to his own vanished wife. Bullitt was independently wealthy; he never thought about such matters as salary.

"Allen knows France'll fall like a house of cards now the Germans are over the border," the ambassador added bleakly.

This was not what he'd told the assembled ministers of French government only an hour ago; for them, Ambassador Bullitt had been disgustingly cheerful. Most of tonight's partygoers had looked as gutted as a bunch of stockbrokers on Black Tuesday. Bullitt had tried to buck them all up with grand phrases about the fighting spirit of the French. Refilled their champagne glasses. Complimented the women. Reynaud and Daladier and the Minister of Armaments, Raoul Dautry, talked hopelessly of a street-to-street fight for the soul of Paris. Suggested that Winston Churchill, who'd been appointed prime minister of Britain only three days before, might send more troops. They planned an official delegation to the Cathedral of Notre-Dame—their defense of the country coming down to this: a prayer to God, who must certainly be French, to send the Germans home.

"If France falls, England'll sink in a matter of weeks," Bullitt continued. "We'll have Oswald Mosley in number ten Downing Street and the Royal Family running for cover. The chief point is to get the British fleet to Canada, as I've told Roosevelt already—for his eyes only, of course. God forbid any real advice should be uttered in public! We have to look neutral, Chrissave us—because of people like Foster Dulles."

Joe Hearst, too, had met Foster once, during a halcyon summer on Long Island in the early thirties: pipe-smoking, reserved to the point of distraction, as emotional as a dead fish. Hearst had been hired to teach Allen Dulles's children to play tennis—and it was true the guy fucked around; he'd seduced a beautiful Russian tennis player that summer, the wife of a good friend. Foster was respected by most of New York, and the long-suffering Clover Dulles was commonly considered to be a saint, but it was Allen whom Hearst had instantly liked—Allen who was just as ruthless as his older brother but who masked his deadness behind a veneer of charm, enslaving children and adults with a single cock of an eyebrow. Hearst had stayed in touch with Allen all these years because a letter from the man made him feel like one of the Brahmin elite—*My friend Hearst. He's something at the embassy.* The letters from New York had been coming thick and fast in recent months, and it was clear, Hearst thought, that Allen Dulles was worried. About the state of Europe. About the state of Sullivan & Cromwell. The state of his brother's soul...

"How I'd love to stick it to Foster," Bullitt mused wistfully. "Smear his pompous little firm all over the world's papers. *Sullivan Lawyer Dead in Sex Den,* or something like that. But it can't be done, of course. There's the young man's family to think of."

Bill Bullitt might dismiss Philip Stilwell as a "queer," but Philip Stilwell had the right money and connections behind him, and in Bullitt's world such things were absolute.

"Miss King believes Stilwell was murdered," Hearst observed.

"Bullshit," the ambassador repeated.

"She showed me a note he sent her this evening. Had it tucked in her gas-mask case."

"Pledging deathless passion? Undying love? Come on, Joe. Men have been lying to women since the first hour in the Garden. Especially when they're queer."

" '*Sally dearest I might be a little late for dinner this evening as I've an appointment with a member of the firm,*'" Hearst recited. " '*This business of Lamont's can't be allowed to continue; it's immoral, it's illegal, and it's going to sink us all.*'"

The ambassador frowned. "Lamont. Lamont?"

"Rogers Lamont," Hearst supplied. "Another Princetonian. Another S and C lawyer. He quit the firm back in September and joined the British Expeditionary Force. He's probably retreating right now from Sedan."

"What the hell's Lamont got to do with two dead queers?"

"Miss King thinks Philip Stilwell stumbled onto

something dirty in Lamont's papers," Hearst said patiently. "Something he shouldn't have seen. She thinks Stilwell was dangerous to people in power. She thinks he was silenced."

"By somebody at Foster Dulles's firm?"

Hearst nodded.

Somewhere in the night, an air-raid siren wailed. Bullitt sank back into the shadows of the great car.

"Find out," he said.

CHAPTER SIX

Emery Morris was nearly fifty years old. He had, by dint of discretion and steady labor, arrived at a certain position in life. If asked to describe the exact dimension and location of that position, the parameters it filled, Morris would have hesitated or demurred. He would have prevaricated. He was not a man who enjoyed being pinned down. Although in matters of law Emery Morris demanded precision, in the personal realm he was tenaciously vague.

But his enjoyment of the position he had attained was predicated upon certain inviolable rules. One was that he be free of all personal entanglements. Entanglements were simply means to an end—in Morris's opinion, the control of oneself by people one despised. His wife, whom he'd acquired as a necessary prop in the business of respectable existence, was included in this category.

A similar rule applied to his clients. Their legal matters might demand Emery Morris's genius, and if he was well compensated for the devotion of his time and intelligence, so be it. The nature of the person who paid the bill—whether he was glamorous or repugnant, sympathetic or evil—was unimportant. Morris would do his job. The standards he set, and the manner in which he reached them, were his alone to decide.

Morris's third law was that he required exactly eight hours of sleep each day. It was the violation of this law that had him twitching now with indignation as he paid off his taxi in the Rue Cambon, at twelve minutes past two o'clock in the morning. He was bone-tired and it was Philip Stilwell's fault.

He waited until the taxi's taillights diminished around a corner. The breathless precincts of Place Vendôme, the hushed portals of the Ritz, the jewelers' shuttered vitrines, the base of the obelisk heavily sandbagged lest Napoleon's statue should fall to a German bomb—were dead quiet at this hour. Elsewhere Paris stuttered in her sleep, but not here, where a single light pierced the blackout shades of the Ritz Hotel. Morris had never felt the pulse of Paris as a living thing and so he turned his back on the square and thrust his key in the office building's outer door. Cursing Stilwell, who was dead, and Rogers Lamont, who might be retreating even now from the enemy at Sedan. Most people thought that Morris and Lamont were friends. The assumption would have surprised both of them.

He yawned cavernously as he mounted the uncarpeted steps. A second taxi in an hour's time. There would be boxes, too heavy to handle alone. He would have to tip the driver.

* * *

Spatz had not watched Emery Morris go. The two men exchanged no pleasantries or clasped hands. They walked away from each other outside the Alibi Club, one toward the taxi idling in the street, the other with his fists thrust in his pockets, as though they did not know each other's name. This indifference might one day be crucial.

Like everyone who chose to navigate the blacked-out city streets, Spatz carried a pocket flashlight with its lens painted dark blue. The night was moonlit, however, and he did not bother to switch on the torch as he walked. His bright bird eyes glittered and his blond head was thrust forward, as though he listened to an intimate conversation. Spatz liked this time of night in Paris, this freedom of the streets, the way the old buildings and all the lives they'd lived were his for the embracing. There had never been a kingdom he'd wanted more than this.

The German's career was a series of entanglements, of leverage bought and sold, of blackmail and emotion and losses he never tallied. He was thinking as he walked of Jacquot dangling from a chandelier and of the way the American named Morris had failed to blink as he talked in a rapid undertone, the words peppering Spatz's cheek like bullets. The crooning voice of Memphis Jones filtered through his thoughts; she would be furious in the morning at his desertion.

He walked for thirty-three minutes, an apparently aimless jaunt that looked like a series of concentric circles—narrowing, narrowing, on a target he had not yet defined. He could have returned to the palatial spread he'd appropriated in the sixteenth arrondissement, but the cousin who owned it was expected hourly and Spatz was not in the mood to see her. War had changed his indifferent relationships, put a price on their heads. For months he'd been coasting on the assumption that nothing terrible could really happen: The German army's breakthrough at Sedan had forced the issue of his future. In a different way, so had Emery Morris.

Morris's problem was a poker chip offered on a silver platter. The lawyer expected Spatz to pass the word about Philip Stilwell to his superiors in Berlin; but Spatz was in no hurry. Stilwell was dead. Much might be made of the opportunities the young man had left behind.

He fetched up thoughtfully in the Rue St-Jacques just as the bells of Saint-Séverin and Saint-Julien-le-Pauvre rang out two-thirty. The huge acacia tree in the Square Viviani was almost as old as the bells. He smoked a little, feeling the spring air tremble around him as though it had turned to deep water. In the silence that followed the churches' clangor, he became aware that his eyes were fixed on a window in the apartment building opposite, two stories above the ground and to the left of the entrance. A blue glow suggested blackout lighting within. A silhouette paced, dark against the darkness of the shade. Stilwell's woman was still awake.

Spatz smiled to himself—amused by the relentless imperatives of the unconscious, which had brought his feet to the very spot Emery Morris had suggested—and tossed his cigarette in the gutter. As he crossed the street he began to whistle a fragment of song—something, had he known it, of Memphis's.

Three stacks of files teetered on the floor in front of Emery Morris: those that meant nothing, those he intended to keep, and those he must destroy.

He had searched every drawer in Rogers Lamont's desk, had rifled the crates stacked neatly behind Madame Renard's reception post, had even jimmied the flimsy lock on Philip Stilwell's small office. The self-conscious diplomas mounted on the plaster wall, the framed black-and-white portraits of the parents, a publicity shot of the girl who'd shown up in the Rue de Rivoli a few hours ago—Morris had met Sally once at the Ritz Bar and disliked her on principle; no decent woman would allow her body to be outlined like that, day after day, would stand quietly before the photographers like a cow in an abattoir. *Cow,* he muttered under his breath as his white hands skimmed over the manila. *Cunt. Whore.* A faint odor of sweat and failure hung in his nostrils.

Forty-one minutes had passed and he understood now what was missing. The one file that should never have been opened. The file that should not exist.

He paused for an instant in the middle of Philip Stilwell's office. The young fool had stolen it from

Lamont's things, of course—but what had he done with it?

Then it came to him, obvious as day.

"The *girl*," he said.

She was leafing through every scrap of paper Philip had ever written to her over the past eight months—stray notes, unsigned fragments, the odd gift card he'd left on her pillow, as though the fine, careless handwriting were ephemeral, as though it might evaporate from her hands like his breath or the light in his eyes. She had kept most of his notes in the foolish belief that they would be cherishable one day, a bit of nonsense she could retrieve from some Connecticut attic with the vague words, *Those are from when I knew your father in Paris, before the War.*

She was drinking Pernod because it was what Philip preferred and she needed some way to reach him. Panic had swept over her like a frigid ocean wave the instant she'd closed the door of her flat, panic that might have come from the blankness of the hour, or from the image of Philip's body she could not get out of her head, but which she thought had more to do with the absolute certainty that she was alone again, alone without prospects or money or anyone to help her and the Germans were marching steadily through Belgium. Sally was feeling maudlin and light-headed, weeping cross-legged on the floor in her bathrobe, because she had never eaten dinner after all and the licorice-flavored fire had gone straight to her brain. Panicking

THE ALIBI CLUB • 55

because she did not know how she could stay in Paris now and she did not want to go back—not to Denver or to the unknown house on Round Hill and the woman who would certainly blame her, simply because she, Sally, had been here in Paris and still Philip had died.

When the knock came on the door it startled her so much that she spilled the Pernod down the front of her robe. Then, *Tasi,* she thought—meaning the woman who lived next door, a Russian émigré by the name of Anastasia who made a dubious living as an escort at one of the nightclubs. Tasi worked all hours and never slept; her apartment was a fog of smoke and samovar fumes. She would know from the sound of pacing that Sally was up, and when she opened the door Tasi would be standing there with a cigarette in her hand, eyes lined perfectly with kohl, hoping for a shot of vodka. Sally opened her mouth to call out, shut it again. She could not face Tasi tonight.

The second knock was harder, peremptory, a summons that would not be denied.

"Mademoiselle King? It is the police. *Ouvrez la porte, s'il vous plaît.*"

The sigh that escaped Sally was almost a sob. They had figured it out, then. *She wasn't crazy.* They understood at last that Philip had been murdered and the whole scene in the Rue de Rivoli was a macabre farce. Maybe the man at the embassy had told them: If the French cared nothing for justice, Americans *did.*

Sally drew the back of one hand across her wet eyes and bounded to the door.

The corridor was dark as though even the blue-painted

bulbs had died, but she registered the man's evening dress, the gentleness of his face and the way he seemed to smile as he reached for her neck with both hands. She gasped as the world went black, like a woman surprised by love.

CHAPTER SEVEN

Joe Hearst had not slept well since Daisy left him. It was possible he'd grown accustomed to the protective cover of his wife's voice, had grown accustomed to receding into the stage set of her world, a bit of fifth business blending with the woodwork. There'd been a comfort in the way he'd moved, unnoticed. Now, in the echoing height of the stripped-down rooms off the Rue Lauriston, he was self-conscious, too aware of silence and his inability to fill it. He caught glimpses of himself unexpectedly in mirrors, furtive and unrecognizable. Took to walking the sixteen hundred square feet in his bathrobe and slippers, the hallways resolutely unlit, humming a jagged tune.

By dawn the morning after Stilwell's death, Hearst was trolling the floor with a cup of coffee in his hand, senses singing. He'd made a list of questions and he was conning it as fervently as any boy had ever learned Shakespeare.

1. Did Stilwell's secretary keep a record of his
   outside appointments?

2. Did anybody ask the building concierge whether she saw Stilwell or his guest(s)?
3. Was there a third man? (Or woman?)
4. What was drunk from the lowball glasses?
5. How did Stilwell die? (What 28-year-old man suffers a heart attack???)
6. Why are Sullivan & Cromwell's Paris lawyers still reporting for work in May when Foster Dulles shut down the office last September?

He could think of at least a dozen more perplexing details that warranted investigation, but they were hounded from his mind and scattered to the four winds by the persistent and haunting image of Sally King's face.

He had seen anguish there last night, but also a keen desire for justice that bordered on compulsion. Had she loved Stilwell? Or had it been just a "good" marriage—a ticket home from a life at Coco Chanel's autocratic beck and call? Had Stilwell and Sally been just a pair of conveniences for each other—the homosexual and the social climber—or had they been lovers?

Hearst had been searching for answers to the nature of love for some time now, but he was well aware that his personal preoccupations—his loitering in the halls of philosophy—had nothing to do with Philip Stilwell. Two men were dead and the Germans were coming. The specifics of Sally King's affair were irrelevant.

He set down the coffee cup—which had lost its saucer somewhere in his travels—and leafed again through the pages he'd been reading as the sun came up over Paris. A letter dated more than eighteen months ago, recounting events that had occurred in the fall of 1935.

"... most inappropriate that we should continue to represent German clients at such a time, when New York firms had already closed their offices or severed relations with agents in Frankfurt, Munich, and Berlin ... I represented to my brother that his dedication to those friends of several decades' standing is understood but that friendship is conditional in the current circumstances ... The personal interest must not be allowed to stand against the public duty ... He maintained that his was a position of principle, well-founded on intellect and experience, and that but for the exploitative and opportunistic leadership of our day these difficulties would not have arisen ... But to accept such treatment of our Jewish clients worldwide, not to mention our Jewish law partners, by National Socialist policies is unacceptable ...

Allen Dulles.

Hearst could almost hear the dry, practiced voice—hear the sardonic phrases with their undercurrent of violence. Allen Dulles was a man of cold temper and controlled passion—which in Hearst's view was far preferable to his brother Foster's talent for feeling nothing.

There had been a bitter scene in the S&C boardroom that day in 1935 when Foster Dulles was forced to shut down Berlin. Allen had tried to reason with him in private. Had told him it looked bad to cater to S&C's Nazi clients when those clients were scapegoating Jews. But Foster refused to listen to his little brother and so Allen had brought the issue to a full partnership vote—and won.

Some people claimed Foster had actually cried.

Then he backdated the decision in the firm's records to 1934.

If Allen raised the matter in his letter to Hearst all these years later, it was not because he liked airing his brother's soiled pajamas or because he was a vicious gossip but because he was not a man to be lulled by false peace. The Berlin office was closed and most of its lawyers had moved. Not back to New York, incidentally, but to Paris...

> *"...naturally, Joe, I would be grateful for any early warning you could give of a deterioration in circumstances..."*

What, exactly, did Allen mean? Early warning of the German advance? Timely notice of the fall of France? Allen Dulles possessed friends in Washington who could cable the news before it happened. Allen didn't need a political secretary in Paris for that. Hearst fingered his coffee cup, empty now, and considered the Dulles he'd known. Ruthless eyes behind steel-rimmed spectacles. A neat mustache. The precision of the sensual lips. The restless fingers. Dulles would know by now that Philip Stilwell was dead—his partner Max Shoop would have sent a telegram immediately to New York. Something oblique and terse, details to follow by personal letter. Hearst imagined Dulles taking a car and driver—the time change would make such things possible—and heading to the Stilwell household in Connecticut to break the news.

Did he sense the threat looming? Did he know that scandal—and all avoidance of it—hinged on his firm's ability to silence Sally King?

It was Tasi Volkonskaya, returning from the Club Shéhérazade at dawn, who found her.

The door to Sally's flat was ajar and blue light crept out into the corridor, which was predictably dim. Tasi rapped on the wood and called out *bonjour* as though she had every intention of breezing past to her own flat, but the lack of response from Sally brought her up short. She peered around the jamb at the small studio beyond.

It had been torn apart.

Papers, scarves, clothing, and books lay tossed on the floor, canned goods and coffee grounds and ink were spilled on the carpet. Even Sally's underthings were scattered across the back of one of her Louis Quinze chairs, the pair she'd found in the flea market with Philip and had painted white like something out of Elsie De Wolfe. Sally herself was lying like a queen on the sofa that did double duty as a bed. With a surge of irritation Tasi realized she'd gone to sleep in the middle of all the destruction, like a child worn out by a temper tantrum. Then she saw the purple bruises on Sally's neck.

Cautiously, she picked her way across the floor in her dance sandals. For an instant she swayed above the prone figure as though afraid to disturb the dead. The eyes were closed and Tasi thought that a good sign—every corpse she'd ever known had been wide and staring. She reached tentatively for one slack wrist and felt for a pulse.

Later, when Mme. Caullebaut the concierge was done screaming and the ambulance klaxon had died away on its careening route to the Hôpital d'Étrangers, Tasi lingered in Sally's empty studio long enough to light a cigarette. It was hard to know where to start. She picked up a book or two, set them in neat piles against the wall, retrieved a vase and discarded some wilted flowers. Freesias, from the market on the Ile St-Louis—that would be Sally's Philippe, always the white flowers of every description filling the corridor with scent. Had her lover given her those bruises, toppled the books from their shelves?

Tasi lounged in the doorway, dragging at her smoke. Sally might never wake up, she might die *enfin,* and there would be family back home that would wish to know the name of the responsible party. She surveyed the flat critically, searching for . . . what?

There was the sleeping divan, the wardrobe with its doors pulled crazily wide, the screen behind which Sally dressed, the full-length mirror. The pair of Louis Quinze chairs. A gas burner, seldom used, and the sink. The communal bath was at the end of the hall.

Tasi's eyes fell on the gas-mask case, tossed like a lump of coal between the wardrobe and the dressing screen. She had frequently envied Sally that mask; they'd been issued to every Parisian citizen, but not to most foreigners. Carrying one was a sign of belonging. She wondered again where the girl had gotten it. *Philippe*, she decided with chagrin—and reached for the case.

Inside, there was the mask—a furled rubber gargoyle—and Sally's papers, her *carte d'identité* affirming she was a neutral American citizen. Blond-haired women could not be too careful these days: German spies were known to be everywhere, Fifth Columnists they called them, and blondes were constantly being questioned by police.

She had dispatched Sally to the hospital without her identity card, a complication for the poor girl; but *tant pis*, Sally could never prove Tasi had been anywhere near her things; she'd been dead to the world when the ambulance crew took her. Tasi pocketed the card—a Jewish woman of her acquaintance would pay anything on earth for a neutral's papers. She probed deeper in the case, hoping for a passport. At the bottom, forty-nine francs in coin. Cigarettes. A powder compact. A lipstick in a shade of shocking pink.

And a single business card with the name *Joseph W. Hearst, Embassy of the United States of America,* engraved on it.

Tasi pursed her lips and fingered the square of heavy card stock. The nearest telephone was in the *tabac* on the corner of Rue St-Jacques, and it was probably still too early to call. She would have to change into something more suitable. Make coffee. Decide exactly what story she had to tell, and how she should tell it.

"Sally King has been attacked."

Bullitt looked up from his desk, where he was scanning a cable from the White House, and scowled at the figure in his doorway. Hearst's hands were pressed against the jamb, head thrust forward like a greyhound's. The ambassador was tempted to snap his head off at the interruption, but he was intrigued by the fury in the younger man's face. Bullitt had never seen Hearst shaken out of his diplomatic manners—not even when they'd chatted, as convention forced them to do, the morning after Daisy's cataclysmic departure. Then, Bullitt had admired Hearst's almost English indifference to pain. Today he was witness to something far less controlled.

"Sit down."

Hearst ignored him, roaming the broad Turkish carpet Bullitt had found in a souk and flung in front of the desk in memory of the palace on the Bosporus.

"She's in the Hôpital d'Étrangers with a fractured skull and a set of bruises that suggest somebody tried to strangle her. They didn't waste time, did they?"

"They?"

"Whoever killed Stilwell! You can't deny the connection, sir. The woman who called—a neighbor—said Sally's place was a shambles."

So it's Sally now, is it? Bullitt mused, and said, "Anything stolen?"

Hearst shrugged impatiently. "God knows. She still hasn't come round—she may never...It's just such a bloody *waste*."

"You think there's a tie to that business over at Sullivan and Cromwell?"

"Of course!"

"—As opposed to a random mugging of a woman who came home too late, without protection?"

Hearst stared at him incredulously.

Bullitt sank back in his massive chair and thrust Roosevelt's instructions aside with his left hand. His reading glasses dangled from his right. "Give it to me straight, Joe. What'd the police say about Stilwell's death?"

Hearst had arrived at the embassy just after seven-thirty that morning and Bullitt was told the young man hadn't even waited for coffee before setting out with a Frenchman named Petie for the *préfecture de police*. Petie was Pierre duPré, a sardonic bastard in a dark blue beret who'd worked for the embassy for most of the past decade. He'd told the ambassador about the trip himself.

"Exactly what we'd expect," Hearst spat out. "Stilwell's death is accidental and his friend's is called suicide. Autopsies to follow."

"But you're not buying it."

Hearst finally came to a halt in front of Bullitt's desk. "Miss King tells us her story, sir, and is nearly killed a few hours later. Her flat is searched with a fine-tooth bulldozer. *Somebody's looking for something. Something they've already killed to hide.*"

"What do you want me to do, Hearst? Call Premier Reynaud and demand an explanation?"

"You might call the Superintendent of Police. Sir."

There was a dry cough, the merest suggestion of an interruption, from the ambassador's doorway. Hearst tensed; Bullitt quirked an eyebrow at his chargé, Robert Murphy.

"What is it, Bob?"

Murphy glanced at a sheet of paper. "We're getting reports of trainloads of Dutch and Belgian refugees arriving at the Gare du Nord. Red Cross evacuation trains, filled with women and kids. Most of them are wounded or dead."

"*Dead?*"

"The Germans apparently strafed the rail lines. Regardless of the fact that the trains were plastered with signs saying *Enfants. Croix Rouge.*" Murphy's eyes met Bullitt's. "Survivors are being taken to various hospitals, sir. I'd like Hearst to make the rounds—talk to whomever he can—see what these people know of the Nazi advance. They're the only eyewitness reports of the Front we're likely to get."

"Goddamn sonuvabitch Krauts—" Bullitt snarled, then gave Hearst a long look. "Joe, why don't you start with the Hôpital d'Étrangers?"

"I'll get my hat," he said quietly.

"One more thing, sir," Murphy attempted, as Bullitt reached for the President's cable again. "I know it's annoying on a morning like this, but he refused to be turned away—"

"Who?"

"Mr. Max Shoop, of the law firm Sullivan and Cromwell. He's demanding to see you."

CHAPTER EIGHT

He reminded Hearst of a cardinal as he waited in the doorway: silently observing, judging them from heavy-lidded eyes. Max Shoop had come to do battle, and he'd already won the first round. Bill Bullitt had agreed to see him.

"*Max*. Pleasure." Bullitt rose and extended his hand. "I don't think we've met since the Christmas party. How's Odette keeping?"

"Quite well, Mr. Ambassador," Shoop returned, "although she's worried about the Germans, naturally. She remembers 1914."

"Take her back to New York for the duration."

Shoop smiled tightly. "I doubt Odette would go."

"You know my political secretary, Joe Hearst?"

"We met at Christmas." Shoop reached for a chair, dismissing the younger man completely.

Hearst's antagonism flared. He wanted to grab Shoop by his starched white collar and say *Which of you tried to strangle her last night?*

"What can we do for you, Max?" Bullitt asked.

The lawyer settled his hat on his knee, fingers carefully balancing. "Well, Bill—we've had an unfortunate thing happen over at S and C. One of our junior people died suddenly last night of a heart attack."

"Philip Stilwell."

"So you know. The police...?"

"The police," Bullitt agreed. "Hearst here has already talked to the Sûreté."

The carefully veiled eyes slid to Hearst's face. Hearst felt the lawyer's calculating intelligence roam over him like a pair of gloved hands, and resented it. He decided to shock the man.

"Miss King appeared at the embassy last night and told us her fiancé was murdered."

"Murdered?" Shoop's expression did not change. "What an extraordinary statement. I suppose she was... overwrought."

"She's in the hospital this morning with a fractured skull," Bullitt observed.

"Good God." A tremor seemed to run through the lawyer's body, but he masked it by shifting his weight in his chair. "I'd no idea. What happened?"

"Somebody tried to strangle her," Hearst said. "He was hunting for something—Miss King's flat was apparently ransacked. Do you know what he wanted, Mr. Shoop?"

Max Shoop did not reply.

Hearst paced slowly across the room and stood over Shoop's chair. "Your lawyer's dead and his girl's seriously injured. It's not a coincidence. It won't be explained away. You'd better tell us what's going on at Sullivan and Cromwell before someone else dies."

Shoop's mouth twisted. "I'm tempted to say I want my lawyer present. But *I'm* the lawyer, aren't I? So that appeal won't help."

He was determined to protect something or someone—a colleague, the law firm, himself? Hearst waited, his eyes fixed on the lawyer's rigid face. He could feel Shoop composing his careful responses.

"Can you promise me that what I tell you will not leave this room?"

"No." Bullitt shook his head regretfully. "My first duty is to the President, Max, as you well know. But if I can hold your confidence without violating *his*—I'll do so. Word of a gentleman."

"If I have the slightest reason to believe Philip Stilwell was murdered and you're implicated," Hearst said, "I'll do my damnedest to see you hang, Mr. Shoop. Word of a gentleman."

"It's the guillotine in this country." Shoop tapped the brim of his hat with one long finger; his expression did not alter. "Very well; I'll take my chances. You know that Foster Dulles, our managing partner in New York, officially closed the Paris office last September, when war was declared between Germany and France."

"But you're still going into the office each day. And eight months have passed. What're you doing there?"

"Spinning straw into gold, Mr. Hearst. Before the Germans roll into France and all the straw goes up in smoke."

"Meaning?"

"Jewish businesses. Jewish banks. Jewish partnerships that govern some of the most lucrative enterprises in Europe. Millions of dollars of assets and stock and financial relationships are at risk once the Nazis take over France, which, as we all know, they're likely to do in a matter of weeks."

"But Hitler confiscates Jewish business," Hearst objected. "It's happened everywhere—Czechoslovakia, Austria, Norway. Germany itself."

"Exactly," Shoop agreed. "Which is why, for the past eight months, we've been working day and night on behalf of our Jewish clients. Fabricating paper trails that suggest their assets and businesses and financial arrangements are *actually* owned by entities in neutral countries. Sweden, for example. Spain or Portugal. Even, at times, entities in the United States."

"You think the Nazis give a good goddamn what the paper trail says?" Hearst spat.

Shoop stared back at him blandly. "Thus far, the National Socialist government has respected the rights and property of *neutrals*. The trick is getting enough neutrals to underwrite our program. We've had to find partners with deep pockets willing to serve as holding companies for an indeterminate period. That's been difficult. A fake transfer of ownership demands a certain level of risk—or a suicidal commitment to charity. The Wallenberg family has been helpful in Sweden, but they're damnably shrewd and we can't be sure they'll honor their agreement when the fighting's done."

"Meaning?"

"There's an unwritten stipulation in every case that when the war is over—if it's ever over—the Jewish partners get their assets *back*."

"And your Jewish clients are willing to go along with this?"

Shoop shrugged. "Some are. The ones who've worked with us longest, the ones who are the most desperate. There are others . . . I've noticed a reluctance to believe the worst will happen. A desire to think that France will halt the Germans in their tracks and business will go on as usual. That's not the picture of the future I've painted to my people, but not all of them are willing to take my advice."

"Does Dulles know what you're doing?"

"Yes." Shoop smiled thinly. "It's business, after all. Foster understands the concept of turning a buck better than anyone in the world."

Bullitt barked with laughter. "Doesn't he just."

"Was Philip Stilwell working on this project to transfer Jewish ownership?" Hearst asked.

"He was."

"Would someone kill him for it?"

Shoop steepled his hands—the Pope, considering the doctrine of infallibility. "Kill Philip in order to *prevent* the transfer of a given company's ownership, you mean? Surely there are less drastic methods. Like waiting a week for the Germans to arrive, and shut us completely down."

"You went to Stilwell's place last night," Hearst persisted. "Why?"

"Philip asked me to come. He wished to discuss a private matter."

"Rogers Lamont's business."

For the first time, Shoop's eyes darted uncontrollably to Hearst's face. He hadn't expected the attack; he thought he'd satisfied them completely with his yarn about property transfers.

" *'This business of Lamont's can't be allowed to continue,'* " Hearst recited. " *'It's immoral, it's illegal, and it's going to sink us all.'* "

"I hadn't realized you were a spy, Mr. Hearst." Shoop rose from his seat abruptly. "That was a private communication between Philip and me. I thought I was dealing with honorable men."

Hearst drew a folded square of paper from his breast pocket. "Stilwell sent this to Miss King before he died. She gave it to me last night. Was he still alive when you got to the Rue de Rivoli yesterday?"

Shoop hesitated. He glanced at Bill Bullitt, who'd leaned back in his desk chair and was staring at the ceiling, as though patiently waiting for the drama to end. Shoop sighed.

"If you've talked to Sally, you know how I found him." He passed a thin hand over his eyes at the memory. "I couldn't believe...I'd never thought of Philip as— At first I figured it was suicide. Something he'd chosen to fling in my face, although I couldn't for the life of me say *why*. But now I don't know—"

Because if in fact he was murdered, you're suspect number one, Hearst thought. "Was anyone else in the apartment when you got there?"

"No. The door was ajar. I walked in and saw the corpse dangling from the chandelier—twisting in the most hideous way, the man's tongue hanging out; I've never seen anything like it, even in the last war—and

I called out for Philip. When he didn't answer, I forced myself to walk through to the bedroom..."

"Was he warm?"

Shoop's eyelids lifted slightly. "I beg your pardon?"

"Did you touch Stilwell's skin? Was he still warm?"

"I...Yes. I touched Philip's neck—the left side, I think—and felt for a pulse. Nothing. But warm, yes."

"What did you do then? Pour yourself a stiff drink?"

"*What?* No, I'm afraid I...left. I went in search of the concierge on the ground floor—Mme. Blum—and asked her to call the police. You undoubtedly know the rest."

There was a brief silence.

Then Bullitt brought his chair to the floor with a crash and said crisply, "Lamont. What about Lamont?"

"I don't know. I never heard. Philip was dead."

"But surely you've got an idea." Bullitt's square head was thrust pugnaciously forward, his unblinking eyes drilling into Shoop's face. "Tell me about the guy. New Yorker, right?"

"Yes. Columbia Law. Before that, Princeton. Captain of the varsity crew. Never married, but much sought after by New York society mamas—one reason he moved to Europe. Rogers resigned his partnership last fall and sailed for Canada. The British gave him the rank of major, I think."

"How'd old Foster Dulles take that?"

Shoop hesitated. "Foster didn't interfere, of course. But I think he disapproved. He sent round a memo after Rogers left, stating that anyone who quit the firm to go to war might not have a job when he got back."

Bullitt's harsh laughter shot through the room. "A true patriot and a gentleman, isn't he? *Jesus Christ*."

"But this business," Hearst persisted, "that's immoral and illegal and will sink you all, the one Stilwell wanted to discuss— What was it?"

The tension in Shoop's body was visible now. He was still protecting something.

"One of Philip's tasks in recent months was to purge the files the firm is boxing for storage. Most of the files were Lamont's. He'd brought his own book of business with him from Germany when the Berlin office closed—"

"Lamont worked in Berlin?" Hearst said quickly.

"For years." Shoop glanced at Bullitt. "Rogers handled German reparations from the last war. Debt payments to American banks. That sort of thing."

"—Then he landed in Paris with his book of Nazi clients, when the Berlin office closed," Bullitt concluded. "And he quit eight months ago, as soon as war was declared, with France, to kill those same Germans. *Interesting*."

Shoop inclined his austere gray head. "I asked Morris about it, but he had no explanation."

"Morris?" Hearst repeated.

"Emery Morris. One of our attorneys. Emery worked with Rogers Lamont in Berlin, and has known him the longest."

"I see. What's happened to Lamont's files, Mr. Shoop? The ones Philip Stilwell was purging?"

The lawyer bit his lip, as though attempting to

swallow the words. "I went looking for them today," he replied. "They're simply ... *gone*."

Later, in the few minutes left to him before touring the city's hospitals, Hearst sat down and drafted a cable to Allen Dulles in New York.

CHAPTER NINE

After they had made love, Memphis fell into one of her uneasy drifts of sleep, sprawled naked and facedown with her arms flung out like a scarecrow, barely conscious of Spatz lying inches away or of the sun that was beginning to force its nose through the heavy draperies. The bed was antique, like all the furniture in the countess's apartment, big enough for the petite forms of the seventeenth century but not the Amazon queen or the *übermensch* from Lower Saxony. She was dreaming of Spatz's penis, she could feel it probing at the mouth of her sex, thick and forceful and supremely satisfying; and as she arched to meet its rhythm, her legs falling open, she was conscious of the blunt instrument sharpening—of human flesh mutating to steel—of the thrust and cut of a bayonet in her vitals. She screamed.

And sat upright, trembling, senses still furled in sleep.

Spatz didn't move.

Had she screamed? Or had the terror she'd ridden with her muscled thighs clamped her vocal cords tight? She stared at him—the perfectly formed profile, the cascade of blond hair freed of pomade, the creases of age in the corners of his eyes. She had a habit of smoothing those creases with her fingertips because age was the man's only vulnerability; Spatz was maybe twenty years older than she was and the weathering of his skin was the single crack in his beautiful aristocratic façade. But she kept her hands to herself now and thought, *Why am I afraid of you? Because you're German?*

Or because there's a smear of blood on your palm?

She pulled the sheet over her breasts and lay down again, quiet as a mouse and thinking. Blood could be anything—a cut, a splinter. Sure, he'd left the Alibi Club last night without saying good-bye, and there were hours unaccounted for between then and the moment she'd pulled up at this Faubourg address just after four A.M., but that didn't mean he'd gone and hurt anybody. She pushed away Jacquot's death and Raoul's desertion and the Germans coming—the Germans coming—

Spatz was German, yes—but a Nazi? *No.* He'd never been the kind who pushed his women around and called it politics when he gave them a black eye. It was the big-ass lawyer and all his questions that had ruined Memphis's sleep.

What does Spatz do, exactly, at the German embassy?

"It's closed, mistuh—has been since war broke out. Spatz is a man of *independent* means. Most of my men are."

She remembered lying back on Jacquot's bed, the dark green velvet of her gown blending subtly with the blue silk of the coverlet, Max Shoop pacing like a judge.

Does he meet people at the Alibi Club?

"He meets *me*. Spatz is a regular. Has his own table. And they ain't cheap to come by, I'll tell you that."

Who does he spend his time with? Other Germans?

"Sometimes. Sometimes French, sometimes English. Tonight he was with an American guy—skinny little fella with a mustache like Hitler's. Don't know his name."

I do, Shoop had said.

Memphis pulled the sheet tighter around her body as she remembered the look on the lawyer's stony face. The kind of look she'd expect a Klansman to wear just before the hood covered his head, the look of an executioner. The easy game of twenty questions, the check for a thousand dollars clutched in her hand, had vanished in a sudden flood of fear and she had wanted nothing more than to get out of that dead man's room.

And so she'd told him what the lawyer never asked to hear, the words tumbling from her lips.

"The American rat—the one who wouldn't drink champagne tonight with Spatz? Only other time I saw him was backstage at the Alibi Club—jerking off Jacquot in the pretty boy's dressing room."

Sally King opened her eyes in the Foreigners' Hospital to a flood of spring sunshine pouring through the casement windows. She grimaced and turned her face away; pain shot like a bolt of lightning through her skull.

"Sally," said a voice somewhere nearby—kind enough

but with an annoying note of insistence in its tone, the voice of a schoolmaster or a parent. "Miss *King*."

Reluctantly she opened her eyes once more. The ward stretched as long as a bowling alley, three times as wide, to a vanishing point of a swing door. Beds full of women were ranked on either side. And this one man: legs crossed in an upright chair, a bunch of lilies in his hand. Her eyes traveled to his face, which she vaguely remembered having seen somewhere.

"Joe Hearst," he reminded her. "We met at the embassy last night."

"Of course—"

She tried to sit up and it was a mistake. Her eyes clenched tight and she allowed her head to sink back as delicately as an eggshell on the stiff bolster of the hospital bed, furiously trying to remember. She was conscious of thirst, of a throbbing and relentless headache, and of embarrassment so acute she wondered if she had all her clothes on. "What happened?"

"I was hoping you could tell me."

The voice was amused and apologetic now; the voice of a lover rejected out of pique.

"It was dark," she said aloud. "Somebody doctored the light bulb in the corridor. He grabbed my neck."

"Who?"

She began to shrug and thought better of it. "Am I a flaming beauty, Mr. Hearst?"

"Bloodstains are all the rage this season. You're lucky to be alive."

"I blacked out."

"Not by yourself. Can you remember what he looked like? The man in the corridor?"

"Tall. Taller than me, and that's not so usual. Six feet, maybe? And strong. His hands were like a vise. But beyond that—"

"Young? Old?"

"Neither. Is there any water?"

He stood and reached for a jug, pouring a glass with his thin, long-fingered hands. They said nothing as he did it, Sally content to watch in silence, Hearst preserving his extraordinary economy of movement. He was restful, she decided; he maintained such perfect self-control.

He waited obediently until she drank it down, then asked, "Fair? Dark? Mustache? Beard?"

She fought an absurd desire to burst into tears. "Fair. No facial hair."

"Laborer? Thug?"

"Evening dress. English tailoring, not French." The realization was momentous, like an unexpected gift. "He had a white silk scarf draped around his neck. And his eyes were bright as a bird's. Glittering at me."

Joe Hearst did not immediately reply. He reached into his breast pocket and withdrew a handkerchief, offered it to Sally. So she *was* crying, then; it must be a reaction to the pain or the awakening or the knowledge that Philip—without warning, an image of Philip's dead body came back to her and she cried harder, a helpless despair engulfing her.

"Is it because of Philip?" she gasped as she dabbed at her face. "Is that why he tried to kill me?"

"We think he was looking for something in your apartment," Hearst said. All amusement and authority had vanished from his voice; he was the wooden diplomat again. She did not think it right to hand him the sodden square of linen he'd given her and so she kept it clutched tightly between her fingers. *Looking for something. He went through my things.*

"Which means," she said carefully, "that whatever he wanted, it wasn't at Philip's place. Or he wouldn't have come to mine."

"Probably true. Did Philip give you anything, Miss King, to keep safe—a document? Something from the law firm perhaps?"

She shook her head. "Not even a ring."

The countess arrived at her Paris apartment at ten o'clock in the morning, letting herself in at the front door with her own key. Her chauffeur Jean-Luc carried the luggage up from the boot of the open car she preferred to drive herself, and was standing deferentially with her lady's maid three feet behind la comtesse as she struggled with the recalcitrant key. When she had thrust open the door and stood drawing off her gloves and hat in the foyer, her piquant doll's face lined with weariness from the early hour of their departure and the general tension of the times, the depressing war news that had met them on their entry into the city— Jean-Luc drew up short in the doorway of the countess's suite and said colorlessly, "Madame."

Her head turned and she was beside him in a few

swift strides, features immobile as she stared at the sleeping pair in her bed. The scent of sex and sour liquor and tobacco assaulted her.

"Very well, Jean-Luc, put the bags in M. le Comte's room," the countess said evenly; but he thought, as he ducked away, that he heard the explosive word *"bâtard"* whispered under her breath.

CHAPTER TEN

Like many Parisians, Pierre duPré was weary of the long economic slump and half in sympathy with Hitler. It wasn't as though the Socialists under Blum had done France any favors—maybe it was time to give Fascism a try. And this war they'd tumbled into, all on account of somebody's promise to Poland, a country Petie had never seen and never wanted to—! A separate peace was clearly the way to go. No more fighting England's battles for her—he'd had enough of that when he was seventeen and nursing trench foot somewhere near Verdun. No, Petie had told Hearst: Give Alsace back to Adolf and bring the boys home.

But with the French army in retreat this morning he was feeling prickly. Reliving old memories. Himself openmouthed in Flanders with a cloud of mustard gas on the wind.

It was the children who were responsible, he was sure—all those blank, scared-witless faces staring back at him from the hospital wards. They ranged in age from eighteen months to twelve years, some of them orphans now in a strange city, their safe Netherlandish worlds blasted to hell by a low-flying Messerschmitt's guns. The nurses had told him that quite a number of mothers were dead—Dutch, Flemish—their bodies stopping the bullets as they huddled protectively around their children. Petie knew the sound of a bullet as it burrowed through flesh, ricocheted off the steel window frames, and ploughed into the padded leather seats. Five trains were strafed as they fled south through Belgium and the morgue was filling up fast; a makeshift viewing area had been set up for identification purposes at a siding near the Gare de Lyon. Some of the families were merely separated, of course—mother in the hospital, kids left behind in the bloody carriages—but with the confusion in Paris and the pressure from the government to move the refugees immediately to resettlement billets in the provinces, who knew if they'd find each other?

"Whaddya know, Petie?" Joe Hearst asked as he pulled the big car away from the Hôpital d'Étrangers. "Do any of us get out alive?"

"You should be packing, Boss," he retorted. "*Now*. Take the car and go south before the roads are shut for good. This isn't your war."

"Bullitt won't let me. It's become a point of pride with him: *No American ambassador has ever fled Paris.* Which means none of his staff can leave, either. He's made FDR promise not to order him out if the government goes—I think he's hoping for a martyr's death on the Nazi barricades. He's already dictated a farewell note to the President to be delivered in the event of his death."

"It doesn't do to joke," Petie insisted. "You're too young to remember the last war, you. The fucking Boches are butchers, believe me. We'll defend the city to our last breath, sure, but with those tanks rolling...If the Line's already broken—"

"There's one big problem with the Maginot Line," Hearst explained. "It's not quite long enough. There's a big blank space near the forest of Ardennes, and if Hitler's thrown his panzers into it we're all screwed. The folks back home imagine something like the Great Wall of China, when in fact the Belgian border is a bunch of martello towers with signal flags and Morse code. You French think in terms of trenches and infantry. But this'll be an air war when it comes."

An air war. Which meant bombs, of course, the beautiful old buildings of Paris tumbled like the footage Petie had seen in newsreels of Poland. Tufts of hair and bits of bone embedded in the leather seats of trains, children of three torn and paralyzed from the waist down. Petie reached for his tobacco pouch and cigarette papers, rolling a smoke with one hand while the other fingered the pistol in his pocket. He'd brought it along to protect the Boss—there was talk of refugees stealing cars, refugees siphoning gas. Petie loved the Boss's car, a dark blue '37 Buick Special shipped over from New York on the *Normandie,* a convertible coupe with a rumble seat and a chrome grille as broad and high as an ocean liner's prow. Half Petie's anxiety for Hearst was really anxiety for the car. *Leave Paris. Pack up and go. I can't bear to see the Buick strafed with machine-gun bullets.*

"If the Boches come by air we'd better get those aeroplanes *l'ambassadeur* has been promising," he suggested with a sidelong glance at Hearst. "Two, three thousand people are saying. Due any day now."

Hearst did not reply. He was nosing the Buick around a horse-drawn cart piled high with furniture, but there was nothing to be said in any case. In a moment of bravado Bullitt had told Premier Reynaud the United States could provide an air fleet, but Roosevelt did not possess two thousand planes he could "lend" France or even Churchill, not to mention American neutrality and Lindbergh's America First movement and the President's battle for reelection in the fall. There would be no help from across the Atlantic, Petie knew. But when his *copains* nudged him or neighbors asked outright, he suggested a secret knowledge. A contingency plan. A confidence he had no business to feel. He'd told his Emmeline to be ready to leave for the coast at a moment's notice.

The Morgue of the City of Paris sat where it had always done, just off the Quai de la Rapée in the twelfth arrondissement, not far from the Gare de Lyon where at least one of the strafed Belgian trains had arrived with its carloads of dead and wounded. Just across the Seine from the morgue there were five hospitals within a two-mile radius, and Hearst was expected to visit them all. He continued to drive while Petie muttered about Messerschmitts and Weygand and running through the marshes of the Marne two decades ago. Hearst was half listening and half studying the traffic, which was worse than usual. Paris was in motion, mattresses strapped to the roofs of cars. A few of them had Belgian plates; but most of those wealthy enough to drive south from Brussels had already done so, streaking through the city under cover of darkness. He thought briefly of his wife, marooned and loveless in Rome. He'd last heard from her a month ago, as Norway fell to the Germans. She'd been desperate for papers, for passage to New York, and asked if Hearst or the embassy might help. He hadn't answered her letter and now, as he stared at the refugees, their belongings piled in wheelbarrows and perambulators, he was awash in remorse and guilt.

He left the car right in front of the morgue, Petie slouched on its prow, pistol raised, as though the Nazis might burst from a side street at any moment. "Don't worry, Boss," the old Frenchman said around the cigarette lodged firmly in the corner of his mouth. "I'll take care of the car."

Bullitt's your boss, Hearst had told him repeatedly. *Bob Murphy's your boss. I'm just the low man on the totem pole.* But the metaphor escaped Pierre duPré and Boss had stuck, despite Hearst's best efforts.

At one time the morgue had been famous for its viewing theatre, the *salle d'exposition,* the corpses laid out on marble slabs far below with a ribbon of the Seine flowing coldly beneath them, a natural form of refrigeration. Up to a million tourists each year had flocked to gaze at the macabre spectacle, some of them deriving an almost sexual enjoyment from the scene; but the *salle* had closed in 1907 and Hearst's erotic tastes ran along different lines. There were stretchers lying everywhere he looked today, some discreetly draped, most exposed to the gaze of strangers: women of every description and age, staring sightlessly at nothing. Well-dressed women, women who'd taken the time to apply makeup before they packed their children into the Red Cross trains and turned toward Paris, women who'd probably thought they'd visit the shops in the Rue St-Honoré before taking up their refugee billets. Elderly women dressed in black, women of twenty. One girl lay face downward on the floor, jet-black hair spilling across the nape of her neck. Hearst stared at the fragile knife of her shoulder blades, exposed by the cut of her light spring frock; stared at the pale smoothness of her skin. He did not want to see her face.

"Stil-ewell," said the man in the lab coat who hovered in the front hall, clipboard in hand. "Dr. Mauriac performed the autopsy. The doctor will have gone to lunch, *tant pis*."

Hearst left Petie standing guard over the Buick, surrounded by a crowd of small boys whose parents, inexplicably, had not yet sent them out of Paris; and tracked the doctor to a café near the railroad station. Mauriac was a mild-featured man with a luxuriant mustache and a head as egg-pated as Bullitt's, a shining, torpedo-shaped dome of baldness. He invited Hearst to join him in a dish of roast lamb, spring peas, the very first potatoes, and a metallic white wine from Lorraine; Hearst declined the food but accepted the empty chair opposite the doctor.

"You will be wanting to know when the body is released, yes?" Mauriac said shrewdly as he forked the delicate pink flesh into his mouth. "There is a family in America?"

"It is customary for the embassy to arrange such things," Hearst agreed. "But the ambassador has taken a personal interest in the matter."

"Ah. He likes his *pédés,* then?"

Hearst ignored the slur—something like "faggot" in English—and said, "The ambassador is acquainted with Mr. Stilwell's father."

Mauriac pursed his lips, nodded once, and tackled a potato. "What do you want to know?"

"How did he die?"

The brown eyes came up to meet his, ferocious with amusement. "He fucked himself to death."

"Dr. Mauriac—"

"You want it tidied? Your young man died of a heart attack. From the looks of his heart, it was not so strong all his life, *hein*? Possibly the damage to the valves from a childhood illness. Rheumatic fever. Scarlet fever. I cannot say. From the contents of the stomach, I would add that he had consumed enough powdered cantharides beetle to fell an elephant."

At Hearst's expression of incomprehension, Mauriac added impatiently, "You would call this Spanish fly. It is supposed to enhance the erection, yes? But it is a topical aid, a substance *d'excitation,* not something one should eat. Young Stilwell must have experienced a turmoil in the bowels before he died. The inflammation of the internal organs was extreme. So, too, was the engorgement of the penis, which persisted even after death. He was a *naïf* or a fool, take your pick, and he paid the price."

"Could he have taken the stuff unwittingly? Say . . . in a drink he'd been given?"

Mauriac lifted his shoulders in a gargantuan shrug, jaws working. "Possibly. There was not a great deal in the stomach. The remains of a hearty luncheon of *bifteck*."

"Any signs of violence on the body?"

"He'd been scourged, of course, but we must assume that was of a piece with the company he kept. Also his hands bound—I saw the chafing at the wrists. They had been rubbed raw, so presumably he was not so happy with this kind of play."

The knot tightened in Hearst's stomach. Bound and poisoned, possibly forced to witness the hanging of the man named Jacquot, and his weak heart pounding with terror—Stilwell's final moments. Had he been gagged to keep him from screaming?

"If I were to bring you a glass from Mr. Stilwell's apartment—could you tell me whether the drink was drugged with Spanish fly?"

Mauriac drained his wine. "You confuse me with a chemist, *monsieur le diplomate*. I suggest you find one in the neighborhood. And now I must return to my work. As you observe we are inundated—these *sales Boches*—and I am quitting Paris this afternoon."

"*Les vacances?*" Hearst asked ironically.

"Mais oui." Mauriac was imperturbable. "A friend with a house near the Spanish border. I will inform the police that your Stilwell's death was due to natural causes. You may ship him home whenever you choose."

CHAPTER ELEVEN

"Has Mr. Morris come in yet?" Max Shoop demanded.

Mme. Renard, the person who *really* ran Sullivan & Cromwell's Paris office, had ceased to jump whenever Shoop materialized beside her desk, but she hated his noiseless tread, the sensation of being watched. For nearly twenty years her perfectly coiffed blond head had been bowed as though in prayer at her station in the firm's reception area, lending the sorry premises a certain amount of chic. Madame did not approve of Americans—childish in their teasing of one another, overly loud, their standards too casual and relaxed. *Her* standards had been learned at the feet of her mother, a forbidding woman, and in the bed of Thomas Cromwell—the elderly founding partner of S&C who'd opened the Paris office purely as a convenience to himself. M. Tommie, as Jane Renard referred to him, had spent the better part of his life in a large apartment on the Boulevard de Boulogne, had survived the deprivations of the Great War by sensibly moving into the Ritz, and had sailed for New York three years ago now, never to return—but Mme. Renard stayed on, her dress exquisite, the rest of the world mere fodder for her contempt.

Except Max Shoop. One appraising glance from under his veiled eyes could raise the small hairs on the back of her neck.

"M. Morris has not seen fit to appear," she answered. "M. Canfield has been taking his calls all morning. There is a message, however, from the Morris wife. I put it on your desk."

Shoop's eyes took in Frank Canfield's open office door, the hum of conversation suggesting he was engaged. The rest of the rooms were dark. Rogers Lamont's was empty; Philip Stilwell's, too; Monod's was dark since the French lawyer had enlisted in the army. *We're dwindling one by one*, Jane Renard thought. *I must make my plans to go, soon.*

"Any sign of those missing files?"

She stared at Shoop coldly. "But no. They have not the legs, to walk them here and there. They will not be hiding, to appear again when we least suspect. The files were removed from this office. That much is plain. Perhaps when M. Morris arrives, he will tell us *why*."

Shoop's eyebrows rose a fraction, as though in shock at her impertinence. Unthinkable, that she should voice the suspicion circulating ever since the files were discovered gone.

"I think," he said carefully, "that you should come into my office, Jane. I have a cable to dictate. For New York."

She picked up her pad and pencil and preceded him through the doorway to the hard wooden chair she preferred, drawn up from the wall to sit menacingly, uncompromisingly, in front of Shoop's beautiful Biedermeier desk. He had so many secrets, this Shoop; so many qualities to his silence. Well, she was done with silence and attitudes of prayer. The Germans were coming and the Americans would all run home. She could feel the panic of their leaving already, hanging in the air around Shoop.

He closed his office door, eyes flicking mechanically to the message from Emery Morris's wife: *My husband is most unwell today, will remain at home until he recovers.*

"You circulated the notice of Mr. Stilwell's death?" he asked, as though it were the day's weather report, or the lunch menu at the Ritz.

The first crack in Mme. Renard's perfect façade appeared; her complexion crumpled and dissolved. "*Pauvre enfant.* It was the heart, yes? Who *knew*? He looked so healthy and strong. My own father, he went that way—"

"Yes, well—" Shoop cut in. "I spoke to the embassy this morning. It's all in hand. The return of the remains. You will order a wreath. Something for the family, with the office members' names on it. Condolences. It can go on the coffin when it sails."

She made a brief note in pencil. "I will take up a collection."

"Is anything else missing?" Shoop asked. "Other than Lamont's files?"

"I did not go over the premises with your small-tooth

comb. No money was taken. No drawers forced. The person responsible possessed a key."

"*Your* key?"

"A copy, perhaps."

"You know more about this shop than anyone. You know which boxes were disturbed, which records of Lamont's work are missing—"

Her eyes narrowed like a Siamese cat's. "Monsieur Shoop, you are not suggesting that *I* disturbed my slumbers to pilfer the office in the dead of night, *hein*? Because if that is so, I have much to do that requires my attention at home, before these *sales Boches* descend upon Paris and make life miserable, you understand? I can leave on the instant!" She snapped her fingers succinctly. "I need not wait for M. Morris to explain what he has done with the law firm's property. It is nothing to me, *comprendez-vous*?"

The clarity of her insight—this fifty-year-old woman with the sensuality of a bordello seething beneath her perfectly fitted suit—had the power to caution him. Shoop had no desire to focus attention on Morris. Or to link him with the missing files. *Or to Stilwell's death.* It would not do for Mme. Renard to talk among the staff.

He sat in his chair, fingers steepled and silver head bowed, the very picture of the aging jurist, and considered the fact of Memphis Jones. The rush of words she'd thrown at him during the night, and the image they conjured: Morris on his knees in his correct Savile Row suit, a cabaret dancer's penis in his hands. That same dancer, hanged in a room with Philip Stilwell. Shoop pursed his lips as though rolling a mouthful of wine. The point, as he saw it, was not to attempt to understand but to contain the problem. And to minimize the potential damage to the firm.

"I merely wondered, Jane, if you knew exactly *which* files disappeared."

She remained rigid in her seat, her beautifully groomed fingers clenched around her notebook. "All of M. Stilwell's. And . . . the I.G. Farbenindustrie files."

"I.G. Farben," he repeated. "The German firm."

"Yes."

Shoop felt a sudden surge of nausea. To cover it, he reached for a letter opener and began to turn it reflectively in his hands, as though he might read the future in its polished surface. Sullivan & Cromwell—Rogers Lamont in particular—served as counsel for an international cartel of chemical manufacturers of which I.G. Farbenindustrie was a member. The cartel also included an American firm, Allied Dye and Chemical Industries; a Belgian concern, Solvay et Cie.; and a British-owned chemical company. The four corporations held chunks of one another's stock and were so incestuous in their governing boards as to be barely distinguishable; but all such relationships had fallen under the ax eight months ago as a result of the war. I.G. Farben was no longer S&C's client. The stolen files were a matter of historical interest only.

—Or were they?

"The files were active up to the week before M. Lamont's departure," Mme. Renard supplied.

Despite the firm's embargo on German business. Shoop's

eyes flicked from the letter opener to the woman's face. "Why?"

She shrugged. "I would be the last to know. M. Lamont never required the services of a secretary. He did all his typing himself, *vous voyez*."

He remembered that habit of Lamont's, the jokes the urbane New Yorker was forced to endure, the comparisons with girl-typists and war correspondents posting bulletins from the front—the suggestion that it was really his memoirs or the Great American Novel he was composing behind his closed office door. He had turned the laughter with his usual wit, never relenting or giving Jane Renard his work to do.

It was Jane, Shoop thought, *who'd started the rumor that Lamont despised women.*

Shoop was a securities lawyer: He understood money, not chemicals. He'd never worked with Lamont or Morris or their clients. But as managing partner of the Paris office he ought to have known of every matter that came across his attorneys' desks. What did I.G. Farben produce? Dye, of course. Nitrates. There was a new process for extracting nickel from ore—Lamont had worked on that patent years ago. So had Morris.

Illegal. Immoral. Sink us all . . .

That meddler in Bullitt's office: Hearst. He was asking difficult questions. He had the annoying air of refusing to back off; Shoop knew his kind. There were always clients who could not compromise, who did not understand that life endured through what was conceded or lost, that such things as firms and wars went on regardless of individuals and their deaths . . .

"The cable, Monsieur Shoop?" Mme. Renard suggested. "The one you wish to dictate for New York?"

He stared at her as though she were a stranger. *Firms and wars,* he thought. *These things must go on.*

"To Mr. John Foster Dulles," he began. *"German army rumored to have crossed the river Meuse yesterday. Stop. Request permission to close office and evacuate firm personnel soonest from Paris. Stop..."*

Philip Stilwell's concierge was a hunchbacked and white-haired woman named Léonie Blum. She glared at Joe Hearst suspiciously when he knocked on her small cubicle door, which opened onto the courtyard of Stilwell's lovely old building, and demanded to know if he was German.

"American," he returned in his diplomat's French. "From the embassy."

"He's a swell from Washington, you old bat," Petie scolded at Hearst's side. *"German,* for the love of God!" He regularly ran interference with know-nothings like Mme. Blum, and figured the Boss had brought him along for the purpose.

She turned to the glass that held her false teeth, popped them into her mouth with dignity, and said, in Petie's same guttural French, "I applied for that visa two months ago. To visit my niece in America. Nothing have I heard. Nothing! I suppose now you've come to deliver it in person?"

"You've applied for a visa?" Hearst said.

"Of course! Two months ago! You know nothing

about it, *hein*? Nobody knows anything when it's an old Jewish woman and the Nazis are coming. But I have a niece! And she lives in New Jersey! You can't stop me from paying her a visit!"

"I wouldn't try. I'm not in the consular section," Hearst explained. He reached for his card case and offered her his name. "I came to talk to you about your tenant. Philip Stilwell."

"Poor boy," she said succinctly. "You'd best come into my place. I have coffee. Cognac."

He told Petie to stay with the car, then followed Léonie Blum inside the dark and cramped ground-floor quarters she called home.

"Poor Philippe," she repeated as she fetched the cups and glasses. "Always such a good boy. Always so respectful. To end like that—"

She stopped short and scrutinized him, the bottle of cognac clutched close to her breast. "You know how he died?"

"I know how he was found."

"Terrible." She shook her head. "I saw. When that lawyer called me—Monsieur Shoop. Shaking like a leaf he was. Pale as a goose feather. And no wonder! Still I cannot believe it."

"You had no notion that Mr. Stilwell was . . ."

"A *pédé*? No. He was in love with the girl—the beautiful one who wears the clothes. And then this—such a spectacle, in my building! I don't believe it. I don't believe it of poor Philippe."

"I don't either, Madame Blum. That's why I'm here."

She poured a thimbleful of cognac for Hearst, offered him oily black coffee. He took a sip of each for the sake of politeness. Was pleasantly surprised by the quality.

"They've roped it off," she volunteered shrewdly. "Philippe's apartment. It's as much as I'm worth to let you in there."

If this was a bid for a bribe, he decided to ignore it. "Have the police been back?"

"No." Under her gaze Hearst took another draught of cognac. "You're not in the consular section, you say. But perhaps you know someone who is?"

"I do," he temporized.

"And no doubt you know exactly where the Germans are right now, and which are the last trains out to Cherbourg harbor?"

Hearst laughed. "I don't know any more about the German advance than you do, Madame Blum. But I imagine you have the timetables memorized."

"My brother lives in Munich, monsieur. Seventy-eight years old. I haven't heard from him in two years. They tell me he's in a labor camp. *Labor camp!* What should he be doing, I ask you, at seventy-eight? Digging ditches?" She grasped his sleeve with sudden urgency. "I must get out of France. Nobody will help me, monsieur. But I *must get out* of France, you understand? My niece—"

"Where does your niece live, madame?"

"A place called Bayonne." She pronounced it as though it were French; the name alone, Hearst thought, would be comforting in its familiarity.

He drew his appointment book from his breast

pocket, opened it to a clean page. "Write down her name. Her address. I'll check on the visa for you."

Mme. Blum stared at him fixedly. She did not, he realized, trust him. There had probably been many careless offers of help, forgotten as soon as they were given. He wondered if Philip Stilwell had made promises he no longer could keep.

"Write them down," he said. "I give you my word."

She poured herself another drink and knocked it back, neat.

Ten minutes later he was standing in the high-ceilinged, light-filled space that Stilwell had loved, thinking involuntarily how well Sally would look against its walls.

The room was in disorder, the furniture pulled out of position to allow the passage of stretchers, the rug trampled by too many feet. The Sûreté had removed both bodies and taken their photographs and noted their measurements, but had left everything else where it lay. Somebody would be expected to pack up Stilwell's effects and ship them home—a lawyer from the firm, or Sally.

He picked his way across the main room, consciously avoiding the space beneath the chandelier where the man from Montmartre had dangled, and studied the crystal drinking glasses.

"Are you always at your desk in the courtyard, Madame Blum?" he asked the concierge.

"I sit there from nine in the morning until I make my

dinner," she said from her position by the doorway, "which is usually around six o'clock. I listen to my radio—it helps to pass the time."

"Did you see Mr. Stilwell yesterday?"

"He left just after nine—cheerful he was, always a hello for me—and then I saw him return, a few minutes before three. That was unusual. That was early."

Hearst drew a linen handkerchief from his pocket and carefully lifted one of the glasses. A caramel-colored syrup the size of a coin had congealed on the bottom. The second glass was the same. He turned and looked for the wastebasket Sally had described—something overturned on the carpet, contents strewn across the floor. He could find nothing. Perhaps the police had taken it.

"And did you see Max Shoop arrive?"

"The lawyer? He came just as I was thinking of dinner."

"Around six," Hearst suggested.

"Give or take five minutes."

"Not half-past four?"

She furrowed her brow. "No, monsieur. At dinner, as I said."

And yet, their meeting was supposed to be at four-thirty. Strange. "When did the other man arrive?"

"Which one?"

"The fellow who died with Stilwell."

Her eyes fell. "I don't know. The police asked the same thing. Well—it must have been between three o'clock and six, when that M. Shoop appeared, *hein*? But I cannot always be at the desk. I have to relieve myself. And there was maybe a tradesman who distracted me—a delivery of flowers to Mme. LeCamier, on the third floor, who recently had the baby. All those steps! And the man would not take it himself, he was in a hurry, so I agreed to carry the flowers to Madame—and then I stopped just a minute to admire the baby . . ."

Any number of people might have entered Philip Stilwell's place, Hearst thought, and murdered him in peace. Even Shoop might have done it. And returned at six to establish his alibi.

Annoyed, he walked into the bedroom and stared at the disordered bed. His mind veered from the picture of Sally's head buried in a pillow, veered from the hazy idea he had of Stilwell, bound and prone with an erection the size of an elephant's. But no terror lingered in this place; no fear. If Stilwell had a ghost, it had already moved on.

He turned back to Mme. Blum. "I need to take those crystal glasses in the main room. Could you find me a bag?"

She was pitifully eager to oblige. In her absence, he strolled again around the apartment. Thinking this time of the answer to the morning's cable he'd found on his chair when he returned to the embassy after lunch.

PHILIP STILWELL WORKED ON TRANSACTIONAL MATTERS, BANKING, SECURITIES. STOP. DO NOT KNOW R. LAMONT PERSONALLY BUT UNDERSTAND HE IS A MAN OF INTEGRITY AND WORTH. STOP. PARIS OFFICE TO BE

SHUT DOWN SOONEST FOR PERSONNEL
EVACUATION. STOP. AVOID SAME PERSONNEL
AND DEAL DIRECTLY WITH ME. ALLEN DULLES.

On this second stroll Hearst found the wastepaper basket, set tidily behind an armchair in the far corner of the salon. It was completely empty.

He got down on his hands and knees and roamed over the carpet. When a fragment of glass drew blood from his palm, he could not suppress a crow of triumph. Tearing a page from his appointment book, he folded it in half and scraped the shattered bits of crystal from the Aubusson's threads. Then he twisted the paper into a tight screw and pocketed it.

"Monsieur," Léonie Blum muttered from the doorway, a cloth grocery bag clutched in her hands. "You *will ask* about my visa?"

"Of course."

"Then I will tell you—" She licked her lips, the poorly fitting false teeth as protuberant as a cart horse's— "This arrived. In the morning mail."

She held out a manila envelope.

"Monsieur Stilwell posted this two days ago. It was returned today. Undeliverable."

The envelope was thick and heavy, as though it contained papers. Hearst stared at the address.

"M. Jacques Allier," he read aloud. "Banque de Paris et des Pays-Bas."

FRENCH INTRIGUE

TUESDAY, MAY 14, 1940—WEDNESDAY, MAY 15, 1940

CHAPTER TWELVE

Jacques Allier no longer worked at the Banque de Paris et des Pays-Bas. He had been given a uniform and transferred for the duration of the war to this uncomfortable cell of an office in the basement of the Ministry of Armaments, its ground-level windows covered with blackout paper and its foundations completely surrounded with sandbags the color and shape of sausages. The basement was wretchedly ventilated and thick with cigarette smoke and the odors of other people's flatulence; it reminded him forcibly of the trench in which he'd endured most of 1917.

Allier still suffered from claustrophobia as a result of the last war and so he was sweating now as he skimmed the morning paper, which had been set aside and forgotten in the chaos of the day: sweating, and allowing a cigarette to burn down to his fingertips, his mild-featured face struggling with the effort to look normal.

Cots had been set up for those who were forced to hold vigil against the German advance, although it was only four o'clock in the afternoon and a French counteroffensive was rumored to be under way. Allier was hoping he'd be allowed to go home, even if it meant he was vulnerable to an air raid. He would begin to scream if he were forced to stay in this airless room with its typewriters clacking like small-arms fire.

"The tanks have rolled right over our fortifications," Dautry was saying to somebody beyond the door. "Concrete shattered like glass, and our best men with it. We're overrun. Nothing to throw between here and Paris except the bodies of two million men."

So much for the counteroffensive.

Allier kept his eyes on the newspaper, as though he were seated over coffee at his favorite café. While other men were screaming, limbs crushed under the treads of German tanks.

The ash of his cigarette burned his skin. Startled, he folded the paper in four and tossed it on his letter tray. A headline on the back page, suddenly revealed, caught his eye.

"Allier," the minister snapped impatiently from the door of his cell. "*Mon Dieu*, so you alone can read the news when the world's about to end?"

"It's the American." He slid the headline under Dautry's nose. "Dead in his flat. It cannot be another accident, *hein*? Like the leak of my cover on the way to Norway?"

Dautry's dark eyes roved swiftly over the lines of text, the innocuous photograph of Philip Stilwell. "They're on to you, the Germans. We've got an informer somewhere in the chain—more than one, *peut-être*. Which means you and every last particle of Joliot's lab will be on the road out of Paris by dawn, understand?"

Allier nodded, relief spreading through him like cool water. *Anything to get out of this basement.* He found he was grinning at Dautry like an idiot, the inner scream transmuted to hysterical laughter.

He went directly toward the laboratory at the Collège de France, the series of rooms where Frédéric Joliot-Curie played with his bizarre apparatus and his odder friends. Allier had never bothered to consider physics until the American boy who lay dead now in the Paris morgue had come to him at the Banque de Paris et des Pays-Bas eight months ago. Tapping on his door with an apologetic smile and a load of documents under his arm. *Excuse me, Monsieur Allier, but they tell me you're the investment officer in charge of HydroNorsk. If you have a moment, I'd like to talk…*

There had followed a concise presentation of advancements in physics, which were coming as thick and fast in recent months as the German planes. The discovery by a German named Otto Hahn that an atom of uranium could be split in two. The suggestion, by the Danish scientist Niels Bohr, in a lecture at Stilwell's old college, that when such an atom split, it triggered a chain reaction capable of unleashing immense force. The word *bomb.*

"HydroNorsk manufactures heavy water," young Stilwell had said patiently. "You're aware that it's extremely difficult to produce, is in extremely short supply, and that some people—your Nobel laureate, Joliot-Curie, is one of them—think it helps to slow down high-speed particles. To control them, maybe. So that the chain reaction can be contained..."

Allier had got the HydroNorsk account as a way of cutting his teeth in banking. It was a small company perched on a remote bay in the northern fastness of the world, of trifling interest to anybody except a handful of scientists who craved its heavy water. The Banque de Paris et des Pays-Bas owned 65 percent of HydroNorsk's stock.

Let Allier have HydroNorsk, the bank's managers had said with the easy assurance of the totally ignorant. *He can hardly screw that up.*

And he would have, but for Philip Stilwell.

The newspaper had reported the American was simply "found dead," nothing about murder or even violence, but Allier was wondering, as he walked briskly toward the fringe of St-Germain, whether Philip was tortured before he died.

If he'd talked—if he'd spilled even one-tenth of all he guarded in his brain—then none of them was safe. Dautry's decision to move, *parbleu,* had come too late.

Who was the informer? *Who? Who?* Somebody at the Ministry—one of the foreigners in Joliot's lab—or Joliot himself...?

Allier broke into a trot, heedless of the curious looks of those he passed or the picture he presented: a slight man but hunted; innocuous, perspiring.

He stopped short near the entrance of the Luxembourg Gardens as though a shell had exploded at his feet.

Frédéric Joliot-Curie was walking by, head down, an expression of acute concentration on his strongly molded face. Pursuing a course along one of the garden's lateral paths as though nothing else existed but the equation he was solving in his brain.

On the point of calling out the physicist's name, Allier hesitated. He glanced at his watch. There was an hour or two of daylight left.

He fell into step behind the man, and followed where he led.

The Foreigners' Hospital discharged her that afternoon, because Sally insisted she was absolutely fine now, and the doctor agreed that her double vision seemed to have waned. In any case, they needed her bed. She'd heard the stories of the strafed trains, how they'd pulled up at sidings on their way into France from Belgium, disgorging the dead and wounded, the bewildered, sobbing children. She caught snippets of French words as she walked unsteadily through the ward in her bathrobe, the eyes of the Flemish and Dutch women following her. More of them, the less serious cases, were slumped in chairs near the nurses' station, and Sally realized they had been there all day. If she hadn't been brought in before dawn she would never have been treated for the insignificant matter of near-strangulation.

She scarcely looked at the form she was supposed to sign, her head throbbing. She had been sent to the hospital without her clothes or gas-mask case, which meant no identity papers or money, but she assumed the system was flexible; how many of the refugees she'd just passed were in a similar fix?

"You'll send me the bill?" she asked in as dignified a tone as she could muster.

"It is already paid," the discharge nurse replied. "By the gentleman who has called to take you home."

Hearst, Sally thought with an absurd little inner leap, and glanced over her shoulder. But it was the austere figure of Max Shoop she saw swinging through the corridor's double doors.

She composed her expression, although her heartbeat quickened. Shoop wore a dark coat with a white silk scarf knotted carefully at the neck, and for an instant she was back in the doorway of her flat with a pair of hands tightening on her throat.

"Sally, my dear." He offered his hand; it was papery and cool to the touch. "I'm so *terribly sorry* for all your trouble. Odette is furious with me. I should never have sent you home last night alone."

"But what else could you have done?" Sally replied reasonably. "There were the police to deal with."

"Yes." He pursed his lips. "You didn't go directly to your flat, I understand. You stopped . . . at the embassy."

"Yes." Sally flushed, aware for the first time how her impulsive visit to the ambassador's residence would look to Max Shoop—as though she didn't trust him, as though she suspected everyone at S&C of murder. But who did he think she was—a little child, to be controlled and rebuked when she disobeyed Daddy? Her embarrassment turned to frustrated anger. *These men, always trying to run my life . . .*

"I felt very alone last night when I saw Philip," she said clearly. "All those French police, shoving me out of the room, refusing to answer questions...I needed to talk to somebody *American*. An objective ear."

"I see." Shoop's shrouded eyes drifted over the bruises at her neck as indifferently as though he surveyed a canvas at the Louvre. "It's not wise to be alone. Odette has made me promise to bring you straight to our place for a good dinner and a comfortable bed. Have you collected your things?"

"I'd rather just go home." She was conscious of rudeness. "I'm very tired, Max, I'd be lousy company tonight and I've only got this bathrobe—"

"Nonsense." His cool fingers grasped her arm. "Odette won't speak to me if I come home without you. She'll lend you something to wear."

A finger of doubt thrilled along her spine. But there was no way to refuse him—he'd paid her hospital bill. That was because of Philip, of course: Shoop was determined to do right by the girl Philip had left behind, even if he'd failed to prevent murder.

"I'm not convinced," she said urgently as he steered her down the hospital corridor, "about Philip. There were these glasses in the salon—"

"That's all taken care of," Shoop interrupted. "I spoke to the police this afternoon. They've ruled the death accidental. They are ready to discharge the remains."

"But—"

He glanced at her coldly. "There *will be* no scandal, Sally. I've booked your passage for New York on a merchant steamer—the *Clothilde,* out of Cherbourg. You will embark with Philip's body Thursday afternoon."

"*Thursday?* I can't possibly be ready to leave France in two days. What about my work?...and all my things..."

"I'll send someone over to your flat to pack," Shoop said. "You will stay with us until you leave."

"But I have to go home!"

"Why?" His gaze sharpened, so that Sally took an involuntary step backward, her hands reaching for the support of the wall.

"Did you leave something there? Something *important*?"

It was Joe Hearst's voice she heard, then, as a kind of warning in her mind.

Did Philip give you anything, Miss King, to keep safe?

"My identity papers and passport," she told Shoop. "They were in my gas-mask case. And I'll need some clothes—"

The lawyer's face relaxed. "I understand your gas mask was stolen. You won't find the papers. But Odette will be delighted to take you shopping."

She went with him quietly in the end. And began, immediately, to consider her escape.

CHAPTER THIRTEEN

The Comtesse de Loudenne had never asked her maid to unpack her bags. She didn't bother to go over the menu with the cook, although there'd been no harsh words at the luncheon table where she'd sat with her cousin, one hand languorously nursing a cigarette. She inclined her head to the black goddess as she departed in her velvet evening gown, but said nothing about finding Memphis in her own bed. It was von Dincklage who showed the girl the door.

"Let's get out of Paris," Memphis said urgently as he pecked her on the cheek. "Get a car, Spatz. Take me away from here. Nobody'll bother you. You're German."

"We'll meet at the club tonight, my darling."

She grasped his lapel. But no more words came to her. She seemed to understand suddenly that her power was limited, and the shock of it bewildered her. A child left too long at a tiring party.

"I'll be there around midnight."

He shoved her firmly out, straightened his tie in the ornate pier glass that dominated one wall, and returned to the countess.

"You've certainly made yourself at home," she observed impassively.

"Isn't she marvelous?"

"That would be one word. A circus performer, I suppose?"

He cocked his head, birdlike, at her: all gleaming gold plumage. "A jazz *artiste*."

"Ah." She crushed the cigarette in the bottom of her cup, eyes fixed on the dregs. "I'd hoped you'd have the sense to get out of here, Spatz. Before I returned. The servants don't like it, you know—a German in the house. And the master at the Front."

He laughed and moved restlessly to perch on the windowsill. "You've never cared a fig for the opinion of servants."

"No." Her eyes came up to meet his. "Very well, then: *I* don't like it. A German in the house. With the master at the Front."

"There'll be Germans all over Paris soon."

"You *say* that to me? You have the *gall* to stand in my own house—"

"Not the gall," he corrected. "The *charm*. We've always told each other the truth, anyway—"

She let him lift her chin and gaze caressingly into her eyes—Spatz, who'd never given a damn about anybody but himself.

"It's not as though I like Germans everywhere," he said reasonably. "I didn't ask them to come. So what's *really* wrong? You're not offended by my . . . circus performer?"

"I'm frightened, that's all." Her mouth set bitterly;

she stood, paced away from him toward the salon. "Jack is in Paris, did you know?"

"Jack" might stand for a hundred different men, of any social class or country of origin, but between the countess and Spatz it signified one person alone: Charles Henry George Howard, the twentieth Earl of Suffolk, who'd once played polo with Spatz at Deauville.

"The mad earl? He's some sort of liaison for the British government, I think."

"—For the British Directorate of Scientific and Industrial Research. He may be wild, he may be *completely* mad—but he warned me away from you, Spatz. Said you've been getting your hands dirty."

"Nell, he carries a pair of revolvers he's named Oscar and Genevieve." His voice was deliberately light. "Drinks champagne morning, noon, and night—"

"Jack said you *weren't safe*."

His expression of amusement died. "God forbid I should be."

"What the hell are you going to do now that the Nazis are coming? What are you going to *do*, Spatz? There will be nowhere left to run, soon. And you can't work for them. You can't."

"Then perhaps I'll come to terms with Jack," he suggested.

She went very still. "What do you mean? You'd... help the British?"

He shrugged, a stretch of the sparrow's wings. "It'd be a change. But I'd need something to sell."

Her mouth twisted. "God, you have an ugly mind sometimes. Does nothing and nobody matter to you?"

"*You* matter, Nanoo." His pet name for her, a memory of childhood.

"Oh, stop it."

"You could help me."

"I?" She turned to him incredulously. "How could I help? Jack is mad for science!"

"You *know* people." He reached for her shoulders, drew her toward him. "*You* could get me something to sell."

"That's why you're still here, isn't it? So you can *use* me." She was silent a long moment. "Very well. Tell me what I have to do."

In the end she sent Jean-Luc for the car, and fled to a hotel for the night.

The man named Hans von Halban saw her standing at the curb, with the car door open and a remote expression on her face. He was a stranger to the countess, his clothes too large for his thin body, his startled brown eyes perpetually wounded, and she did not acknowledge him or even glance his way. He was struck by the dark, glossy hair that swung to her chin, and by her delicate profile. But then the German skipped down the stone steps and bent to kiss her cheek; and von Halban thought *Ah,* with a sense of bitter resignation. Spatz always cherished the most beautiful women in the world.

The two men had met five years before, when both

of them adopted Paris as their shining refuge, a place to speak German without saying *Heil Hitler*. Spatz's French was perfect and von Halban's poor; Spatz was at home everywhere, and von Halban the perpetual alien. They shared the same given name, however, and a love of jazz. A predilection for haunting Montmartre. They'd met at the Alibi Club, long before Memphis Jones came to stay, during a lull in the acts when the sheer joy of speaking their native tongue had forged a sudden and simple bond. Spatz had attended von Halban's wedding; his French bride was entranced with his charm. But if von Halban had tallied what he really knew of Hans Gunter von Dincklage—set it down like a calculation in the lines of his lab note-book—he'd have come up with little. A few anecdotes, a stray fact or two. A world of speculation and innuendo that followed Spatz like his personal entourage, acknowledged but never owned.

Von Halban stood now before the curbside tableau with his hat in his hand and a sickening anxiety on his face, wondering why he'd come. His French always deserted him in moments of acute embarrassment.

"Hans!" Spatz darted across the paving, hand extended. Not for him the Nazi salute.

"I . . . hope I'm not disturbing you."

"You're not. I was just going out for a drink. You'll join me?"

"With pleasure." He ducked his head wordlessly toward the unknown woman, who slid behind the wheel of her car, one hand fluttering farewell as she pulled out into the street.

"My cousin," Spatz explained. "The Comtesse de Loudenne. I've been using her place while she was in Bordeaux, but she turned up rather unexpectedly this morning."

"And now she must leave again?"

"She's worried about her husband. He's at the Front."

"Ah," von Halban managed. He'd heard of Spatz's cousin. Never realized there actually *was* a husband.

"You look ill, Hans." Spatz cocked his alert blond head. "Joliot-Curie works you too hard in that lab!"

"If it were only that!"

He glanced distractedly at the wide boulevard, wondering why it was that this street was empty of life. The rest of the city had been flooded all day by increasing crowds of people, refugees from the north with blank expressions and exhausted steps, shuffling with children on their hips and dogs tied to their belts, clothes and pans and a few bandboxes of treasures piled into wheelbarrows. *Wheelbarrows!* It was unbelievable and appalling to Hans, but he was paralyzed with indecision: to stay and support Joliot to the last, or to run, run as his wife demanded. Annick would leave without him anyway—she would take the girls to her parents' place in the country that very afternoon; she'd said he could come when he'd found a way to save them. He did not know how to begin to tell Spatz all this, Spatz who looked as though nothing could shatter his inner serenity, who was beautifully dressed and searching for alcohol in the neighborhood café as though his life were one long holiday.

The quiet of the Passy quarter was broken suddenly by a powerful engine. A car, long and sleek and black, flung itself south down the Rue de Longchamp.

"Belgians," Spatz observed. "They'll be in Spain by tomorrow. It's always the wealthy ones with the fast cars that outrun disaster. Have you got a car, Hans?"

Von Halban shook his head, dread choking his throat.

The two of them walked without speaking along the beautiful and privileged streets of the sixteenth arrondissement, the Rue des Belles-Feuilles, the Avenue Victor-Hugo. The Place du Trocadéro was aswarm with vehicles, the base of the Chaillot Palace sandbagged. Spatz stopped short, his hands shoved carelessly in his trouser pockets, and stared at the massive building; it had been completed only a few years before, and favored the Fascist style of architecture.

"There's no physics to speak of, in Spain," von Halban said, as though concluding a conversation held long ago.

"There'll be none here, soon." Spatz tossed aside the stub of his Dunhill. "It comes down to this: You'll leave because the path of honor lies elsewhere and you're an honorable man. We both know that, Hans. Your wife *can't* want you to stay and work for Himmler and his crowd."

Heinrich Himmler, as they both knew, commanded the SS—the elite and criminal corps of the Nazi Party. The SS, and Himmler, had denounced *Jewish Physics* in recent months with such ferocity that even Werner Heisenberg—no Jew and Germany's best hope for an atomic bomb—thought his career was over. There would be no future for Hans von Halban in a world of Himmler's ordering.

Spatz seemed to know everything important already—and Hans was unsurprised. For years, rumor had linked the idle Sparrow to Admiral Wilhelm Canaris, the head of the Abwehr—Germany's intelligence network. Spatz was a spy. How else could he have attached himself so vaguely to the German embassy in Paris, lingering years beyond the natural end of a foreign ministry tour? How else could he come and go like the heir to a principality, free of conventions or expectation, of the need to earn a living? A bird of passage, a bird on a wire. That was surely why they were standing together on the edge of a major intersection, staring at a monstrosity in the Fascist vein of architecture—because Spatz needed what Hans knew.

"You're a fine physicist, Hans," Spatz said thoughtfully. "One of the best Europe's ever produced. You're Austrian, of course, but the Anschluss made that distinction irrelevant. We're all happy brothers in the Reich now, aren't we? The real problem is that your mother is Jewish, and as a result it's illegal for any German or Austrian institution to hire you. *Verboten.* As much as one's life is worth."

He didn't wait for von Halban to agree.

"...So your decision to become a full French citizen and marry in kind was probably a good one. Or would have been, if the French army hadn't decided to refight the last war instead of Hitler's. Do you know the Allied infantry has no tanks? And they're facing the largest tank brigade the world has ever seen? Do you know the Luftwaffe outnumbers French planes ten to one?"

"Churchill will send British planes."

"Churchill's keeping every last one. He needs them to fight off the invasion of Britain, once France falls."

Von Halban licked his lips. "There are too many rumors abroad. One has no idea what to believe."

"Unless one has read the telegrams," Spatz said ruthlessly. "The German embassy is closed, as we both know, but believe me when I tell you there's an underground German force in this city. I talk to them daily."

"*Your* loyalty to the Fatherland must be suspect," von Halban retorted, stung. "God knows what you find to tell your . . . *underground*."

"Lies. Truth." Spatz shrugged, an impatient flick of the wings. "Depends on the day. For years I've kept my head down and my ass out of Berlin, Hans. Only now Berlin's on my doorstep and you think I *like* it? You think I want to see the boys in *feldgrau* uniforms goose-stepping down the Champs-Élysées?"

"But—" He groped for words, his mind always filled with numbers. Particle speeds. Equations. "You just said—"

"—That I'm buying time. *Yes.* If I look like I'm cooperating maybe they'll leave me alone, long enough for me to make other plans. My cousin knows people in the British legation."

Being German was a sick joke, von Halban thought. There was Spatz: the perfect Aryan, with his taut physique and gilded head. But Spatz's mother was British, his ex-wife was Jewish, and like Hans himself,

Spatz had a nobleman's *von* in his name. Any hint of aristocratic background and you were suspect by birth, grist for Hitler's warped mill. There were at least three counts against Hans Gunter von Dincklage and every file in the Reich would list them in ink.

Von Halban began to move again, aimlessly, as though his feet could actually save him. "*Gott in Himmel,* what must I do, Spatz?"

"Decide your future. Because it's got a half-life, as I think you people would say, of a couple of days. By that time you'd better be elsewhere."

But I have no money. No car. A wife and two children.

"Will Canaris protect you?" he asked.

Spatz's boss hated Hitler; everybody in the Abwehr did.

Spatz just looked at von Halban. "Will Minister Dautry protect *you?*"

Von Halban drew a quick breath. Spatz knew even this, then: that Hans's work in Joliot's lab came directly under the authority of Raoul Dautry and the Ministry of Armaments. Unbidden, Joliot's face, hollowed and bony, surged into his mind: Joliot's eyes, piercing as God's. *No word,* the Great Man was saying, *no word of what we do here must* ever *leave this room.*

"Maybe," Spatz suggested, "we could protect each other."

"How?"

"—By pooling our resources." He stopped short, attention focused on the tip of his cigarette. "I have money. Access to transport. I could get Annick and your girls out. And you..."

"...have information," Hans concluded. His throat constricted so severely it was a full moment before he could speak. "Information certain people would pay to know. You have planned this for some time, Spatz. Yes?"

The Sparrow slipped his gold lighter into his jacket.

"Since the night your people stole my water out of Norway," he answered.

CHAPTER FOURTEEN

Joe Hearst stared at the envelope he'd placed squarely on his desk, the heavy manila corners slightly bent with misuse and too much mailing. He was in a quandary about this envelope, sent two days before by a dead man. He'd tried to make good on Stilwell's intentions—had taken the package confidently from Léonie Blum and driven by the main office of the Banque de Paris et des Pays-Bas—where he'd asked for Jacques Allier and been told, icily, that Monsieur was no longer employed by the bank.

End of story, no further information given.

He thought next of Sally King—perhaps this letter was as much her property now as the unknown Allier's—and phoned the Foreigners' Hospital.

"Gone," the nurse said simply. "A gentleman called for her. Paid her bill, too. I suppose, with a face like that—"

Fighting a surge of jealousy, now, alone in his chancellery office, Hearst confronted the problem of the undeliverable envelope.

Gentlemen do not read each other's mail, he thought as he stared at the scrawl of ink before him. Henry

Stimson—the career diplomat who'd coined that phrase—deplored spying in any form. Stimson would have burned Stilwell's correspondence and thought nothing more about it.

Hearst reached for his engraved letter opener, and inserted the silver tip under the resistant flap.

There was a knock at the door: soft, determined, like a kiss on the ear. *A woman's knock,* he thought with a flare of hope. *Sally?* He slid Stilwell's envelope hastily into a drawer.

"Come in."

A face appeared around the jamb. "Mr. *Hearst,* I believe?"

He rose politely, inclined his head. "And you are?"

"Emery *Morris.* Of the *law* firm Sullivan and Cromwell." He was a compact figure, perfectly groomed, but fussily prim. "Bob Murphy *said* I might walk back—"

"Certainly." Hearst motioned to a chair. "You know Bob?"

"The entire *world* knows Bob, I believe," Morris observed. He bent down and eased a large cardboard box across the threshold. "I was able to *serve* him on a trifling *legal matter* at one time."

"You're here about Philip Stilwell, I guess—the morgue agreed to release his body. Your firm should decide whether it wants to book passage for the remains, and if so, whether you need our consular section's help. An undertaker should be retained, of course—and a casket purchased..."

Morris looked up from his box; his nostrils twitched above the toothbrush mustache. "*Convey* that suggestion to the managing *head,* Mr. Max Shoop. I do not *anticipate* returning to the Sullivan and Cromwell offices *myself.*"

"No?" Hearst eyed him curiously.

"And as for young Stilwell's *remains*—I do not give a *damn,* sir."

"I see." He did not invite the man to sit down again. "What can I do for you?"

Morris smiled. "No, *no,* Mr. Hearst. The question is what *I* can do to help *you.*"

"I beg your pardon?"

"This *box.*" The lawyer nudged it lightly with his shoe. "It contains several *months'* worth of *files* from Philip Stilwell's office. I *removed* them last *night,* on the strong assumption that if I did *not,* Max Shoop certainly *would*—and Shoop, Mr. Hearst, would *never* have delivered them to *you.* He would *burn* them first. These files, you see, could *destroy* Max Shoop."

"In what way?" Hearst sank cautiously into his chair.

"They record, in *excruciating* detail, how Shoop has systematically *violated* the American Neutrality Act, by *aiding* and *abetting* the French government in the present *war.*"

Hearst quelled an impulse to laugh. They were all aiding and abetting the French government, however little they admitted it in public. "And you brought the files to me?"

"The American Embassy *ought* to *know,*" Morris said acutely. "Stilwell was Shoop's *tool.* Hand-in-glove with the *French.* That kind of *collaboration* with a *belligerent* is hardly Sullivan and Cromwell *policy.* Mr. Foster Dulles *closed* the Paris office last *September* precisely to *avoid* this kind of thing. Shoop has been *lying* to Dulles. Pursuing his *own* sympathies and interests in *direct violation* of American *law*. He was using *Stilwell* to do it."

"Why didn't you go to Foster Dulles with this?"

"Oh, I *will*," Morris assured him. "Shoop's career at S and C is *over*. But with life in Paris so *uncertain*—with the Germans across the Meuse and everyone scattering to the *four winds*—I thought the chancellery the best place to keep the *evidence*. In case Shoop *runs*. Before he can be *prosecuted*."

"For what? Violating the Neutrality Act?"

"No, *no*, Mr. Hearst." Morris smiled sickly. "For *murdering* Philip Stilwell."

There were eight files in all, one for each month of the war, filled with the oddest assortment of documents Joe Hearst had ever seen: notes penned in Stilwell's scrawl that made sense only to their author; articles snipped from what appeared to be scientific journals; short messages signed *MS* that he interpreted to be from Max Shoop; and oblique letters addressed to the Banque de Paris et des Pays-Bas.

It all boiled down to a list of dates Hearst found in the final file, written in what he assumed was Philip Stilwell's longhand.

March 1939:
• *Bohemia and Moravia annexed by Germany.*
  Note: this region sole source of uranium in Europe,
  now under German control.

- *Joliot and colleagues show that splitting of uranium atom by a single neutron results in the emission of more than one neutron. Suggests chain reaction possible, <u>for use as energy source—or explosive.</u>*

<u>*April 1, 1939*</u>*: Joliot receives telegram from U.S. colleague begging him to stop publishing results of experimentation, due to threat of war from Germany.*

<u>*May 1, 1939*</u>*: Joliot takes out 5 patents on construction and use of nuclear reactors. Von Halban and Kowarski co-applicants.*

<u>*June 1939*</u>*: More than fifty articles to date published worldwide on <u>atomic fission</u>. Experimentation at breakneck pace.*

<u>*Sept. 1939*</u>*: I arrive in Paris. France and Britain declare war on Germany.*

<u>*Nov. 1939*</u>*:*

- *Joliot called up for military service. Captain, Group 1 Scientific Research.*
- *Requests French government minister Dautry purchase 400 kg uranium from Metal Hydrides, Inc., of Clifton, Massachusetts (Sullivan & Cromwell client). Also requests purchase of <u>entire stockpile of heavy water currently stored at HydroNorsk facility in Norway.</u> (HydroNorsk owned 65% by Banque de Paris et des Pays-Bas. <u>Sullivan & Cromwell client</u>.)*
- *Clients ask advice of S&C. Shoop refers matter to me.*
- *Discover heavy water already in play for purchase by HydroNorsk's secondary shareholder, <u>I.G. Farbenindustrie (25% of stock. Sullivan & Cromwell client.</u> See files of <u>Rogers Lamont</u>.)*

<u>March 1940</u>: Bank officer successfully negotiates loan of HydroNorsk stockpile to France.
<u>April 1940</u>:
• Germans invade Norway, seize HydroNorsk facility.
<u>May 1940</u>:
• Hostilities begin on Maginot Line.
• <u>Warn Joliot about vulnerability of his cyclotron.</u>

Here the list abruptly broke off.

Hearst sat quite still at his desk, Stilwell's notes in his hands. He knew next to nothing about physics but he remembered something Bullitt had said once, not too long ago—about Albert Einstein. The man was in exile at Princeton and he was a weird fish by all accounts. Nonetheless, he'd written a letter directly to Roosevelt, warning him that the Germans were working on an atomic bomb. Something that could destroy the entire city of New York with a pound or two of explosive.

Roosevelt, Bullitt said, had no idea whether to take Einstein seriously. Most of the scientists the President had consulted agreed there was no feasible way to make such a bomb.

Until Philip Stilwell and the French had found it.

"Max Shoop looks capable of murder," Bullitt said placidly when Hearst hunted him down in his office. "Think there's any truth in Morris's claim?"

"Nothing I can prove—yet. But the files are confusing; they're full of atomic research. *French* atomic research."

"That'd be Joliot-Curie." Bullitt reached for a glass of water. He'd been burning documents in his tole wastebasket all afternoon and his eyes were streaming.

"You know him?"

"Slightly. —Bit of a snake-charmer, in my opinion, for all he won the Nobel. Chummy with the damned Communists. Got a Russian working in his lab."

"And plans for a bomb," Hearst said, "that could level Berlin. Or London. Or New York."

"That's not possible." Bullitt set down his water glass. "We've checked."

"Joliot-Curie would disagree. And with the Germans on their way to Paris—"

The ambassador's office was cloudy with smoke and Hearst could barely discern Bullitt through the thickening gloom: domed head, impeccable suiting, neat fingers with their polished nails. Bullitt was no fool, but the demands on him were endless. He hadn't slept in days and he could not be blamed, Hearst thought, for ignoring a branch of science so theoretical only ten people in the world truly understood it.

"The Germans have already taken Czechoslovakia—Europe's main source of uranium," he persisted. "They just took Norway—the one place in the world with heavy water. Now they're taking *Paris*. Joliot has the only cyclotron on the Continent and the brains to design this bomb. I think we should be concerned, sir. I think we should inform the President."

Bullitt refilled his water glass. "Tell it to the Brits, Joe. We're not even in this war."

"Will Roosevelt see it that way?"

"Roosevelt's far more worried about the Allied retreat from the Meuse," the ambassador retorted, "and the fact that I've got Winston Bloody Churchill flying into Paris on Thursday for a quick conference. The PM seems to think he can buck up the French and send them back into battle. He doesn't know yet there's a hole a hundred kilometers wide on the border and the Germans are pouring through like turds in a sewer. Nobody's stopping them."

"The French counteroffensive..."

"Is pure shit." Bullitt reached for a pile of letters and dropped them into the flaming wastebasket. "I saw Premier Reynaud an hour ago. He's on the point of resigning. I'm ordering all non-essential staff and family to Bordeaux tomorrow. You can book passage to England from there, maybe even New York."

Hearst digested this. "*I* can book passage, sir?"

"I want you in Bordeaux, Joe," Bullitt snapped. "I need Carmel Offie and Murphy here and a couple of guards and telegraph operators—but you and Steve Tarnow and the others must go. No sense in all of us dying."

"Do we even *know* whether Paris is the German objective?" Hearst burst out. "There's no accurate reporting from the Front! The panzers could be heading west toward the Channel."

"I can't wait for news that may never come." Bullitt coughed gutturally, the phlegm of a smoker. "Reynaud's considering fallback positions for his government—somewhere in the Auvergne—and if he's getting his people out, so should I."

"The Auvergne?"

"Vichy, to be precise. The premier has some vague notion that German panzers won't be able to penetrate the mountains of the Massif Central."

"What about *defending the city, street by street,* as he claimed he'd do?"

"That's an army's job, not a bureaucrat's." The ambassador's eyes flicked up at Hearst, flat and hard as glass. "Find Petie. Take the chancellery's fleet of cars and plan a convoy for the Bordeaux road. Leave no later than tomorrow night, Thursday morning at the latest. Protect the women and kids if you can. It'll be slow going."

Hearst did a mental calculation. He'd be babysitting nearly fifty women and children, with assorted male hangers-on, the occasional servant, all of them squabbling about belongings and privileges and exactly what *kind* of boat would be available in Bordeaux. They'd need food. Bathroom breaks. Petrol. When there was no petrol to be found anywhere in Paris.

"What about Philip Stilwell?" he asked. "He's still lying in the Paris morgue."

Bullitt waved dismissively. "Shoop's got the corpse booked on a tramp steamer out of Cherbourg Thursday. Told me so this afternoon."

"Jesus *Christ,*" Hearst muttered. "And Sally?"

"Why don't you invite her on a romantic getaway?" the ambassador suggested blisteringly. "I hear the wine country is lovely this time of year."

He took the Buick and went straight to the Rue St-Jacques, hoping to find her home. But the concierge had gone to bed and when he tossed a rock at a random window, it was the neighbor, Tasi, who appeared at the front door.

"Sally never came back from the hospital," she said, her slanted eyes narrowing.

"She was discharged this afternoon."

"Then perhaps she's left town?"

"Without her things?"

Tasi shrugged, bored and weary of the pettiness of men. "She was *attacked*, monsieur. She is frightened, no? And then, *pauvre Philippe*, it was in all the papers..."

"She's sent no word?"

Tasi laid a delicate hand on his arm and shivered. "It's so cold outside, monsieur, even if it *is* spring. Would you like to come up? I will make you some real Russian tea..."

"Do you know any of Sally's friends? A woman or... a man, for instance, with whom she might be staying?"

"Always it was Philippe, you understand? She has gone to a hotel, *peut-être*."

"She had no money to pay for one," he said brusquely, his anxiety soaring.

What *was* it these fool women were searching for, running off into the blue, alone and unprotected? Daisy had done the same thing—skipping out the front door with her laugh still bubbling on her lips. No farewell kiss, no forwarding address. *His fault*, of course—his enduring sin that his wife had run into the maw of violence, beyond all hope of saving. He'd failed her. As he was failing Sally. Grieving, frightened, wounded Sally—

The tears streaming down her cheeks in the Foreigners' Hospital. The man who'd put his hands around her neck...

Hearst left a note with Tasi and three hundred francs. He felt no confidence that Sally would ever receive either.

CHAPTER FIFTEEN

When Joliot caught a glimpse of her in the Luxembourg Gardens a few minutes before five o'clock, she was turning briskly into the path that led toward the Boulevard St-Michel. He thought he'd raised a ghost—or an incubus, rather: the embodiment of all his brutal yearnings.

It could not be Nell. Not Nell in the flesh, in Paris—

He stopped short, his eyes narrowing to follow her as she passed under the shade of the young elm leaves. Her waist, narrow and coy, might belong to any woman; so, too, the insubordinate legs; but two things screamed her name across the years of separation and distrust: the bones of her neck, fragile beneath that too-clever hat, and the decided way she stalked the paving. Her heels clicked in syncopation: sunlight, shadow, sunlight, shadow, the water trickling somewhere in a fountain and his errand gone in the second of recognizing her.

He called out. *Nell.*

The footsteps did not falter; her head was down, her mind lost in thought. She was bent on reaching

Boul-Mich. Maybe she had an appointment there. But suddenly it occurred to him she'd seen him, too; had seen him even before he scented her presence, and had deliberately walked in her fierce English way as swiftly as she could toward the promise of escape.

He began to run, his papers flapping, the pencil he kept behind one ear plummeting unnoticed to the ground. Called her name urgently this time, so that a clutch of pigeons took clattering flight.

Her head turned—one gloved hand clenched spasmodically on the strap of her handbag. Then she halted, waiting for him.

"Ricki."

It was *her* name; nobody else had ever called him that. To the world, he was Joliot, to his colleagues, Frédéric. Fred to his mother and wife. *Le Professeur Joliot-Curie* to the students who listened to his lectures at the Collège de France, four blocks away. Ricki was the name she'd given him fifteen years ago in Berlin as he stood, light-headed from gin and lack of sleep, with his back against the wall of the club she'd insisted they visit long after everyone else was longing for bed. *Ricki*, she'd said, *I want your lighter. I need some heat at the tip of my cigar.*

She'd been dressed like a man that night in 1925, in good English suiting borrowed from her brother: the Honourable Nell Bracecourt, daughter of an earl, slumming it in the backstreets of Berlin with a polyglot bunch of freaks. This was not her usual scene—talk of radium and Bohr's model and quantum jumps—and Joliot could feel her boredom curling like a cat between them. Twenty-one years old and already tired of life.

She'd made certain he knew just how irrelevant—how impossibly old—he really was.

"What are you doing here?" he demanded, his breath coming in tearing gasps.

"Is it *yours*, then, the Luxembourg? Nobody else allowed to set foot in it?"

"Nell—"

A smile pursed her lips, something acid on the tongue. "You never change, Ricki. Always that sense of outrage. As though I offend the world simply by walking through it."

"You know that's not true." He'd spoken English to her out of long-dead habit, but his command of the language was sporadic, and he groped for words, tongue-tied and overwhelmed. "It's wonderful to see you, Nell. You look . . . very well."

She was older, he could not deny it: the luminous quality of youth had drained from her skin, leaving it taut across the bones, mapping the infinite beauty of her cheek and brow, the swallows' lift above her blue eyes. She must be somewhat more than thirty-five, he thought. Her form was unchanged: light and contained and perfectly controlled, the body of a disciplined athlete. How she came by it he never understood; Nell was rarely disciplined or controlled.

"Thank you," she said crisply. "I don't make a point of advertising my perfect misery to the crowd. You're keeping well, I take it? Still swotting away at your atoms and such?"

"Yes." The question recalled him with a thud to reality: the lab; the errand he'd intended to run; the war.

For a second he wanted to tell her everything: let the words come tumbling out, the urgency of his life in these last days, how the certainty of the German threat had thrown every choice he'd ever made under the glare of an interrogator's bulb, like silhouettes projected against a blank screen. All the regrets and compromises were redeemed by only two things: the purity of his work. His children.

He nodded distractedly, staring over her shoulder. He did not realize she was frowning, eyes searching his face, until she spoke.

"Let me buy you a *fine*, Ricki. In the Boul-Mich. We can talk there."

If he had ordered the cognac himself it would certainly have been lousy and he would hardly have noticed, the burn at the back of the throat being something he expected now, of a piece with the general shoddiness of things. Even the café owners were sending their stores out of the city for safekeeping, or bricking up their cellars. But Nell demanded quality: her *domaine* in Bordeaux supplied some of these people with their wines and she knew everyone within a twenty-mile radius of the Seine, from old Edouard at the Dôme to Héloise at Café Flore to the legendary André Terrail of Tour d'Argent. She knew exactly what was hoarded in the *cave* beneath their feet and she ordered it straight up, her French accent somewhat better than his English.

"You're in Paris for pleasure?" he asked as they were

abandoned at their table, sitting directly opposite the main entrance of the Sorbonne and in full sight of a host of colleagues who might wonder why the celebrated Nobel laureate was drinking in the early evening with a woman manifestly not his wife. "You've come to shop, perhaps? To see friends?"

"In the middle of the German offensive?" she returned coolly as she lit a cigarette. *Nell's hands.* Slender and artistic and pampered. His wife's were covered with radium burns.

She glanced at him through the smoke. "There's a consignment of wine casks I have to get back to Bordeaux before the Nazis confiscate them. Very expensive, very new Nevers oak. Twenty of them in a hired van. You'd like to think I'm useless—one of those decorative parasites you've made a practice of hating, Ricki—but nobody can run a vineyard merely on privilege and good looks."

"Bertrand—"

"My husband is at the Front." Clipped words, thrown up like a shield in front of her face: *I do not want your sympathy.*

"I didn't know."

"Naturally not. You haven't exactly kept in touch." She stubbed out the cigarette, although it had barely burned. "Bertrand hasn't written in weeks. I think he's not allowed. Which means, of course, that it's bloody awful where he is."

"You still love him so much?"

"God, no. I simply hate to be ignored, Ricki, you

know that. Why else did *you* cut me off so completely—if not because it hurt?"

In that instant, Nell's hand poised over an ashtray and the slanting light of May gilding her chestnut hair, it was all alive again between them: the jealousy and the betrayal and the aching need. He wanted to circle her neck with his fingers and tell her, once and for all, that she would never belong to anyone else. No matter how much time passed. No matter who else they fucked or married.

"Have you noticed only the old men are left in these wretched places?" she said conversationally, her eyes flicking from the street to the approaching waiter. "It's the same in Bordeaux. Not an able-bodied laborer to be had, the vines setting fruit. It's going to get worse. *Salut.*"

She drank as he remembered: the amber liquid swallowed neatly as an insult. Then she set down the glass—nothing but bitter lees hunkering in the bottom—and said, "How's Irène?"

It was a deliberate ploy. Mention the wife and cover him with shame. But fidelity had never been *his* problem: Nell had left him first, fifteen years ago, on a train platform with a packed suitcase and a ticket he methodically shredded over the rails until his hands bled. He'd read of her marriage in the newspapers.

"Irène's not well. She's gone to Brittany for a rest cure. With the children."

"You astonish me."

Irène frightened most people. Kept them safely at

arm's length with her reputation for genius. Her silence and self-sufficiency. Her dreadful clothes.

He guessed Nell was a little bored by her.

"It's not the war she's running from," he explained. "It's our...occupational hazard. Leukemia. Her mother died from it. Irène's persistently anemic."

"And you?"

He shrugged. "I'm too busy to be sick. I was called up last September. Like Bertrand."

"Only *you're* safe in Paris."

"For the moment. My front is the laboratory."

"Christ," she muttered viciously. "Is this the bomb I've heard whispers of? Splitting the atom?"

Nell would know, of course. She was not like most people. She'd grown up around physicists, her brother chief among them—the Honourable Ian Bracecourt, who'd slaved away with Rutherford at Cambridge. Ian had sent a telegram of congratulations when the Joliot-Curies won the Nobel in 1935. But Nell's words returned him to self-awareness: to the life he really led. The desperate secrecy. The patents he'd drawn. The Germans on the border and the things he could not tell even to his wife.

"There is no such thing as an atomic bomb," he whispered.

Nell threw back her head and laughed.

He set his cognac aside, unfinished; raised a hand for the waiter. "Is there anything I can do for you while you are in Paris? I know Raoul Dautry—the minister. He might be able to get news of Bertrand."

"Stay with me," she said, unexpectedly. "I won't run this time, I promise you."

He dragged his eyes from his billfold to her face.

The words were uttered so quietly they might not have been said. There was denial in her careful expression: She was prepared to ignore her words if he did.

And if she had not run all those years ago—to Bertrand and his title and the fortress in Bordeaux—what then? Would he have gone slowly mad with wanting and hating her until nothing but death could save him from himself? He'd been obsessed. *Obsessed.* With her caprice and her charm, her refusal ever to yield, her sweet liquid sex smelling of violets. He could have eaten her alive in that bed in the Rue Martine.

Go to the lab, Joliot. Something sterile and white, not that fragile neck between your teeth.

He paid too much for the cognacs, bills slipping from his fingers.

Night fell as they left the café. They skittered like leaves through the shadowed garden.

CHAPTER SIXTEEN

Hans von Halban was dreaming of Joliot's cloud chamber when the doorbell rang: water vapor clinging to the glass cylinder, Joliot in his white smock with his hands balled in his pockets. The room at the back of the laboratory was dim, the mood hushed—Joliot's shrine, Kowarski called it. Kowarski stood to the left of Joliot, enormous and hunched, his fists like mallets, his face the usual Russian blend of brutality and madness. Joliot was talking reverently of particles: how the tiniest trajectory could be traced through the condensation on the glass, the hand of God in the scattering of droplets. Von Halban tried to interrupt—tried to stop Joliot from reaching for the piston—but it was too late. The mechanical thing leaped forward, uncontrolled. The glass shattered violently as it had never done before and Joliot was screaming, his hands over his eyes, blood streaming between his fingers.

A chain reaction, von Halban thought. *Gott in Himmel, it will kill us all.*

He sat up in bed, panting, with the sound of the buzzer in his ears.

"What is it, *cher*?" his wife murmured, not really awake—not really caring, just waiting for the disturbance to go away. Her attitude toward most things.

He threw back the covers and reached for a robe—it was his habit to sleep in the nude. Annick rolled over, her blond head shining silver in the moonlight, and immediately fell back to sleep. The clock on the bedside table read 1:19 A.M.

The summons in the night, Hans thought bitterly. *The knock on the door.* He had been waiting for it for months. But not even the Germans could be here already.

He walked toward the front hall, his muscles tensed. The buzzer trilled again, violent as the trajectory of a particle or bullet. The sound slammed against his eardrum.

He opened the door a crack, waiting for the boot against the jamb, the overpowering force thrusting him backward, the black-clad storm troopers surging through.

Nothing.

He peered into the corridor. The block of flats was silent and dark—no sound of traffic rose from the street below. The dead hour. A mild-faced Frenchman hovered.

"Monsieur von Halban?"

"Yes?"

"Jacques Allier. Ministry of Armaments."

Allier. He knew the name: Allier who'd worked for the Banque de Paris et des Pays-Bas—one of the biggest French banks, powerful, allied with government. Allier was a lieutenant now in the army. *A spy.*

"I'm sorry to disturb you at this hour of the morning, but I could not find *le Professeur* Joliot-Curie, and—"

"You have tried the lab, yes?" von Halban interrupted stiffly.

"It's closed and dark."

"His home? It is south—in Antony." Still Paris, but closer to the suburbs of Orly; Joliot liked living a distance from the lab, liked leaving his work behind when he could.

"I drove out there an hour ago. He's not there."

"And you found me—how?"

"The Ministry must know where its leading scientists are at any given moment, *vous comprendez*." Allier shrugged, his hands spread wide. "In the current climate—"

In the current climate, keep the foreigners under surveillance. They all hate our guts.

Von Halban stepped back and ushered Allier inside. He had no other choice.

The lab at the Collège de France had been placed under the Ministry of Armaments in September, just after the declaration of war. Fred Joliot's work—Joliot the Nobel laureate—was that crucial. Which made it awkward, Hans von Halban thought, that his principal assistants were Russian and Austrian. Enemy combatants, as it were. Suspect.

He and Kowarski had actually been sent out of Paris while this fool Allier—a *banker, mein Gott,* who looked as if he couldn't harm a fly—had been off on his hush-hush mission to Norway. Kowarski dispatched to the island of Belle-Île, off the coast of Brittany, and von Halban to Pôquerolle, in the Mediterranean. Just to be certain they could not conspire against the French, or betray what they did not know.

"Joliot has been called away, perhaps, to Brittany." Von Halban heard the German edge to his own words, the unmistakable syntax of the alien. "His children are there, yes? His wife, too, one supposes. You are acquainted with Irène?"

"By reputation," Allier returned dismissively. "I placed a trunk call to Arcouest. He's not in Brittany."

Von Halban studied the other man. Allier might have fidgeted; might have paced in agitation before the perfunctory hearth that graced Annick's rigidly modernist room, the chrome tables and leather chairs—instead, he preserved a remarkable stillness, mild brown eyes fixed on von Halban's face.

"I came to inquire whether there might be another address where Joliot-Curie could be found."

"You will tell me what is wrong, please," von Halban demanded bluntly. "Fred was as usual when he left the *labo* this afternoon. If you call there again in the morning—around nine, yes?—no doubt you may talk to him then."

"When did you last see Joliot-Curie, Herr Doktor?"

Von Halban winced at the title. "Four. Four-thirty perhaps. He was to deliver a letter to the president of the college. He did not return."

"He was seen at a café in the Boul-Mich at half-past five. He left with a woman—not his wife. Nobody has been able to locate him since. You understand, now, why I ask for an alternative address."

How perfectly French, von Halban thought. *How stupid of me not to have seen it coming.* Joliot, whose only mistress was his cloud chamber—that and the magnetron he was building with the parts ordered from Switzerland. *And if he did take some woman to bed? What business is it of mine or this petty Ministry spy's?*

"I cannot help you," he replied firmly. "If it is as you say, he has gone to a hotel, yes? Or to the woman's place. Come to the lab in the morning."

There was a delicate pause.

"Or perhaps . . . I may be of assistance?"

Allier was still studying him with that suggestion of inner quiet, a man completely in control of himself and his emotions. His face betrayed nothing, but the silence itself spoke volumes: the Frenchman was considering how far he could trust this scientist with the German name, this man in Fred Joliot's pocket, this too-ready ear in an hour of crisis.

"I am a French citizen," von Halban asserted, still too stiff from pride and anger. "My wife is French. My children also. My sympathies. I have lived and worked here for years."

"Have you got a key to the laboratory?"

"But of course."

"Then perhaps you would be so good as to dress. We're under orders to remove everything—*everything,* you understand—before dawn. If we're lucky, Joliot will join us there."

"Do you remember the night at Birchmere Park?" Nell asked him. "The way we huddled on the roof tiles, Ricki, waiting for the sun to rise?"

How could he have forgotten it? Her father's house, generations of English noblemen born and dead between its stone walls, a thing of turrets and wings flung out through the centuries. Nell's family was always pressed for money and the roof tiles were broken, but they had taken some blankets from an old linen press at three o'clock in the morning, the two of them and her brother Ian with a bottle of claret, and they had listened in companionable silence fifty feet above the ground while some small animal below was crushed in the jaws of a fox, screaming. The fen country: flat as Holland, sodden underfoot, a line of dikes keeping the whole thing from sinking. Her father had not wanted the football player with the hooked nose and the graceful body for his Nell. The earl needed money. Joliot had none.

She sat now in the deep window of her room at the Crillon, wearing nothing but his shirt. Her bare legs were drawn up under her chin and she was brooding on this other dawn as the Place de la Concorde woke beneath them, the first hush of tires circling the square. They had made love during the long hours of the night, lying in a doze and waking to this deep hunger Joliot had known only once before in his life. Bertrand's people had always stayed at the Crillon and Nell ought to have been more discreet than to have taken Joliot there; but it was possible, he realized, that she wanted them to know that *Mme. la Comtesse* did as she pleased. She was English: nobody ruled her.

"Will you go back?" he asked. "To Birchmere? Now that the Germans are coming?"

"I want them to come," she muttered. "I'm sick to death of this phony war. I want things *decided*. No—I won't go back. Whether the vineyard's called French or German is unimportant. If I stay, I can do some good there. You'll laugh, Ricki, but I've come to love Domaine de Loudenne. I won't have it taken from me. I *won't*."

Her voice broke on the word and in the sound he heard all the fear of the past winter, the news from Sedan where even now her husband might be dying, the helplessness and the tension of waiting. He stretched out his hand to stroke her head but she started up, turned her shoulder to him, walked abruptly to the bath. She did not want his sympathy; it was salt in a wound.

This was what was different about Nell, he thought: the fierce bitterness beneath her beauty. Maybe it was age or Bertrand's indifference or the lack of children, but the mark of the survivor was cut deep into her eyes. It hurt him to see it there.

She was running water in the tub. He almost considered picking up the shirt she'd discarded on the tiles and slipping away while she bathed. It would be a relief, after the demons that had dogged him all night, her skin beneath his hands, the coiled wire of her body. A relief to be alone.

If it was commonly held that every Frenchman had a mistress, then Frédéric Joliot-Curie was the exception to the rule. He had been faithful to Irène from the first day of their meeting in 1925—she absorbed in an experiment mounted on her bench at the Laboratoire du

Radium where he had been newly hired as Marie Curie's assistant; he, Fred, bruised and sour in the aftermath of Nell's defection. He had courted his wife in walks through the forests of Fontainebleau; during ski trips to the Alps where she removed her clothing in the most perfunctory manner and obligingly offered him her virginity; at her mother's house in Brittany where he learned to sail; in the lab where they both pursued matters too obscure to be explained to outsiders. Irène cared nothing for the usual things: jewels or clothes or flirtation or intrigue. From childhood she had been raised by two of the most formidable minds in physics to hone the organ of her brain. When Fred thought of Irène it was in the form of Picasso before the Cubist period, her limbs massive and heavy-flanked, her face devoid of emotion. She regarded him as a good means of having children—"that remarkable experiment," as she called it. They now possessed two.

Irène had continued to work in the lab during her pregnancies—had won the Nobel Prize with him in 1935. He was more often called by *her* name than his own, and though it rankled to be viewed as secondary to his wife, she'd been his passport to respect and acceptance. Frédéric Joliot, who'd failed his first qualifying exam, who'd been granted an indifferent degree from an inferior school, was of very little interest to the French scientific establishment. But Frédéric Joliot-Curie—allied with the most famous female name in France—was a man nobody could ignore.

Did I do it for that? he asked himself now, with the scent of Nell's body still on his skin. *For success? A career?*

It was something. A partnership. A life. And I do love her. But not to the point of madness...

The bathroom door opened. Nell stood there, warm and silent, the hawk peering out of her eyes. He walked slowly toward her. And ripped the towel from her body with his restless hands.

CHAPTER SEVENTEEN

The Shoops lived in a gilded set of rooms off the Rue de Monceau, overlooking one of the entrances to the park. They had been living there nearly twenty years, without children, the interiors gradually acquiring the peculiarly French patina that comes with exquisite taste and unlimited means. Odette Shoop was superbly fitted to her home, as though she'd been chosen along with the Sèvres china to ornament the place. She was petite, gamine, perpetually vivacious, and quite in the manner of Mlle. Chanel, whose salon she patronized. Sally recognized the careless jersey dress Odette was wearing; she had worn it herself during last autumn's shows.

"My poor child," Odette said firmly as she brushed each of Sally's cheeks in turn with her cool crimson lips. "You have suffered an enormity. You will have a hot bath, a tray of supper brought to your room, and an early bed. Tomorrow, we will set out for the shops and equip you for the voyage home, *oui*?"

She had not bothered to argue, not with Odette or even with Max himself during the brief ride from the hospital to Parc Monceau. The *Clothilde,* he'd repeated, *Cherbourg Harbor, Thursday. Your tickets are waiting at the shipping office near the docks.* He had never threatened her with anything; she did not believe herself to be in physical danger; and yet, every fiber of her being resisted his plans for her. It was vital to Max Shoop that she stay away from her studio in the Rue St-Jacques, vital that she embark with Philip's body on a merchant steamer the day after tomorrow. Sally did not like it when older men tried to order her existence. Her father had tried once and she had simply left the country. Now, she was increasingly inclined to thwart Max Shoop by staying.

The bath was heaven; dinner, a simple affair of *magret de canard* with a glass of excellent burgundy; the room to which Odette conveyed her, a perfection of rose and green silk brocade. But the colors reminded Sally of her Schiaparelli dress and she lay awake long after the rest of the house was doused in sleep, while the bells of Saint-Philippe-du-Roule rang the successive hours. It might be possible to slip away from Odette tomorrow in one of the crowded stores of the Boulevard Haussmann, or perhaps she could excuse herself from the tea table at Fauchon's—but when the bells sang out three A.M., she thrust back the covers and set her feet noiselessly on the carpet.

The flat was an enfilade of rooms: bedchambers at one end of the wide salon, servants' quarters and kitchen at the other. Sally shut her bedroom door quietly and crept down the hallway in the clothes Odette had lent her. A ridiculous pair of borrowed dress slippers dangled from her hands.

The bolt driven home in the front door's lock did not even squeak as she pulled it; still holding her breath, she stepped onto the landing. The blue glow of blackout bulbs fell like sainthood around her.

There were no taxis until she reached the Opéra, and even then, she had no money to pay a fare. The eerie silence of the world magnified her footfalls until she could almost believe the buildings trembled as she passed. The chief danger was that her solitude would attract the attention not of thieves but of a gendarme, who would certainly demand to see her papers. Sally had none. She kept off the main boulevards, hugging the side streets and narrower ways.

Just before three-thirty in the morning she crossed the Seine at Pont Alexandre Trois, the heavy dome of Les Invalides looming in the blackout sky; the moon had set. And yet some movement as of a bird across the dim vault attracted her attention; she stopped short near the parapet of the bridge and stared upward. A plane droned ominous as thunder. It had to be German—no one else would make this sortie over sleeping Paris, the city exposed like an indolent nude beneath the stars. Sally stood rooted, her face uplifted, waiting for the whistle of the falling bomb, the flaring leap of fire.

Dawn was breaking fresh and golden over the narrow streets of the Latin Quarter as she closed the door of her flat for the last time and set out, suitcase clenched firmly in one hand. She was smiling faintly to herself because, incredibly, Tasi had left Joe Hearst's letter with its three hundred francs unviolated on the little dressing table in Sally's studio and now, please God, she could buy a cup of coffee. The tone of Hearst's note was puzzlingly brusque—*If you receive this, contact me immediately at the chancellery*—but it was nice of him to think of her.

Sally's ankles were aching from all the walking she'd done in dress slippers, and the suitcase would begin to feel heavy soon; but the pounding in her head was gone and with it, all uncertainty. She felt light of heart, as though she'd cut some rope that held her. Swimming steadily out to sea.

Other people with suitcases in their hands were trudging along the pavements. None of them looked as cheerful as she did. And what reason did she have for this rising joy? The man she had meant to marry was dead. Her city was on the cusp of destruction. But as she approached Philip's old apartment—Mme. Blum the concierge already up and sweeping the threshold of the massive courtyard doors—she began, softly, to sing.

CHAPTER EIGHTEEN

"I don't understand at all what you people do," Allier was saying in an absent sort of way as von Halban prepared coffee over a gas burner he kept in his corner of the lab. "My superiors tell me what I should do about it. *C'est tout.*"

Liar, von Halban mentally replied. *You understand physics well enough to have explained it all to the British in London only last month. G. P. Thomson and Oliphant and Cockcroft—who said it couldn't be done and who'll steal our work, now. Our colleagues and competitors. Our allies in this war.*

"We each have our *métier,*" he countered hollowly. "I know nothing about banking, myself. I am always in want of money."

"But that would be your wife! Women are always spending more than they ought, *n'est-ce pas?*—and your wife is French, I think you said?"

You knew that before you rang the buzzer at my door, Allier, you know everything about me, and this subtle conversational approach does not deceive me at all. I remember being sent to Porquerolles while you adventured your way through

Norway. I remember the shame and fear of it, my wife refusing to come with me and taking the children to her mother. The look in her people's eyes.

He turned, beaker raised, and offered the steaming brew to his enemy.

"I don't suppose you have milk," Allier suggested mournfully.

Von Halban did not reply. Dawn was breaking over Paris in the watery, opalescent fashion of spring and they had been at it for three hours: collecting lab papers and the canisters of heavy water Joliot had stored at the Collège for a month. There were twenty-six of them in all, handmade by an artisan in Norway for the specific purpose of being smuggled in thirteen suitcases: Allier's work, again. The canisters were waiting by the doorway of the lab, ready for transport, if transport could be found.

The uranium metal was a trickier proposition, and von Halban had refused to let Allier anywhere near the lead boxes in which it was stored. The Frenchman would simply have to take his word for it that all four hundred kilograms were assembled and accounted for.

"The cyclotron cannot be moved," he'd told Allier firmly. "The magnet alone took two years to build in Switzerland, yes? It cost the earth and weighs a ton. You will never disassemble it."

"It's the only cyclotron in Europe," Allier retorted. "We cannot allow it to fall into German hands."

As von Halban drank the scalding coffee now, he was thinking not of magnets or particles but of Joliot: of this unknown woman rising in ecstasy above him. Of an impossible happiness entirely of the flesh. Thinking of how it was all to be ruined, and how he was the agent of Joliot's ruin.

"These names," Allier persisted. "Year after year. These discoveries. Fermi, the Italian. *Nobel Prize*. Niels Bohr, the Dane. *Nobel Prize*. Albert Einstein, of no country and every country—*Nobel Prize*. That German and his Uncertainty Principle. What is his name?"

"Heisenberg. Werner Heisenberg."

"—One of the few, I might point out, who is not a Jew."

Is he waiting for me to laugh heartily? von Halban wondered. *To agree that Jewish Physics, as Hitler calls it, is a perversion and a farce? The Nazi hatred of Jewish Physics is the world's best hope, because the Nazis will kill the very science that could win their war.*

"Fermi spent his Nobel prize money escaping from Italy with his wife," he told Allier. "They left like thieves in the night, with a suitcase full of cash, and sought asylum in New York. This is what a laureate has come to, in the present age."

Allier was silent, his spectacles focused on the surface of his coffee cup.

"My mother is Jewish," von Halban persisted, overly loud. "Because of that my father has fled to Switzerland and I am unable to work in my native country ever again. I speak of Austria, you understand. Perhaps you did not know, Monsieur Allier, that Austria since the Anschluss has also closed its doors on Jewish minds."

"Oh, I knew," Allier replied easily. "That's the reason you gave for requesting French citizenship—that, and the expensive French wife. You've worked with him some time, *je crois*?"

Him being Fred the Seducer of Unknowns, lover of Russians and Apostate Jews: *le Professeur Joliot-Curie.*

"Five years."

"Ah. And he's taken out patents for all this...business, I assume? Or he's applied for same?"

Business being an amorphous term for the subtleties of atomic energy. They'd discussed it last October and agreed: Scientists had certain rights to the fruits of their work. Intellectual property.

"We all signed the requests for patents," von Halban said tiredly. "Fred and I and Lew Kowarski. We are a team, yes?"

Defiant words. The team might be broken tomorrow, at a word from this man. The French banker's smile was genial; Allier was concerned, von Halban thought, for Fred's gullibility. Did the banker know about the sealed document they'd signed and deposited with the Académie des Sciences?—The design for a sustained nuclear reaction, the first of its kind in the world?

Which either Kowarski or I could take back to our native land, von Halban thought, *and sell to the highest bidder. So fuck you, Allier. My intelligence has no ruler. No allegiance you can command. In this war, it's every Jew for himself.*

They heard him long before the key rattled uselessly in the unbolted laboratory door and he stuck his long nose around the heavy steel jamb; heard him because he was singing.

Von Halban saw it all: the fear that rose sharply in Fred's eyes, the reserve that followed like a shot bolt. The clothes he hadn't changed since yesterday and that seemed, in the meticulous—the fastidious—Fred, to be a greater declaration of betrayal than any words might offer. In his mind's eye von Halban saw again the form of the unknown woman, a joy entirely of the flesh—and felt a shudder pass through his body. *Gott in Himmel. Poor Fred.*

Being human, Joliot seized on the most obvious reason for their presence in his lab at dawn.

"Irène?" he said. "Something's happened to her? The children?"

"I spoke with Madame Joliot-Curie a few hours ago," Allier offered smoothly. "She seemed well enough. Concerned, of course, when I mentioned I could not locate you—*mais, assez bien* . . ."

Von Halban watched his friend shade his eyes with one thin hand; his lips were moving in a curse or fractured prayer.

"Then what have you come for?" he muttered. "What is it today, Allier?"

"Marching orders," the banker said briskly. "Dautry says everything in the lab must go to the Auvergne, Joliot—including, of course, *you.*"

As the morning wore on, Joliot found that his hands were shaking—either from von Halban's coffee or per-

haps the panic rising in his throat. He had lived a settled life for so long: the milk cart pulling up to the
service entrance of the house in Antony, the bluish liquid poured from buckets into the scullery maid's tin,
Irène insistent that the milk must be boiled to prevent
the spread of tuberculosis, and the girl slacking, always,
at this incomprehensible job. The children in their
school uniforms with their hair brushed and gleaming.
His work clothes laid out on their double bed, hers
nearly always the same: a starched white shirt smacking
of the convent, a formless black skirt with an ample
waistband for those rare occasions when, as she put it,
she ate too much and made a pig of herself. Two pairs
of sensible shoes, somewhat scuffed, beneath the mari-
tal dresser. It might have gone on this way indefinitely,
both of them grayer, their vitality consumed by method
and science, but for the war. War had left him single for
the span of too many hours, exposed to the possibilities
of chaos.

Von Halban had gone home to tell his wife about the
lab's evacuation but when Joliot walked him to the
door he'd paused on the threshold and muttered,
"Fred. I'm sorry. I did not intend for this man to violate
your privacy—"

"It's not your fault, Hans."

He nodded once, eyes sliding away from Joliot's
guilt. He was a reticent man; he would never ask questions; but the nebulous matter would lie between them
and a kind of unease would grow, a lack of confidence.

Impulsively Joliot said, "I was with an old friend. An
old...*flame*." It was the only word for Nell. "I knew her

before Irène. Loved her...Oh, God, Hans, I'm such a fool."

"No," he said gently. "Never a fool. And you do not have to tell me."

"She's an Englishwoman. Married to a comte. I'll probably never see her again..."

Von Halban's nostrils had flared slightly and he'd said, with sudden nervousness, "Not...not the Comtesse de Loudenne?"

Merde, Joliot had thought viciously. *The whole world knows already.*

"Be careful, Fred," von Halban said. "Her cousin is a Nazi spy—and I think he was her lover once, too..."

So he was listening now to Jacques Allier as the banker-lieutenant talked of war matériel and places of safety, but it was Nell he saw in his mind's eye: Nell the coiled wire of passion, Nell the bitter flame.

"...considering the town of Vichy," Allier was saying. "Reynaud and Daladier believe that if we can put the Massif Central between ourselves and the panzers, we could survive indefinitely."

"I don't know of any lab in Vichy," Joliot managed.

"Time enough to worry about that once you've got your apparatus down there." Allier sipped tentatively at his coffee, as though radioactivity had a taste that could be identified, sour or sweet on the tongue. "The vital thing is to get the water and uranium out of Paris, *n'est-ce pas?* I've wired the manager of the Banque de France in Clermont-Ferrand—the capital of the

Auvergne—and he's willing to store whatever I ask in his vault. That should do for your water. Complete security and complete discretion, no questions asked."

A bank vault, Joliot thought mordantly. *I'm in the hands of financiers, just another commodity for trade. How do I set up my cyclotron in a steel vault surrounded by money changers? But I'm forgetting. The cyclotron is immovable. The cyclotron stays. Which means that so, ultimately, do I.*

"We can start the canisters on the road to the Auvergne tonight and you can make your way down there with the rest of the lab equipment once your wife returns from Brittany," Allier decreed. "I'll rent you a villa big enough for your personnel and their families."

"Henri Moureu should take the water," Joliot said. "He's my deputy here at the Collège, and you can have no question about his loyalty—his father played a key part in the last war. He was called 'the Marshal of French Science,' I believe. Moureu knows the Auvergne fairly well. But he'll need a truck."

"I am familiar with M. Moureu," Allier said.

…Down to the size of his underwear, Joliot thought. *Have you measured all our balls? Do you know exactly what we boast in combined inches? Damn you and your necessary impertinence.*

"And the uranium?" he asked. "It should go with the water. I can't do much useful work without it."

"The water and metal must be separately stored," Allier said. "The world just isn't *safe* for your kind of science."

Joliot looked at this mild-featured banker, accustomed to caution, and felt a wild impulse to laugh.

Science was a leap into the void that had nothing to do with safety. Irène's mother had died leaping, her body glowing with radium, and it was fated that Joliot would follow her into that abyss. All the Curies decayed with a half-life both gorgeous and deadly.

"You want me to do *nothing*, then, for the duration of the war?" he said with sharp intensity. "My work goes nowhere without supplies. I thought that was understood."

"Your work is important, *bien sûr*. But so is the need to keep it out of the grasp of the Germans. *Your work*, as you call it, could destroy the world, Joliot."

"Nonsense! We've no idea yet what's possible—what these atoms could do . . . Fuel an entire country's electrical grid, perhaps. Heat all of Europe in winter—"

"Level a city the size of Paris," Allier concluded implacably. "With every living soul buried beneath it."

Joliot bowed his head. "To what bank vault does the uranium go?"

"The minister wants it out of France—one of our colonies in North Africa, perhaps. Our job right now is simply to get it to Marseille. And await orders."

"Uranium is dangerous," Joliot said. "Nobody but a trained scientist should handle it. I'll have to send Kowarski. Or von Halban."

"No."

"You do realize," he persisted, voice rising, "that von Halban and Kowarski are unavoidable vulnerabilities for you, for Dautry? *Everything I know, they know, too.*"

"Then they will be interned." Allier said it quietly.

"Kept under lock and key. There's no other acceptable solution."

"Are you going to lock up their wives and children?"

"If necessary."

"Then you lock me up, too. I refuse to cooperate. I refuse to ... *lend* myself to something so despicable as the betrayal of friends."

Allier said nothing for an instant, his gentle eyes dim behind his spectacles. "But perhaps the betrayal has already occurred."

"What do you mean?"

"There's a leak," the banker said patiently. "We've been aware for some time that a spy is selling our secrets. Someone at the Ministry, maybe. Someone *here*. I've come under suspicion myself, I'm certain of that, and the fact I survived my trip to Norway is no excuse. I *shouldn't* have survived and the water should never have made it out of Oslo. But it did and the leaks continue. We think they're meant to continue. Until the Germans have the information they need. We're all being kept alive—kept on a string—*watched*. Like laboratory rats."

Joliot swallowed hard, cotton-mouthed. "What kind of leaks?"

Allier shrugged. "The less you know the better. But I assure you it is entirely possible that someone on your staff—someone with knowledge and divided loyalties—has systematically betrayed you. I think we could name several possible turncoats, yes? That Russian, Lew Kowarski. The Austrian, Hans von Halban. Possibly—forgive me—yourself or your wife. Both of you have professed sympathy, after all, for the Communist system."

"Von Halban must take the uranium metal," Joliot said flatly. "Send a watchdog if you like—go yourself, I don't give a damn. But allow him this chance to prove himself. Unfounded suspicion will kill a man; it hangs over his life like poison gas. I won't do that to Hans. He's too good a physicist."

"I doubt that the minister will allow it."

Joliot's lips quirked in a wintry fashion. "The minister has no choice. I outrank you, Lieutenant Allier. Tell Dautry I issued my orders."

When the banker left, Joliot faced the task of calling Irène.

They were apart only on rare occasions, and when they communicated it was usually by letter. For this, however, he required the telephone and there was only one in the building, in a wood-paneled cubicle in the main hall. A trunk call was a tedious affair of dictating the number to the national operator, who placed the call to Arcouest and then phoned him back with Irène on the line. His wife's voice astonished him: disembodied, breathless with tuberculosis, the voice of an elderly woman. "I'm sorry Allier disturbed you last night, my darling." He was relieved that she could not see his face.

"No matter," Irène said complacently. "I wasn't sleeping. I knew you must have been out for a walk. I know your habits. How restless you are when the children and I are away."

How neatly she solved the problem for him, he thought. He had composed the lie carefully in advance:

the German bomber suddenly in the sky, the air-raid sirens wailing, himself in the communal shelter in Antony below the baker's, all of them sitting shoulder to shoulder in the dark with the smell of warm bread in their lungs. Irène would have enjoyed that, she'd have told the children how their father's tummy had rumbled while the bombs fell through the sky, but in the end her more prosaic imagination had sufficed, his invention was unnecessary, he had simply gone for a midnight walk.

"I trekked for hours," he said. "Working on something."

She coughed in a way that would have split a lesser woman in two and in that instant he saw the blood spotting her handkerchief, the dreadful pallor of her face.

"Come home," he said urgently. "Bring the children with you. I miss our life."

He sat in the empty lab for perhaps another hour, perfecting his plans. Then he rang Nell at the Hôtel Crillon.

CHAPTER NINETEEN

Those who'd looked for Memphis Jones at the Folies Bergères, or stood in line for hours outside the Alibi Club, were destined for disappointment. Memphis had behaved in a way utterly alien to her: She'd spent last night at home alone.

Rumors were flying round the nightclub world that Raoul had killed his wife's partner and run to the south of France one step ahead of the police, or the Nazis, or both. The motive was unclear, because nobody thought Jacquot would toy with Memphis—everybody knew what kind he was—but the knowledgeable guessed the *pédé* had come on to Raoul and that the killing was tantamount to self-defense. Jacquot's body was released Wednesday morning by the Paris morgue; nobody claimed it. The glittering *garçon* of the *boîte de nuit* seemed destined for a pauper's grave.

Memphis learned all this from An Li, her Vietnamese chauffeur. He had brought her a tray in bed at ten o'clock Wednesday morning: frothy hot milk, café, a porcelain plate of orange segments. The morning mail, which contained nothing but a sheaf of bills. Memphis flipped through them indolently, the fine linen sheet drawn up over her breasts, as though unconscious of An Li's wordless presence; but she detected in his immobility a new kind of silence, watchful and deadly. He reminded her of the big cat, the jaguar sleeping at the end of her bed, both of them ready to pounce.

"Tell the morgue we want Jacquot buried in style, no expense spared, and the bill sent to M. Raoul," she said. "Then call the club and tell everybody on staff to show up at the funeral. Whenever it is."

"Will Madame be in attendance?" An Li asked.

"Of course. Make sure it's in the afternoon, now—I got somewhere to be this morning. And An Li—send Madeleine in. I want a bath as soon's I've had breakfast."

"Madeleine gave notice yesterday."

She stared at him apprehensively: the black eyes she'd never been able to read. Raoul gone, and now Madeleine. How long before he, too, deserted her? But all she said was, "Stupid bitch. You'd think Memphis couldn't take a bath by herself or dress herself neither. What I want with Madeleine? *Shit.*"

"Now that Master has left, Madeleine said there is no money and none of us will be paid. She has gone to be a *fille de joie,* at one of the closed houses in Clichy; the Sphinx, I think she said. With so many German soldiers coming—"

"—She'll be walking like a cowboy for the rest of the war. Screw Madeleine. She thinks bein' a prostitute's so great, that's her life dream? Be my guest. You go on, now, An Li, and take Roscoe for a walk."

Roscoe was the jaguar. In his sinuous, shape-shifting way the big cat hauled himself to his feet, tail sleek as a hangman's rope, heavy jaw working. He did not look at Memphis, did not seek her attention; she was already dead to him. *I'll send him to the zoo,* she decided as she bit into an orange segment, juice spurting over her lips. *Can't take a cat south to Marseille, North Africa, a ship to the States.* Roscoe thudded to the ground on mallet-shaped paws, swaggered toward An Li. Neither of them was indifferent to the plans she made. But they would die, she knew, sooner than give her power over them.

An hour later she emerged from a taxi before the Chancellery of the United States. She would not allow An Li to drive her, would not let him guess that she was desperate for assurance, for passage home, for somebody to tell her it would all be okay. She was afraid to lose him, this last voice in the empty house, the echoing rooms and corridors, her stylish heels clacking on the naked floors. She expected An Li to be gone when she returned to the Rue des Trois Frères. She'd made him take Roscoe to the zoo; the driver's smoldering look suggested that this casual treason—one creature bartering another—smacked of slavery and death. She had no time for his nonsense. She was playing for survival.

"I want to see the ambassador," she said loudly to the Frenchwoman who vetted guests at the chancellery entrance. "You tell Mr. Ambassador that Memphis Jones has come to call."

The woman looked down her French nose at

Memphis's gown, a gorgeous thing of bugle beads and silk more appropriate to the night but fitting her body like a ripe banana peel. Unimpressed, she went off and presently returned with a man who was disappointing: not the ambassador.

"Robert Murphy," he said, extending his hand. "The ambassador is at the Élysée Palace, I'm afraid, consulting with the French government."

Memphis was adamant. She did not allow Robert Murphy to lead her to his back office, away from the curious eyes of various governmental departments. She stood in the middle of the marble foyer and demanded her passage home. Some kind of safe conduct. A ticket for a first-class cabin on the next ocean liner out of France.

"There are no ocean liners anymore," Murphy said gently. "Only troop transports and merchant convoys."

"You want to know what happens, mistuh, if Memphis Jones gets caught by the Nazis? You'll have race riots in the streets of Kansas City. Flames in every building in uptown New York. You'll have blood on your hands, mistuh, you and your fine ambassador, and the whole world'll be askin' what the hell *you* were doin' in Paris when the greatest jazz singer in Europe was asking for help. Understand?"

Murphy inclined his head. He assured her he would speak to Bullitt himself. But Memphis could smell the burning paper on the air; she'd seen the chaos of desk chairs and boxes stacked in the hallways beyond the elegant reception hall. The chancellery was clearly shutting down. Murphy suggested that she try the Gare

St-Lazare—he understood women were getting seats on trains, although it helped to be the mother of a child; she couldn't borrow one, by any chance?

Memphis parked herself in a chair in front of Bullitt's door and declared defiantly that she'd wait. It was then she heard the word *coon* and the word *nigger,* not from Robert Murphy but from a sneering woman who was destroying papers in an office two doors down from the chargé's, a rail-thin upper-class bitch in a cashmere twinset and tweed skirt.

"If only they *would* go back to Africa," Mims Tarnow said in an audible undertone to the French receptionist, "and stop embarrassing Americans the world over. I'd buy her a ticket to Tangier myself—if I didn't have ten better places to put the spare change."

Memphis longed to claw the woman's narrow face, wanted to push her nose in a toilet, wanted to spit in Mims Tarnow's eye and make her beg for a little kindness; but her knees were suddenly like water, unstable and gaping; her knees were ashamed and she sat fixed in her chair, remembering the woman who'd burnt her hands with scalding water when she was eight years old and working as a dishwasher, remembering the man who'd beat her for the fun of it behind the trash cans at her mama's laundry, pulling her skirt up over her head until the white underpants showed, slapping his broad flat palm on her ass and chortling while his other hand gripped her hair, his erection stabbing her side. She remembered all of this and a hundred sordid things the years of silk and comfort had failed to blot away, her cheeks flaming with hatred, and a voice inside her mocked, *What the hell you thinkin', a white man's gonna help you, Memphis? They all Nazis by another name anyway.*

She walked without a backward look out of the chancellery and down the broad marble steps to the paving, careful of her heels where the steps had worn shallow. The Place de la Concorde spread before her like a place of worship, the obelisk in the center where heads had rolled, and she stood there uncertain, aware that she could no longer think. Trying, trying.

"Mam'selle," said a voice at her elbow. She turned. He was an elderly Frenchman, all mustache and soiled beret, his eyes watering.

"Pierre duPré at your service." The old man lifted the beret, set it back on his gray hair. "You must know the Americans leave tomorrow. Everybody but Bullitt and a few others, gone at dawn. They hope to make Bordeaux. I could find you a place in the baggage cars, perhaps. A seat among the household servants. It is not much, *tant pis,* but..."

"No, thanks," she said distinctly. "I'll make my own way. I always have."

Then she hailed a taxi for the Alibi Club.

CHAPTER TWENTY

Sally was too exhausted to care much about Mims Tarnow, who glowered at her in the chancellery foyer, her arms filled with codebooks from her husband's office. Mims was supposed to chuck them on the bonfire roaring in the chancellery's rear courtyard, but Sally had stepped smack in front of her, ignoring the look of exasperation curdling the other woman's face.

Sally said again, louder this time: "I need to see Mr. Hearst. *Please*. On a matter of urgent business."

"Joe's in a meeting with British Liaison," Mims snapped. "You'll have to come back later."

As though the chancellery would be open later, Sally thought, as though the courtyard bonfire would not still be burning by morning. A cord of barely suppressed panic was tightening around everyone scurrying through the building; Mims's cashmere sweater was stained dark with sweat. The chancellery smelled like an animal house at the zoo, rank with fear and untamed ferocity.

She had forced her way past a surly and muttering crowd of desperate people, shouting *Je suis americaine* to

the armed guards controlling access on this final afternoon of business. American military police from the
Department of the Army held down the back courtyard, so that Mims Tarnow could throw her codebooks
in safety and nobody would steal the last remaining
gallons of petrol from the chancellery's storage tanks.
Bullitt had authorized snipers on the roof if the crowd
got ugly when the front entrance was finally locked.
The ambassador suspected the work of Communist
agents.

Sally had no intention of leaving.

She took Mme. Blum's hand—Léonie Blum, who
had chosen a few cherished belongings: a prayer shawl
for keeping Sabbath in the New World, a few pictures
of children long since scattered, the gold teeth of her
dead husband. She had set out with Sally an hour before, walking through the increasingly crowded streets
with an old black leather satchel, toward the promise
Joe Hearst had made only yesterday and completely
forgotten. The promise of her visa.

"We'll wait," Sally informed Mims Tarnow.

There were no seats to be had in the foyer. Sally
inched her way nearer to a marble column that seemed
to demarcate the public from the private space. A soldier with a gun stood between her and the inner corridor. The French receptionist was gone from her desk;
perhaps she had resigned. Mims frowned prodi-
giously—Sally would *never* be admitted to any of *her*
sororities in future—and clicked her narrow-skirted
way through the courtyard door. Her silhouette charcoal against the flames.

Sally walked up to the armed guard blocking the corridor. And began to scream Joe Hearst's name.

Hearst had started the day early with a demitasse of espresso near his neighborhood pharmacy. Max Shoop could ship Stilwell's body out of Cherbourg tomorrow if he liked, but Joe Hearst was still investigating murder. His reading of Stilwell's files made the truth too important to bury. He didn't know the *pharmacien* well, and the man wore the hunted look of every Parisian waiting for news from the Front—but he accepted the paper twist of shattered glass Hearst had scraped from Stilwell's carpet, and agreed to analyze the fragments. Hearst told him time was short, the matter one of poison.

From the pharmacy he drove to Sûreté headquarters and found the police detective who'd handled Stilwell's death. He gave the man—whose name was Foch—two crystal lowballs he'd pilfered from the Rue de Rivoli.

The detective was furious.

"It is *most* improper, that the concierge should have let you invade Monsieur Stil-ewell's apartment, *hein*? It means nothing that you are from the embassy. Nothing."

"It is our delegation's duty to ensure that every American in France is treated in a manner consistent with justice," Hearst replied. "Check those glasses for prints."

The request was less outrageous than it seemed. Since the outbreak of war, identity cards were mandatory for every resident of Paris—and each applicant was fingerprinted by the police. Which meant that Max Shoop's prints were on file. As were Stilwell's and Jacquot's. And Sally King's.

"Justice is immaterial in the present case!" Foch spluttered. "It was an accident—if not suicide! There will be the prints of the two dead *pédés* on the glass. So we will learn they drank together before dying. *Bon*. I could tell you as much without recourse to finger-prints. It is your American obsession with *le roman policier*."

"Maybe so," Hearst agreed in his flawless French, "but you'll do the fingerprint analysis all the same. If you refuse, *monsieur l'ambassadeur* will be on the phone to the Minister of Justice, who has formed the habit of dining weekly with *l'ambassadeur* at his château in Chantilly; and you, my friend, will be at the Front firing a gun at the Nazis before you can say *vas te faire foûtre*."

Or *go fuck yourself,* in the common tongue.

Foch said grudgingly he'd get on the prints.

Now Hearst was waiting for the telephone to ring, with news from the pharmacy or the Sûreté—anything that might give him a thread to follow, a soul to damn with murder. His pulse jumping, he listened to British Liaison read him the riot act about Frédéric Joliot-Curie, while the pungent odor of smoke permeated the office.

"I've been jauntering all over France for the past month," Liaison drawled bitterly, "looking for chaps like your Fred. I've got a *list*, you know. Long as your arm." The Brit thrust his right hand at Joe Hearst, cuff riding upward to expose a tattoo of a curled viper cut into the wrist. "Cream of the French scientific establishment. Imperative we get them all to England before Hitler snaps them up like rats. I've had to promise some of them the earth, I've had to sell my old mother on the public street corner, I've had to pull out Oscar and Genevieve and hold a bloody bullet to their heads—and you just sit here and *wait*. For a . . . *treasure trove* . . . of documents to simply *fall* into your lap. There's no *God*, Hearst. No God at all."

"If that were true, Jack, I'd have sold the whole box of files right back to the Germans," Hearst retorted mildly.

Charles Henry George Howard, twentieth Earl of Suffolk, was known as Mad Jack to his friends, partly because he'd never behaved much like a peer and partly because the name suited him: tattooed, limping from an old hunting injury, broad-shouldered, bristling of mustache. In another age he'd have gone to sea and set fire to ships. In this one, he'd married a cabaret dancer from the Alhambra and taken a First in pharmacology at Edinburgh. Drugs being his century's answer to privateer's booty.

The earl poured himself a third glass of champagne—he never stirred without a bottle—and settled his boots on Hearst's desk. Oscar and Genevieve—a matched set of dueling pistols, remarkable for their beauty—were trained on the office door. A raft of papers was scattered all around him, most bearing the S&C letterhead. Ambassador Bullitt's quandary—to call FDR or the British embassy about the French atomic program—had produced Mad Jack: His Royal Majesty's official Paris representative, British Scientific and Industrial Committee.

Hearst assumed the title was cover for spying. Not for the first time, he wished the United States had an intelligence service. But there was none, had been none for years: just Joe Hearst and Pierre duPré, with their fingers up France's ass.

"Do you understand physics?" he asked.

"Not at all." Jack peered nearsightedly at one of Philip Stilwell's papers. "But I *quite like* bombs. I've taken to sapping in my off-hours, you know. There's nothing like defusing a bloody great wad of wires and explosive that's tumbled into the back garden. Gets the juices flowing, what?"

"Anything in these papers? —That might cause murder, I mean?"

The earl drained his glass. "*No*sir—but I'll send them off to G. P. Thomson in London. He'll make sense of this lot in two shakes of a lamb's tail. Well—bottle's empty! Time for me to be going."

He thrust his boots to the floor, wincing slightly as his game leg made contact with Hearst's carpet, and shuffled the papers together with deft hands. The earl's mind, Hearst thought, was probably similar: quick as a conjurer's. The rest of the swashbuckling package—part Wodehouse, part Gilbert and Sullivan—was merely a cultivated distraction.

"I'm not sure I can let you take those. The files don't

belong to—" Hearst stopped in mid-sentence, listening to something he alone heard. A woman's voice, screaming his name.

He rose abruptly and threw open the door.

He could just see her outlined at the far end of the corridor, struggling against the grasp of a chancellery guard, her face very white except for the two spots of feverish color burning high on her cheekbones. *She had come to him, after all.*

"Sally!"

The guard was thrusting her out of Hearst's sight, hand raised to strike this absurdly hysterical woman. She wasn't dead. The pictures he'd seen in his mind—the fragile shoulder blades thrusting through a light spring dress on the cement floor of the Paris morgue—were nightmares for another man's sleep.

He strode toward her. "Miss King! It's about time. I don't suppose it ever occurred to you we'd be *worried,* here at the embassy, given what happened to you two nights ago—that we'd like to know you were safe. I don't suppose you even thought to contact us. Until you needed help again, right?"

He saw her wince at the harshness in his voice, the brutal anger on his face, and felt a poor stab of triumph. He would not be tricked into caring about this girl who went off with any man who paid her bills, who was too stupid to sit tight when people were dropping like flies around her. He would not watch another Daisy dance out the door with his heart in her hands.

"I—no, I never..." she stammered. "That is, I got

your message. At my flat. You said to contact you—I brought Mme. Blum..."

He glanced from her wounded eyes to the old woman stooped behind her. Remembered, suddenly, his easy promises of yesterday. And felt sharply and miserably ashamed.

"Of course. The visa. Sally, I'm *sorry*—"

"Don't be silly," she said, in a tight, careful voice. "It's my fault entirely. I didn't know I was expected to report my movements to the embassy staff. I don't need your help today, Mr. Hearst—I rarely need anyone's help—but Mme. Blum *does*. Are you available?"

"Yes."

Mad Jack was easing his elegant bulk out of Hearst's office, his gaze roaming openly over Sally's figure. He waggled a farewell in Hearst's direction, Stilwell's files tucked discreetly under his arm.

"Sally—don't go anywhere," Hearst said. "I've got to talk to you."

"Naturally, I'll wait for Mme. Blum."

She would not look at him as she adopted a leaning pose against the chancellery wall; and he was reminded of an imperious child, clinging to dignity to keep from crying.

"I'm sorry," he said again, inconsequently—and led Léonie Blum into the chaos of the consular section.

CHAPTER TWENTY-ONE

Joliot found Nell's warehouse only with difficulty, after a few wrong turns and a series of explosive obscenities. The streets of Les Halles were narrow and strewn with every imaginable kind of refuse: pig offal and wooden crates, bales of hay and butter churns, cheese hoops and cattle hooves. Les Halles was the belly of Paris, the great open-air market in the shadow of Saint-Eustache that stretched for blocks in every direction, lined with warehouses, fringed with bakers' ovens and wine cellars and butchers' back rooms, the gutters running with blood at an early hour of the morning, all manner of fowl screaming their last day to the sun, the somnolent eyes of rabbits trussed and hung upside down by their feet from wooden dowels, the fresh goat cheese covered in ashes, the winey smell of apples kept too long. The people who haunted Les Halles were unlike any Joliot encountered in the rarefied air of the Collège de France: round-shouldered men with shapeless clothes and shambling gaits; heavy laborers wedded to the land and the warehouses, for whom market day was an ancient and sacred rite; women whose hands were broad and pitted as river rock, who thought nothing of wringing a goose's neck or cutting the liver from its live body. He shoved the truck's fender cautiously through the milling hordes, packing up now, the makeshift stands coming down, the raucous goats tethered to posts. These people looked untroubled by war, though their sons must certainly have been packed off to the Front months and months ago—like so many trussed rabbits, their world turned upside down. Every man Joliot saw in Les Halles was over the age of sixty. Anyone younger was elsewhere, with a gun in his hands.

He inched the truck forward, searching for the street Nell had told him to find, the yawning entrance to the warehouse, thinking idly of harvests and planting, of the shortage of labor in the countryside and what it would do to his children's meals in a very little while, regardless of whether the Nazis reached Paris. Joliot, too, had endured a childhood of war, and he remembered the pinched stomach, the constant growl of hunger. Today, however, with Hélène and Pierre still in Brittany or possibly starting on their road home, he felt curiously suspended in his truck cab, above the swirl and flow of foot traffic, insulated from the noise and smells of the market stalls, alone in his deceit.

As soon as Jacques Allier had left the lab, Joliot carefully siphoned the heavy water, all twenty-six canisters, into sterile glass jugs. He refilled the canisters with ordinary tap water from the lab's spigot and put them back in place, where Allier expected to find them. Then he loaded the heavy water into the back of the truck delivered by the Ministry of Armaments only half an hour before, an official-looking army transport with a dull green canvas cover. Only then did he set out in search of Nell.

He pulled up before a pair of vast wooden doors and leaned on the truck horn. There was a pause; some cursing from a belligerent vendor whose passage he was blocking, which Joliot ignored; then the doors swung open. Two elderly men stood inside, staring at him, their hands dangling uselessly at their sides. He leaned through the cab window.

"Mme. la Comtesse," he said. "She's expecting me."

The nearest nodded, stepped back. Joliot drove carefully through, not wanting to look for Nell, not wanting to betray the pulse throbbing in his temples, the dryness of his mouth.

She was standing before a massive stack of wine barrels bound together with rope, her nose pressed against a stave of wood that had been torn from one of them, her eyes closed. Drinking in some elusive scent Joliot had never dreamed of, drinking in the oak. The growl of the truck engine brought her head around, however, and she walked toward him as he braked, turned off the ignition, swung down. He could see from her eyes and expression that she had herself firmly in hand; this was business now, they were in front of her people, the vineyard workers she'd sent from Bordeaux to requisition these things. He must not reach for her, fold her into his arms, smell the teasing scent of her hair.

He stood woodenly, waiting. She wore trousers, something he'd never seen on her, the effect both exotic and unexpectedly erotic. Her whipcord body and bobbed hair suddenly those of a disciplined boy.

"I'd given up on you," she told him. "Henri is ready to load."

"I don't know Les Halles."

"Naturally. You're the kind who always shops in stores, aren't you? Or your maid does. Despite your dedication to Communism. Very well—what do you need from me?"

She was determined to treat him cruelly. Pretend the night did not exist. Cut the cord with a jagged blade. "Send your men away. Henri. The other one."

"Why?"

"Because I ask you to, Nell."

She held his gaze, considering whether to fight for the sake of fighting him. Instead she swung around abruptly and called out in French, "The oak's fine. Not the best quality and certainly not what I paid for, but it will have to do. God knows, if this year's vintage is as dreadful as the last it won't matter a damn what we put in the barrels. Start loading."

He followed her up a rickety staircase and through a doorway in the warehouse loft, to a small office entirely deserted of people, where Nell scrawled her signature on a bill of lading, then flung herself into a chair. "Have you got a cigarette?"

He found one for her, lit it.

"You said you wanted me to carry something. To Bordeaux."

"I do, yes."

She drew on the smoke, waiting.

"My colleague—von Halban...knows your cousin. The German.—What's his name?"

"Hans Gunter von Dincklage," she returned. "One of my old playmates."

He winced at the word, imagining every carnal possibility, Nell's leg pressed to the man's mouth, his lips working at her sex, Nell's head flung back, her teeth bared.

"Our mothers are sisters. We practically grew up together at Birchmere when I was a child, but I lost touch when Spatz went to university. And then I married and came here," she said succinctly.

And then you married. After five torrid months of sprawling in my bed. Not even a footnote, Nell. No mention of Ricki and the empty train platform.

"Von Halban says this...cousin...is staying with you."

Her eyelids fluttered impatiently. "Oh, *God*, Ricki—not this, again. Not your pathetic possessive jealousy, when you've got the Ice Queen at home and two perfect children. *Not* now. I've more important things to deal with."

"It was *you* who asked me to stay last night. *You*, Nell. I'm not in the habit of picking up women, in case you wondered. I don't do that sort of thing easily; it mattered to me, it wasn't a casual lay—"

"—But now you're suffering agonies, you're wallowing in remorse, and you want me to tell you it's all right. Well, I *won't*, Ricki. I don't slip in and out of bed with anybody who crosses my path and I resent your notion I'd sleep with a man I regard as a brother, as though I'm that desperate or that much of a slut. So fuck off, Ricki, and take whatever you've got in your truck back home, all right?"

"I'm sorry, Nell."

She was stabbing out her cigarette. She refused to look at him.

"I'm not asking what you've done or would like to do with your cousin. I'm asking what you've told him."

"*Told* him?" She glanced up, fingers suspended over the ashtray.

"He's the enemy, Nell. What's he doing in Paris right now, for God's sake? The police must stop him daily and demand to see his papers."

"Oh, I don't think it's as bad as all that," she said coolly. "He's not in uniform and he's spent most of his life in France. He's got a better accent than I have. He's probably not questioned above once a week. And when he is—he gives them my address. Tells them he's family. Just visiting."

"Visiting? *Sacre bleu*— He's a Nazi agent, isn't he?"

"Don't let your jealousy run away with you, Ricki." She eyed him lazily. "Spatz is nobody's boy but his own. He frankly loathes Hitler and his set and I think he's seriously considering working for the Allies, so don't report him to your minister *just* yet, there's a pet."

"Nell—"

"You'd better tell me quickly why you're here."

She had given him no assistance, no reason he could cling to that would make it all right, his defection from Allier to a woman he hadn't seen or heard of in years, whose loyalty he had every reason to mistrust.

"We have to get some lab supplies out of Paris. Before the Germans arrive."

"And I have a truck heading south."

"Heading toward Bordeaux, which is where we need our supplies to be."

"Why?"

"The port. It's more sheltered than Calais, and if we eventually have to get something to England—"

"Don't ask me to carry uranium," she inserted sharply. "I won't do it. You'll radiate my wines for a century to come, as though I didn't have enough already to deal with. Prices for top Bordeaux on the world market are *half* what they were a decade ago, and between the chemical shells we're still digging out of the soil from the last war, and the phylloxera blight that decimated the vines, the *domaine* hasn't turned a profit in years. Bertrand would have sold the place long ago if I hadn't insisted, if I hadn't taken over complete responsibility for the place and forced it to meet the standards for *Appellation Contrôlée*. It's been years of effort, Ricki, and now the war's taken all our field hands and thrown them at the German guns, it's taken the copper sulfate for dusting the vines—"

"I wouldn't ask you to carry uranium," he said swiftly. "It's water, Nell. Twenty-six glass jugs of water, sealed by my own hand. If you're stopped and searched, smash the bottles and let it run into the ground, understand?"

"In the final seconds before I'm arrested?" She tried to laugh but her voice broke and she placed a shaking hand over her mouth.

"You won't be stopped. *Please*, Nell."

She nodded once, her hand still pressed against her lips.

"Once you've got to Bordeaux safely, you'll write to your brother Ian at Cambridge. Ask the Cavendish people if they'll make room for it in their lab. In the event we can't stop the German army."

"It's all ending, isn't it? No matter what brave words we throw into the wind? I can't bear it, Ricki."

He reached for her then, took her in his arms as he'd longed to do, held her wordlessly with his face pressed against her hair. *Here at the end of all things I pledge you my reason, my sanity. I give you my soul, Nell, who've always had it in keeping.*

"What will happen to you?" she asked. "Will they arrest you? Deport you to a camp?"

"I don't know."

"Come with me." She gripped his shoulders hard. "Come with me and your water. We'll get you both to Bordeaux. To Cambridge if necessary."

"No."

"Ricki—"

"I have children, Nell. A wife. Who's on her way home right now."

Her hands fell. She stepped backward. "And so you'll walk willingly into the Germans' trap? You'll accept their plans for you?"

"Have I any choice?"

"We all do. But your choices were always different from mine."

CHAPTER TWENTY-TWO

The spring color faded from street and sky by cocktail hour. In the lower reaches of Montmartre, at the base of the funicular, a discarded sheet of baker's paper tossed fitfully in the wind, still laced with sticky white icing. Tired and disheveled people—refugees, Spatz thought— had collapsed with their backs against the street lamps, their eyes staring dully ahead of them. A pregnant woman with two children; an elderly man in a newsboy cap, whose right leg was bandaged and spotted with blood. *Shrapnel wounds. A Messerschmitt.* Spatz understood the reasoning of the German High Command: Send a million people from the Lowlands south in panic, flood the main highways leading in and out of France, cut off all possibility of swift maneuvers for the Allied army—but he found that he preferred to hunch his shoulders and ignore the unblinking eyes. He kept his gaze fixed on the tips of his shoes.

Until the woman said, in French, "Please, monsieur. Do you know where I might find a bed for the night?"

She was alone, but no *fille de joie,* this one—no prostitute opening early for business. Her simple cotton dress was smeared with blood and what looked like mud; more mud spattered on her cheekbone and the fingers that clenched convulsively as they dangled at her side. He recoiled from her, from the accusation in her look.

"Have you tried one of the train stations? I think the city has set up cots," he said.

"How do I get there?"

He turned and pointed to the Métro, the entrance of furled iron and glass. "There is a map of the system on the wall."

"I have no money." She said it blankly, a raw statement of fact. "I was robbed yesterday, after the planes went over."

"Are you alone?"

"Except for my children."

Spatz glanced around. Other than the exhausted pregnant woman he'd noticed earlier, nobody had children in this corner of the city. "Where are they?"

"I forgot. *Mon Dieu, I forgot.* I buried them with my own hands beside the road. Both dead! *Mon Dieu, mes enfants—*"

Her eyes closed tightly and her mouth fell open as she sank down onto the paving stones, keening uncontrollably. In sudden horror Spatz backed away, tossing franc notes at her feet. His hands were shaking.

At this twilit hour, Montmartre stirred and women in dressing gowns emerged to sweep doorsteps filthy with vomit and grime, the tinny sound of phonograph records drifting from tired kitchens. For the most part they ignored the refugees who'd sprung up like dandelions overnight; what to do in the face of so many? It was the perfect theatre for suicide, Spatz thought, remembering the mother half insane with grief; he had never been able to bear Montmartre in daylight.

The Alibi Club was wedged into a corner of the Place du Tertre, holding down its cobblestoned bit with flaring neon and garish red lintels. The square was deserted but for a man sipping something at a table in the central café; Spatz studied him: soft hat, modest overcoat, large mustache, eyes that ignored his newspaper and swept easily instead over Spatz: well-heeled, too large for this kind of life. Spatz cocked his blond head and entered the club.

He could hear Memphis singing.

It was a mournful sound, something of Billie Holiday's, the kind of tune Memphis never chose. Memphis didn't cry into a heroin cocktail: She sang the world Cole Porter invented—rich white women, dancing till dawn, and champagne in bed. But today her voice ripped along Spatz's spine with jagged fingernails, and he stood rigidly in the empty room, noticing the forlorn little tables, chairs akimbo, one white linen cloth trailing. She was singing in her dressing room. And a man—utterly different from the café loiterer outside—sat primly on her elevated stage.

"Morris," Spatz said.

"Von Dincklage," the American acknowledged. "I *hoped* you would come."

"I'm never in the quarter at this hour." Spatz removed his fedora, laid it lightly on one of the tables. Reached for his cigarette case.

"But then I *summoned* you. Through that *woman* in the back room."

Spatz lifted his eyes coldly.

"It is *imperative*," Morris continued, jumping down from his perch on the stage, "that we *talk*. Don't you think? For the *greater good* of the Reich, and our mutual survival?"

"What do you want, Morris?"

"My *documents*." The lawyer smiled thinly. "You *have* them, I believe. Please sit down."

"I wouldn't want anything of yours."

Morris sighed, a man long tried in patience. "I am *speaking* of the papers Philip Stilwell *stole* from my firm's *files,* and which I presume you then *lifted* from his lady friend's *flat* when you nearly *killed* her two nights ago."

Spatz concentrated on striking the match without burning his fingers. "There were no papers in that room."

The lawyer's lips compressed while Spatz nursed his flame, the tip of his Dunhill glowing warmly, his indifference sharp as a slap.

"I sent you there to *retrieve* my property. Hearing *nothing* from you for *far* too long, I went to the place *myself* this afternoon. A Russian *slut* let me into the room for a small . . . gratuity. I searched it *thoroughly*."

"And found nothing."

"I want my property *back*." Morris placed his hands on the table: small, feral, moist with desire. One of them held a snub-nosed gun.

Spatz stared at the weapon coolly. This pathetic little man found it necessary to threaten him.

"If you do not *choose* to help me, von Dincklage, I will be *forced* to call upon the services of *friends,*" the lawyer persisted. "Your...woman...is not of the most *Aryan* kind. She would grace the Führer's *work* camps admirably."

"You're wasting time. I never saw your file. I didn't take it. I do not know where it is."

"Are you *acquainted* with Reichsführer Himmler?" Morris inquired.

Spatz went still. His eyes drifted over the lawyer's face: the small, wet eyes; the pursed lips quirked with malice. "Are you?" he countered.

"Our paths have *crossed*. I was able to *render* him some...small service. The Reichsführer chooses to say he is under an *obligation* to me. I *flatter* myself I have the Great Man's *ear*."

"The head of the SS is obliged to nobody. Think otherwise, and you won't live till tomorrow."

"Hah! Very *good*, von Dincklage! I *applaud* your wit!"

"So it's Himmler's papers you've lost? No wonder you're worried. I wouldn't like to give the Great Man, as you call him, that news."

"I said *nothing* about Himmler and any *documents*." The gun wavered in Morris's hand. *"Nothing."*

"You didn't need to." Spatz drew on his cigarette. "If I had the papers, I'd give them to you for a price. Believe me. But I don't have them. So where are they?"

"It comes down to the *girl,*" Morris said fretfully. "I'm *sure* of it."

"Why?"

"Because Stilwell would *never* have destroyed them, and I've *searched* everywhere else. The *firm*, both *apartments*—"

Through the thin walls, he could still hear Memphis sing.

"*...don't know nothin' 'bout blue skies, mistuh, my sky's all gray...'cause my man done gone away...*"

Spatz thought of that body he cherished, the supple curve of muscle and bone bowed under the steel of Sachsenhausen, the way in which she could be torn in half by the casual hands of a thousand men.

"If the Allies have got Himmler's papers," he countered, "I wouldn't give you three hours after the Nazis take Paris."

For once, Emery Morris had nothing to say. They both knew the violence of Great Men.

"It's a pity. With such a relationship—the ear of Himmler himself—you might have done much when the Germans arrived. Made yourself indispensable. Shown them all the best whorehouses in the city. But now—you have no choice but to run."

"Are your choices any different?" Morris spat.

"I never saw those papers. I avoid Himmler and his kind like the plague." Spatz's eyes were calculating. "I could still help you, of course."

"How?"

"You're looking for Stilwell's girl, correct?"

Morris leaned toward him avidly.

"Follow the body. Stilwell's corpse. It will either be consigned to French earth or shipped across the sea.

The girl's sure to go with it. You have only to ring the Paris Morgue to learn the funeral arrangements."

The lawyer shot to his feet. "Thank you, von Dincklage."

"From now on, my friend," Spatz answered acidly, "you will leave Memphis Jones alone."

The man who'd been drinking an apéritif in the small café in the Place du Tertre had long since drained his glass. He was sitting in a square that had once served as the forecourt of a Benedictine abbey. Shackles and gallows had stood there, centuries ago; but now it was merely a place for sin and coffee. Some instinct of caution prevented him from ordering a second Pernod; he had missed his lunch and the alcohol sat uncomfortably on his empty stomach. The glass, like the newspaper folded beside him, was primarily chosen for cover, a plausible excuse for keeping a solitary man in an uncongenial bar.

He surveyed the war news, a concoction of bravado and rumor—*the Grand Army of France is fighting with extreme bravery to repulse the German attack*—passed by the government censors in a despairing attempt to fill the page—and declined politely the offers of a prostitute who wove her way like a shadow down the Rue St-Vincent.

The Alibi Club door opened, and Emery Morris stepped out.

The lawyer looked like a man of purpose: neatly tailored, trim of figure, one hand casually in his trousers pocket and his gaze fixed on the middle distance. He walked briskly down the paving, oblivious of the watcher in the café as he rose from the table and crossed the square at an angle designed to intersect the American's path. Only when the stranger was abreast of him did Morris glance to the side, his face impassive.

"Monsieur Emery Morris?"

"Yes?"

"Etienne Foch. *Sûreté National*. I must ask you to accompany me. We have questions regarding the death of your compatriot, Monsieur Philip Stilwell."

For an instant Morris did not move, as though he were parsing the meaning of every accented word. Then he withdrew his hand from his trousers pocket and fired a gun directly at Foch.

The bullet tore into the detective's stomach. He gaped at Morris, his hand instinctively moving to the bunched fabric of his jacket. *A lawyer. Such a little man—*

And then the revolver flared again.

CHAPTER TWENTY-THREE

"Where's Madame Blum?" Sally demanded as Hearst swung down the corridor from the consular section, alone.

"I sent her home with an embassy driver. She was completely exhausted and she'll never get a taxi in this city tonight. The entire world's in the streets."

"I know. I walked here today, remember?"

"Then I'll drive you now," he said, "wherever you want to go. But not back to your flat. It isn't safe."

"You're awfully high-handed, Mr. Hearst." She bent down and picked up her suitcase. "But as it happens, I don't need a ride. I can walk to the Latin Quarter."

"And wait for the killer to call again? Don't be a fool, Sally. You've been hurt enough."

"Mother of Mercy," she muttered. "What *is* it about men? You and Shoop. Always telling me what to do—"

"Max Shoop?"

"He checked me out of the hospital yesterday. Then checked me into the hands of his wife. I sneaked out of their place in the dead of night. I don't like it when people try to run my life, Mr. Hearst. *Especially* men."

"You were with *Shoop*?" The possibility had never occurred to him. He was oddly unsettled; she hadn't run off with an unknown guy, some lover from the past. He'd been thinking of Sally, and seeing *Daisy*. The clear awareness of jealousy—the way it distorted his judgment—left Hearst momentarily speechless.

"People make all kinds of mistakes about me," Sally said tautly. "I wear these impossible confections, chiffon and silk, with diamonds at my throat. Hair piled high on the top of my head, a little veil over one eye. Gloves. I look like a dream, Mr. Hearst. Men *think* I'm a dream. They have no idea I was raised by a rancher out West, that I can break a horse inside of a week and ride two days without water if I have to. Most men have no idea who I am. It's the dream they pay for, at Chanel and Schiaparelli—but Philip saw beyond the silk. Philip saw *me*. And...loved me all the same..."

"How could he do anything else?" Hearst reached for her suitcase. She allowed him to take it. There were no tears today, only fierceness; but from the pallor of her face he guessed she was at the end of her rope.

"I have something for you," he said. "Something of Philip's. Come with me now, and we'll talk about it."

He drove her directly to his flat in the Rue Lauriston. With another woman and in different circumstances the move would be awkward: Highhanded Joe Hearst, seducing a girl with no place else to sleep. From what he knew of Sally, however, she cared little for proprieties. She had a fund of sense behind her sculpted features, a supple strength. When he told her she'd never get a hotel room in refugee Paris, she agreed without a murmur.

"Shoop would find me in a hotel, anyway." She helped herself to the triple-crème Camembert he'd placed on the coffee table. "It'd be the first place he'd look, after mine."

"Are you hiding from him?" Hearst concentrated on mashing sugar into the bottom of a martini shaker. They both needed a stiff drink by this time and gimlets reminded him of Long Island summers, Daisy in a halter-strapped dress and a wide-brimmed hat. He could picture the sculpted bones of Sally King's tanned shoulders emerging from a bit of torrid-colored silk. The *dream,* again. Paris's best designers ought to pay the earth for it.

"Shoop wants me out of Paris. *There will* be *no scandal, Sally,*" she intoned in a fair approximation of the lawyer's Brahmin voice. "He wants to pack me off to the States with Philip's body tomorrow."

"So you know about that."

"The *Clothilde.* Philip to be retrieved by chauffeured hearse at the morgue tomorrow morning. Tickets to be retrieved by me at the Cherbourg shipping office. I'm sending Mme. Blum home in my place."

"You're not!" He frowned at her, all the afternoon's frustration resurging.

"She needs the trip. I don't. I'm staying in Paris, Mr. Hearst."

"Call me Joe."

She eyed him, amused. "I suppose I might as well. Since I'm sleeping on your couch tonight."

"Look, Sally—" He handed her the gimlet and waited for her to taste it. "You've got to make that boat tomorrow. Don't sit here waiting for the Germans to kill you."

The implacable words stopped her cold. "They're really coming?"

"Any day."

"Then—" She swallowed the last of her cheese as though it might choke her—"nobody gives a damn about Philip, do they? That he was murdered, I mean. They'll chalk it up as suicide. We'll never find out…"

"—Who did it?" Hearst shrugged. "I've done what I can. A pharmacist told me Stilwell's drink was laced with Spanish fly. I've got the police checking for fingerprints. But with everybody in Paris running for the exits—I don't think we'll get much action."

There had been no message from Foch that afternoon. Hearst was fighting an urge to call the Sûreté.

"Are you running?" Sally demanded sharply.

"Not by choice." The question took him aback. "Bullitt has ordered me to Bordeaux in the morning, with a convoy of embassy dependents."

Hearst watched her absorb the news of complete desertion—every last American in Paris headed south and west—and down the gimlet, neat.

From the look on her face the world was becoming an increasingly scary place. He was conscious of the impulse to reach for her; he quelled it immediately. He was nothing in particular to Sally King; just one more man who was *not* Philip Stilwell.

"Go to Cherbourg," he said gently. "It's for the best. Truly."

She handed him her empty glass. "What was she like?"

"Who?"

"The woman in the portrait."

He had spent so much time walking the flat in the middle of the night, all the lights doused, that he'd almost forgotten the grace of this drawing room—the Louis Seize boiserie, the pooled silk curtains. The sketchy splash of oils, all suggestion and random lines, that held pride of place above the mantel.

"She was...*is*...a simpler person than I ever realized." He refilled Sally's glass.

"Your wife?"

"For a while. She left me about six months ago."

Sally might have said, as so many of his acquaintances had done, *I'm sorry,* or *How could she do that?* But instead she allowed a silence to seep between them. And naturally he filled it.

"I failed her. First in my marriage, and then after she left."

"How?"

"You talked about mistaking the dream for the woman. I think I did that with Daisy."

He had never voiced his doubts and guilt aloud; had never betrayed to anyone that he gave his wife's defection a second thought. It was not part of his training—his diplomatic life—to admit a vulnerability.

"I don't need many people," he said somewhat jerkily. "I've always been self-sufficient. But Daisy loved parties. Dancing. The admiration of a multitude. She took up with a bohemian crowd here in Paris—painters, writers." He gestured toward the portrait. "That was done by one of them. Before she ran off with an anarchist to Rome."

"You're blaming yourself, Joe," Sally observed. "That's another mistake. Women make their own choices, too, you know—and sometimes we even learn to live with them."

"She wrote to me a month ago. Asking for help. I never answered the letter. And now—" He met Sally's eyes with naked guilt in his own—"nobody can find her. I've wired the embassy in Rome. Can you believe it? Joe Hearst, hunting for his errant wife through all the back channels State can offer. It's pathetic. Every time I see one of those refugees—"

"That's why you were so angry." She set the gimlet down deliberately on the table. "This afternoon. That's why you took my head off in the middle of the embassy. You couldn't save Daisy, so by God you're going to save me. But the cases are not the same, Joe."

"That's true," he said. "I know *exactly* where you are, for instance. And I know there's a berth on a U.S.-bound ship with your name on it. You're going to Cherbourg tomorrow, Sally."

"What did you want to show me?—That belonged to Philip?"

He was tempted to tell her she couldn't change the subject all night—but he had lured her to the apartment with the promise of the manila envelope. He retrieved it from his briefcase and placed it in her lap.

"Your Mme. Blum gave me this yesterday. It's probably the last thing Stilwell mailed. Does the address mean anything to you?"

"Jacques Allier?" She shook her head. "Probably a client. Give the thing back to Max Shoop."

"Can't do that. It might be exactly what Shoop wants."

She studied his face, that perfect façade. "You think Philip died for this," she said suddenly.

"Yes. I think the man who attacked you was looking for it, too."

She shoved the package across the cocktail table as though it smelled. "Open it, then."

He ripped the manila flap, withdrew a slim bundle of papers, and read the cover sheet aloud.

13 May 1940
Dear M. Allier:
  You asked for the original letter that started my highly improper search through my colleague's files. Here it is, along with a few stray documents I uncovered in the archives. Keep them safe with the rest—and for God's sake, get all of this in front of somebody with power at the Armaments Ministry, Dautry or the like, if you're still in touch with him after Norway. Nobody here has the courage to deal with it.

  Cordially,

  Philip Stilwell

"The original letter, as he calls it, is in German," Hearst remarked. "It's signed by Rogers Lamont."

"I don't read German."

"As it will probably be the official language of Europe before the year's out," Hearst observed bitterly, "it's fortunate that I do."

12 May 1939
Rue Cambon, Paris
My dear Juergen:

It was a delight to hear from you last month and know that you and all of my old friends from Berlin are managing to thrive under the present system. I understand the risk you took in getting your letter out by human carrier pigeon. I will employ our mutual friend in the same manner for this reply. I have no love of official censors myself, and it appalls me to learn that you cannot avoid them, even for a friendly note.

I, too, remember our days of trekking in Switzerland with immense fondness. I hope before very many months pass we may meet again over a good glass of beer and a strong-smelling cheese and exchange our stories of the past two years without worrying that anyone might overhear us.

I was impressed to learn of your appointment to the Ludwigshafen factory; it's a major concern. I hope the strains and demands of the present situation don't wear you out. Try to take time for yourself, old fellow, or you'll be of no use to anyone.

Regarding your query: I can think of no reason why

*you're being asked to supply so many pressurized
containers of carbon monoxide to the Reich Security's
main office. It's a fairly useless substance, after all,
except for scientific research, and even then, might be
regarded as of limited value. One wonders if they meant
to order carbon <u>di</u>oxide for the drinks bar! But the fact
that the canisters themselves are supplied by a different
company—Mannesmann Röhrenwerke, I think you
said?—suggests a more organized effort than a couple of
clowns with a soda siphon. Somebody in the purchasing
department at the Criminal Technology Institute is
signing an awful lot of invoices. If you're truly
concerned—and from the care you've taken to get this
letter out, you obviously are—I'll try to learn what I
can on this end.*

> *Best to Dagmar and the children—*
> *Rogers Lamont*

"I don't understand," Sally said. "Carbon monoxide? The stuff that comes out of a car's tailpipe?"

"Flowing freely through every highway and city in the world. So why buy the stuff in bulk?"

She shrugged. "What else have you got?"

"Something that looks like an official memorandum," he said as he surveyed the next sheet of paper, "from the German Interior Ministry. Dated August of '39. It's about something called . . . how would I translate this?—*The Reich Committee for the Scientific Study of Severe Hereditary and Congenital Diseases*. Apparently if you give birth to a child with any kind of deformity, you have to register it with them. Or so this memorandum says."

"And?"

"—And I've no idea what that has to do with Lamont's letter. Except that he's initialed this memo and scribbled *From Juergen* at the bottom. Maybe this was Lamont's 'Juergen' file."

"Next," Sally ordered, draining her gimlet.

"A list of hospitals, as far as I can make out. '*Stuttgart Samaritan Foundation*: Grafeneck Castle. *Facility for Care and Nursing*: Bernburg-an-der-Saale. *Linz*: Hartheim Castle. *Facility for Care and Nursing*: Sonnenstein-bei-Pirna.' Any of those ring a bell?"

"Philip never mentioned them, if that's what you mean."

"And finally—" Hearst handed her a fourth sheet of paper, this one a flimsy copy of what might have been an invoice. "A purchase order for a fleet of buses, on behalf of the *Charitable Society for the Transportation of the Sick*. Headquarters, Berlin."

"That's all?"

Hearst waggled the empty manila envelope.

"But Philip told Allier to keep these papers *safe with the rest*—which means there's more," Sally argued. "Pieces of the puzzle we don't have."

"You think more pieces would help?"

"Philip wasn't murdered for car exhaust."

"Looks like somebody else was."

Hearst held out a fragment of faded newsprint that had been tucked into one of the document's folds. A square scissored by conscientious hands. It was a photograph of a sober-looking man, neither old nor young, in the uncompromising black eyeglasses of an engineer.

Juergen Gebl, the death notice said. *Manager, I.G. Farbenindustrie, Ludwigshafen. Killed 25 August 1939.*

CHAPTER TWENTY-FOUR

None of them could eat that night, Joliot or young Moureu, who was pale with excitement and the burden of being tried; von Halban and the big Russian they called Lew—pronounced *Lev*—all of them standing under the laboratory lights around the map Jacques Allier had spread on the chemistry bench.

Allier had brought in fresh loaves of bread and a couple of good cheeses from a shop near the Ministry. He'd also brought several bottles of white burgundy and two uniformed military police with guns, who stood silently surveying the group of physicists as he talked.

"You, Monsieur Moureu, are familiar with the Auvergne, I understand?"

"My grandparents kept a cottage there when I was a boy." Moureu was much younger than the rest, with a prominent Adam's apple and a shock of unruly hair; he looked overly eager, on the verge of hysteria.

"The roads, I'm afraid, are not much improved," Allier continued. "You will want to stick to the main turnpikes. Head south by the Porte d'Orléans to Orléans itself, and then by degrees to Bourges and

Limoges. From the Limousin, you may proceed due east to Clermont-Ferrand. You should reach the Massif Central by daylight."

"It was my father's habit to take the Dijon road," Moureu objected, "to Lyon and then west—"

"—But with the entire force of the German army spreading like a disease in that part of the country," Joliot said gently, "it would be wiser to do as Allier says."

"We aren't coming back, are we?" Lew Kowarski looked challengingly at all of them from under his bushy black eyebrows.

"Is that an existential judgment, my dear Lew—or a question?" von Halban asked with ponderous humor.

The Russian shrugged. "Take your pick. Me, I don't expect the *sales Boches* to stop until they reach the Atlantic. Once the deuterium's in the Auvergne, do we hunt out a good place for temporary quarters? Find a spot for Joliot's cloud chamber?"

Allier stabbed at his glasses with relief. He had been dreading some kind of scene—Kowarski demanding assurance of his family's safety, forcing the subject of their internment for the duration; Kowarski and von Halban refusing to submit. No decision had been made yet about the fate of these foreigners—the minister was too harassed with waves of tanks and Reynaud's insistence on keeping his precious planes in reserve against some greater German thrust yet to come; he had no time for a couple of scientists. However much Allier argued *treason*.

"Minister Dautry has authorized the rental of a suitable villa that might house your staff and equipment," he answered. "On a temporary basis, of course. Once you've located such a place, you may send for your families. But first, the water. The branch of the Banque de France whose vault we will be using lies here, in Rue Gregoire de Tours." He pointed with the tip of his pen at a map of Clermont-Ferrand. "A Monsieur Boyer is the manager. You are to refer to the water as Product Z. Boyer has no idea what it is."

"I'm taking my dog," Kowarski said suddenly. "A borzoi. He'll tear the throat out of any German who comes near the truck. You like dogs, Moureu?"

"If he's bathed."

"And you, Joliot?" Kowarski turned. "What do you do while we risk our necks with the Boches on back country roads?"

"I'll be packing up the laboratory," Joliot replied. "Deciding what stays and goes."

"The cyclotron?"

"Impossible."

Kowarski swore colorfully. He loved Joliot's cyclotron the way some men cherished cars or women.

"You and Monsieur Moureu will do most of the trip tonight." Allier's mild brown eyes were fixed on the Russian. "Spell each other driving. Joffroi and Méleuse—" this with a nod at the armed guards—"will ride in the back of the truck with the water. They have orders to kill anybody who tries to steal it. If they're overwhelmed, they're to destroy the supply."

"Am I also to have a personal army?" von Halban asked the banker.

"There is a slight disagreement about that."

"I've told Lieutenant Allier that I cannot be responsible for the ill-effects of radiation," Joliot said smoothly. "You know, Hans, that we who work with uranium on a daily basis are all dead men—it is the price we pay for science—but can we ask innocent soldiers such as these—" with a theatrical gesture at Joffroi and Méleuse—"to share our sentence? To ride all night in an enclosed compartment with *poison*? To undertake the duty of destroying it—and how in God's name would they do so without the gravest bodily harm—in the event of being intercepted by the Nazis? I refuse to have blood on my hands. I refuse that burden for you, Hans. And I have told the lieutenant as much."

He was not a theatrical man, despite the gestures, despite the lofty words, and he intended poor Hans to read in his artifice the desire to protect him. The desire for implicit trust. For Hans and his freedom to head south in a car, blessedly alone, to do what he chose in safety with the uranium Joliot had moved heaven and earth to obtain. He could not have trusted von Halban more if he'd handed him his own son, if he'd given him Pierre to bundle onto a ship in Marseille; he wanted von Halban to know this, tonight, as they stood there in the company of strangers. In case, as Kowarski said, nobody ever came back.

"How much uranium must be moved?" the banker asked.

They stared at him, surprised, having assumed he would know.

"Four hundred kilograms. We purchased it not six months ago, from a source in America."

"Not *natural* uranium?"

"Metal," von Halban corrected. "It's a relatively new process—and produces a higher-density form, which means the neutrons have a shorter distance to travel."

"*Do* they travel?"

"In a chain reaction." Joliot was not looking at the banker but at von Halban. "You'll need another truck. Allier will get you one."

"Of course." The banker reached into his briefcase and withdrew an envelope. "The minister has agreed that you may take this dangerous metal alone, Herr von Halban, because *le Professeur* Joliot-Curie has insisted on it. But we retain the right, *voyez-vous,* to direct your movements. Read the contents of that envelope and then burn it. Share your instructions with no one."

Von Halban clicked his heels together and bowed his head—in the manner of an Austrian nobleman—and recognized too late that he might as well have screeched *Heil Hitler.*

"Hans," Joliot said a few minutes later as von Halban prepared to leave—there was luggage to pack, his wife to kiss good-bye, the Ministry letter to read and burn—"no matter what Dautry's people say, you have only one mission. Hide it somewhere safe, where no one can steal it and no one can be hurt by it. And don't tell me where it is until the war's over."

Joliot lingered in the darkened lab, afraid that if he left the Collège de France his feet might carry him through the darkness to the Hôtel Crillon. He did not want to ask for Nell and have her deny him; he did not want to learn that she was no longer there.

He pulled up a stool and set it in the doorway of the room that housed his cyclotron—a massive machine, the first in Western Europe. He knew from friends in Germany that the Nazi government had considered commissioning one. They had invaded France to get his. It provided a beam of deuterons of energies up to 7 MeV—exceeded only by a machine at Berkeley, where Lawrence had first invented the cyclotron. A scientist named Paxton—a colleague of Lawrence's—had actually come to France to help Joliot build the glove box and oscillator. The magnet had been made in Switzerland at the Oerlikon works. It was a magnificent machine, worthy of a Nobel laureate and his Nobel laureate wife. Joliot hated the thought of it broken down and shipped in crates to Dahlem or Berlin.

"And what problem, exactly, were you solving while you walked all night?" a voice asked from the laboratory behind him.

He turned, caught her face pale and floating in the dim light; the heavy mass of her black hair, the unblinking focus of her gaze. Irène was capable of staring at the evidence of particles without blinking for moments on end; his wife could face down any natural anomaly and provide a theory for its existence. He could not say whether she understood love.

"I was considering how to prevent the Nazis from taking what matters most."

"Your cyclotron?"

He shook his head. "You. Hélène. Pierre."

"But are people *really* critical, Fred? In the individual rather than the mass?"

She was making a scientist's pun—*critical mass*. It was the sort of thing he might once have celebrated gently, admiring her detachment. Tonight, however, he was too tired and lonely to take refuge in the cerebral.

"We all die," she continued reasonably. "Only our discoveries outlive us. Science will endure long after it kills us all."

It was possible that Irène, who was so much sicker than he, whose anemia and chronic tuberculosis were constant cause for concern, whose diet was restricted now and whose activities were limited—it was possible that Irène had found the study of death more profitable than love.

"And your conclusion?" she asked abruptly. "On your long walks in the depths of the night?"

"The question is whether to stay or go, Irène," he said simply. "Stay—and face the consequences of working under German rule, in the hope that France survives—or go. And lend our talents to other worlds."

"I will never leave France. I do not want to be buried in strange ground."

She turned away, walked toward the laboratory door. Upright in solitude, monolithic and impenetrable, like the death that held her hand.

"Where are the children?" he called after her.

"Arcouest. With Tatin. Until things are...clearer, here."

Tatin was the nursemaid. He thought of the small

faces—Hélène and Pierre, with buttercups under their chins shining liquid yellow—and yearned toward them.

"That was wise," he said.

She turned and looked at him one last time. "The Comtesse de Loudenne is in Paris," she said. "Did you know?"

CHAPTER TWENTY-FIVE

When Spatz rang his doorbell, von Halban was packing—a few freshly laundered shirts, an ascot for the days when ties would be questionable, two suits, and the laboratory coat he always wore while working. He threw three scientific journals into the leather satchel he'd had since Swiss boarding school: *Nature*, *Comptes Rendus* (from the Académie des Sciences), and a recent issue of the *Journal de Physique*, in which he himself had a modest article—"*Mise en évidence d'une réaction nucléaire en chaîne au sien d'une masse uranifère*"—co-authored with Kowarski and Joliot. But he was not really thinking of these things. His wife was standing in the doorway, studying him. He felt like a thief in the night.

"Are you taking the saxophone?" Annick asked.

It was a symbol of everything frivolous and casual that would be destroyed by war, von Halban thought: the gleaming brass instrument he'd struggled to master and had always loved, breathing through the tube at odd hours when the children were asleep, filling the stairwell of the apartment building with sinuous threads. He was too stiff for jazz, too archaically formal, a man of method and classification, a Germanic sensibility that never relaxed or let its hair down, a despairing poet who craved strict form. Why he cared for the music at all—why it spoke to him of what he would never be—had something to do with the unruly blood in his veins. The elements that were not Austrian, were not even European, but far older: blood that remembered desert sun, frenetic bazaars, the hawking and spitting of camel vendors, women's hips undulating in the light of oil lamps. His Jewish blood, quietly triumphant in the untracked hours when he struggled for improvisation.

"There will be no use for saxophones where I'm going," he answered.

"And where is that?"

He tossed a set of undergarments in the satchel.

"I broke our lease this morning," Annick said with bitter triumph. "I informed Mme. Jaunne. *We are leaving before these* sales Boches *destroy Paris,* I told her; *before the bombs start to fall. Thank God my parents can take care of me, even if my half-Aryan husband refuses to do so.*"

"Annick—"

But she had turned from him, left the hallway empty. The clanging note of the front doorbell hung in the air; somewhere his daughters' laughter.

He sank down on the edge of the bed. He had no answers for his wife: no destination, no length of stay, no likely date of return. No advice to give in her own predicament: Remain in Paris? Run to the in-laws in Pontoise? Had he been his own master—no Joliot, no Ministry of Armaments, no uranium in lead-lined coffers waiting to be transported across the sea—he would have gathered his family in his encircling arms and left in any small plane he could find for England, or America: somewhere the Germans had not yet reached. He could not say this to Annick—there was no plane, no freedom from Joliot's mastery. No spare change to speak of. He made a decent salary in the lab but it was hardly enough to dress Annick in the style a Parisienne thought necessary. He was careful with the monthly accounts, he often went without some minor luxury, but they were always in debt. There was no slack to take up now, no fund to pilfer, no berths to be bought on the last ships out of French harbors.

"Hans," she said abruptly from the doorway again—and he looked up to find her nostrils flaring, her anger so immense it nearly stopped her breathing—"visitors have come to call."

"*Who?*"

"That German from our wedding. Perhaps he intends to recruit you. And *such* a woman—"

He thought of the cousin. Some message for Joliot, perhaps. He rose quickly, too eagerly for Annick, who snorted her contempt. But it was not the Comtesse de Loudenne who stood with Spatz in his living room.

"Good God," he said blankly, staring at Memphis: the embroidered silk of her traveling suit, the ostrich gloves, the snakeskin shoes. She looked magnificent, like a goddess descended from a mountain to their spartan home—a sordid space of chrome tubes and black leather. She smiled, and all he could think of was the night he'd seen her at the Folies Bergères: dancing bare-breasted with a belt of bananas slung around her waist.

"Good evening, von Halban," Spatz said easily from her side. "Forgive me for persuading your beautiful wife. You're packing for a trip, I understand. Business?"

"Of a sort."

"And where are you going?"

You will proceed directly to Marseille by the western route through Tours, veering east only once you are south of the Auvergne, and in Marseille will proceed immediately to the destroyer Foudroyant, *under the command of Captain Bedoyer... You will give your supplies into the captain's keeping and return immediately to Paris...*

He had burned the Ministry letter as instructed.

"That I am forbidden to tell, Spatz."

"Ah. And you, *ma belle*?" The bright blond plumage, the glittering bird's eye, were cocked at Annick. "Are you bound on this journey, too?"

"My wife is promised to her parents," von Halban said stiffly.

"I see." Spatz studied Hans a moment, keenly aware as always of undercurrents and what could not be said. "Time is short, my dear fellow, and I will not abuse your kindness by wasting it. I have a proposition for you—for you and your wife, I should say—"

Annick drew a sharp breath. "Me? You want to recruit *me*? But this is too much!"

"But I forget my manners," the German exclaimed regretfully. "Mademoiselle Memphis Jones—Annick von Halban. Doktor von Halban."

Memphis slipped her leg backward in an elegant, if

wholly theatrical curtsey, and von Halban said hurriedly, "Of course. Charmed. A great honor—"

Annick's nod was glacial.

"Mademoiselle Jones is forced to leave Paris quite suddenly," Spatz continued, "having no more desire than you, Madame von Halban, to entertain Germans. It is of the first importance that she reach Marseille as soon as possible. And so I thought of *you*, my dear Hans."

Von Halban frowned at him.

"Mademoiselle Jones has a car but no driver. She never learned the art of motoring herself. Nor does she have any petrol; it's scarce as hens' teeth. Of course, for one traveling on *government* business...You, I believe, are headed for *le Midi*?"

"How did you know that?"

"My cousin tells me that Joliot is breaking down his lab," Spatz returned evenly. "It makes no sense for any of you to head north or east—"

"And thus you deduced *south*."

Spatz smiled. "When you leave this evening, would you take Mademoiselle Jones?"

The request was so shocking it deprived von Halban of breath. He stared at his friend, his mouth working.

"Her company might prove valuable," Spatz said smoothly. "Her car certainly would. Your official vehicle—I'm right in thinking you drive one?—is certain to attract unwelcome attention. Whereas if you drive south in Mademoiselle Jones's car...the escort of a famous entertainer...no one will question your motives in the slightest. You're pleasure-bent, with suitable company, and why else seek Marseille at this time of year?"

Annick made an impatient sound, half disgust, half jeer. "Decidedly, this is too much! I have never been a party to your debauches, *mon cher,* at those places you frequent in Montmartre—but if you mean to set up your mistress for this disgusting holiday, if you've *bribed* this man to mock me in my own home—"

Von Halban strove toward her—his helpless brown eyes implored her—but Spatz was before him. Spatz, with his effortless grace, reaching into his jacket and withdrawing a wad of banknotes such as von Halban had never seen, offering the money to Annick as though he were a page and she a queen.

"I know that for a family such as yours—young children, a father unavoidably absent on duties too dangerous to be voiced aloud—many difficulties may arise. Who can say when the banks will close altogether? Who can say when the decision to leave Paris might be taken too late? Please, Madame von Halban. Accept this small token of my esteem and respect." He had the courage to brush her rigid shoulder. "For the sake of your girls."

Von Halban watched her attempt to calculate the possible sum in the thick wad; watched her revolve the possibilities the money could bring, and the horrors all lack of it made certain. Then, like a snake, her hand darted out and snatched the notes from Spatz's hand.

"For the sake of the girls," she said tightly. And turned toward the children's bedroom.

The three of them stood in silence while the door slammed closed.

Von Halban found that he was perspiring, his heart racing. He had agreed to nothing, he had compromised nothing—and yet, it had happened! He was taking this unknown woman—this harlequin of fleshly desires, this siren on the rock—with him to Marseille that night. He was actually going to drive her car. He was going to collude and bamboozle the Minister of Armaments, Raoul Dautry, and ditch his official van somewhere outside Paris. Nothing had been said and yet everything was decided. He heard himself begin to plot, felt the vertiginous power of rogue action, of working counter to a system that would undoubtedly entrap him, given half the chance.

"The car—it is where?" he heard himself say.

"In the Rue des Trois Frères." This was the first phrase Memphis Jones had spoken, and her husky voice was intoxicating, a susurration of foreign French full of backroom smoke and half-learned songs.

"Meet me at the Gare du Montparnasse," he told Spatz, "at midnight. It will be a rare pleasure to escort your friend south."

BRITISH EFFICIENCY

THURSDAY, MAY 16, 1940—TUESDAY, JUNE 18, 1940

CHAPTER TWENTY-SIX

The Médoc, where Nell had lived for much of the past decade, lay north of the city of Bordeaux, a sandy, windswept spit of land bordered to the west by the forest of Les Landes, and to the east by the bank of the river Gironde. Beyond the great conifers and the massive belt of dunes was the Atlantic; the main road ran straight and narrow through a string of hamlets, most of them impoverished, to the seaport of Le Verdon-sur-Mer. It was a place of quiet beaches and brackish lagoons, of lone birds on lakeshores, of campsites that sprang to life in the summer months and were deserted the remainder of the year. It had a history of contraband smuggling, cross-Channel passages by moonlight, lives eked out through storms and fishing. The most legendary earth in the history of French winemaking lay at the southern end of the Médoc—where the châteaux Margaux, Lafite, Latour, and Mouton-Rothschild laid down their bottles—but Loudenne was firmly in the north, almost falling into the Gironde, and its wines merited only the most basic Médoc appellation. They were known as *cru bourgeois*—middle-class drinking wines—and the quality of the land they sprang from would never rise any higher.

Nell's husband, Bertrand, who had inherited the château with its charming, rose-colored walls and its forty-eight hectares of vines, loathed Loudenne. It was too scrubby, too remote, too lacking in chic; the neighborhood was abysmal. The fields were pocked with unexploded shells from the last war, when Le Verdon had been used by the Americans for landing troops and pummeled by German guns. The river docks were decayed and sagging. He'd intended to sell the *domaine* until the day Nell arrived, fresh with the disillusionments of marriage. The place reminded her of the fen country where she'd grown up, with its flooded cow pastures and dispirited gulls. She recognized Bertrand's hatred, saw immediately that Loudenne was cause for war. She staked out her position—she with her desultory workers and her vines riddled with phylloxera. When Bertrand gave her jewels, she sold them to fund the vineyard. She grafted old French vines onto disease-resistant American rootstock in the shattered greenhouses near the château. She learned how to dust with copper sulfate against the mold that spoiled her grapes. She brought in electricity, restored the tumbledown *chai* and *cuverie*—the outbuildings where the wine was made—and installed a proper English bath in her suite of rooms. Bertrand, who loved Paris and gin and the Jazz Age even after the Depression made such things irrelevant, gave his jewels to other women and came home less and less. But Loudenne was kingdom enough for Nell: It bottled loneliness of a *grand cru* class.

She was yearning for it already as her lumbering truck broached the outskirts of Bordeaux. They had been driving for sixteen hours and had covered a distance of more than four hundred miles, from Paris to Chartres, to Tours and eventually Poitiers, and on down to Angoulême. The truck's fastest speed was a firm thirty miles per hour. In the dead of night Nell and her driver, Henri, ran afoul of very few refugees—and saw no sign of German troops. There might almost have been no war. Except for Henri's constant fear: that the truck would run out of fuel. He had hoarded petrol in tin canisters for weeks before this trip, and could not understand Nell's insistence that they keep to the back roads. Highways were faster, better paved, kinder to thirsty tanks. He had been driving at a pitch of anxiety, his gaze constantly flicking between petrol gauge and the rapidly draining cans, most of the night.

Nell guessed that Joliot-Curie had access to petrol through the Ministry of Armaments. But she'd been reluctant to ask him for it. She was angry at Ricki—he had disturbed her loneliness and for that she could not forgive him. When she'd called to him from the past, that day in the Boul-Mich, she'd done it on a whim: a test of her old power over him. She'd done it because Spatz had asked her to. She'd meant to take Ricki and drop him again just like before—and tell Spatz everything he needed to know. Unlike Ricki and Bertrand, the German had never promised her anything, had never demanded fidelity, had betrayed her as casually as she betrayed him. She understood Spatz: He was as greedy and solitary as herself.

She had never understood Ricki. Her desire to own and dominate him—to possess that searing look in his eyes, the burn of his touch—was like a wound she could not stop fingering. He had given her his glass jugs full of water. A second chance at contact, a promise. She would not ask for petrol, too.

"Would Madame la Comtesse wish to stop for coffee?" Jean-Luc was wedged into the space behind the front seats, knees almost up to his chin, with Nell's maid lolling sleepily on his shoulder. Nell had left her beautiful little car with Spatz and was bringing the elderly chauffeur home. Jean-Luc was too old for the Front, too old to find other work, and she was determined to make sure he was safe. But there was not enough fuel for two vehicles to drive south and no justification for a chauffeur anymore. The Germans would ruthlessly commandeer everything on wheels—even bicycles—once they marched into Paris. Better that Spatz should drive her beloved two-seater.

"I'd kill for a cup of coffee," she replied, "but I think we ought to press toward home. Don't you, Henri?"

The old man merely grunted. Words, like fuel, were not to be wasted.

They skirted Bordeaux, wistful under spring sunlight, a haze of salt air off the sea. They drove steadily north, through the gentle gravel hills of Margaux, across the streams of Pauillac and through the rolling plateau of St. Estèphe, Nell's heart rising as they turned toward the Gironde. It did not matter that last fall's harvest had been the worst in memory, or that she had no hope of tending her vines, with most of the labor force gone to the Front. She was *home*.

She had not expected the cars pulled up on the gravel drive, waiting to greet them.

Three cars, to be exact: one a lumbering black Daimler of uncertain vintage; a neat little dark blue sports car; and a Silver Cloud Rolls with uniformed chauffeur.

This last belonged to the leader of the group. She was slim and tall, with a disciplined mouth and gloves on her hands. Fair-haired, clear-eyed, in a short, fitted jacket and jodhpurs—as though she'd intended to go riding that morning, rather than journey north through ill-kept roads with a party of relative strangers. It was all of fifty miles to Mouton-Rothschild, where the woman lived, and she was not in the habit of changing her schedule for anyone. She had refused to change so much as her name for her husband, the Baron Philippe de Rothschild; her title outranked his. She remained the same Vicomtesse Elizabeth de Chambure to her friends after her marriage, as she had been before it.

Nell had exchanged only a few words with her at various aristocratic functions, years ago when Bertrand had taken Loudenne more seriously. Elizabeth de Chambure de Rothschild was not one of their acquaintance. And so Nell was frowning even before the truck had come to a stop, her mind racing, wondering what the Vicomtesse wanted.

Near the group, there were two children of perhaps four and six playing in the gravel around the dried-up fountain, and a girl whose job, it seemed, was to look after them. Behind Vicomtesse Elizabeth stood three men: dark, elegant, fastidious, foreign-looking men, whose eyes followed the truck as Henri navigated the rutted drive. Three men who did not move as Jean-Luc jumped down from the cab and held the door open for his mistress.

Nell did not get out of the truck immediately, although she was keeping the chatelaine of Mouton-Rothschild waiting in the midday sun. Instead, she said to Henri: "Take the truck around to the *chai*. I want the oak barrels placed in the first-year room, understand? The jugs of water we brought from Paris must go down in the cellar beneath. *Far back* in the cellar, *oui*? With insignificant bottles—poor vintages—in front of them that nobody would want. *Comprends?*"

"*Oui,*" Henri muttered, and the truck was already in motion as Nell stepped down, rocking away from her with its secrets at a steady if agonizingly slow pace.

"Madame la Vicomtesse." Nell managed the French words with her usual grace, but her body was aching from the strain of the ride and she badly craved a bath. "My apologies. My housekeeper should never have left you standing outside—"

"The children preferred it," Elizabeth de Chambure cut in indifferently. "And indeed, we thought you were from home, and were on the point of leaving. May I introduce you to my friends? The Comtesse de Loudenne—Julian de Kuyper, from Holland."

One of the men—the eldest, Nell guessed—bent low over her hand. *"Enchanté."*

"—and his cousins, Moïses and Elie Loewens."

These two nodded austerely. Neither attempted to approach her.

"Mr. de Kuyper has his family with him. He and the Loewenses arrived by boat two nights ago at the port of Le Verdon, having fled Amsterdam ahead of the German army."

"Then they were fortunate," Nell said.

"Julian and Moïses are very old friends of my husband's." Without warning, Elizabeth de Chambure switched from French to English. "I had to take them in when they showed up at my door. But I've brought them to you, Nell, because I need your help. I won't disguise it. I'm at my wit's end."

"I see." Nell studied the other woman's face. "They're . . . Jewish?"

The vicomtesse nodded. It was well known that unlike her husband, she was of venerable French pedigree and Christian blood. "Bankers of a very high order. The Baron has had countless dealings with them."

The Baron. Nell suffered a faint sensation of dizziness—the aftereffects of her abominable night, or perhaps the force of memory: Philippe de Rothschild as she had last seen him, racing a Bugatti to death-point at Le Mans, his fine hands splayed on the wheel, his mouth sardonic. He was a consummate daredevil, a charming and profound intellect, a lover of dogs and women who strode through the *domaine* he'd created in a chevalier's flowing cape. He was a second son of the

English branch of the great banking family, and Nell had glimpsed him once in the enclosure at Ascot. But she had never known him, never had a foothold in his charmed circle. And while she was indifferent to Elizabeth de Chambure's existence, she'd have given a great deal for a few hours at Philippe de Rothschild's side. There was no man alive—had been no man in three hundred years—quite like the Baron.

"Where is he now, your husband?"

"Paris. He offered his help to Reynaud. They won't let him leave now that the German army...And your husband? The Comte?"

"At the Front," Nell replied brusquely. "Does the Baron know you're here? Handing his friends to a relative stranger?"

Elizabeth de Chambure stiffened, drew herself up—as though she might hurl a blistering reply at Nell and drive off immediately in her Rolls—but then she shook her head. "He expects me to keep them at Mouton. And my daughter is there—she's still so young!—If the Nazis take Paris, they'll take Mouton. You know they will. They steal everything that is...*Jewish*..."

"And if you're harboring fugitives, it will be that much the worse for you," Nell said slowly. "Whereas nobody will look twice at Loudenne. It's not the prize that Mouton-Rothschild would be. And it backs directly to the river, if your friends are forced to escape."

"You understand!" the other woman cried eagerly, and grasped Nell's hand. "I *knew* I could make you understand."

"Did you?" She glanced over at the silent knot of

men, certain from their expressions that they comprehended English perfectly, knew they were being sold. "I have a price. For helping you."

"What is it?"

"A team of workers. Mouton and the other great houses—Latour, your cousins at Lafite, the Maihles at Comtesse de Lalande—all of them snap up the few remaining hands first, and leave none for the rest of us. In this wretched district I can't find a soul to help. The commune of St-Yzans is deserted."

"But we're not even close to harvest time!"

"I have to rack my wines. Fine them. There are countless jobs in the *cuverie,* and only myself and three others to do them."

The two women stared at one another, neither willing to give ground. Elizabeth de Chambure's lips thinned.

"You English," she said bitterly. "You do *nothing* without something in return."

"Neither do bankers." Nell smiled at the three men, the children tossing stones in her decaying fountain. "Take it or leave it, Vicomtesse."

CHAPTER TWENTY-SEVEN

She was wearing a charcoal wool suit Mainbocher had given her after his final show last autumn—wrong for May, but terribly chic and just the thing, Sally thought, for following a hearse.

She was standing on the pavement in front of the Paris Morgue, staring at the long black car with its square back end, its plated glass, its curiously immobile burden of high, domed sarcophagus so like a mammoth cigar—Philip, in fact, laced with whatever chemicals the mortuary had flushed through his system, bloodless at last, his eyes closed. She could imagine him as he had been Monday night—staring, aghast, at the spectacle Death had made of him. Or she could imagine the cigar-box Philip: hands folded prayerfully across his chest, expression blank. Both were equally remote and beside the point. Philip had dropped his body like a soiled pair of trousers and floated away.

At night—the rare nights since Monday that she had slept an hour or two—the whisper of his presence had flitted across her pillowcase, mosquitolike in its persistence.

Sally. Sally. Pay attention, Sally.

"To *what*?" she would mutter, and wake all at once in another unfamiliar bedroom, a different quality of dark, the recognition of Philip vanishing.

This war that had been only a rumor the night he died had opened like a pit and swallowed him up. A small thing, really—the violent death of one man, when so many millions were torn from their beds, thrown onto the roads of Belgium and France, their children riddled with bullets. But Philip's brutal death would never lose its power over Sally—never quite fade to gray. There was justice somewhere, and she would have it. Perhaps then he would stop haunting her sleep.

A second car had pulled up to the curb, equally black and imposing, with a liveried driver of benign aspect. This was the car she was expected to enter, with the elderly concierge Mme. Blum, and allow to carry them at a sedate pace all the way to Cherbourg.

The driver of the hearse was smoking, hips propped against the door of his vehicle; he'd exchanged a few curt pleasantries with the limousine's chauffeur, something about the weather or the *sales Boches,* Sally hadn't exactly heard. He was a man not quite old enough to have avoided the Front, but she noticed that he kept his right arm tucked close to his rib cage as though it were only partly functional, and she imagined some sort of trench wound in his twenties that had relegated him to driving the dead for the rest of his days.

Mme. Blum was late. The limousine driver had already looked twice at his watch. Sally had adopted the mannequin's slouch—one leg cocked, hips sidelong, hands clutching her bag. A suitcase sat docilely at her feet. She was staring as though bored in the direction from which Mme. Blum ought to come, a beautiful woman whose indolence might be read as any number of moods. Not necessarily worried.

It was Joe Hearst who broke her fixed indifference: emerging quietly from the bowels of the morgue with consular paperwork in his hands. His lanky frame was unconsciously graceful, as though while unobserved, he was the kind of man who tap-danced to a tune only he could whistle. His face, however, was deathly pale and there were complicated shadows under his eyes, purple and gray. This, Sally thought, was the face he would wear for the rest of the war—eternally responsible for what he could not save. Like herself.

That woman who'd ditched him had a lot to answer for.

She felt a pang of guilt; she was too interested in the complexity of Joe Hearst for a woman who'd just lost her fiancé. The consciousness of her life and energy reasserting itself even as Philip lay quietly decomposing ten feet away brought a rush of color to her cheeks.

"Mme. Blum's not here, Joe."

"Probably found another ten things she absolutely needed in Bayonne," he said briskly, "and is struggling to get them into her suitcase. Listen, Sally: The reports from the Front this morning aren't good. We can't tell whether the Germans are heading south toward Paris or veering west, to the sea. It's possible they're doing both. Either way, you've got to get on that ship in

Cherbourg today. This may be your last chance to get out."

"No," she said.

"I'm leaving Paris in forty minutes' time. Shoop and everybody at Sullivan and Cromwell are right on my heels, heading for Bordeaux. Every American expat in France will be desperate for a berth in another week, and you'll be back here in Paris trying to figure out how to escape without a car or gas, your money dwindling. Don't be a fool. Get on that boat with Stilwell's body. Go home."

Tears pricked at the corners of her eyes and her whole body felt hot, now, her throat constricting like a rebellious child's. "How long have you been in Paris, Joe?"

He was taken aback. "Eighteen months."

"I've been here four years. A sixth of my lifetime. It's the most gorgeous life I could ever lead, and it dropped right into my lap. I've been Cinderella in Paris, I've been the Evil Stepmother if I wanted, I've been one hell of a princess in any kingdom you could name. *I was never going back*. To the place where I'm just somebody's daughter. Just Sally King."

"You can come back when the war's over." Hearst slipped his arm around her shoulders; at his touch, she felt an unaccustomed shock.

"I'll be married to some chump by that time," she said bitterly, "and weigh a hundred more pounds."

"Get on the boat." He released her. "I need you to carry Philip Stilwell's documents to New York, Sally. It's the only way they'll get there."

"The things we read last night? You think they're that important?"

"Somebody murdered Stilwell for them."

The words lingered in the air between them. Sally glanced involuntarily at the too-quiet hearse.

"I need you to deliver them to Allen Dulles at Sullivan and Cromwell's New York office. He'll figure out what they mean. Your ship will reach Manhattan long before any other kind of mail."

He'd already decided what her life would be, how she'd cross back over the Atlantic with her dead dreams, deliver his convenient parcel for him. But she noticed, all the same, the twist of pain at his mouth. This cost him something.

"Getting that file out may be the only thing you can do for Stilwell," he said gently. "The only kind of justice you'll find."

"Give it to me," she said. And walked away from him toward her funereal car.

And so Léonie Blum arrived at last, puffing with the exertion of dragging her suitcase down into the Métro and up again, her forearms damp with sweat. Hearst saw her safely into the capacious limousine and listened while she clucked in sympathy over Sally, who exerted herself to make the little old woman feel welcome, a valued companion. Sally did not look at Hearst, however, as she said her good-byes, and he detected a lifelessness beneath the good manners—a kindling of despair. He did not care if she wept all the way across the ocean, provided that she went.

He stood on the paving after the two cars pulled away, both traveling too slowly for his taste, and cursed the day Sally King had walked into Bullitt's embassy.

"Now that's a looker," Petie said dreamily from the front end of Hearst's Buick, where he'd been standing guard. "Nice little thing, too, Boss."

"She's not little," Hearst said abruptly, "and she's in love with a dead man."

He had just lifted the chrome handle of the car door when someone called out his name. He turned his head toward the morgue, scanning the drift of people crisscrossing the pavement. There it was again: *Hearst*.

A slight figure, almost indistinguishable from the pale limestone of the surrounding façades; a soft-brimmed gray hat like any other. Only Max Shoop's eyes commanded attention today, arresting Hearst where he stood. They were blazing with malice and fury.

"She's gone?"

"Sally? A few minutes ago."

The lawyer swore, unexpectedly and viciously.

He knows she has the papers, Hearst thought. *He knows.*

"You couldn't have warned her?"

"About what?"

"Emery Morris." Shoop walked to the edge of the paving, shading his eyes as he stared west. "He's on the run—and wanted for murder."

CHAPTER TWENTY-EIGHT

On the morning of the day war really came to France, Memphis awoke in a small, white-plastered room tucked under the eaves of the inn at Alise-Ste-Reine. She thought it was a weird name for a tiny village lost in the folds of the hills—*Alise, the Sainted Queen*—when nobody now alive could remember exactly who Alise was. The hamlet had held maybe five hundred souls before its men were hauled off to the Front; a farming village, close to Dijon, and notable for a grand bronze statue of Vercingetorix in its neat central square. Hans had told her Vercingetorix was an old fart who'd died fighting Caesar—every statue in France, it seemed, commemorated some lost and bloody cause.

Sunshine streamed through the casement and the scent of roses swam headily on the wind, but neither sun nor scent had awakened her. It was engines—revved high and loud, repeatedly gunned as though to emphasize a point—and the voices of men rising through the open window. She got up and scuttled to the casement, peering down on the square.

Gilles Martin was standing in front of the inn with

his son, only a kid in his teens for all he worked in the bar. The innkeeper had looked her up and down without speaking a word last night, as though she'd dropped out of the sky, dropped from Mars maybe, in her shining coffee skin and her Parisian clothes. His wife had demanded sharply if von Halban was with the German army, and when he denied it, she'd examined his French papers narrowly and muttered something about Fifth Columnists and reporting him to the local gendarme. Hans had quietly explained that he was a French citizen, a resident of Paris, that he was conducting Miss Jones to Marseille, where she was engaged to perform—and from the look on the innkeepers' faces they expected a strip routine, something bare-breasted and gyrating like the posters of Paris from the twenties. The wife had put her arm firmly around René's shoulders—that was the son—and pulled him out of harm's way, back into her kitchen. At first Gilles had insisted there were no rooms, the place was full up, though even Memphis could tell the town was deserted now the war was on, Sedan only a couple hundred miles to the north. Hans had unrolled some of Spatz's money and pushed it into the man's palm. He'd shut up at that point. Found not one, but two rooms.

Hans was standing a little behind Gilles and René, as though he'd just walked out of the inn after breakfast: eyes squinting into the sun and that expression of caution on his face that Memphis had learned to recognize. He went through life looking wary, as though every day was one big chilly pond he was forced to stick his toe into, as though something nasty might bite him. She was beginning to feel affection for him after all these days in his car—or *her* car, rather, piled high with trunks and bandboxes and a satchel or two, Hans hunched over the wheel patiently negotiating traffic. They'd been on the road for nearly three days, ever since that hurried meeting at Hans's place Wednesday night: a confused departure from her echoing house on the Rue des Trois Frères, Spatz silently smoking, all her costumes and feathered boas, spangled brassieres and towering hats shoved willy-nilly into the depths of the Vuitton trunk, too many pairs of shoes left behind, the satchels needed for her precious sheet music.

"Where did you get that money?" Spatz had asked her with deceptive unconcern, as she counted out the cash she'd taken from the man at the American Express office.

"From one of my fellas," she'd said coolly. "You don't know him." Not about to tell how she'd talked to the lawyer named Shoop. The memory of that desperate conversation in the wee hours, Jacquot's bedroom and the look of death on Shoop's face, still made her squirm. But she'd cashed the man's check all right.

"You use everybody, don't you, my sweet?"

"Same as you use me," she retorted. "You think I don't know you're sticking this guy Hans in my car for a reason? Which one of us you watching, Spatz? Me or the German?"

"Hans is Austrian. And of course he's there to watch over you. I want you out of Paris safely."

He'd come to stand behind her as she tossed her jewelry in the depths of a handbag, golden head cocked in amusement. She raised her head and met his bright, birdlike gaze in the mirror. His hand caressed her shoulder. Gooseflesh rising.

"And while you're on the road, my darling," he said, "I want you to keep in touch. Call me whenever you find a public telephone. Tell me *exactly* where you are. Just in case I need to . . . rescue you."

What had surprised Memphis during the long hours of travel was how restful she found Hans von Halban. The Austrian might look at the world as though it were going to savage him, but behind the wheel of her car he was comfortable enough: rarely speaking, companionable in his silence, never expecting to be entertained. She had spent most of her life entertaining somebody—she'd done it at three for her sisters and brothers, she'd done it at thirteen the first time she got married—she'd done it in London and Manhattan and up and down the Champs-Élysées. She'd come to think of men as idiots whose mouths were always hanging open, waiting for some woman to dangle her tit. Hans was different. When he talked, he figured she had a brain in her head. It was a novel sensation.

"How come you friends with Spatz?" she'd asked that first night, as they turned in the opposite direction he'd been ordered by the Ministry to follow, and headed resolutely east, into the teeth of the advancing German army. His plan, as he'd vaguely sketched it, was to take the fastest route to Marseille so as to get home sooner to his wife and kids, and the fastest route was east and south. He was counting on the fact that not even the panzer divisions could cover many miles in two days, and anyway the rumor was the Germans were headed for the Channel. He was just brushing the edge of Champagne, turning toward Troyes and then Dijon, but what he hadn't reckoned on was the whole French army scattering like a pile of windblown leaves, south from the Ardennes and their failed counteroffensive into Troyes and every other town in Champagne, the roads clogged to a standstill with exhausted men and jeeps and village people struggling to get through the ranks to Paris. Hans had pushed on for a few hours in the dark of Wednesday night until, at last, he pulled off to the side of the road and they both watched the columns of sagging soldiers trudge by. Moonlight glinting on the barrels of their guns. Memphis had opened a bottle of cognac she'd brought along for the ride and they'd passed it to each other, wiping the bottle's rim with one of her gloves.

"I became Spatz's friend the day I understood I could never be French," he said then. "It is not enough to take the citizenship or the French wife. When your loneliness is unrelieved—when you feel invisible to most others—just the sound of your native tongue can bring tears to your eyes, yes? You have felt this also, I think, Miss Jones?"

They were speaking French because his English was poor and her German nonexistent, and when she heard his words, everything twisted inside her. She'd said she didn't care if she never went back to Tennessee, she could stay in Paris the rest of her life, but the truth was there were times she wanted nothing more than to sit down at her mother's table in the humid forenoon of a Memphis July, rest her elbows on a crumpled paper bag, and shell peas into a bowl. She wanted the food only her mother could make, she wanted the lilting patois of her dusty, run-down street—the speech that had rocked and curdled her infancy, that had shouted her out of town, that rang in her ears in her worst midnight dreams. She understood all too painfully what Hans von Halban meant: Sometimes even an enemy looks like salvation if he calls you by your name.

The Enemy was standing in the square right in front of Gilles Martin's inn, now, at forty-three minutes past seven o'clock in the morning, Saturday the eighteenth of May. Three soldiers in what Spatz called *feldgrau* uniforms: gray wool tunics and trousers, gleaming black boots rising to mid-calf. They wore helmets and goggles and thick black gloves and they had arrived on the backs of three motorcycles—young René was openly admiring these, all the complicated mechanics of a German machine. The fact that the trio represented the advance guard of a formidable force was obvious to Memphis, as she stared from her attic room: They were too self-assured, these three who'd conquered a town just by passing through it. There were more where they came from.

One of them—the commanding officer, she guessed—spoke French, and he was speaking it very loudly, as though to compensate for his lousy accent.

She gathered that he was recommending that the entire remaining population of Alise-Ste-Reine pick up and hit the road before the German army arrived. He was also demanding petrol for the motorcycles. There was a snag at this point—Hans and Memphis had already discovered there was no petrol to be had in Alise-Ste-Reine. In point of truth, theirs was the only car in the entire village. Hans had stolen some fuel in the dead of night from a storage depot on the outskirts of Troyes, but that was a day ago and Memphis was beginning to worry about the distance ahead: the ascent into mountainous country around Grenoble.

Gilles motioned to Hans, pleading for an interpreter, and with that familiar look of wariness Hans stepped forward and broke into German. And at that moment, a shot rang out from somewhere beyond the square: a single, sharp crack of a rifle. One of the German motorcyclists dropped to the ground like a stone.

The officer glanced at the fallen man—blood spurting from the neck, the second soldier bent over the prone body, shaking his head—and then without much thought or apparent effort he grabbed Hans, grabbed Gilles and the boy René, and dragged them into the center of the square: a human wall between himself and the unknown sniper. As Memphis watched, the German muttered something to Hans, who in turn spoke confidentially to Gilles Martin: The innkeeper called out in French, high and desperate.

Hold your fire! Come forward and surrender your weapon! If you do not—there will be consequences!

A silence settled over Alise-Ste-Reine. Memphis

watched the little group, standing like statues in the early sunlight. A bird settled on the head of Vercingetorix, lazily stretched its wings.

The German officer pulled a knife from his pocket and slit the boy René's throat from ear to ear.

Gilles they shot in the head.

CHAPTER TWENTY-NINE

It was difficult to know what to burn and what to save. Allier had told him to start sorting the research reports he'd compiled for the Ministry, file the essential data in folders and boxes but destroy the reports themselves, with their incriminating trail of responsibility, and Joliot meant to do so. He even constructed an ideal arsonist's chamber far from the volatile chemicals of the lab, a steel drum that must have held something important at one time but was mere refuse now, suitable for flames and ashes. He was used to constructing infernal machines. Every physicist was one part auto mechanic, a tinkerer with toys, and Joliot was no exception. He'd made his own cloud chamber. Installed his own Hoffman electrometer. Blown and cut glass. Assembled the cyclotron. All examples of his patient ability to waste time—since everything must be abandoned now. The futility of his life kept him on his knees in front of his desk, surrounded by papers, unable to decide what should be consigned to flames. His citation from the Nobel committee, perhaps?

It was there that Mad Jack found him.

Joliot had never met Mad Jack. It was Allier who served as the Earl of Suffolk's pilot fish—his entrée to the Collège de France. Once he'd devoured the Sullivan & Cromwell papers, the earl wasted no time in locating Jacques Allier, through contacts at the British embassy and the various French ministries. Mad Jack knew the French johnnies would have plans for a star like Frédéric Joliot-Curie, not to mention his wife, and it was vital he scotch those plans while they were yet in the making.

"The Earl of Suffolk is to be trusted," Allier told Joliot in a lowered voice as Mad Jack lifted tubes and peered into beakers, happy as a clam at high tide. "I am ordered by my minister to give him every facility, you understand?"

It was late Saturday afternoon. Irène hadn't bothered to come to the lab today; she was at home in Antony, resting. Joliot was self-conscious now around her, exactingly polite. Terrified of embarking on any conversation that might tumble him, willy-nilly, into a confession of love for another woman. She had never raised the issue of Nell again after that first evening, as though everything that needed to be said was already understood between them. She was aware of his guilt much as she might visualize each facet of a scientific theory before undertaking the burden of proof. That was why she'd left the children in Brittany. She did not want them contaminated. He was suddenly and forever radioactive.

"Got the heavy water safely out of town, I take it?" the earl inquired.

Frowning, Joliot glanced at Allier. The banker gave a barely perceptible nod. It was true that Moureu had awakened Joliot at seven o'clock the previous morning with a telephone call, to say that he and Kowarski were in Clermont-Ferrand; Product Z was tucked away in the Bank of France's vault; he was on his way back to Paris while Kowarski tracked down a suitable location for the temporary Auvergne lab—but that was privileged information. Not something to toss like confetti at a virtual stranger. Even if Moureu's canisters *were* decoys.

"Good of you to consider the HydroNorsk stockpile," Mad Jack observed. "Very astute. Forward-thinking. We were no end bucked when Allier came to London to tell us all about it. Couldn't have pulled a neater operation ourselves. And then when the Germans simply rolled over Norway—"

"What is it you've come to say?" Joliot interrupted.

The Englishman propped himself on a metal stool and fished a hard salami out of his tweed pocket. He gave it all his attention, a small knife in his hand.

"I'm inviting you to Cambridge, old chap. The Cavendish laboratory, perfect for a man of your brilliance and reputation. I can offer you every assurance of professional support and private accommodation—help with resettling the wife and kiddies, the esteem and collaboration of the best minds in England. And you'd have the comfort of knowing you were fighting Jerry instead of walking right into his trap."

"It is by no means certain the Germans will prevail." Joliot glanced at Allier, whose face was expressionless. "It could be a very long war."

The earl shook his head. "Honor you for the sentiment. Shows proper feeling and all that. But rather a forlorn hope, what? Your man Reynaud told our P.M. Thursday that his army was done for. Had no choice but to give up the ship. Actually read Churchill the riot act for not sending more planes! I've never seen the Old Man so incensed. No, I'd say it's all over but the shouting."

Joliot set down the papers he'd been holding and strolled toward the laboratory windows.

"And yet you've got this plan for a bomb," the earl mused. "Taken out a patent on it. I think we're all agreed we can't let any particle of that research—hah! no pun intended—fall into Jerry's hands."

"Reynaud will never give up Paris," Joliot said.

"But he has instructed our ministry, *voyez-vous,* to prepare to fall back to Tours," Allier interjected. "From what I understand, every branch of the French government is making evacuation plans. We have people burning papers even now at the Armaments Ministry. There's no telling when the word will come. You've got to be *prepared,* Joliot."

"I agreed to go to Clermont-Ferrand—"

"That may not be far enough. You *do realize* that you, yourself—that brain in your head—are as much of a danger to France as your heavy water and your cyclotron? If you fall into German hands? We can't guarantee your safety, *mon ami.* Or the safety of Irène and the children. We can't even guarantee we can get you out. But the earl is willing to try."

Joliot wheeled around and stared at the banker.

"Take my boys," he said. "Take von Halban and Kowarski. They're first-class minds and they need a place to work. The Germans will simply kill them."

"To be sure they will," Mad Jack agreed. "But don't think they won't kill *you,* too, Joliot—once they've learned everything they need to know. Extraordinarily efficient soldiers, the Germans. Damnably efficient."

He had finished carving his salami and he offered Joliot a slice, his eyes thoroughly hard. The earl might sound like Bertie Wooster, but Joliot understood suddenly that the Englishman was no music hall character, no readily dismissed fool.

"How long until I must decide?" His eyes remained on the earl and his tattooed arm, the bright blade of the knife in his hand.

"I'll give you a day or two." Mad Jack grinned. "Unless Jerry gets here first."

CHAPTER THIRTY

Monday, the twentieth of May, and the German planes swooping low over Cherbourg harbor again.

The captain had ordered them all into the hold of the ship—not the true hull, which was packed with crates of cargo because the *Clothilde* was a merchant steamer—but the lowest passenger area that could be reached. The uppermost deck was covered with sandbags against the possibility of fire. All around their berth were French naval ships, manning antiaircraft guns; once in a while they brought down a German plane, which plummeted like a sizzling phoenix into the sea. To the cheers of those watching.

The bombs had been falling for four days, ever since Sally and Mme. Blum first came aboard Friday morning, and she was sick of the stench and the heat inside the *Clothilde*'s hold, sick of the hundreds of desperate people who'd overwhelmed the Dutch crew and forced their way onto the ship.

Sally and Mme. Blum had arrived thirteen hours late for their scheduled departure, having fought their way through tides of retreating soldiers, most of them

English, on the Cherbourg road. The exhausted men had parted for the hearse out of some vestigial respect for the dead, but both long, black cars had proceeded at a snail's pace through the ranks, the four-hour trip lengthening and lengthening until darkness fell and Mme. Blum began to snore in the limousine's corner and Sally was ready to scream with impatience. They gave rides to a few soldiers in the massive expanse of the limousine, boys of eighteen and twenty talking carelessly as the car crawled toward Cherbourg through the evening hours. Sally learned their names only to forget them, she heard rumors of the German advance, saw the delicate trembling of fingers as each lost boy stepped back out of the car, saluting. The whole world was staggering toward the English Channel and the Nazis were on their heels.

At three o'clock in the morning they'd pulled off the road so that the driver could sleep. Both cars were parked on the verge of a crossroads leading nowhere through the apple orchards of Normandy, Léonie Blum murmuring in her dreams and Sally restlessly dozing. A stutter of sound, and then the hailstorm of strafing bullets: Messerschmitts. She started awake, screaming.

When the planes had flown on, bodies and vehicles littered the road. The lucky ones had dived into ditches; a few cars had overturned. But the silent figures in the middle of the highway told their own story. She had been showered by Death and the raindrops had missed her.

"Why would they do such a thing?" Mme. Blum

raged. "How *could* they? With women and children on the road?"

"They're clearing it," Sally said. "For their tanks and armored vehicles. It's the most efficient way. We've got to get off this highway somehow."

Their driver—elderly, appalled, tears streaming down his face—threw the limousine into gear and turned abruptly into the side road. They followed the apple trees to nowhere for the rest of that night.

"I'd rather he just put the damned boat to sea and took his chances," Léonie Blum declared now in the *Clothilde*'s hold. "We could die here as easily as crossing to Southampton or Folkestone. What is the man waiting for?"

"Orders." Sally reached into her purse and passed the old woman a handkerchief—not too badly soiled. They had yet to spend more than an hour in their cabin; meals were sporadic affairs of water and crackers doled out by the overworked crew; and Sally had no idea where their luggage had gone. "The captain told me he's under orders from the French navy not to leave. That's the only reason he was still at anchor when we got here on Friday. I don't think the poor man's life is his own."

She had spoken to the captain only twice. He was a harassed and despairing individual who could not go home again to Holland, which was occupied by the Germans now, without being impressed into the German navy or having his ship confiscated. He wanted to reach the safety of England. Draw breath for a day or two. Decide the best way to fight or even whether he wanted to.

He had refused to accept Philip's coffin. Sally had given him all the money she had to take it on board. It was stowed now in the area of the ship reserved for meat—a refrigerated unit, although the captain, whose name was Anders, had turned off the generator to conserve his battery power. She avoided thinking of Philip's body rocking gently in the bilge. Instead she said to Mme. Blum: "We won't stay here forever, you know. Tell me about your niece. She's in her forties, I think you said? With two children?"

"Two boys," Léonie Blum corrected. "David and Saul. Growing like weeds. She sent me pictures...Saul for my brother, the one in Munich. I haven't heard from him in nearly two years..."

Sally knew all about the old man in Munich who'd been sent to a labor camp. Mme. Blum had been talking about him fretfully for days, as though the decision to leave Europe, to turn her back on an entire existence and plunge, at the age of seventy-six, into the unknown, had come to be symbolized by this brother whose face she would never see again. Sally let her talk. Her own thoughts wandered to Bordeaux and Joe Hearst. He must have reached the city by now, with his collection of household effects and whining children. Maybe they were already at sea, the rest of the Americans—already bound for New York—while Sally was adrift in the Atlantic with Hearst's precious file and her dead lover in a box.

But she had been faithful to Joe in her way. Uncertain exactly where her luggage was, crushed by the sheer numbers of people crammed into this boat that had never been intended for passengers, she had tucked his manila envelope under the wilting spray of white flowers Sullivan & Cromwell had ordered strapped to the top of Philip's coffin. She figured the documents were safest there, guarded by a corpse in the refrigerated hold.

The *Clothilde* shuddered violently.

"Mon Dieu," Léonie Blum gasped, clutching at Sally's hand. "We've been hit! The *sales Boches* are sinking us!"

"No." Sally was listening, her whole body straining toward the surface. "I think that's the engines, not a bomb. We're *moving*."

She pushed her way up on deck. It was important to stand facing France as the *Clothilde* moved out of Cherbourg harbor, to drink deep of the salt air and the fumes of burning, to stare until her eyes ached at this spit of land where the quaint old buildings of the town spilled into the sea, to witness the fires on the neighboring ships and stare at the Dutch seamen as they beat out the smoking embers not ten feet away from where she stood. It was important to say good-bye to this country she was abandoning. The *Clothilde* wallowed and heaved; a German plane soared low over Sally's head and she stared up at its belly fearlessly, seeing the gunner's face as he aimed through the transparent turret.

"Get *down*!" a sailor shouted, but he spoke Dutch and she did not understand the words.

The German plane passed over her head without firing.

"I'll never be afraid of dying," she said aloud, watching the plane into the horizon. "It can't be worse than leaving France."

"But you're *not* leaving," a voice said close by her; an intimate, insinuating voice. "Haven't you *heard*? The captain's been *ordered* up the *coast*. We're supposed to *evacuate* the army. If the *Germans* don't sink us *first*."

She turned and stared at the man: a neat figure despite the privations of the past four days; his eyes overly wet and bright above a toothbrush mustache.

"Excuse me," she said. "Do I know you?"

He smiled primly and bowed. "Emery Morris. I worked with *Philip,* at Sullivan and Cromwell."

CHAPTER THIRTY-ONE

Nell stood in the cool center of the *cuverie*—the long, dim shed where her first-year wines were stored—and watched old Henri topping up the casks. It was a methodical process, undertaken almost daily as the aging wine evaporated into thin air: the glass stopper removed from its bunghole and extra wine ladled into the barrels, to prevent an excess of oxygen in the mix. These casks were several years old, culled from the forests of Tronçais, not the brand-new ones of Nevers oak she'd just hauled from Paris. Those were reserved for the harvest to come in four months' time, for the grapes that had not yet set on the vines that had not yet flowered. Most vineyards in Nell's part of the Médoc preferred to use only old oak, mellowed and saturated with years of wine, but she considered new oak essential to the aging process—a concept she'd borrowed from Baron Philippe at Mouton-Rothschild. The wood imparted flavor and scent; its raw tannins shortened the aging period. She'd had difficulty convincing Henri that her instincts were right—it was he who blended Nell's wines—and only time would truly tell if her penchant for the new was preferable to his fidelity to the old.

Château Loudenne's red wine was part Cabernet Sauvignon, part Merlot, a little Petit-Verdot and Malbec. Henri varied the mix from year to year, drawing on different sections of the vineyards according to the quality of that season's grapes. He'd been doing it from the age of fifteen, having followed his father through the trellised rows since he could walk. Henri's son had no winemaker's palate—no sixth sense for what an untamed crush might be in twenty years—but the old man's nineteen-year-old grandson was born with a cork in his mouth, and Henri intended for the boy to take over at Loudenne when the time came. Young Roger was somewhere in the Ardennes right now, in command of a gun emplacement. Part of Bertrand's company, in fact.

"I put the new folk onto spraying the Merlot vines," Henri told Nell as she stood silently watching him. "La Baronne sent us some copper sulfate, along with her people. Good of her. All the copper in the world's been commandeered by the Armaments Ministry. She must have had a storehouse full of it at Mouton. That'll be the Baron, of course—only a Rothschild could get copper sulfate in time of war."

"Are they any good?"

Henri glanced at her from under his bushy eyebrows. "The new folk, you mean? They know which end of the vine the grapes hang on. She didn't send us the lame and halt, if that's what you're asking. They'll do."

The day after Nell agreed to harbor Julian de Kuyper and the Loewens brothers, five winery workers had arrived from Mouton-Rothschild: two men in their sixties, a boy of fifteen, and two women of indeterminate age. Nell had turned them over immediately to Henri, who found them places to sleep above the *chai*. He'd set them tasks over the past few days and quietly assessed their talents: this one to help rack, this one to stand patiently with a bowl full of casein while Henri fined the second-year wine, this one grafting in the greenhouse. He was careful with the women and joked with the men; the boy he took instantly under his wing.

Nell had been left with very little to do. She spent her time worrying about how she would pay these people—five more salaries to meet—and where to find food for her rapidly expanding household. Between her domestic staff, the visitors from Holland, and the winery workers, they numbered twenty.

"I'll just have to sell something," she muttered, as she walked back up the gravel drive toward the château. "A painting, perhaps. A piece of silver. I'll find a buyer in Bordeaux."

Thirty yards from the entrance she stopped short. The strains of a violin were wafting through an open window—painful, melancholy, fleeting. That would be Elie Loewens, the youngest of the three Jews from Amsterdam. A trained musician who spent his idle hours practicing, practicing, as though if he could perfect this difficult passage of Berlioz he might be able to control what happened to him. Nell closed her eyes as she listened, the violin blending with the wind-stirred leaves and the call of a bird somewhere in the distance.

"I didn't know you ran to concerts at Loudenne," remarked a voice behind her.

She turned abruptly—but her ear had not deceived her.

"What are you doing here, Spatz?"

He had driven her little car south from Paris, taking the trip in stages over the past two days, and it was clear he'd brought news.

"I know nothing of what's happening," she said. "I have a radio, but the national broadcasts are so stupid—repeating rumors and lies. What's going on in Paris?"

Spatz cocked his sleek blond head. "Not much. Reynaud is still hanging on, but the army's in full retreat. I drove through enough French soldiers on the road south to overthrow Hitler myself. Pathetic."

"But you must know more than that! Your people—"

"—Tell me that your husband's company surrendered three days ago, on the outskirts of Rouen," he said brusquely. "Bertrand's a prisoner of war, Nell."

"Surrendered?" She swayed slightly on the gravel drive, and Spatz gripped her arm. "But *why*?"

"No other choice. You have no idea what it's like, Nanoo. Entire battalions are surrounded. The few poor bastards who make it to the coast grab any boat they can find and put out to sea. They don't come back."

Nell looked around her blindly, groped toward a stone bench that sat under a great Médoc pine. In the house the violin had fallen silent. She could imagine the Loewens brothers peering warily through the tall windows at this blond stranger standing over the countess, the sudden terror that already they were betrayed.

"You don't even know if he's alive, do you?" she said. "Just that his company gave up."

"I'll find out—what his status is, where he's sent. I know you care about Bertrand, no matter how much you two...despite your past differences..."

"Yes." She looked up. "Oh, God. *Henri.* His grandson Roger serves under Bertrand. I'll have to tell him—"

Spatz nodded. "I'll wait for you in the salon. I drove most of the night and I'm tired. Is your housekeeper still here? Do you have any eggs?"

The salon.

Some memory of the violin—the two children playing in the formal box garden behind the house—brought Nell to her feet. Her heart was racing and for the life of her she could not say what Spatz would do with the information she was about to give him. She only knew that she was honor-bound to protect her refugees—out of simple decency, out of fellow feeling, all the bargains with Elizabeth de Chambure forgotten.

"There's something I have to tell you," she said slowly. "I have visitors, Spatz."

CHAPTER THIRTY-TWO

Joe Hearst rolled into Bordeaux at the rear of a convoy of fifteen cars and two vans, all packed with people and luggage, more than a week after he'd left Paris. It was Saturday afternoon, the twenty-fifth of May. A trip that should have required two days of travel had been prolonged by an unexpected outbreak of measles just shy of Orléans. With seven children and two adults quarantined in the village of Châteaudun, and no possibility of finding rooms for the rest of his forty-odd Americans, Hearst had twiddled his thumbs at a local campsite and fretted about the loss of time. He'd called Paris repeatedly from Châteaudun's single public telephone: Bullitt's office, Shoop's office, Sûreté headquarters—anybody who might be able to give him news of the hunt for Philip Stilwell's killer. But there was no news—Morris had not been found. Which meant that if Sally King *hadn't* boarded her boat, she was still in danger.

Now, on this Saturday afternoon, Bordeaux under a lowering threat of rain, with the end of his responsibilities in sight, Hearst was irritable as hell. He was fed up with whining and feverish children. He hated being far from the nerve center of war. He was lonely and yet surfeited with people; he wanted quiet and a bottle of good red wine—a '29 Margaux, if possible. He left the convoy sprawling in the Esplanade des Quinconces, the reviving children chasing one another among the fountains, and stalked off under the plane trees to the American consulate.

It was housed in an imposing eighteenth-century building, not far from the Bordeaux Préfecture—the town hall and city offices. The consul-general was a fussy little man named Noakes—"spelled with an *a*," he assured Hearst primly—whose previous life had revolved around drinking wine, negotiating the sale and export duties of wines, and recommending the best vintages and *domaines* to American tourists traveling through his province. He lived in the consulate itself, and his bachelor existence had been a thoroughly happy one; he was unprepared for war and the demands it brought. Indeed, he was overwhelmed.

"I may say I received a letter from the ambassador—Mr. Bullitt—some five days ago, advising me of your probable arrival," he fretted when Hearst presented his card, "but I am afraid I can offer little in the way of help. The whole town is overrun with those looking for accommodation and passage home. Channel shipping is all at sixes and sevens, you know, whether one hails from New York or Southampton, what with the Germans harrying any vessel that so much as dares to thrust its prow out of the harbor."

Hearst listened, and hoped devoutly that Sally had

gotten on the *Clothilde* in Cherbourg. She ought to be safe in New York by this time.

"No, no, my dear Mr. Hearst—the only possible thing to do is to turn around and head back to Paris," Noakes assured him. "You'll be much more comfortable there, and once this silly dispute with Herr Hitler is settled—"

"Nothing would induce me to get back on the road to Paris with *that* group," Hearst replied.

It was only by the exercise of immense patience that he prolonged the interview. Over a glass of Margaux— the '34, if not the '29—he eventually learned that Hoddard Noakes had done one thing in preparation for the embassy evacuation: He had consulted with the British consul in Bordeaux, who advised that he lodge his people at one of the vineyards outside the city, preferably northward along the Gironde estuary. Hearst leaped at this sensible suggestion.

"We have tents," he said. "We'll be no trouble."

"I hope you have money as well," Noakes observed with surprising shrewdness. "There isn't a vineyard proprietor in the Médoc that isn't hurting. The '39 harvest was dreadful—the peasants insist a bad crop presages war—and now with labor so damnably short-handed—"

"We'll buy provisions here in Bordeaux," Hearst suggested, "and shift for ourselves if necessary. What we need is a place to wait for a likely ship—and your help in securing our passage."

Noakes scribbled a few words on a piece of paper. "Your best bet is to work with the wine-shipping companies. They all have offices here, and they move tons of cargo over the Atlantic every year. Mention my name. If you pay them enough, they'll even telegraph New York and find out when the next big boat is due at Le Verdon. You'll want to be standing on the quai waiting for it when it arrives. Otherwise, you'll never get aboard. Reservations or no."

Hearst scanned the slip of paper: two addresses of shipping companies scrawled across the top. "And this third one?" he asked, straining at Noakes's handwriting. "Château..."

"Loudenne," Noakes replied. "It's a smallish place, quite out of the way—but it backs right down to the river. Good for your purposes. Not one of your great wine houses, mind—produces nothing but *cru bourgeois*—but it's virtually empty. An Englishwoman runs it. She's sure to find room for fifty Americans on her grounds—especially if you've got some hard cash. The Countess de Loudenne is not exactly flush."

"Will she know we're coming?" Hearst asked.

Noakes smiled thinly. "The *domaine* is not on the telephone. Much better to simply present the countess with a *fait accompli,* don't you think?"

Hearst was wrong: Sally King was not in New York.

At the very moment he thought of her, she was gripping the *Clothilde*'s rail and saying to Léonie Blum: "Look at them. Thousands and thousands—we can't possibly take them all—"

The merchant steamer was wallowing in the swells just off the coast of Calais. The beach was black with moving ants—company after company of French soldiers who'd fled west before the German armored divisions until they'd abruptly run out of land. The *boom* of enemy guns reverberated from the inland hills; the air was thick with the whine of circling Messerschmitts. There were other planes in the air now, too—British fighters, always too few for the black cloud of German planes, but fretting at the flanks of the massive force, bringing an occasional enemy plane down in a spiral of smoke and fire into the sea, and plummeting themselves to the shocked moans of the people watching on board the *Clothilde*. At times the ants returned fire from their positions on the beach—occasionally a French *tricoleur* waved—but as the day wore on, it was clear the beachhead would be overwhelmed.

"Poor boys," Léonie Blum said heavily. "Poor abandoned souls. We must do for them what we can."

She and Sally had emerged from the stinking hold to witness this war. If Death came, each of them preferred to meet it in the open air, like the pilots of the RAF planes. The *Clothilde* had turned north, not west, when it slipped its moorings in Cherbourg, and for the past several days had hugged the coast. The French naval ships based at Cherbourg had been ordered south, to Gibraltar and the relative safety of the Mediterranean. German fighter-bombers strafed the ports and German submarines trolled the Channel. Their object, as Emery Morris explained, was only partly to terrify the retreating French troops into surrender.

"They're *determined* to keep Churchill from *landing* his reinforcements," the lawyer said. "They'll sink *everything* that moves in these waters *first*."

And so the *Clothilde* went on: moving north at a snail's pace, mooring at night in secluded Norman inlets, her crew flinging themselves at every spark or blast the ship sustained, as though the ship were Noah's ark and the world's sole chance for survival.

"Stand by to launch lifeboats!" Captain Anders cried in hoarse French over the ship's loudspeaker. "All passengers below!"

"He can't be planning to take those soldiers off the beach," Sally said in disbelief. "My God—they're desperate enough to sink every one of his boats."

Léonie Blum did not answer. She was staring at Emery Morris, who stood about ten feet away from them, also against the rail, also studying the shore. He was smoking a cigarette; an acid little smile flitted over his face.

"I don't like that man," she whispered to Sally.

"Morris? But he worked with Philip. He's a lawyer."

"I don't like him," the older woman repeated. "He follows you with his eyes. There is something not right about that one, look you."

A qualm of fear ripped through Sally. She refused to encourage Mme. Blum's fantasies, but she knew what the woman meant: Morris was watching her. Four hundred people were crammed inside the *Clothilde,* and yet he was always hovering at her elbow. She'd caught him once with her handbag in his hand, and he'd chided her with false amusement for leaving her belongings behind, on such a ship, where any number of thieves might be lurking among the motley passengers. There was a falseness to his tone, a too-keen interest in her things, that she understood was dangerous.

Philip's file, she thought. *He wants Philip's file.*

There was no reason she should suspect Morris. He'd explained he was simply trying to get to New York—that his wife had gone on before him, and he was expected to join her. But her uneasiness persisted. The one night she and Mme. Blum were allowed to sleep without interruption in their tiny cabin, she'd awakened a few hours before dawn convinced she'd heard the door click closed—convinced someone had been standing over her bed, probing with sweating palms beneath her mattress. The revulsion of fear, the sense of doom descending—Sally hadn't slept again. She'd told Léonie nothing about it at breakfast.

Ten lifeboats were strung out now, across the waters of Calais, the crewmen pulling with the shorebound current. Sally watched as the first of them nosed into the shallows, the soldiers on the beach not even waiting for the boat to make landfall before surging into the waves to meet it, a horde of them flinging themselves over the gunwales. The cries of the crew and the desperate men were like the screech of gulls carried on the wind. Another boat, and another, all nearly swamped, and the *Clothilde*'s sailors reduced to flailing at the crowds with their oars, one of them knocked overboard and his place at the stern seized by a soldier, the boat turning and pulling back for the ship with men still wading deeper into the surf.

"They'd rather drown than be taken by the Germans," she muttered.

"Then *most* of them *will* drown," Morris said indifferently at her side. "The captain *told* me the British are *signaling* over the radio for *any available* boat, fishing or *otherwise,* to take off their troops from Dunkirk. That's a little *north* of us, it seems. The *entire coast* must be *filthy* with *cowards.* There aren't enough boats in the *world* to save them."

"You want the Germans to win, don't you? You like all this...desperation. You like witnessing the pain. You enjoy...*death*..."

He stared back at her implacably, the familiar smile curling at the corners of his tight mustache, and in that instant of calm she understood how he had watched Philip die, how Philip's terror and pain had excited his sexual frenzy, so that he had desecrated the bodies of the two men before leaving them in the sordid misery of their own blood and gone home to his unsuspecting wife in the suburbs. She understood it all without Morris having to say a word. The certainty of it clenched in her stomach with the conviction that his presence on the ship was no accident, and that she was in the most mortal of dangers.

But *why?* What was it about Philip's papers that had driven Morris to murder?

"My dear," he said gently, "I *know* I will enjoy *your* death very *much.*"

Sally heard and lost his words in the terrible whistling rush that filled the air, as though a demon had split the sea and was rising in a wave to engulf the

Clothilde. The torpedos—there were two of them, fired from a German submarine cruising just offshore—tore through the hull and the passengers huddled against its steel walls, penetrating the boiler room and cutting the propeller shaft in two, before exploding with a rush of fire and steam that shot up through the bridge, killing the captain as he watched the first of his lifeboats return.

CHAPTER THIRTY-THREE

The German officer was named Krauss, and his corporal was Bagge. Krauss drove with Memphis next to him in the front seat, while Bagge and von Halban held down the rear. They talked little and made frequent stops, so that Krauss could announce the coming of the Third Reich in any village square that would listen, while Bagge stole petrol at gunpoint when it could be found. Krauss was under orders to reach Marseille in advance of his company; it had become a kind of game with him, a test of how many miles he could put between himself and the German army. He often left a corpse in his wake as a calling card: *Krauss was here.* Von Halban had decided the man was insane.

The two soldiers had abandoned their motorcycles in Alise-Ste-Reine and left the dead infantryman lying in state in the town hall. Hans guessed they'd intended to take Memphis's car, luggage and all, but when they learned who she was—Krauss had liked jazz in his university days—they adopted her as a kind of mascot, an exotic prize awarded to the conquerors. She'd insisted Hans come along for the ride, and because he was

Austrian by birth the Germans assumed his French papers were false; he was some kind of Reich spy, a Fifth Columnist poised for insurgency. He and Memphis were more afraid of losing the car and its contents than of riding with Krauss, and so they'd driven off, leaving the dead boy with his severed throat and the look of blank horror on his murdered father's face, the woman screaming behind them.

They had been traveling now for days.

Krauss avoided large cities where the French population might actually kill him and kept to the back roads of the Rhône valley. Their days had fallen into a kind of pattern: arrive at the next stop by lunchtime, terrify the populace with the German army's approach, steal food and fuel, shoot anyone who complained. They'd drive on until late afternoon, when Bagge would set up camp in a deserted spot and Krauss would chart his progress through France on an army map, plotting at a guess where his division might be. He thought perhaps after Marseille he would single-handedly take North Africa, but his military map ended at the Mediterranean. He would talk as he studied his geography, about the superiority of the German race and the inevitability of the Thousand Year Reich; after they'd eaten something Bagge had stolen, Krauss would order Memphis to sing. She never refused.

Von Halban had learned a good deal about Memphis Jones in the past few days. How she'd survived, for instance. How she'd clawed her way to the top of a world populated by scoundrels. Watching her smile at Krauss, watching her charm the unhinged killer in the well-made uniform, von Halban had understood that to Memphis, all men were the same. They were brutal, they exploited everything they touched, they would kill her as casually as ripping petals off a rose—or they could be used. This was how Memphis had always lived. It was von Halban who found the situation confusing, who suffered in his soul. Von Halban who might not survive.

He'd had only a few chances to talk about their situation because they were never alone. At night either Krauss or Bagge stayed alert on sentry duty, and by day they were all trapped in the car. It was at their most public moments that communication was easiest. When Krauss was shouting his heavily accented French in a village square—Villars-les-Dombes or Pérouges or eventually, several days later, in Grignan—with Bagge standing at attention, Hans could whisper in Memphis's ear.

"We will never reach Marseille, Miss Jones. We will be shot long before."

"I wish I could call Spatz," she muttered. "He told me to call. He'll be worried sick."

While they drove through the Rhône valley or ventured higher into the fringes of the Alps, von Halban made his plans. It wasn't enough to simply escape on foot. He couldn't carry the trunk full of uranium—the trunk Memphis had claimed as her own when Krauss inspected the boot. She'd shown the German her feather boas and satchels full of albums, and when he'd tired of looking at women's things she'd remarked carelessly that the last trunk had a lot of shoes in it. Memphis was partial to shoes. Von Halban knew it was vital to steal the car itself: Leave the two Germans stranded and never look back. But Krauss slept with the ignition key in his pocket.

Hans hadn't considered Memphis. Naturally, she was making plans of her own.

"Am I right in thinkin' it's Sunday?" she purred as the car swept along the road toward the Vaucluse. "The twenty-sixth of May? Where *has* the time gone?"

Krauss assured her that she was correct: It was the sixteenth day of the assault on France. The twenty-sixth of May.

"Then it's my birthday! I'm twenty-six on the twenty-sixth! We gotta have a party, Captain!" She turned and flashed a blazing smile at Bagge. "You look for some bottles of wine when we get to the next town, you hear? *Red* wine. That's the only kind that'll do for Memphis. This girl's gonna celebrate."

Hans had noticed that Krauss was scrupulous in avoiding drink. Perhaps he preferred beer, or did not fully trust himself or his passengers under the influence of alcohol. He congratulated Memphis on the anniversary of her birth but said nothing about finding wine in Châteauneuf-du-Pape, which despite the fame of its name was a small enough village to serve Krauss's purpose. When they pulled up in the Place du Portail and Krauss got out of the car, Bagge at his back with his gun poised, Hans leaned forward and whispered, "Miss Jones. It is in truth your birthday?"

"Shit, no. But we gotta get these boys real happy, you know what I'm sayin'?"

He did. He also knew Krauss was unpredictable. Alcohol might turn his simmering nuttiness into something worse. But when Bagge returned from his daily jaunt lugging cheese and bread and an entire case of wine, von Halban tried to look pleased. Bagge had even stolen wineglasses. They opened the first bottle on the way to Avignon.

She was singing "Ain't Misbehavin'," and the lyric sweetness of the tune—its cagey backhanded seduction—was working on all of them. Memphis was swaying in the firelight in a costume from the Folies Bergères, spangles on her breasts and a triangle of silk over her ass. She'd never worn that kind of thing performing at the Alibi Club, and von Halban was astounded at the raw power of her body.

They'd been drinking steadily for the past hour, although he'd been careful to nurse his glass and make it last. Bagge clutched a bottle by the neck and tipped the wine straight down his throat, singing jaggedly off-tune in German. Krauss was lounging near the fire, tunic unbuttoned; his eyes were narrowed as he watched Memphis. She pulled him up to dance with her, and von Halban saw with disappointment that Krauss was still steady on his feet, still in perfect control. He was leaning toward Memphis as she moved, with the same narrow-eyed, watchful look—and then he reached out and grasped her breast, hard, in his hand.

Von Halban thought an instant of shock flashed over Memphis's face, but her smile only widened and her body seemed to fold into Krauss's like a liquid thing. Krauss mouthed her neck, tearing at her skin with his teeth—and Hans rose, unable to watch anymore; his stomach was cramping with fear. And with something he was sure was envy.

Bagge was standing now, too, his glazed eyes fixed on Memphis. Before Hans could speak or stop him, he hurled himself at Krauss and smashed the bottle of Châteauneuf-du-Pape over his head.

Krauss should have dropped like a stone. Instead, he seized Bagge by the throat and strangled him.

Memphis had stepped backward while Bagge choked and gasped, a look of horror on her face. When Krauss threw down the limp body of his corporal, she turned and stumbled away on her high heels. Von Halban could hear her retching.

He waited, motionless, just beyond the fire's circle of light, until Krauss had crashed through the underbrush after her. Then he bent down quickly over Bagge's corpse, hunting for the man's gun.

CHAPTER THIRTY-FOUR

It was Elie Loewens, the violinist, who became a go-between for Nell with the rest of the Dutch group. It was not that they lacked a common language—all of them spoke French—but the six remained aloof. It was as though they were paying guests and she their landlady. The chilliness both irked and amused her: She could not quite figure out if the Jewish banking clan regarded her as socially inferior, or thought themselves unequal to a countess.

They were unfailingly polite, taking their meals without commenting on the monotony of the food, the gaps in what might have been expected to grace a château's table. But they did not unbend. No conversation flowed, though Nell made an effort in those first few days to inquire about their lives in Holland, their plans for the future. Not even the girl—whose name was Mathilde—responded to Nell. She was Julian de Kuyper's young sister. His wife had died some years before. It was three days before Nell was even sure that Mathilde had a voice.

But she noticed the excellent quality of the girl's

clothes, which spoke for her: They had certainly been made in Paris. The men's suits came from London—Nell could never mistake British tailoring—and they carried themselves like men of standing, men who had a prominence in their world.

Only Elie Loewens looked as though he understood just how completely that prominence had melted into nothing now that the Nazis gripped the Netherlands. There was a hollowness in his eyes that said there would be no going back.

The morning after Spatz had come and gone—Spatz who treated the Dutch Jews with indifferent charm, filling their silence with anecdotes of Amsterdam and his opinion of Rembrandt—Nell decided it was vital she hold a council of war. The strains of the violin had begun as soon as Spatz disappeared down the long gravel drive in Nell's car. She followed the sound until she discovered Elie, standing in his shirtsleeves on the rear terrace. His eyes were closed and his long, sensitive fingers fluttered with the sixth sense of the blind.

She waited until he raised his chin from the instrument and looked at her.

"What is that you're playing?"

It was not what she had intended to say, but he had been practicing the same piece over and over, ever since he'd arrived at Loudenne, and obsessions made Nell curious. They were what defined people, after all.

"*Death and the Maiden*. Schubert. Is there something I can do for you, Countess?"

"I'd like to talk to your brother. And Mr. de Kuyper. Would you find them, and meet me down at the *chai*?"

The young man studied his fingertips, the mark of the strings embedded in the pads. "I'm afraid I don't understand the meaning of that word. *Chai.*"

"The outbuildings—the winery. I'm going ahead to make sure that none of my staff are there."

She turned without waiting for his reply. As she walked toward the *cuverie,* part of her was listening for the strings and the bow, the resumption of frenzy. But the terrace was silent.

They appeared a quarter of an hour later: three men in dark suit jackets, correct and wary. Elie had left his violin behind. Nell was leaning against a massive oak cask, waiting for them, and the scent of grape must and the sugar of fermentation were heavy on the air.

"You know that my cousin, Herr von Dincklage, is German," she said without preamble. "He's no soldier and I would never describe him as a Nazi—although he certainly joined the party years ago. He wouldn't have a career if he hadn't."

"Is he a spy?" Julian de Kuyper asked.

"I assume so." Nell met the banker's eyes. "I didn't know Spatz was planning to visit Loudenne, and I had no time to conceal your presence from him. I asked him to keep your visit a secret. But I cannot promise that he will do so."

"The Germans will take France just as they took Holland," Elie said. "They won't stop until they've driven us into the sea. But do you understand, Countess, that we're running out of places to go?"

"I've heard stories," Nell said slowly. "Of what the Germans did to people in Poland. People who were . . ."

"Jewish," de Kuyper finished. "I've heard those stories, too. Thousands were rounded up. They were shot beside open graves."

"I think we ought to have a plan," Nell said. "A place you can hide. The obvious choice is right here."

"*Here?*" Elie strolled forward, his eyes roaming among the casks, each as tall as a man. "I don't understand."

"This is the first-year room," Nell explained. "Where the wine blended from last year's harvest is sitting in oak. But beneath it is the cellar. Any Germans who come to Loudenne will naturally find it—they'll be looking for the wine. But they'll take the bottles. Not the casks. Even Germans aren't that stupid."

"I want to see your cellar."

She took them downstairs, into the cool, grottolike depths with the arching stone vaults, where the thousands of bottles laid down by Henri over the years were stacked, waiting to be opened or sold. The cellars ran for hundreds of yards beneath the foundations of the *cuverie* and even the château itself, beneath the green lawns that stretched to the Gironde, beneath the gravel drive; a vast series of man-made caverns that were the true heart of Château Loudenne. They ended at the riverbank, in a water gate, where the barrels could be rolled onto boats. The Gironde had always been the primary *route du vin*.

"I brought these casks from Paris ten days ago," she told Elie as she led the three men past the racks of bottles to the fresh oak barrels Henri had stored there. "There's nothing inside them. I intended them for this year's wine. But if I were to set aside a few—enough to hold each of you, Mathilde and the children—"

"For the rest of the war?" Julian de Kuyper burst out.

"At least until the danger has passed. Until the Germans—if they come—have moved on..."

De Kuyper turned away, his hands clenching.

"God in Heaven," he muttered. "Is this what we've come to?"

Three days later, the Americans arrived.

Joe Hearst led them in his beautiful blue Buick, straight from the Esplanade de Quinconces. He'd waited only for Noakes, the consul, to write his note of introduction to the Countess of Loudenne before rounding up the children who played by the fountains and their parents lounging in the sun. It was an hour from Bordeaux to the part of the Médoc where Nell lived, and Hearst knew that if she agreed to take all fifty of his refugees they'd be pitching tents in near-darkness. He'd told every adult in his group to put three hundred francs in the countess's kitty; he hoped it would be enough to buy them room.

Nell was having tea alone in the salon when the cavalcade appeared—tea being the one British custom she could not abandon, however many years she lived in France—and for an instant her heart came into her mouth as she heard the rumble of wheels. She was certain Spatz had betrayed her.

"Do you hold Public Days at Loudenne," Elie Loewens

asked from the doorway, "or are there still tourists in France?"

Nell set down her teacup, and went to meet the strangers.

By nightfall, there were seventy people sheltering at the château. Nell saw no reason to explain the Dutch guests—who merited rooms inside—to the diplomats wandering the grounds. This was not, after all, an American war.

"You want a boat?" the agent repeated, "to cross the Channel? You might as well ask if we can get you to New York. Or the moon. Haven't you heard the radio broadcasts, monsieur?"

It was Tuesday, the twenty-eighth of May, and Hearst was standing in one of Noakes's suggested shipping offices in the heart of Bordeaux. He'd recovered something of his usual good temper in the past few days at Loudenne, but the incredulity in the agent's voice—the disbelief bordering on mockery—raised his hackles instantly.

"No. I haven't heard a radio. What's happened?"

"The Germans have reached the Channel. Every available boat has been told to report to Dunkirk. There's a massive evacuation on. They say half a million soldiers are fighting for a place in line on the beach. Half a million! Now tell me we haven't lost the war."

"Are you saying there are no boats coming into Bordeaux? None at all? What about merchant ships?

Transatlantic steamers? We'll skip the Channel and head straight for New York if we have to."

The shipping agent grinned at him. "Be my guest, monsieur. You'll be sunk before you leave Le Verdon."

"German subs?"

"They torpedoed a Dutch steamer a few days ago— the *Clothilde*—off Calais."

"What did you say?"

Hearst was gripping the man's desk now, his body gone cold. *Sally,* his mind screamed. *Sally. And I made you go.*

"I only mention it," the agent continued, looking curiously at Hearst, "because they brought the survivors in this morning. They're down at the *préfecture,* having their papers checked—"

Hearst was out the door before the man could finish.

There were fifty-nine people huddled in the waiting room of the *préfecture* building in the center of town: twenty-nine men, twelve children, and eighteen women.

None of them was Sally King.

CHAPTER THIRTY-FIVE

At the moment the torpedo hit, Sally was hurled from the *Clothilde*'s deck into the sea.

It was a long fall; if she had been standing on a passenger liner—the *Normandie*, for instance—she would never have survived it. But the *Clothilde* was a smaller class of vessel and the distance from rail to waves was roughly equivalent to a jump from a high-diving board. Her body shuddered as it slapped the water. She was conscious of surprise as she plummeted through: struggling against her own momentum, eight feet down, twelve feet, her ears pounding with pain. Just short of twenty feet below the surface she kicked upward again.

Her head broke into the air and she screamed—more from shock at being alive, from the sheer terror of survival, than anything else. She shook the water out of her eyes.

The *Clothilde* was engulfed in flames. The stern was already below water, the bow keeling high, and the air was filled with the crackling of fire and the confused shouting of people still struggling on the ship. She glanced around wildly, searching for Léonie Blum.

Floating near her in the water were pieces of the hull, blasted out of its living sides. There were bodies and bales of sodden hay from the livestock hold and one horse, nose high, swimming desperately in circles. No Léonie Blum. Then she saw something familiar: the domed lid of a coffin.

It bobbed sickly a few yards from where she was treading water. One end had been torn away and she could see the soles of Philip's shoes. As she watched, the sea poured through the opening, and with unconscious mimicry the casket upended like the ship, sliding stern-first under the waves.

Oh, God, she thought, kicking toward it frantically. *I'll never find you in all this water...your mother...I promised to take you home...*

She dove, eyes straining through the murky sea, the dimness humped and horribly peopled with the dead and their belongings, hair streaming like seaweed, everything falling in slow motion, a million bubbles rising. The coffin was gone. The sheer pain of it made her gasp and she bucked skyward with a mouthful of water brimming in her lungs.

He was gone, completely gone. She could never save him now from the killers who'd snuffed his life, Morris and Shoop and all the others at S&C who cared more about money and silence than they did about Philip. The lies and the waste. *Justice.* She'd failed.

The back of her head slammed into something solid and hard.

The hull of a lifeboat.

She glanced over her shoulder, flung out an arm. The

lifeboat must have held the crew or some of the French soldiers the *Clothilde* had tried to take off the Calais beach, but it was empty and capsized now. The hull curved toward the sky like the shell of a peanut. Her fingers scrabbled over the wood, which was slick with water and the fresh oil paint the ship's crew had constantly applied to it. The sea current was dragging her under the overturned boat; if it succeeded she would die, confused by the solid weight above her, unable to surface. She dug her nails into a crack between the hull's planks and hung on.

She'd lost her shoes when she hit the water. Her bare legs flailed beneath the waterlogged cotton of her spring dress. And then her feet touched something else.

Some*one* else.

Another person was hanging from the opposite side of the lifeboat, clutching the hull like Sally.

With a leap of hope, she cried out. "Hello! Is there someone there? Can you reach me? Can you help me right the boat?"

Her companion might have laughed.

A hand clutched at Sally's wrist: a hard, strong, and cruel hand, that bent all its will in prying her fingers from the wood that might have saved her.

"*Poor* Miss King," Emery Morris rasped. "Didn't I *tell* you I would enjoy watching you *die?*"

It was a strange little drama that played out off Calais: the two of them keeping the twelve-foot hull between them, fighting each other with their feet and their hands. Circling the boat as though it were a dinner table, Sally clutching with her fingers at the gunwale when she could not grasp the keel. Once in a while Morris grunted with exertion, and she could hope he was tiring. The numbing cold of the Atlantic was taking its toll in the increasing stiffness of her limbs.

He wanted to catch up with her, to reach her side of the capsized boat before she reached his. It was a foolish waste of energy on Morris's part; the sea was far more likely to kill her than he was. Darkness was falling now and it had begun to rain. The flaming wreck of the *Clothilde* was gone, in a sudden rushing whirlpool of water that sucked down all debris within twenty yards of the ship: bodies, crates, the struggling horse. Sally and Morris were beyond that danger, beyond any capability of saving the passengers who dove from the prow in its final seconds—the Channel current was ripping them surely south, the lights of Calais dwindling. Sally knew there were other boats near the ship, lifeboats filled with Dutch crewmen and French soldiers, with no room for survivors; salvation did not lie that way. Because she was growing tired, because panic was climbing into her mouth and her brain with the falling dark and the sound of Morris's panting, constant and ever closer, she almost gave up.

Then she remembered Philip.

"Why did you kill him?" she gasped out. "Why did Philip have to die?"

"Because he couldn't *mind* his own *business,*" Morris snapped. "Nosing around in my *files. Questioning* everything."

"I.G. Farben. The dead German engineer."

"I.G. *Farben*," he repeated sarcastically. "The only ones with the strength of *will* to do their *job*. But if you know all about *that*, you've read my papers. Stilwell *gave* them to you, *didn't* he?"

He was nearly upon her. Sally decided it was time to stop struggling.

She waited until he rounded the stern of the boat, until she could see his face and look him directly in the eye. The surprise of her capitulation brought him up short, his hands motionless on the hull, staring at her.

"Philip gave the papers to the American embassy," she told him. "They've already sent them to Allen Dulles in New York. Soon everyone will know what you've done." It was a lie, of course—the documents were at the bottom of the sea—but Morris didn't need to know he was safe. "You're being hunted for murder."

His face convulsed—with rage? Or laughter?

Sally filled her lungs and thrust herself under the capsized boat.

It was utterly dark here, the curving height of the hull punctuated by the cross-planks of its seats, but a bubble of air remained between boat and water. She reached out and felt the sides, four feet across. He would wait for her to emerge or he would come after her; one of the two. She was betting he would follow, and she would be ready for him when he did.

She was wrong.

The boat suddenly crashed down on her head, forcing her underwater, the pain of it nearly knocking her senseless. She had a sharp vision of Morris, hurling himself onto the hull with all his weight and failing energy, forcing the boat deeper, preventing her escape. Drowning her.

She reached out blindly for the gunwale and found his ankle.

He kicked wildly, but Sally grasped the leg with both hands, dragging it down.

All his weight was on the hull: He was not a large man, but a wiry one, with desperate strength, clinging like a limpet to the wood. As Sally pulled, Morris clawed the capsized boat over.

He may have realized what he was doing as it happened, but the momentum was too great to reverse. The boat righted with a sudden spring, like a cork popping to the surface.

Morris lost his grip; with a cry, he fell into the sea.

The unexpected release thrust Sally deeper underwater, still clutching the man's leg. He kicked out savagely at her head. The pain burst through her brain. She released him.

The blackness of the sky at the surface disoriented her. With no light from above, she could not tell if she was reaching upward toward air or swimming deeper. Her lungs were bursting and she could see Death now, could feel it in an iron band around her chest: the desire to drink water as though it were air.

Her head broke the surface. Shuddering drafts of rain swept overhead; the waves were jagged and surging. Another time, the sea might have terrified her. Not now.

She drew breath in starving gasps. And after a few seconds, looked around for Morris.

A dipping wave revealed him ten feet away, the lifeboat spinning out of reach. As she watched, he howled, threw his arms up to the sky, and sank like a stone.

My God, she thought. *He can't swim.*

Her own part in this—the way she'd dragged him from the boat—knifed through her sickeningly and she began to crawl against the heavy seas that separated them. She could not watch another man go under the waves like a scuttled ship. She screamed Morris's name through the rain and blackness. The wind or perhaps the drowning man, invisible now, screamed back. The lifeboat they'd fought over vanished into a trough of wave. Sally shouted again and again, the ocean slapping into her mouth, until her voice gave out.

Her strength was ebbing. Morris was gone.

She drifted with the current, alone in all the vastness of the sea, aware of the great cold that had cut off sensation in her bare feet, the animal chill that wracked her body. It would be like falling asleep, she thought—like drifting into the night for good—and it occurred to her that they would both lie here forever, now: she and Philip.

She thought once of Joe Hearst with a warm sadness. He would blame himself.

CHAPTER THIRTY-SIX

Von Halban roared through Avignon as though Hell and all its demons were at his heels, through the quiet streets of St-Rémy, driving past Arles and down along the Rhône into the marshland of the Camargue. Every settlement or whitewashed *cabane*, every tumbled Roman ruin, was blacked out completely under the ink-colored sky of the Côte d'Azur.

He knew that even now there might be German warships, German submarines, in the waters that curled far below this high cliff road. He drove with the painted headlights throwing a ghoulish blue glare over the roadbed, and he met no one—not a single truck or even bicycle—until twenty-three minutes past five o'clock in the morning, when a solitary woman plodding at the verge shook her fist at the car as it plunged toward Marseille.

Memphis was swaddled in one of her evening coats, the first thing she'd been able to lay hands on, a black velvet cape of enormous proportions. For a while Hans thought she was sleeping but a faint tremor in the surrounding air told him she was trembling uncontrollably, her jaw clenched, her face rigid. Krauss had caught up with her twelve feet from the campfire, and by the time von Halban had stolen his dead corporal's gun there was no pulling the German off Memphis's body; he'd pinned her facedown and was sodomizing her. Memphis screamed like a tortured dog, and von Halban shouted orders that Krauss ignored. In the end Hans raised the revolver and shot Krauss point-blank in the base of the skull.

He fell heavily on Memphis, his penis still thrust into her body, and von Halban had been forced to drag the perfect athlete's frame off her, his own hands almost incapable of working, his fingers sliding on muscle and bone. She crawled away like a crushed bird; she forced herself to her feet and stumbled on into the woods as though even von Halban might kill her. When he reached her he said nothing. He did not even try to touch her.

She had curled into a fetal ball, as though if she hugged her nakedness she might be fine, she might be a baby somebody loved, not a hunk of skewered meat. He took off his jacket and laid it gently over her. They sat like that, two stones in the night, for almost an hour, the smell of semen and blood rising around them.

"Marseille," he said, as the prison of Château d'If rose from its island in the sea. "They will not find us here."

The German soldiers who'd taken their car might be dead, but the whole German army was somewhere behind them, and neither Memphis nor von Halban would ever again feel safe.

"Let me out of this car," she whispered. "I got to get out of this car."

He had been thinking about the problem as he drove. Her husband was supposed to be at the Hôtel d'Angleterre, but so much time had passed that von Halban expected the man to have gone on to North Africa. For his part, he was ordered to find the *Foudroyant* and hand over the uranium to Captain Bedoyer. Neither errand seemed as important as the woman shivering beside him now.

"You need a doctor, I think."

She shook her head furiously. "There's nothin' wrong with me that a hot bath and good coffee won't cure."

"Miss Jones—" He slowed the car and brought it to rest on the narrow shoulder above the cliffs, the whole Greco-Roman settlement of Massilia spread out beneath them, coral-colored and filthy in the first light. "It would be well if I found your husband, yes?"

"Fuck Raoul."

"Or we could call Spatz. You wished to call Spatz, I think."

"Fuck him, too." She opened the collar of her velvet cape with swift fingers. "If this is what Germany plans to do to France, I want no part of it, understand?"

He nodded wordlessly. Her skin where it was visible in the cleft of her cape was shining. Her profile was as timeless and ancient as the old city at their feet, the profile of a Cleopatra.

"What would you have me do?"

"Whatever you came south for, mistuh," she shot back. "I'll go my own way."

He said nothing as the light lit the sky. Her shuddering had stopped, but she was still huddled beneath the enveloping cloak. Eventually she would look at him, would acknowledge everything that had occurred, that he had witnessed her rape and had killed her attacker, he who'd never felt that kind of violence, who'd never panicked and shot a man dead. Eventually she would acknowledge that he was scared to death, too.

She said, "What've you got in that trunk you told them was mine?"

"Four hundred kilos of uranium metal encased in lead."

Her head came around. She was exhausted and in pain and she had no idea what uranium was.

"They would have murdered us both, had they known what we carried," he said apologetically. "It is worth the whole bloody war, Miss Jones."

She put her hand to her mouth and gnawed at her fingers.

He looked away, out to sea. "I would never have saved it without you. I would not have reached Marseille alive. But if I could have spared you this horror, Miss Jones— death or dishonor would be nothing."

Spatz's money bought her coffee and a bath in a hotel that was not the d'Angleterre but a quieter place off the Rue des Oliviers. Von Halban approached

Reception with the breezy confidence of a man who has shot his enemy at close range, the agent and representative of a celebrity swathed in black velvet, defying the authority behind the desk to comment on his travel-stained clothes, the smear of blood on his trousers.

"Miss Jones intends to embark for North Africa. She wishes only to rest before her journey. Two rooms, please."

In the end it was the quantity of luggage and the fine motorcar pulled up before the door that convinced the hotel to find Memphis a spare suite. They gave von Halban a room on the ground floor usually reserved for servants.

"Is the fleet in port?" he asked.

Reception's small black eyes flicked over him, registered the traitor's accent, shrugged. "The *French* fleet, monsieur, hauled anchor three days ago. But *your* U-boats are in the Channel."

Not my U-boats, he wanted to say; but could no longer make the effort to explain himself. He was not German, but he felt complicit. He had stood by and watched a woman raped.

Memphis slept for nine hours. She ordered dinner brought to her upstairs. Von Halban spent the intervening period walking the docks in a vain search for the *Foudroyant,* wondering what in heaven he ought to do. He could not sit and wait for the Germans to come; he could not turn around and go back to Paris with his dangerous cargo. He was terrified to board a boat for Marseille and lose his family forever.

At bedtime, he received a note summoning him to Memphis.

"What you gonna do with that trunk?" she demanded. She was dressed in silk and propped up on a sofa. "You can't take it back to Paris."

"Maybe I will throw it into the sea."

"Me, I'm going to Casablanca. M. Etienne at the front desk arranged it—bought my passage himself—for only four times the cost of a lousy ticket. I call that a bargain in time of war. I think he's *afraid* of that accent of yours."

"You are shrewd, Miss Jones. You will know how to survive."

She gave him one naked look. "I should be dead. We both know that. I never thanked you. I never— So I'm saying it now: Come with me?"

"To Casablanca?"

"You could bring your trunk. Get it where it needs to go."

"Miss Jones—"

"I don't need an answer tonight. But we'll have to pay the man soon if you want a ticket, understand?"

Hans thought of Annick and his daughters. Of Joliot-Curie, that final night in the lab: *Hide it somewhere safe, where no one can steal it and no one can be hurt by it.*

"Thank you," he told her. "I will think what we must do."

CHAPTER THIRTY-SEVEN

The shipping agent's face had grown more lined and weary in the past few days, and Hearst knew before he spoke what the news would be.

"No ships?" he suggested.

"*Non et non et non,*" the man snapped. "Surely you are not an imbecile, Mr. American. How can there be ships in Bordeaux when every boat in Europe is moored off Dunkirk? Five days it has been going on, the small fishing boats and the private launches moving back and forth between England and France, and still there are hundreds of thousands on the beaches. They are all French, I understand, the ones who are left behind—because of course, the *English* run the boats and they take their own people first. That is always the English way, *hein*? They start these wars with the Boches and then they run—"

He stopped short, his expression changing. "*Bonjour,* Madame la Comtesse."

Nell had dressed for this trip into Bordeaux in one of her narrow Parisian suits and a hat that swooped like a palm frond. She was not the same woman Hearst had watched stride around her vineyards this past week, stopping to talk to the embassy children or the strange Dutch refugees, fending off Mims Tarnow's presumptions with a satiric lift of her brow. Mims was determined to be invited into the château for tea, or perhaps a real bath, and Nell was equally determined not to admit her.

"*Bonjour,* Monsieur Vingtain," she said briskly. "I, you observe, have not run."

"Of course not, Comtesse. I did not mean—"

"Perhaps you would be so good as to cable London or New York about transatlantic vessels expected to arrive in the next few weeks? We'll check back in an hour to learn what you've heard, *bien?*"

"*Oui, c'est bien,*" the clerk replied, his face flaming. "And madame—I am desolated at the news of the comte's capture. We were all sorry to hear—"

"Thank you, monsieur."

She said the words with dignity, but as they left the small room Hearst saw the lines around her mouth tighten.

"Will you stay here?" he asked as they walked toward the quai. "Even if it's all over, soon?"

"Where else should I go? Loudenne is my home."

"I thought—family in England, perhaps."

She shrugged. "They're no safer than we are here. And I would never leave without word of Bertrand and Roger."

"Your husband and..."

"Henri's grandson. Henri keeps the whole vineyard going but he's really only living for Roger. I feel so culpable." Her face twisted with a sudden, sharp pain. "The boy's only nineteen. He joined Bertrand's company as soon as war was declared. God knows what could happen to him in the hands of those people. We don't even know if they killed them, or—"

They'd reached the city quai, busy and commercial and lined with elegant town houses, the river narrow enough here to imagine pitching a stone to the opposite bank, a manageable waterway utterly unlike the wide, swift sweep of the Gironde estuary to the north.

"I owe Henri everything," she continued. "He's kept Loudenne together for years, even when Bertrand— He's not just someone I've hired. He and Roger are family."

It seemed to Hearst that she was more concerned for her *maître de chai* than for her husband. Nell had been schooled in the life of great estates, where the ties between landowner and dependent were timeless and fundamental. She saw herself at the center of a constellation of people who knew no other world than Loudenne. Nell was responsible. Nell would not run.

"It's different for you," she said. "This isn't your war. You should go home as soon as you can."

"That's what I told Sally King," he said, staring out over the river. "But she wanted to stay. Like me, she knew that home was here. I should never have—"

He bit off the words *meddled in her life*. He'd told Nell about the *Clothilde*: torpedoes striking, the deck shattering in flame. The image of Sally slipping under the waves . . .

"You blame yourself," Nell observed.

"Of course I blame myself!"

"She had an extraordinary presence. I saw her pictures often, in magazines."

"There was far more to Sally than just a pretty face."

"You were in love with her?"

He laughed harshly. "I never once allowed myself to ask that question. There was no time, and it seemed self-indulgent in the middle of the German invasion."

"But when the whole world is on the point of death," she persisted, "the truth is all that matters. Answer my question, Joe. If only to yourself. Even if she *is* gone."

He caught the passion in her voice and wondered at it. Was this for Bertrand? Or someone else?

"Listen," she said, her hand suddenly on his arm. "That fishing boat. At the far end of the quai. They're calling for help."

"Must be Dunkirk. They've got stretchers on the deck. But why bring evacuees here? They're supposed to go to England."

"Maybe they're French," Nell said, then broke into a run.

Hearst went after her. She was thinking, he knew, of her husband or perhaps of the boy Roger, hoping against hope that the reports had been wrong, the company hadn't surrendered, they'd been pulled off the beach like so many others. His heart was wrung for her—for the way hope reignited even when it ought to be dead. And then he stopped short.

A stretcher was rising in the hands of the Bordeaux fishermen: a limp figure in a sodden dress, eyes closed, face pale as death.

"*Sally,*" he whispered.

It was nearly three hours before a doctor appeared in the crowded corridor of the Bordeaux hospital, but Nell insisted on waiting with Hearst. It was Nell who'd gotten the story out of the fishing boat's crew as they unloaded the rest of the casualties from their latest run up the Brittany coast: a platoon of lost French soldiers trapped by the German army well south of Dunkirk, and three people washed up on various beaches. One of these was Sally. The Channel tides in the grip of a twilight squall had swept her south and thrust her firmly toward shore somewhere off the Côte d'Albâtre of Normandy, where she had come to grief on the rocks.

A boy found her in the bright Sunday morning, a boy who'd gone to look for soldiers on the beach; she was lying as though dead with the cold spring surf washing over her, facedown in the chilly sand. Hearst listened to the story in the fisherman's heavy Médoc accent and imagined the girl in the morgue, hair cascading off her vulnerable neck, the swan's arc of shoulder blade through the thin cotton dress.

She was not dead. She'd been unconscious, however, from the time she was carried into the village of

Fécamp four days ago. It would be the rocks, the fisherman said; the limestone cliffs of the Alabaster coast. That would explain the broken arm, as well.

It was her left arm, swollen and bruised and bent at an alarming angle, as though she had reached out to clutch or fend off a cliff face and the rocks had slapped her hard in retribution. There were bruises and gashes on her face and legs. The long exposure in chilling sea had inflamed her lungs and she burned with fever, her breathing wracked and painful. Hearst tried to sit by the stretcher, but his gaze would shift inevitably to Sally's eyelids, fluttering with her dreams, the wild rolling of her eyes beneath the protective skin, and he would rise impatiently and pace, shoving his long, lean frame through the waiting wounded.

"You should find Noakes," Nell told him tersely. "He could cable her family. Inform them she's alive. They may have heard about the *Clothilde*. They will want to know."

The thought gave him direction and served to kill an hour of time. When he returned from the U.S. consulate, Sally still had not awakened. And so he paced, stifling the impulse to demand a doctor at the top of his American lungs.

The fishing boat had put in to shore north of Dieppe in response to a signal from the company of marooned soldiers, a transport crew who'd abandoned their vehicles and supplies and had only their guns and a case of wine for moral support. They'd come through Fécamp on their way to the beach and heard of a woman in desperate need of a hospital. The German army was nearly in Dieppe and so the fishermen decided to evacuate Sally, too.

"Severe concussion," the doctor told them. "Pneumonia as well. We'll set the arm. There's little else we can do for her."

"Will she live?" Hearst asked.

"Look you, monsieur," the doctor said bitterly, "I stopped playing God when the Germans arrived."

CHAPTER THIRTY-EIGHT

Spatz was angry as he walked the Marseille waterfront in search of them, but he was masking his feelings well. No frustration in the Sparrow's genial smile, the direct and inviting gaze.

He considered himself a good judge of character, but in recent days his judgment had failed him badly. Nell had seduced Joliot-Curie but refused to betray him, and when Spatz reminded her that he needed information if he was to sell his soul to the British, she'd said, almost as an afterthought, that their old friend Mad Jack knew everything about the French bomb already.

That had rocked him badly.

Nell knew more than she was telling, but she was obsessed with her Jews and bored by physics. She was harboring love like an illness, Spatz thought. He would have to consider how to control her. It might be the gift of Joliot's freedom; it might be Bertrand's.

Perhaps it would be the Jews.

But this Friday, the thirty-first of May, he'd come to Marseille in search of Memphis. It was her car he saw first.

The sleek touring sedan was pulled up inside the cordon that separated the Moroccan ship from the crowd of swaying and frantic people attempting to board it. Von Halban was leaning against the front fender, one foot crossed casually over the opposite ankle, his back to the press of refugees. He may have been conscious of the wave of people behind him, of the insults and pleas hurled in seven different languages; his expression was almost too dignified. There was only one trunk left in the car and Spatz recognized it as von Halban's own—he'd help to load it the night they left Paris, heavy as lead. The uranium must be inside. Von Halban had failed, then. He hadn't delivered it.

His heart lifting, Spatz adjusted his hat and thrust through the crowd. He had only to mutter in German, conscious of the language's frightening power, to part the mass as easily as the Red Sea.

Von Halban reached into his breast pocket and withdrew a packet of tickets. The noise of the quai was preying upon him: stevedores and sailors, the passengers and their friends who'd gathered to wave good-bye, the press of fingers at his back. *Refugees.* Which was what he was now, he realized, cut loose from his mission and his home. He felt a kind of vertigo, as though he were standing on the parapet of a high window and had no choice but to jump. He must leap across the eight-foot span of water separating the dock from the boat and claw his way on board. It was madness to go back. He would be deported to a labor camp as soon as he reached Paris.

"Hello, old man," Spatz said.

The cordon had opened for him as readily as the Alibi Club. He was smiling at Hans, but von Halban smelled the danger in the air around him, bitter as cordite.

"How did you find us?"

Spatz shrugged. "Followed the blood."

It was a shock, the words thrown so carelessly on the ground between them. He thought of the two dead Germans, nodded weakly.

"Where is she?"

"Inspecting her cabin. Miss Jones is very careful about her luggage."

"No kidding." He drew out a cigarette, offered one to Hans. "But your luggage stays," he observed. "You're not going with her?"

"How is Annick?" von Halban asked. "My girls?"

"Fine."

"They reached her parents, yes?"

Spatz did not reply. His eyes came up to von Halban's. There was a taunt in the man's gaze that reminded von Halban of the way a cat looked when it played with a mouse.

"That luggage," Spatz mused. "I thought when I helped you load it in Paris that it was heavy as lead. I'm right, aren't I?"

The vertigo pitched and roared in his ears; he was suddenly too tired to fight it anymore, to keep pretending. "Spatz—why do you make a woman your personal spy? Why not put yourself beside me in the car, if you want what I carried so badly?"

"Because you would never have agreed to take me," the German answered reasonably, "and you would never have opened your mind to me as you did to Memphis. I knew you would. I was always certain to use that."

In one blinding second, von Halban saw it all: the woman vulnerable, suffering despite her defiance; his own guilt and pity. The naïve way he'd assumed that shared danger meant shared truth. He'd shifted the uranium from his own trunk to hers in the belief it was the sole chance he had of getting it out of France. He'd handed a jazz chanteuse the future of French science. To turn over to her lover at the first opportunity.

She was coming down the gangplank toward them, smiling brilliantly, as though Spatz were the only man in the world she'd ever wanted—as though the day was complete merely because he'd arrived. Von Halban watched, and it seemed to him that even the clamor of the desperate people pressing at his back ceased for an instant, as though the raw animal grace of Memphis's form, the intoxicating wildness of her look, had the power to silence even war.

"Hey, baby," she said softly, and wrapped her arms around Spatz. "I got a bunk big enough for two."

CHAPTER THIRTY-NINE

"You've made yourself *bien confortable* here," Jacques Allier observed as he stepped into the drawing room of Clair Logis.

The villa sat on Rue Etienne-Dollet, not a bad part of Clermont-Ferrand. After disposing of Product Z, as Allier persisted in calling it, Moureu and Kowarski had mounted a hurried hunt through town for vacant properties. Clair Logis was a summer place, owned by a family who lived in Paris. The house agents had been only too glad to take cash down, with times so uncertain—and Moureu was authorized to sign a month's lease.

Kowarski had transformed the house in the subsequent two weeks. His Russian wolfhound, Boris, had a bed in the main salon, where half of Joliot's lab was already up and running; the villa's dining room table was now a bench for experiments. Even the kitchen had a gas-fed torch in one corner for improvised glassblowing and welding.

Kowarski hadn't shaved in days. He seemed to be living in his lab coat, with a hunk of bread permanently stuffed in one pocket and his reading glasses in another.

He was happy in the belief he'd left war behind and could work now in peace. He told Allier he was pursuing what he called a divergent chain reaction, in a mixture of uranium oxide and heavy water. Allier thought he could guess where Lew had obtained his deuterium; he decided not to inquire about the uranium oxide.

"Have you heard from your colleague—Herr von Halban?"

"Not a word," Kowarski said cheerfully. "But Hans is all right. He'll turn up one day. How are things in Paris?"

"*Très mal.* You heard the Belgians surrendered?"

"Three days ago. The twenty-eighth of May. I had the radio on." Kowarski preferred his phonograph records, which he'd managed to bring—along with his wolfhound—south in the truck. His taste ran to experimental Russian composers, dissonant and jarring, a corollary to the random paths of nuclear particles.

He bit off a hunk of bread. "Fucking *Belges.* Between them opening the front door and the Brits running out the back—" He shrugged. "What German *wouldn't* drive down for a look at Paris?"

"There have been grave errors on the government's part," Allier said slowly, as though the words were treason. *"Vous n'avez aucune idée—"*

How to tell the scientist about the poor intelligence, the errors in judgment, the squabbles and fear of old men? It didn't matter anymore. Everyone at the Armaments Ministry knew the war was lost. The government would be gone in a matter of days. There were tanks lying along every road out of the Ardennes and two million French soldiers, killed or abandoned to the enemy. Only the French people continued to believe.

"It's a grand country, this." Kowarski sighed. "I'd never seen the Auvergne before. Moureu, now—he was practically raised here as a boy. Loves these hills. Even the air is different, Allier. Stronger and fresher. I can't wait to bring my family down."

Allier could have told Kowarski he was a heartbeat away from internment, and all his family with him; but though he'd been willing to face death alone in a Norwegian aerodrome, he was a coward in other things. When the time came to take Kowarski in the night, Allier would be far away.

"Don't send for your wife," he advised. "You may have to move on."

"But I've already told her we've got Clair Logis for a month!"

"I hope," Allier said sharply, "that you never refer to the villa by name. Particularly when you correspond with Joliot. If you must mention the place, say only *Rue Etienne-Dollet*. It's safest that way."

Kowarski threw back his head and laughed, but at that moment there was a knock on the door and both men fell silent, staring at each other. It was after nine o'clock at night and the entire town was under blackout darkness.

The wolfhound scrabbled to its feet, hackles rising.

"Moureu?" Allier whispered.

Kowarski shook his head. "He's gone back to Paris. To help Joliot break down the lab."

"Who, then?"

"I'd better answer the door."

Allier watched Kowarski follow his dog to the door in unreasoning panic. He carried a gun in the pocket of his coat, but he'd left that in his Simca; he'd had no time to unload the luggage. For no reason he could name he wanted his gun very badly right now.

Boris whined like a child and Kowarski threw open the door.

"Hans!" He spread his arms wide in a Russian bear hug. "How good to see you! You survived the trip south, eh?"

Allier could see von Halban's face, too white and disembodied in the blacked-out doorway. No lights on the threshold, no lights at the villa's entrance or in Rue Etienne-Dollet, and behind von Halban was the wealth of Auvergne night.

Von Halban looked strained and unnatural, he seemed rooted to the threshold, and when his eyes found Allier's, there was a beseeching terror in them.

Allier began to move. He was too late.

Von Halban stepped woodenly through the door of Clair Logis, his hands reaching for Kowarski. There was another man behind him—a tall blond man that, to his horror, Allier knew.

He'd last seen him running after the wrong plane, two months ago, on a night of cold and death in Norway.

The man was smiling, indifferent to Allier's presence. It was possible he'd forgotten the planes for Perth and Amsterdam, the Italian girl shot down over the North Sea. He had a gun at von Halban's back.

"I'm sorry, Lew," von Halban muttered. "I'm so sorry. He has come for the water, yes?"

CHAPTER FORTY

When Allier finally reached Frédéric Joliot-Curie four days later, the physicist was standing on the paving stones behind the Labo de Physique, watching the documents burn.

He had come to the end of six years' accumulation of paper, everything thrown onto the blaze from the conviction that nothing was worth saving anymore. The important things were in his brain, or had already been published long ago; if the rest of his jottings were lost to posterity, so much the better. The vacuum he left behind would provide other men with something to discover, something to invent, in the happy delusion of originality.

He reached into his lab coat pocket and withdrew a bundle of letters. They had lived for the past decade among his lab notes, too incendiary to store with socks and undergarments. He traced his own name, written in Nell's careless and jagged pen; the foreign stamps posted from England. In the midst of so much despair and ending, he yearned for the sound of her voice.

It occurred to him to wonder if Irène had read all these words, years ago. It hardly mattered now. Nell was no longer his private country, his sea for voyaging. He had bartered that secret self for the privilege of seeing his children.

He tossed the letters into the flames.

When Allier told him about the German from Norway who'd appeared at von Halban's back, Joliot did not immediately share the truth: that the heavy water was safe at a Bordeaux vineyard. He listened to Allier in silence—to the bitter self-recrimination, the certainty of betrayal among foreigners, the hatred for von Halban, who'd been thrown into an Auvergne jail once his German friend left with the water. When Allier was done, Joliot said only, "Let him go."

"Are you out of your *mind*?" Allier retorted savagely. "Will you never see the truth, *enfin,* even when it lives in your pocket?"

"Let him go," Joliot repeated. "It's obvious the Nazi must have threatened his family. Or me. Yes, perhaps it was me. I was to be killed in some horrible way, and von Halban got noble at the wrong moment."

Allier stared at him impotently, his mild banker's face bewildered. Joliot said, "It's only water, Jacques."

"Which I very nearly paid for with my life!"

"On two separate occasions. I know. And I'm grateful. But the whole country is going to the dogs before our very eyes. We tried our best. We failed."

"We were betrayed."

Joliot shook his head gently. "We were *found.* Nothing more than that. It wasn't Hans's life that was at stake—he's the sort who'd die gladly. But he would never bargain with someone else's life. I know the man, Jacques. I know the man."

"You can't be wrong, can you?" Allier snarled. "The great Frédéric Joliot-Curie, Nobel genius, the man who married fame for the sake of his career—"

Without turning, Joliot said, "Did you find the uranium?"

"What?"

"The uranium metal von Halban was supposed to deliver to the French navy. Did he tell you where it is?"

"He refused."

Good man, Joliot thought. And walked away.

He ran Mad Jack to earth in a suite at the Hôtel Meurice, entertaining three women. Joliot suspected they were *filles de joie* or perhaps chorus girls from the Folies Bergères, but he remembered Allier saying the earl's tastes in women were varied and quixotic. He declined an offer of champagne but accepted a slice of pâté de foie gras. The earl escorted the women to the door with a bottle in each hand.

"Well," he said as he sat back down at his dining table and thrust his game foot onto a neighboring chair, "have you decided to jump? Are you coming to England?"

"No." Joliot eyed the warm bread lingering between them and realized it had been days since he'd eaten properly. The food shortages had begun with so many grocers and bakers closing their shops; the hemorrhage from Paris since the first of June had been painful. "Somebody has to stay in France. Otherwise we'll start thinking it was always German."

Mad Jack smiled, and Joliot watched the sensual curve of his lips, the possibility of humor or cruelty they held. Generations of inbreeding were responsible for the man's eccentricities—and his acute intelligence.

"I might have gone to Dunkirk, you know," the earl said. "Or dodged Messerschmitts all the way across the Channel. I won't wait here long enough to be hanged by Jerry. But if you change your mind in the next few days, give me a jingle. I'll make arrangements for you and your family."

He offered the bread basket. Joliot took a slice.

"What I chiefly need," he said, "is a boat."

Mad Jack laughed. "You and every bloody Frenchman. There's two hundred thousand of your countrymen looking for a ship at this very moment, and I'm sorry to say they're dashed out of luck."

"I don't want it for myself. It's for the heavy water we took out of Norway. It ought to be sent to England before France falls."

The earl's bright blue eyes rose to meet his. "I understood the stuff was shanghaied."

"I sent decoy canisters to the Auvergne."

"*Did* you, now." Mad Jack whistled softly. "What a bright boy you are, Joliot-Curie."

June 5: Churchill withdrew all his attack planes from France, convinced that French air bases would fall at any moment. Irène was inclined to regard this as typical of the British, *l'Albion perfide,* who'd quit ferrying their boats to Dunkirk now that all the English soldiers were saved. Hundreds of thousands of Belgians and French were still stranded on the beaches.

"I will never go to England," she vowed. "I will never allow my children to be reared by the English."

June 9: Ambassador Bill Bullitt sent one of his remaining aides to Lisbon to procure twelve submachine guns for the defense of the embassy, convinced a Communist mob would sack the city once the Germans approached.

Moureu arrived back at the Collège de France an hour after breakfast, disheveled and weary, having driven all night against the waves of refugees heading south. He had come to help Joliot finish the packing and to collect his wife. There were, he said, a million people on the roads. Perhaps more.

He was a scientist and did not inflate his data.

The French government packed up and quite suddenly was gone. The ministries tossed belongings from their upper windows all day, and small columns of smoke could be spotted, as though a general leaf-burning was under way. By nightfall, the beautiful stone buildings echoed and the bureaucrats were on their way to Tours. Parisians still sat in the sidewalk cafés under the blacked-out sky, drinking when no food was available.

Irène withdrew all their money from the Banque de Paris, and hid it carefully in the lining of her suitcase.

June 10: Premier Paul Reynaud, after assuring

Franklin Roosevelt that the French would fight "in front of Paris; we shall fight behind Paris; we shall close ourselves in one of our provinces to fight and if we should be driven out of it we shall establish ourselves in North Africa to continue the fight," left town, as quietly as a thief.

Irène wrote a letter to her nanny but could not mail it to Arcouest; the post offices were abandoned. She carried it by train to a friend who lived south of the city, a friend bound for Brittany, who promised it would arrive.

She and Joliot had heard nothing of their children in days. And the Germans were in Brittany now, too.

June 11: Mussolini declared war against France and England.

The last pieces of lab equipment were sent south to Clermont-Ferrand: a galvanometer, an ionization chamber, a spectroscope. Joliot had sent ten cases of equipment to the Auvergne altogether, worth something like two hundred thousand francs. He was convinced he might as well have thrown everything into the trash. It was impossible to know if it would arrive.

Allier came to say farewell. He'd waited long after the Ministry of Armaments had left Paris, hoping he could persuade Joliot to head straight to Bordeaux and a boat for England. Joliot had told him nothing about Mad Jack's offer or the decoy water canisters.

"I released your colleague," Allier said abruptly, "from the prison in Riom."

"Why?"

The banker looked away, unable to meet Joliot's eyes.

"Your uranium was delivered to the French governor in Morocco by a woman—an American negress—in a suitcase full of shoes."

"I see. So it's safe?"

"*Oui.*" Allier swallowed with difficulty. "But we've had word . . . through certain sources . . . that all your research reports—copies of the ones you've burned, *copies sent to the Ministry*—were found by the Germans."

Joliot's stomach somersaulted in shock. "Where?"

"In a railroad car near Charité-sur-Loire. *Mon Dieu.* They were almost certainly left there by prior arrangement."

"You mean they were sold."

Allier nodded.

"So your leak—your German spy—is in the Armaments Ministry. *Not* in my lab."

"It looks that way."

Joliot stared out at the twilight visible beyond the open laboratory door. Moureu was carefully packing the boot of his Peugeot, as though a perfect job might get him out of Paris.

"We leave tomorrow," he said.

It was dark when he and Irène locked the doors of the lab for the final time. It had been dark all day: The petrol refineries along the Seine were burning. Heavy, black smuts fell from the skies, coating the fresh chestnut leaves in mourning. Oil was in Joliot's hair and all over the surface of his car. The Germans were reported to be only fifty miles away.

Moureu and his wife were waiting for the small convoy to start. Irène was clutching some gold and platinum she'd brought from the laboratory, precious stuff to anybody but essential to a physicist's work. She had her mother's gramme of radium stored in a lead-lined box. She could not stop coughing; the oily air had lodged in her weak lungs and clotted her throat; the tension of the past few days had exhausted her, and her placid face was torn with anxiety and pain. Joliot did not speak as he sat at the wheel of the Peugeot, hoping she might sleep once they hit the open road.

He pulled away from the Collège de France a few minutes before three o'clock in the afternoon. The Latin Quarter and the Boulevard St-Germain were empty; so far, so good. Moureu kept steadily behind him although his Peugeot was less powerful than Joliot's. They turned into the Boulevard Raspail, heading for the Porte d'Orléans, and came to a shuddering stop.

A sea of southbound vehicles stretched before them, not only on the side of the road heading toward Orléans, but completely filling the northbound lanes as well. The entire boulevard had been given over to the mob fleeing Paris, and nobody was moving. A few gendarmes waved ineffectual arms, panic on their faces.

They're wondering, Joliot thought, *why they can't leave, too.*

He rolled down his window and called, "How far does the blockage go?"

"Two hundred miles, monsieur," the man replied.

Irène collapsed into coughing.

The car inched forward under Joliot's feet.

He settled in, resigned to waiting.

At four in the morning he realized he had managed to crawl twenty miles over the past twelve hours, a foot at a time. A stream of humanity was trudging by the stalled cars on both sides of the Route Nationale No. 20, the broad highway that ran from Paris to the south of France; he had an impulse to abandon the Peugeot, take to his feet with Madame Curie's radium stuffed into his shirt, and walk to the Auvergne.

"They say it's General Weygand's idea to block the road with refugees," Irène observed dispassionately, "to keep the Germans bottled up in Paris. It will take days to clear this road."

Joliot heard her words; he might have responded to them with a murmur of agreement, an exhausted grunt, but the sound of engines came to his ears, too: cutting the sky in half.

"Get down!" he screamed, just as the Messerschmitts flew over.

From the surging roar came a *rat-tat-tat* of machine guns, strafing the immobile traffic on the Route Nationale; the horrible staccato that was like hail, and yet not hail, the hulking shape of the machine just visible through the blackout, flame spitting from its guns. His car was in the outer lane of traffic and Joliot could just jerk the wheel and send it over into the ditch, but the car next to him was hit—he saw the driver jerk back and forth as the bullets pierced his body.

Irène screamed—a low, guttural sound that became relentless coughing. Her body doubled over. The Peugeot lurched wildly off the road and Joliot counted three planes, seven, then he could not count anymore and the noise was suddenly gone.

The car was filled with the raw sound of breathing.

"Moureu," Irène gasped.

Joliot threw open his door, staggered out unsteadily, pelted backward to the spot where he'd last glimpsed Moureu's Peugeot. It was not there.

"Moureu!" he called, desperation cracking his voice. *"Moureu!"*

He glanced wildly around. A tide of moaning rose from the wreckage, the flicker of flames. A figure crawled toward him on its knees through the packed and riddled cars—

And there was Moureu's car, nose-down in the opposite ditch, Moureu sprawled against the steering column. His wife bending over him.

"I think he's knocked out," she said when Joliot reached her. Her teeth were bared like an animal's. "The impact of the crash. I don't think he was hit."

"We've got to get off this highway," Joliot muttered.

There was no help for those left behind. No way to send for help. Joliot went on, a foot at a time, hoping for a crossroads where he could turn. Irène's eyes were closed and she spoke only once, to ask if she could pee in a field somewhere. Joliot waited almost an hour before he pulled the Peugeot off, desperate to make some progress, and the sun was high in the sky when he helped her out of the car and up the highway's bank. She squatted in the grass, indifferent to the entire population of Paris inching by her. And the sound of the planes came again.

"Irène," he shouted. "Lie down!"

He curled behind the parked car and waited. But the *rat-tat-tat* never came; only the rising whine of the engine, cutting out once, the buzz of a thousand hornets settling down somewhere near him.

He stood up, looking for his wife.

She was flat on the ground with her hands over her head. Beyond her was a plane, idling in the middle of the field. A man was climbing out of it—climbing with difficulty, because one of his legs was bad and the cockpit could hardly hold his large British frame.

"Mad Jack," Joliot whispered.

He began to run across the field toward him.

CHAPTER FORTY-ONE

The fever broke on the third day, when Hearst had almost given up hope.

He'd taken to driving the fifty miles between Loudenne and Bordeaux each morning, Petie sitting in the passenger seat beside him. The old Frenchman would buy provisions in town: food, charcoal for the camp's cookfires, milk if he could find it—and drive back to the Americans scattered under the château's pines, while Hearst sat vigil in the overcrowded hospital ward. After dinner Petie would return, and fetch Hearst back to lie on the hard ground under the June stars, certain Sally would be dead by dawn. He never asked Petie how he found the petrol to fuel the Buick, and the old Frenchman never told him.

The doctors worried about Sally's fractured skull, the possible swelling of her brain. She was excruciatingly thin, her jutting bones more painful than elegant, her skin rough with dehydration. She thrashed in uneasy dreams. More than once Hearst caught the shouted name of *Morris*.

When he could not bear it any longer he would walk

out of the hospital and down to the docks. He talked up the fishermen, hoping to learn further details of Sally's story and whether anyone had seen a man of Emery Morris's description. No one had. So many refugees flooded Bordeaux now that nobody looked hard at any of them. It was after one of these disconsolate strolls that he returned to find Sally's eyes wide open.

"Joe," she said hoarsely. "Did you die, too?"

From that point on, her progress was swift, although she did not immediately recover her memory. It was another two days before she could tell him about the torpedoes and the way Morris died, the lawyer's admission of guilt in Philip's murder—and then, with fresh horror as the image returned, of how the casket sank beneath the Channel waves with its burden of missent documents.

She asked daily if Hearst had any news of Léonie Blum, but he never did. The old woman had vanished.

He tried to suppress all talk of the war, believing it might increase her fretfulness at being confined to bed, but on Friday, June fourteenth, he could no longer hold the world at bay. He arrived at the hospital to hear the radio blaring the German army's triumphal march down the Champs-Élysées.

"They won't stop there, will they, Joe?" Tears were streaming down her face; it was as though Philip had died all over again.

Hearst thought of Bill Bullitt, sheltering from air raids in his embassy's wine cellar, and said, "We've got to move on, Sally. As soon as you're able. There's a ship due any day, the *S.S. Milwaukee* out of New York, and we're all going to get on it."

"Not another ship," she protested faintly.

"You can't walk across the Atlantic."

"What about the Pan Am Clipper?"

"You'd still have to get to London. Which means another ship. And after all—nothing could possibly be as bad as what you've already experienced."

She shook her head. "I'd rather go back to Paris. I'd rather live with the Germans all around me than trust myself to the sea."

"First things first," he temporized. "Let's get you back on your feet. I'm taking you home to Loudenne today."

Light broke on her face and a new kind of hope seemed to sustain her through all the tedium of discharge and the wrangling over her lack of documents— a detail Hearst would have to address with the American consulate at the earliest opportunity. But the long ride over the rutted and narrow roads was difficult, and when he finally pulled up before the château door, she had lost consciousness again.

"Worn out, poor poppet," Nell said briskly as she helped Hearst carry Sally up the wide marble steps. "Will she be ready to sail by Monday?"

"Monday?" he repeated.

"The shipping agent sent word. Your *Milwaukee* is expected the seventeenth."

"Good God," he said blankly. "She'll *have* to be."

Sunday night at dusk, the sound of tires on gravel alerted Hearst they had visitors.

He was ambling toward the house for dinner with Sally, who was sitting up now and eating rather well for someone who'd cheated death, when the small green Simca bowled down the drive.

Elie Loewens's violin, filtering through the château's open windows, fell silent.

Hearst stopped abruptly under the pines. He knew the vineyard workers' ancient jalopies and Henri's truck and the vehicles owned by distant neighbors. None of them drove a Simca.

The château's massive front door clicked quietly closed. He looked up. Nell stood watchful in the twilight. Her small, catlike face floated palely above her work clothes.

The Simca's side doors opened simultaneously to disgorge two men.

"Hallo," Mad Jack called cheerfully to Nell. "It's been ages. How're you keeping, old thing?"

CHAPTER FORTY-TWO

That same night, Frédéric Joliot-Curie kissed his wife's cool forehead, adjusted the reading lamp so that the glare would not hurt her eyes, and said, "You'll be all right?"

She stared back at him coldly from the crisp white sheets. It had not been Irène's idea to check herself into the sanatorium, hastily found in a small town in the Dordogne; it was Allier's work, Allier who had appeared suddenly out of nowhere that Sunday afternoon when they were just getting settled into the villa called Clair Logis. The banker had roared up on Fred and Moureu as they walked the high road to the Puy de Dôme in the bright June sunshine and told them: The final collapse of French forces was only hours away. Nothing could hold the Germans back. They had to move on from Clermont-Ferrand, from the Auvergne altogether. It was time to make for Bordeaux. Time to find a ship.

It was then Fred had produced the Englishman, the one who called himself an earl, and told the little banker all about his deception with the heavy water, how he'd put it in the hands of his lover—he had not called the woman that, of course, but Irène knew everything; she had known his heart for years, and she observed the small flicker of his eyelids as he said the countess's name. He had deceived the government, it seemed, as well as his wife, and for an instant Irène was acutely sorry the heavy water had survived, that Fred would be rewarded in this way for his betrayals. But Allier was overjoyed; he embraced Fred and kissed him on both cheeks, as though if he could he would award the man a medal, and then he'd shaken the Englishman's hand. It was the earl who informed them he'd found a ship capable of transporting the water, the Scottish *Broompark,* waiting now in Bordeaux harbor and bound for Southampton in a matter of days.

"You could get a ship," she'd observed shrilly, "for the world's supply of heavy water. You English were willing to take that. But not our young men, *hein?*"

"Irène," Fred chided. "Remember how much we owe Lord Suffolk."

It was true the earl had set down his plane on a field near the Route Nationale and plucked them all out of the deathtrap of cars waiting for the Messerschmitts; it was true he'd flown them right to the Auvergne and landed safely at the airstrip in Riom, where Kowarski was waiting with a car; but Irène no longer cared. He'd left the Peugeot behind and God knows when they'd ever have another. It was probably in the hands of the Germans now.

"*Certainement,* you must be on that ship when it leaves," Allier told Kowarski and von Halban. "It will be your privilege to present the deuterium to the British authorities. There is nothing in France for you now. Joliot—"

Fred refused to discuss the matter of emigrating to

England. There was a discussion of wives and children, annoying appendages that must be sent parcel post from a variety of locations, some of them now behind enemy lines. Moureu was silent and pale, his eyes flicking nervously toward his wife, who said nothing; probably she liked the idea of London and the shops.

Irène raised her voice to denounce them all for betraying France, for running like cowards, but her breath gave out and she was coughing again, painfully and convulsively, nearly choking on the violence of her own hatred for the war, for her failing body, for the husband who had never loved her enough.

When she came to her senses again, she lay in this bed: a private room in a private sanatorium, no sound of artillery or screaming in the distance, a clean and well-lit place to die.

"That man wants you for England," she told Joliot. "You've left me here so you can run."

"Will you be all right?" he repeated.

"Of course. I have everything I need." *Except love.* "You'll come tomorrow?"

"If I can."

Painfully, she thrust herself upright. "You're going to *her*, aren't you? To that English whore in Bordeaux."

"I'm going to help move the water. Allier and the earl are already there."

She lay down and turned her back to him. He could die for all she cared, without a word of forgiveness; she hoped he would. The spasms began again, choking her; she reached for a glass of water.

He touched her hair once, and left.

* * *

It was three A.M. when Joliot reached Loudenne in Kowarski's car. He navigated the silent, blacked-out avenue with caution, groping toward the house. He had never been to the place—it was another man's patrimony—and even now he felt he was trespassing.

He was aware of the odd, humped shapes of tents scattered about the wide grounds that ran between château and vineyard, but he had no idea what they might be or why they were there. It was very late and he was drained and aching with both guilt and the dangerous euphoria of seeing Nell again.

He mounted the stone steps and tried the front door handle.

It opened to his touch.

He pushed the heavy oak wide, and stepped into a deeper darkness. His heels rang suddenly on marble. He stopped short, mouth dry. He would be taken for a thief. He should find the salon and sleep there on a settee or even the floor, perhaps, without waking the household.

A candle flame materialized in the darkness above him.

He glanced up.

"Ricki," she breathed. "They said you would come."

She began to descend the stairs, a strange and unknown creature clothed in white, a votive with her candle, eyes burning clear above the flame.

He stood still in the middle of her floor, and let her come.

CHAPTER FORTY-THREE

They were ferrying people from the port of Bordeaux, which sat on the narrow Garonne river, to the ships moored out in the Gironde estuary, on flat, bargelike craft normally reserved for casks of wine. Bordeaux fishermen and laborers were pitching in wherever they could, to get the refugees out of France. It was a cloudy Monday morning, the seventeenth of June, and the Germans had arrived.

The attack planes dove in low over the moored ships and the ferries jammed with passengers and without hesitation dropped bombs on them. Sometimes the bombs went wide, but the river was so packed with vessels that most bombs struck something: A boat would explode into a shower of debris and body parts. It was a complete crap shoot, Joe Hearst thought, whether any of them would make it out alive.

"I'm not going," Mims Tarnow said flatly. "You're nuts even to suggest it, Hearst. We've got children here!"

She glared at him fiercely, her arm around her son, as though Hearst intended the boy for cannon fodder. He did not answer Mims, his eyes fixed on the crowd of small craft choking the port. It was impossible to see the *S.S. Milwaukee*—it was too far out in the estuary. He hoped the captain had waited for them.

He'd brought Sally King to Bordeaux that morning in the Buick. Mims and the rest of the Americans followed, bickering over Hearst's orders to leave their cars and baggage in the care of Consul Noakes, for transatlantic shipment later. Hearst had told Petie to siphon the fuel from the convoy's tanks once the cars were parked at the consulate. He'd need all the petrol he could steal, to get back to Bullitt in Paris.

"I'd bet anything you could name that Noakes will sell our Chrysler to the Germans," Mims Tarnow said acidly to her husband, Steve. "Maybe we should just sit tight."

"Mims," Hearst interjected, "unless you want to eat lunch with the entire German army, you'll stop complaining and get on the launch, okay?"

"What's so awful about the German army, anyway?" Mims retorted. "It's not like we're at *war* with them. We're innocent bystanders."

"Tell that to the bombers," Sally muttered.

One of the flat little barges nosed into the stone quai in front of the café where they were huddled. At the prow, standing like a figurehead, was no local fisherman but an actual sailor in a crisp white uniform, *S.S. Milwaukee* embroidered on his breast.

"Thank God," Mims declared. "Somebody who knows what they're doing, at last." She clutched her son's shoulder and three suitcases she had culled from her wealth of baggage and hurried forward. The rest of the Americans began to follow her.

Hearst put his arm around Sally—gently, because of her cast and sling—and said, "Time to go."

"No," she replied.

"It's the right thing to do."

"How do you know?" She turned a furious face on him. "You said that the last time I got on a boat, and you were wrong. I'm tired of being *sensible*. I'm tired of doing what I'm told. I'm not that kind of woman anymore."

The whistle of a bomb, hurtling through the air. A hundred yards upriver, a quai burst into a shower of stone and wood. The barge heaved from the shock wave and everybody screamed.

"Go!" Hearst shouted, thrusting Sally toward the precarious grasp of the sailor. Steve Tarnow and two others jumped the widening gap of water between quai and barge, the weight of their bodies rocking the edge dangerously. The sailor stumbled backward, Sally in his arms, both of them lurching into the mass of people pressing toward the bow. Tarnow recovered his balance, and reached for the mooring rope.

Hearst tossed it to him. He waved farewell.

It was then he saw Sally, white-faced, her eyes fixed on his. He'd never told her he was staying behind.

She threw his name desperately across the water, straining toward him. The *Milwaukee* crewman grasped her good arm but she surged forward, shaking herself free, toward the stern of the barge.

Hearst saw what she meant to do.

"Sally, don't!" he cried. *"Don't!"*

For the first time since they'd met, she ignored him, and jumped.

Joliot had awakened as the last of the American cars pulled out of Loudenne.

Pale sunlight on a white ceiling, a furl of bedclothes over his loins. The place where Nell had been was empty. When he touched the sheets they were already cold.

He pulled on his clothes and got himself out of the room. He could not be found there, by a servant or another guest—Allier or Mad Jack. Whether his impulse was to protect himself or Nell—himself or Irène—he could not say.

He moved silently down the marble staircase and followed the sound of voices to the kitchen.

It was an old-fashioned block of a room with scrubbed oak tables and bare white walls: the province of a staff far larger than Loudenne now boasted. He wondered how often Nell came here, and why she had seen fit to entertain an earl in the château's scullery. Mad Jack had made himself at home, however, propped at the table in his shirtsleeves with a map of Bordeaux spread out before him. Oscar and Genevieve were loaded at his side.

"The *Broompark* is presently moored at the quai in Bordeaux," the earl was saying. "I intend to bring a smaller craft up the Gironde to your docks here at Loudenne, and shift the jolly jugs of water out around nightfall. I shouldn't like those bombers to catch us ferrying suspect goods."

"What bombers?" Joliot asked from the doorway.

Three heads swiveled toward him. Nell smiled her secret smile; he could not acknowledge it under all those eyes.

"You're here!" Allier cried, and rose from his chair. He alone had shaved that morning; he looked neat as a pin. "I confess I hadn't hoped for it, Joliot. Where are von Halban and the others?"

"On their way. I came directly from the Dordogne. I left my wife in the sanatorium you found."

"Poor lady," Mad Jack mused. "Hell of a cough. TB, I suppose?"

Joliot nodded. "You've made your plans?"

"We have. I'm to fetch the boat while you and Allier stand guard over the goods and await reinforcements. The *Broompark* leaves with the dawn tide and the captain waits for nobody. We'll hope your chappies make it."

"Where is the water?" Joliot asked.

In all the heated hours of the night he had never once remembered the reason for his errand, never asked whether Nell had kept his precious stuff safe. He'd awakened now from his dream, and it was the night that was no longer real.

"That's why we held the Council of War in the kitchen," Nell said quietly. "Come. Let me show you."

She lit an oil lamp and led them through a doorway at the rear of the pantry.

"All the cellars at Loudenne are connected underground. These are the stairs to the château's main cellar—where we keep the bottles we don't intend to sell, the ones laid down by Bertrand's father and grandfather."

"Any port?" Mad Jack inquired with sudden interest.

"Next to none. But there's some very good Lafite," Nell replied dryly. "If we're successful this evening I'll crack open a bottle. Gentlemen?"

They followed her single light down the stone steps into the arching depths of the château, the chill settling immediately in Joliot's bones. They walked on, past shadowed *cave* after shadowed *cave* filled with dusty bottles. Once there was the scrabbling of small feet, and Joliot imagined a mouse with its nest among the fifty-year-old classed growths. The silence and the stale air reminded him of a crypt, and he understood suddenly why Nell loved Loudenne, why it had a sacred power over her. This was her cathedral, her broken bread and spilled wine. There had been ritual, too, in their lovemaking last night, Joliot thought—as though without speaking they both understood it would be the last time.

The passage before them widened suddenly, the lantern light welling. "This is the passage from the *cuverie*," Nell said. "It joins the tunnel from the house. If we move on you'll see the water gate just ahead."

Massive casks, smelling of toast—Joliot recognized the new wood she'd paid a fortune to bring from Paris. And then, past the rank upon rank of barrels, the sound of the river. A ramp descending to a hatch with an iron grille.

"There are tides in the estuary," Nell said. "This gate can only be opened at low ebb. That, too, is why you should wait for darkness."

"And my jugs?" Joliot asked.

She turned and looked at him, her face immobile. "Packed in straw. I had Henri open two casks and store them there. He resealed the tops so nobody would know. We can roll them right down to Jack's boat, when he brings it."

Joliot nodded.

There remained nothing to do but wait.

He spent much of the day in writing to his children, in the hope that somebody might be able to deliver a letter.

Mad Jack disappeared in the green Simca, bound for Bordeaux, but Allier moved restlessly around the château, colliding with Nell's other guests—the Jews from Holland—and conversing at length on the subject of Schubert. Joliot noticed how Elie Loewens's eyes followed Nell even as he listened politely to Allier, fingers grasping the throat of his violin; and Joliot thought, *Ah. Another of the fallen.*

He took a walk among the vines and discovered a playhouse erected from two flat stones and the broken staves of a barrel. Sheltering inside it were a small boy and girl belonging to the Dutch, already speaking passable French after a few short weeks at Loudenne. Joliot made the girl a daisy chain and carried the boy on his back. He could hear the rumble of bombs and guns in

the distance—coming from the south, near Bordeaux—
and wondered at the children's calm.

Toward evening, the light still strong in the sky, he
strolled down toward the river to check on the tide. He
was shocked to discover a mass of boats in the Gironde,
a vast fleet of river traffic, and veering out of the mass
was one small craft: Mad Jack at the wheel.

Joliot ran to the end of Loudenne's pier.

"Catch hold, there's a good fellow," the earl called.

He looked more than ever like a pirate, his tattoos
flashing in the last sunlight, his pistols shoved into the
waist of his trousers. He was grinning hugely, in love
with this adventure, better than any service at the Front
could be. Joliot caught the rope. He had spent enough
holidays in Brittany to know how to tie a sailor's knot.
The water level was so low now, that the dock was at the
Englishman's shoulder.

"Von Halban arrived? Moureu and the Russian?"

Joliot shook his head. "They may not make it. Too
many Germans between here and the Auvergne."

"Like shooting fish in a barrel," the earl agreed cheerfully. "Let's open Nell's wine and then load the water,
hey? The tide should be low enough."

They walked together toward the darkening bulk of
the château, Joliot matching his pace to the earl's limp.

"I've known Nell for donkey's years, you know," Mad
Jack confided. "Grew up together. Had our wilder days.
Attended her wedding to Bertrand, though we grew
apart after that. What I mean to say is, Joliot: She told
me about you."

"Told you what?" he asked.

"That you were the flame to her moth—the most dangerous air she could breathe—that sort of thing. Has a kind of passion for you. Thought you ought to know."

"Thank you," Joliot said with difficulty. "I, too, have known Nell a long time."

"I don't suppose you'd use your influence with her? Get her to leave on the *Broompark* when it goes? I don't feel right abandoning her to Jerry. All manner of terrible things might happen."

"If I had any influence to use," Joliot replied, "I would persuade her to stay here forever."

"I see," the earl said. And they walked on to the house in silence.

It was as they were finishing dinner—a hasty affair of rabbits Henri had snared in the park and the cook had stewed in wine—that the whole table was thrown into silence by the sound of approaching vehicles.

"Von Halban." Joliot thrust back his chair and followed Nell into the hall.

She was standing at the door when the first of the German staff cars rolled to a halt, and Spatz stepped out into the sweet night air.

He raised his arm and smiled.

"*Heil Hitler,*" he said.

CHAPTER FORTY-FOUR

"Quickly," Nell breathed. "Get back into the house. Find the Dutch. Get them to the tunnels as quick as you can. *Do as I say, Ricki!*"

Joliot turned and raced back to the dining room. "Germans," he muttered. "Five cars at least. We've got to move quickly."

Mad Jack was already brandishing Oscar or Genevieve, but Allier grasped his wrist and urged, "The water gate. *Vite.*"

Joliot wheeled. He made for the back staircase near the kitchen, aware of the sound of bright chatter in the château's entry, of Nell at her most aristocratic, speaking French for all the world as though she were not an English citizen and an enemy national of the twelve men who came striding into her house.

"Hello, Spatz, darling," he heard her say, and thought to himself, *Her cousin. Has Nell betrayed us?*

Elie Loewens was standing mute in the upper hall, his fingertips reaching for the walls as though he could channel sound through the heavy plaster.

"Get your family," Joliot whispered. "Down the back staircase. Before it's too late."

"The children," Elie said. "*The children*. They're not in the house."

Joliot swore under his breath. "I'll take care of it—I know where they might be. *Go*. Quickly. To the cellar."

She led them into the dining room and apologized for the fact that dinner was already over—rang the bell for the housemaid, who would not respond, terrified of invasion and rape. Nell begged them all to sit down, so tired as they must be after such a journey, she would get some food and wine herself—and felt Spatz following her as she made for the kitchen.

It was empty. But she knew that at all costs she must keep him out of that part of the house now, because it was the only route of escape. She turned and placed her hands on his good wool tunic. Bracing herself against his chest and stopping him cold in the butler's pantry.

"What in bloody hell are you doing here?" she demanded.

He smiled down at her, with the usual careless warmth in his birdlike gaze, and dropped a kiss on her forehead. "Sweet Nell," he said. "You're a sight for sore eyes. The amount of death I've had to witness since I last saw you—"

"But why? Surely you should be in Paris?"

"I'm saving my apostate soul," he answered lightly. "I'm kissing up to the Gestapo. Some of the most violent men in Germany are sitting at your dinner table right now, Nell, and they want your vineyard. Your wine cellar. Your house. I gave it all to them as a sort of grand gesture of reconciliation. They are, after all, the Master Race."

She stepped backward, bile surging into her throat. *"What?"*

"Did you know two million French soldiers are missing or taken prisoner?—That nearly a hundred thousand are dead? Two hundred thousand wounded? And all in six weeks. The German war machine is something even I can't oppose."

"Spatz—"

"Loudenne was all I had to offer them, Nanoo. Because you failed me. You were supposed to find something to sell." He gripped her shoulders. "But nobody wants to help little Spatz anymore. The nigger girl—my *circus performer*—stole a fortune in uranium once I got her out of France, and I *believed* in her, Nell—I waved good-bye on the dock at Marseille while she took off with the trunk I thought was mine. Then I got Joliot's deuterium, but it turned out *that* was a fucking mistake—I took dirty tap water from Clermont-Ferrand all the way to the German High Command outside Paris and they *laughed* at me, Nell, once they'd tested the first three canisters. They almost laughed me all the way back to Berlin and I'd rather die than go there, you understand? I'd sell my mother and my child if I had one and I'd even sell *you*, Nell, before I'd face Hitler in the Fatherland. *Comprends?*"

"Oui," she replied, her body cold as ice. "I understand. But I can't give you Loudenne. It isn't mine."

"Those men in the other room'll take it anyway. They hammered out the Occupation zone with old Pétain this morning—he replaced Premier Reynaud, he's the Führer's lapdog now—and it's hilarious, you'd laugh if you saw the map; it includes the best wine regions in France. Yours among them. So pack a bag before my friends at the dinner table decide they want your lingerie, my darling. Or you, perhaps. You'd make a passable fuck for one of them until Bertrand comes home."

"Don't do this, Spatz. Don't trade your soul—"

He reached for her, kissed her brutally on the mouth, caressed the drop of blood on her lower lip.

"I have no soul, dearest. Now pack, before I sell them your pathetic little Jews."

He'd eased breathlessly down the back staircase, groping his way with his palms against the wall, listening as Nell's world fell in ruins around her.

When Spatz tore at her lip with his teeth he almost rushed forward and choked the man, but then he fought back the red miasma clouding his sight and thought, *Science, Ricki. The voice of reason. You need it now.*

There was something of Irène's dispassionate habit in the way he ignored Nell's anguished face, the door to the butler pantry swinging closed behind the tall blond German as he returned to entertain his jackals, and continued down the stairs into the wine cellar. He ran steadily in the dark, and turned sharply left where the passage from the *cuverie* fed into the one from the house. He could hear low voices in the distance: Allier and the Dutch bankers, negotiating barrels.

He climbed up into the first-year room and out into the June darkness.

What was it that had driven the children from the house?

He thought of his own daughter and son, Hélène thirteen years old now, Pierre a few years younger, both overwhelmed by the violence of the adult world. The little de Kuypers knew too much about flight and death; too much impermanence; so they finally made a home for themselves. How much safer it must have seemed than anything the grown-ups could provide.

They were shivering and slightly damp with the sea air when he found them, huddled together under the barrel staves and stones. Six years old and maybe four, staring from their den with the eyes of foxes.

"Les allemands," the little girl whispered, holding her brother close. "They've come for Papa."

"You must be utterly quiet," Julian de Kuyper said softly to his daughter as he settled her in the huge oak cask, "and even when the barrel rolls, you must not cry out. Promise?"

The girl nodded; and her aunt Mathilde stepped into the cask beside her, enfolding both children in her arms. The *maître du vin,* Henri, wrapped a blanket he'd brought from his cottage around her, and Joliot caught one last glimpse of Mathilde's bowed head as the old man nailed the cask lid closed.

Henri had appeared without warning minutes after Joliot arrived at the water gate with the children. Mad Jack nearly shot off the cellar master's white head, looming noiselessly out of the darkened tunnel. Henri explained that the countess had ordered him to be at the water gate for low tide, as a shipment must be moved downstream to Bordeaux. He'd brought none of the Mouton workers with him, and he asked no questions, even when the expensive new oak barrels were broached and filled with the countess's house-guests.

"Sad news," the old man murmured as he hammered down the lids on first Elie and then Moïses Loewens. "They say Mouton and Lafite are in German hands tonight. Baron Philippe has been thrown into one of Pétain's prisons. But they won't get these, eh?"

Nobody answered him. They could all hear the sudden tramp of feet pacing toward them: It sounded like the entire German army was on the move. Headed straight for the water gate.

"Quickly," Mad Jack said. "The casks!"

And Mathilde's barrel rolled slowly toward the river.

Nell raced through the *cuverie* and down the steps to the aging room, her heart pounding. It was Spatz who'd invited the Nazis into Loudenne's wine cellar, and as the Germans were still waiting for dinner it seemed like a good way to kill time. The conquerors were in the mood for celebration. They wanted to gloat over this prize they'd won.

Spatz led them down the kitchen steps to the cellar while Nell melted into the hall, waiting only for the last uniform to disappear before she pelted out the front door and across the lawn. There were many entrances to Loudenne's cellars.

She had farther to go than the Nazis did but she was running now, and they were pausing at every arch of the *cave* below the house to study the bottles and their labels, talking of vintages and classed growths and whether German beer was not after all superior to French wine.

She could hear their voices echoing in the cellar as she flitted like a shadow past the passageway leading up to the house. A few yards more and she would reach the water gate.

A shot rang out and she reeled backward, right shoulder exploding in pain. *Oscar,* she thought despairingly. *Genevieve.* She reached for the wound and felt the warm blood welling under her fingers.

"You idiot!" she called furiously in English as she stumbled toward Mad Jack. "You'll bring them down on you like a pack of wolves!"

And already the sound of voices behind her had stopped, the hammer of feet had begun.

"Get on the boat," she ordered the four of them—Allier, Joliot, Henri, and the earl—as they stared at her in horror.

"Nell—you're bleeding!"

"Spatz is with them," she persisted. "He'll recognize you, Jack, and if he does you're all dead men. *Get on the boat.*"

Allier grabbed Joliot, who seemed unable to move, and pulled him over to the last barrel. They shoved it furiously toward the laden barge moored beyond the water gate, which was already rising; the tide had turned.

"Von Dincklage? Good Lord—I haven't seen the bastard since my polo days in Deauville," the earl said blankly. "The blighter always cheated." He raised one of his pistols as though measuring the distance between the river and the enemy.

"I'll take that," Nell said, and pulled it from his hands with her good left arm. "Now go. I'll hold them off."

In the end it was not Spatz who killed her as she stood with the earl's gun leveled before the hatch leading out onto the Gironde; Spatz still wore civilian clothes and his pistol, secure in his suit jacket, was mostly for show. But neither did he stop the Nazi officer who raised his arm and shot the Countess of Loudenne at point-blank range.

There were times for choosing sides, and this was one of them.

CHAPTER FORTY-FIVE

"You're staying behind?"

Allier turned and studied the man standing on the pier with his hands in his pockets. Rangy and fine-boned, with deep-set eyes. He'd spoken in flawless French, but from the carelessness of his clothes Allier thought he must be foreign. A woman with a broken arm stood beside him.

"Yes," he answered. "As are you, Monsieur . . . ?"

The man extended his hand. "Joe Hearst. American embassy. And this is Miss Sally King. Our people left Bordeaux yesterday."

"I see," Allier said. He bowed to the woman.

"We were camping at Château Loudenne," Hearst persisted. "I saw you there Sunday night. The green Simca. Is the countess all right?"

Allier glanced at Joliot-Curie, who stood wretchedly on the quai a good twenty yards distant, and said softly, "I think she is beyond all worry at present."

"Please give her my regards when you see her again, Monsieur . . ."

"Jacques Allier." He offered his hand. "Ministry of Armaments."

Something in the American's face changed. He looked swiftly from the quai to the *Broompark,* which was just slipping its moorings and backing into the Garonne with the entire French physics establishment on board. But it was Sally King who spoke.

"Allier!" she said. "Then you must have known Philip!"

"Pardon, mademoiselle?"

"Philip Stilwell. My fiancé. He sent you some papers before he died—" She stopped short, and glanced up at the man named Hearst.

Allier fingered his spectacles. *"Le pauvre Philippe.* You have all my sympathy, Miss King. He was murdered, I think?"

"Yes," she said firmly. "And the papers he meant you to have are gone. They sank in the Channel when my boat was torpedoed."

He glanced at Joliot-Curie, who seemed almost a separate country; there was nothing more Allier could do for the man, now that he'd refused Mad Jack's final offer of asylum. And so he began to walk slowly away from the river, his work there finished.

"What exactly were these documents, *s'il vous plaît?"*

"A list of shipments of carbon monoxide." Hearst fell into step beside him, his arm protectively around Stilwell's girl. "One of German sanatoria and hospitals. Something about bus routes. The obituary of a chemical engineer named Juergen Gebl, who worked for a company named I.G. Farben..."

Allier pulled the collar of his coat closer about his neck. The *Broompark* was dwindling behind them and Mad Jack's voice carried over the whine of the German bombers. The earl was singing a sea chanty. He'd lashed the wine casks holding the heavy water to the *Broompark*'s side; if the ship was hit, explosives would scuttle the heavy water before the barrels fell into enemy hands. But Allier no longer worried about the heavy water or the people who sailed with it.

"Would you tell us why Philip died?" Sally King's voice rose above the persistent bombers, the engines' whine. "The carbon monoxide? I realize it means nothing to you in the face of all this..." She gestured to the splintered fragments of boats in the harbor, the shattered quais. "One death in the midst of so much...but to *me*..."

"...to you, it is as though all light was extinguished," Allier said. "And you hope for justice. For meaning. *Bon.* Your fiancé was murdered because there are people who did not wish the world to know what he had found. That these Germans—" he glanced over his shoulder at the chaos of the Garonne— "are killing their infirm and unfit citizens like so many diseased cattle. Polio victims. The mentally ill. Epileptics and tuberculars. Pensioners or children—it doesn't matter. They're all wrenched from their loving families for 'special treatment,' and the next thing you know, a death certificate's in the mail."

"My God," Hearst muttered. "But you can't just..."

"Euthanize people? That's what they call it in Berlin. The word means *beautiful death*. The Master Race needs to look absolutely flawless while it devours the world, *mon ami.* So the authorities bus their medical failures to certain centers—hospitals, mostly—where they're locked in a room fitted with pipes full of carbon monoxide. A slow and messy death, Mr. Hearst. Courtesy of I.G. Farben. They're turning a healthy profit on auto exhaust."

"That's hideous," Sally King said faintly. "It's...inhuman. If it's true..."

"Oh, it's true, I assure you. That engineer, Juergen Gebl, witnessed it. He wanted to know where all the carbon monoxide was going. He saw children of ten and fourteen taken off those buses. That's why he had to be killed, you see. A gang of 'Communist thugs,' I think they called them, beat him to death one night as he walked home. It's all detailed in my file."

"It should be stopped. If you published it—"

"Your Philip thought so, too." Allier turned. "Particularly as I.G. Farben was once a Sullivan and Cromwell client. It enraged him that American lawyers would treat the murder of innocents as just so much commerce. But some in his firm did not want the truth disclosed. And so Stilwell, too, had to die. In a manner so shameful that no one would investigate."

"Emery Morris," the woman said. "He was paid by I.G. Farben."

Allier nodded. "His old partner, Rogers Lamont, refused to represent Farben any longer. Juergen Gebl was a friend of Lamont's."

"But if Morris had to kill Stilwell," Hearst mused

"—if silence is so vital—the Nazis must *still be doing it.* Gassing people."

"In the midst of the invasion of France?" Allier laughed harshly. "Why kill civilians when there are so many Allied soldiers to shoot? They've traded gas for Messerschmitts."

Somewhere out in the harbor, a shell exploded with a flare of black and orange. They could no longer see the *Broompark*.

"Mr. Allier," Sally King said, "we're staying here, Joe and I. We'd like to help you with this war."

"In that case, mademoiselle," he answered gravely, "I will certainly find something for you to do."

And they walked on into the heart of conquered France.

EPILOGUE

Transcript of the interrogation of Frédéric Joliot-Curie, Nobel laureate and member of the Collège de France, by General Erich Schumann, professor of military physics, Berlin University, scientific advisor to General Keitel. General Schumann was accompanied by Dr. Kurt Diebner, nuclear physicist, Kaiser Wilhelm Institute of Physics, and Wolfgang Gentner, physicist, who trained under Joliot-Curie from 1932 to 1935. This interrogation took place at the Collège de France on August 13, 1940. Dieter Wolfe, transcriber.

Question: Where is the heavy water?

Joliot: I put it on an English ship in the port of Bordeaux.

Question: And the name of this ship?

Joliot: I have no idea. I heard your bombers sank it a few hours after leaving port.

Question: Our records show you purchased a supply of uranium metal from the United States. Where is it now?

Joliot: The Ministry of Armaments took the

uranium. You'd better ask them what they did
with it. You have a spy in the Ministry,
I believe?

Question: Don't toy with us, Doktor Joliot. You
of all people must know where the uranium is.

Joliot: I'm the last person the Ministry would tell.
They don't trust me at all, I'm afraid. I'm a
Communist.

He was enjoying the interrogation; it pleased him to
lie with such abandon now, he who'd always found it so
difficult to deceive. Schumann had used the correct
word—he was toying with them, throwing his knowledge of their spy and his complete indifference to the
truth right in their faces. It was his testament of love
and loyalty to Nell, as much as to France.

"Think twice, Fred," Wolfgang Gentner warned him
privately when at last the others had left. "They can
make life impossible for you, you know. I've asked to be
placed here in the lab so that I can protect you, but
I don't know how long they'll leave me here. I've been
denounced once already for my democratic tenden-
cies."

"Poor Gentner." He clapped his old friend on the
shoulder with sincere affection and pity. "Shall we meet
later, in the Boul-Mich? I don't promise to tell you the
truth. But we might talk of our children."

Gentner smiled at him sadly. "Those men will be
back. They won't leave you alone. They want your

cyclotron and your expertise. Most of all they want your mind."

"I don't think even the Nazis have figured out a way to steal that."

Gentner turned at the door. "You're wrong, you know, about the spy at the Ministry. I understand the source of their information was someone much closer to home. Watch your back, Fred. As well as your front. You're vulnerable on all sides, now."

He lingered alone in the lab, his empty and echoing lab, stripped of its equipment and its vivid life. *Someone much closer to home.* But she had not yet returned from her rest cure in the Dordogne; they were both, he realized, delaying the reunion as long as possible.

He had a month before the children came from Brittany and Irène would be discharged. A month to heal his wounds, and go on as before: as though the war had never happened, as though his own wife had not risked the annihilation of the world by putting his research into German hands.

It was remarkable, he thought as he turned out the laboratory lights and set off to meet Gentner in the small café where he'd once drunk with Nell, what crimes a person could commit in the name of love.

AFTERWORD

Any number of outcomes might be imagined for the fictional characters that fill these pages: Sally King, Joe Hearst, the Loewens brothers, and the de Kuyper family to name a few. For others, however—characters drawn from actual people who lived through the events—the future played out in ways that can be told.

Mad Jack, the twentieth Earl of Suffolk, succeeded in getting the heavy water lashed to the *Broompark* safely into Southampton harbor a few days after its departure from Bordeaux. With a logic comprehensible only to the British, the water was eventually placed under the care of Windsor Castle's librarian. Mad Jack was killed a year after the events described in this novel, while attempting to defuse a bomb.

Frédéric Joliot-Curie supported the underground Résistance movement by offering the use of his laboratory at night for the clandestine construction of bombs, despite the fact that four German scientists were sent to work with him at the Collège de France. He joined the French Communist Party after the war. His role as a pioneer of atomic physics and even his name have been forgotten by many. This may be due to his constant efforts to bridge the gap between Soviet scientists and the West during the height of the Cold War; his political affiliation made him suspect in the United States and among some colleagues in Europe. He died in August 1958.

Irène Joliot-Curie worked in her laboratory throughout World War II, supported and shared her husband's political views, and died of leukemia in the spring of 1956. There is no evidence to suggest that she betrayed her husband's research to the Germans. The mystery of the leaks in the Ministry of Armaments remains unsolved to this day.

Hans von Halban and Lew Kowarski contributed to British atomic research while at Cambridge and returned to France at the war's close. They enjoyed distinguished careers in physics.

Jacques Allier survived the war and returned to banking.

Rogers Lamont was killed by a German sniper in the British retreat to Dunkirk. He was the only Sullivan & Cromwell partner to die in World War II, although many served. A plaque to his memory as an oarsman and a scholar is mounted in the boathouse at Princeton University.

I.G. Farbenindustrie continued its work in chemical warfare, moving from the supply of carbon monoxide to the production of Zyklon-B, the prussic acid extermination gas used at Auschwitz and other concentration camps. The company reorganized after World War II, and is now known internationally as BASF.

Documents pertaining to the use of carbon monoxide in domestic euthanasia programs, as well as I.G. Farben's role in Hitler's Final Solution, are retained in the company's archives.

Hans Gunter von Dincklage—Spatz to his friends—sat out the war as the vaguest of spies. He lived in the Ritz Hotel, where one day he met Coco Chanel in the lobby. Chanel is said to have admired Spatz's flawless French and excellent tailoring; despite the fact she was twelve years older, the two became lovers. Chanel moved into Spatz's suite at the Ritz (she'd been evicted from her own by the Germans) and became an ardent supporter of the Occupation. Before Paris was liberated in August 1944, Spatz fled east. Chanel was denounced as a collaborator, arrested, and interrogated by the Free French. She and Spatz eventually reunited in Switzerland, where they lived in exile for many years before drifting apart. Chanel returned to Paris in 1953 and, at age seventy, reopened her fashion house after a hiatus of fifteen years, with a collection that took the world by storm in the spring of 1954.

The end of Spatz's life remains obscure.

Château Loudenne still sits on the banks of the Gironde in the Médoc, but it has not boasted a count or countess for many years. The Gilbey family, of British gin fortune and fame, bought the estate in the late nineteenth century, and it is still owned by their successors. A cooking school operates in the rose-colored château, and although the wine remains *cru bourgeois,* it is of good quality.

Mouton-Rothschild was occupied by the German

army throughout the war. Baron Philippe de Rothschild was thrown into a Vichy prison, from which he managed to escape to England and join de Gaulle. His wife, Vicomtesse Elizabeth de Chambure, spent the war in Paris—where she was arrested by the Gestapo in the final weeks of France's Occupation and dragged away from her young daughter, Philippine. Elizabeth de Chambure was exterminated at Ravensbrück concentration camp a few weeks later.

On his return to Mouton after the liberation of France, Baron Philippe requested a labor party of German POW's to repair the extensive damage to his château and construct a new drive through the park. Forever after, Baron Philippe referred to it as the "Road of Revenge."

Memphis Jones is based on the jazz performer and cabaret legend Josephine Baker, who fled Paris for North Africa at the German invasion and joined de Gaulle's Free French forces as a spy. Baker was later decorated for meritorious service by de Gaulle, and remained in Paris until her death in 1975. Throughout her life she collected lovers and adopted children of diverse ethnic backgrounds, whom she called her "Rainbow Family."

Ambassador William Bullitt served as Provisional Mayor of Paris once the French government abandoned the city to the Germans. He witnessed the capitulation of French forces and is said to have served champagne to the Government of Occupation when it entered Paris, despite his well-known hatred of Nazism. He left Europe in July 1940, and was never given another post under Roosevelt. Despite his close friendship with the President, Bullitt's blunt style and penchant for gossip irritated and distanced FDR, as did his expectation of being appointed Secretary of the Navy in a war cabinet. A devastating car accident damaged his health; his Freudian study of Woodrow Wilson was roundly panned by critics; and he died of cancer in 1967.

Max Shoop closed the Paris office of Sullivan & Cromwell and sent his American colleagues home to New York on what is described as the last ship out of Bordeaux. He and Odette eventually left Paris for Switzerland, where he ran intelligence operations for the Office of Strategic Services under his former Sullivan & Cromwell partner, Allen Dulles. After the war he returned to Paris and joined the international firm of Coudert Brothers. He died in 1956.

John Foster Dulles served as Secretary of State under Dwight D. Eisenhower, thereby ensuring that an international airport would one day be named for him. His brother, however, gave up his S&C partnership in 1940 to join the OSS. Allen Dulles was sent to Berne, Switzerland, in December 1942, and spent the next three years running intelligence operations throughout Europe, using in many cases old contacts he'd made through the Sullivan & Cromwell network. Allen's flair for intrigue and deception—formerly practiced against his wife—found a natural outlet in espionage, and following the war he was made Director of Central Intelligence. Dulles ran the CIA for a decade, during the high watermark of the Cold War. Perhaps more than any other single man he left his mark indelibly on the organization.

Allen Dulles later founded a quiet little watering hole where gentlemen spies could gather in the heart of Washington, D.C.—roughly on the site of the present-day International Spy Museum.

He called it the Alibi Club.

About the Author

FRANCINE MATHEWS spent four years as an intelligence analyst at the CIA, where she trained in operations and worked briefly on the investigation into the 1988 bombing of Pan Am Flight 103. A former journalist, she lives and writes in Colorado, where she is at work on her next novel of historical suspense, *A Flaw in the Blood*.

If you enjoyed Francine Mathews' electrifying *The Alibi Club*, you won't want to miss any of the novels she writes under her own name or under the name of Stephanie Barron. Look for them at your favorite bookseller.

And read on for an exciting early look at the newest Stephanie Barron novel of historical suspense, *A Flaw in the Blood*, coming soon from Bantam Books.

A FLAW IN THE BLOOD

by Stephanie Barron

On sale March 2008

A FLAW IN THE BLOOD
On sale March 2008

Chapter One

The carriage made little sound as it rolled beneath the iron portcullis of Windsor; the harness and wheels were wrapped in flannel, the paving stones three inches deep in sawdust. But its arrival fell upon the place like an armed attack, shaking the ostlers out of their torpor. They sprang to the horses' heads before the equipage had even pulled to a halt, as though Patrick Fitzgerald brought tidings of war.

Fitzgerald made no move to step down into the sawdust. His hands were thrust in his coat pockets for warmth, his eyes fixed on the flaming torches and silent men beyond the window. Once before, he had been to the great stone pile west of London—summoned, as tonight, by the woman who ruled there. But he was thinking less of the Queen now than of the man who lay in her private apartments, shuddering with fever.

"Let me come with you." Georgiana's gloved hand—that supple hand, so deft with the knife blade—reached for him. "I want to come with you."

"No."

Darkness filled the carriage. Only the gleam of her

eyes suggested a presence; she had drawn the hood of her cloak close about her face, like a thief.

"It may have nothing to do with you, Georgiana. You cannot always presume—"

"And what if *I* have something to do with *it*?" she interrupted. "With *him*?"

"Georgie—"

But she'd turned her head away, profile outlined against the squabs. She was biting down hard on anger, as though it were a haft of iron between her teeth.

"And she'd never let you near him," he attempted. "You must know that."

"Then she's a fool!"

The coachman stumbled as he jumped from the box; the noise reverberated against the chilled stone like a gunshot, and the ostlers stared in outrage. *Silence in the Old Quadrangle, in respect of the dying.* Fitzgerald caught the coachman's indrawn hiss of breath, ripe with fear, as he pulled open the door.

"Wait," he told Georgiana. "I shan't be long."

She didn't attempt to argue. She would be freezing soon, he thought, despite her layers of petticoats. But Georgie would never ask for a hot brick, a brazier of coals. Her pride would kill her one day.

A footman led him into Windsor by the lower entrance, and there, too, the stone floor was blanketed with sawdust. The castle was known for its menacing silence—the vast, carpeted halls absorbed every footfall, and its people trafficked in whispers. Fitzgerald neither spoke nor offered his hand to the man who awaited him—William Jenner, court physician and eminent man of science.

"You took your time," the doctor snapped.

Fitzgerald handed his gloves and hat to the footman before replying. "I was in Dublin but two days since."

"And you stink to high heaven of strong spirits."

"Would you have had me miss my dinner, then? I only received your summons at five o'clock."

"It is nearly ten! As I say—you took your time." Jenner's eyes were small and close-set, his jowls turned down in perpetual disappointment. He surveyed the Irishman's careless dress, his unkempt hair, with disfavour. "It may be that she will not receive you, now."

"I didn't ask for the audience." Fitzgerald shrugged indifferently. "Is it so necessary?"

"I would not thwart her smallest wish at such an hour! I fear too much for her reason."

"And your patient? How is he?"

"Typhoid."

Jenner had made his reputation, years ago, by distinguishing typhoid fever from its close relative, typhus. The physician was the acknowledged expert in the thing that was now killing Prince Albert.

"The Prince will rally," Jenner said.

From the vehemence of the doctor's words, Fitzgerald concluded there was no hope.

He followed Jenner up a narrow staircase. Through shadowy passages, and paneled doors. The final hallway was remarkable for its dimness; oil lamps burned low. A pair of footmen stood immobile by one chamber. He was led beyond, to the Red Room.

"Wait," Jenner ordered, and stalked away.

To sit would be forbidden. Indeed, it was a testament to

the chaos of this night that he was left alone at all, in such a place—that he should have the freedom of Windsor—and for a wild instant he was tempted to fly back into the passage, to trust in the footmen's trained invisibility, to roam at will over the seat of British power and take from it such tokens as he chose. But Patrick Fitzgerald was not quite the savage young man he'd been on his first visit, more than twenty years ago. He was six-and-forty years now, he had earned a reputation at the Bar, there was talk of a university appointment back home or a safe seat in the Irish parliament. For an instant, Georgie's eyes rose before his mind and he wished with all his heart and soul that he was still raw, still young, still braced with hope. Then the rustle of silk proclaimed her coming.

"Your Majesty." He went down on one knee.

"Mr. Fitzgerald."

She had taken up a position behind the sopha. The plump white hands grasped the wooden frame; had her grip been less fierce, the fingers might have trembled. She was a short woman of forty-two, with sagging cheeks and a mass of dark hair dragging at her temples; but once, she had been a dab of a girl—a joyous girl, tricked out in silver net and flashing diamonds, her hand coquettish on her husband's arm as he led her into the opera. A bruising rider on her gallops through the park—a passionate performer on the pianoforte. The unkind and malicious said she ate like a glutton. That she was given to odd fits of temper and caprice, like her mad old grandfather. They said a woman was too weak to rule. Fitzgerald knew better. Weakness had never been Victoria's failing.

"I am here at your command." He chose his words carefully. "Pray inform me how I may serve Your Majesty."

With a gesture, she bade him rise. "You know of our great trouble? Of the Prince's . . . illness?"

"You have my deepest sympathy."

A blank expression of terror in her eyes; contempt as she looked at him. "We do not *want* your sympathy, Mr. Fitzgerald! Our doctors assure us there is every cause for hope."

"There must be, while Prince Albert breathes."

Her eyes slid away from his face. "He *will not* fight it as he ought. He has no tenacity for life. If it were *I*—"

"Your Majesty should have rallied days since."

Perhaps she had been speaking only to herself. She flashed a look of pure hatred in his direction, as though he had been dangling at her keyhole.

"Good God, that we should waste our precious moments in *this*! Mr. Fitzgerald, some two decades ago you inserted yourself in our affairs, on the occasion of an attempt on our life in Green Park. You undertook, during the summer of 1840, to insinuate yourself among those who were not our friends—to purchase scurrilous information—in short, to besmirch the reputation of the Royal Family—with a view to vindicating the wretched creature who would have murdered his Queen."

She had torn him to shreds in just this way, all those years ago. Then he was an ill-dressed solicitor's clerk, cap crushed in his hands and heart pounding in his chest. And the dupe, Oxford, had waited to be hanged in Newgate Gaol.

"I was a servant of justice, Your Majesty!"

"You were an uncouth lackey of the Irish rabble, she retorted. "And your late success has not improved you one whit. I know what you are, Patrick Fitzgerald. I know that you have chosen to insert yourself *again* in my affairs—that you will not rest until you have toppled this monarchy!"

Angry heat mounted in his cheeks. "That is a lie! *Yes*—though the Queen herself says it!"

"I would not spare a blackguard such as you one second of notice," she continued, "were it not for the Angelic Being who lies wasting in the next room! Were it not for the ravings he has uttered—"

She broke off. She closed her eyes, swaying slightly.

"Ravings," Fitzgerald repeated. "The Prince has ... wandered, in his fever?"

"Oh, God," she murmured brokenly. "My reason—*my reason* ... Do you care nothing that I shall go *mad*?"

She sank heavily against the back of the sopha, her nails raking the silk.

"Majesty..." He crossed toward her, afraid she would collapse at his feet—but one upraised arm checked his steps.

"Do not even *think* of touching me." She said it venomously. "Get Jenner. He will tell you what to do."

She pulled herself upright. Drew a shuddering breath. And, without glancing again in his direction, left him.

"What is it?" Georgie asked the moment he slid into the forward seat of the coach and the muffled wheels began to turn. "What did she want? What did she ask of you?"

"It doesn't matter."

"Tell me! I've waited nearly an hour—" Georgie bit her lip. "*Please*, Patrick."

"I was ordered to sign a bit of paper," he answered. "Affirming that every fact I discovered, every witness I deposed, every rumour I substantiated in the summer of 1840, was nothing more than a fabrication of my own treacherous Irish mind. And that, having repented of my calumnies, I hereby swear to lead a better life in allegiance to my Crown, so help me God—"

"No!" Georgie gasped. "But that is . . . that is *wicked*! You did not sign it?"

"I threw it on the fire, lass."

"Why does it matter? Why should she care about that old business? With the Prince so ill?"

"Lord alone knows. Poor thing was half out of her mind, I think." He glanced at Georgiana—her luminous skin, her eyes filled with intelligence and fatal truth. "She talked of conspiracy. Accused me of trying *again* to topple the monarchy. As though I ever have!"

"There must be some mistake. A misapprehension—"

"The Prince is raving, seemingly. In his fever."

"And when you refused to recant?"

"Jenner threatened me. Informed me my life has no more purchase than a sparrow's." Fitzgerald smiled faintly. "If I'd signed, of course, he'd have made me an honourary Englishman."

Humour for Georgie's sake, but she knew Jenner, and she seized on his significance at once.

"He was there—attending on the Prince? Then it *is* typhoid." She reached impulsively for the carriage door. "We must go back, Patrick. You know I could prevent the spread of contagion—"

Fitzgerald's heart twisted. All her passion in her beautiful eyes.

"Georgie love," he said gently as the bells of Windsor began to toll, "the Prince is dead."

Chapter Two

It is true that I was a dab of a girl at twenty, a coquettish young thing on Albert's arm. I loved the attention of men, the interest and conversation of brilliant blades like William Lamb, Viscount Melbourne, who taught me when I first came to the throne how to think on every subject of importance. I loved Melbourne like a *father*—the father torn from me too early—and but for the impertinent who dared call me *Mrs. Melbourne*, might have lived entirely in his pocket, as the saying goes. He was such a droll character, despite a tendency to talk to himself or snore in church—and so clearly handsome at sixty, that I must have been quite overpowered to have met him in his prime. I was, however, not even thought of then—and he was his wife's devoted slave. Lady Caroline Lamb trampled Melbourne's character and name in the dirt, offered every possible exhibition of indecency to the wondering eyes of the *ton*, and destroyed all hope of future happiness by producing an imbecile son almost as recklessly as she seduced Byron—but Melbourne stood by her until her death.

In this, too, Melbourne most *truly* taught me the

meaning of the word *gentleman*: One who backs his wife to the limit, however grievous the peccadillo or infraction; one who, having loved, can never recant or betray.

I may declare that Melbourne loved *me*, in his fashion—and had the political Whig losses not utterly divided us, might have continued to haunt my Windsor walks until his death. As a woman's first Prime Minister, he was all that could be desired. And though in later years he resented Albert's monopoly of my interest, and a coolness fell between us, indeed I am *very fortunate* to have known him—

But I was speaking of myself, not dear William Lamb, who has been dead now these thirteen years.

I am capable of the most profound and intense love, but must confess that I am capable of loving only *one person* at a time. As a child, I adored dear Lehzen, my governess, and *quite hated* Mama; when Albert came, Melbourne was forced to quit my heart. So it has always been. And that is how it happens that I am lying here, with my cheek on Albert's breast, my hands clenched in the bedclothes Jenner drew, at the last, over his *dear face*—I must endeavour to explain how love, the *purest love*, for that Angelic Being, has brought me to this parting.

Perhaps I was a little drunk early in my reign, with my first sips of independence and power—I had banished Mama from my household and thought the credit of a Queen equal to even the most *daring behaviour*. I played favourites; snubbed those I ought to have embraced for political reasons; circulated scandal; laughed at the scoundrels of the press. I loved to dress, too—dearly loved the feel of silks and satins next to my skin, loved jewels and the way they took on the warmth of my full breasts, swelling above the line of my gowns. I was *never* beautiful, not even at twenty, my features too lumpen and bourgeois for beauty; but Albert was extraordinary—tall and graceful and muscled—and when he looked at me I felt as bewitching as the most celebrated courtesan in London.

My mother was sister to his father. Albert and I were delivered by the same midwife, a continent and a few months apart. We watched each other grow with the disinterest of children. For years, my cousin thought I was a spoiled little frump; for years, I considered him fat and stupid. His elder brother Ernest was far more *dashing*—Albert preferred books to flirtation. Until that day in October, more than twenty years ago, when he traveled from Germany straight to his doom, knowing he must accept my hand in marriage whether he wanted it or not. The Family—the Saxe-Coburgs, our Uncle Leopold most of all—said it was his *Duty*. The idea of Duty fascinated Albert as flagellation haunts an ascetic; it meant Sacrifice. Otherwise, Duty would have been called *Pleasure*—and Albert would have had nothing to do with it.

He came reluctantly to London. He hated the English damp, missed his friends and his hunting grounds *acutely*. He despised women on principle and was keenly aware that I was graceless—too short in the neck, too full in the cheeks, my chin receding. He had only just completed his studies at the University at Bonn, and was so serious and melancholy he looked like a martyr of old. I could not drink in his beauty enough as I stood at the head of the stairs, *stunned*, to receive him. I was of an age when I *craved* the touch and passion of a man—and here was a god, handed me on a silver salver!

For a matter of weeks, *everything* about our lives was perfect. We two seemed lost in a rosy world of our own, which nothing—not the hatefulness of Parliament, the ridicule of the press, the jealousy of my relations—could influence or mar. Mama, of course, loved him from the first. He called her his *Dear Aunt*, as was most proper. We sang duets, we rode together, Albert sat by my side as I wrote my tedious letters—asking only for the privilege of licking the stamps. And when we were left alone at last, he would take down the pins in my hair and let it tumble across my shoulders, *wanton* as he loved to see it. Clasp my face between his palms to kiss me.

In body and soul ever your slave, he wrote the night of our betrothal. No mention, then, of the *abandonment* of Death. And I did not apprehend, as I cried over his passionate note, that it was the slave I was marrying—Albert's Master, always—Duty.

In the morning, I would be barred from this room; Albert would be given over to Löhlein and MacDonald, his valets; to the hideous men of the undertaking firm. Now, as the bells continued to toll, negating the individual hours, I could lie with my face pressed into his groin. Drinking in the last warmth of his soul as it fled through the darkness of Windsor.

I sobbed aloud. I reproached him bitterly for leaving me helpless—and of course he was unreachable, as he always was when passion deranged me. How many times in the past has he shut himself up in his private study? How many times has he locked the door and taken meals on a tray, while I screamed into my pillow? He wrote me long lectures, like a remote Papa; and I reproached him for that—for growing *old* without me. He even called me *Dear Child, Dear Little One*—I, the most powerful monarch in the world—and thought the condescension charming!

But I am no longer, and never will be again, a dab of a girl.

Children came between us so early. I was pregnant with Vicky when Oxford tried to murder me, a mere four months after my wedding, on Constitution Hill.

We were driving to Mama's. I remember the softness of the June air. I had retched three times that day and already hated the change in my body—I felt betrayed by Albert, by the *intensity* of the pleasure I took from his sex, the way animal need had produced such misery. That day he almost carried me to the carriage, determined to get me out of doors—and indeed, the air improved me. My head felt clearer. I could look about and nod to the people in the Park who stopped to watch us pass.

And then without warning Albert seized my head, forcing it down, as the ball whined benignly over us.

He would have protected me if he could. That was his nature. But I fought his hands, staring without fear at Edward Oxford, a half-mad son of a mad mulatto labourer. I defied him to shoot as he raised his second pistol. The coachman did not drive on. Albert cried out in German. The second ball sang wide.

It was Providence, I suppose, that preserved me. And I read in that preservation a *sign*: That I am ordained to rule. That it is God's will, for me to endure as Queen of England.

The lunatic Oxford was seized by passersby, and the whole episode devolved into the sordid business of *courts* and *newspapers*—of men like Patrick Fitzgerald. Men who owe no one loyalty. Who *profit* from conspiracy. Who believe a killer may be innocent, simply because he is mad.

Would death then, in the full flower of my youth and love, have been preferable to this abandonment? This grief cutting a trench through my heart?

All those years of pregnancy—child after child after child, eight in all; the deep abiding depression that rode me like a curse; the weight I could not shed; Albert more remote with every birth; the demands of Royalty I refused to face; the way he became King without ever needing the crown.

Only once in recent memory did I recognise the ardent lover of the year—the youth who took my face in his hands and drank from my lips. It was the day he nearly perished in the wreck of his carriage, and the mistress he pursued was Death.

Did Albert feel that same clarity, as his horses raced toward the crossing bar last autumn? Did he stare down the train as I had Edward Oxford? Neither of us lacked courage. It was for Death to decide whether to take us.

And now I have given Her my Albert. No one

will shield me any longer. No one will treat me like a child. It is for me to suppress his ravings, the mad words that drowned him at the end—for me to protect what he was, at last—from such *villains* as Patrick Fitzgerald.